I0725863

Ten Feet Tall and Bulletproof, Alaska Natives:

Blazing the Iditarod Trail

by Judy Ferguson

and the Yukon-Koyukuk School District

Text by Judy Ferguson. Cover by Sue Sprinkle, 5th Avenue Design & Graphics, Inc. and Voice of Alaska Press. Map, sled dog illustrations, and family tree title page by Justin Maple, Tammy Holland, Nikola Kocic, and Judy Ferguson. Family trees by Susan Paskvan and George Yaska, Jr. Editor: Martha Eliassen Bristow. Cultural consultants: Susan Paskvan and George Yaska, Jr. Editorial consultants: all thirteen featured dog mushers. Layout and design: Judy Ferguson. Layout overseer: Justin Maple. Photos credited in captions.

Front and back cover: painting by Iditarod competitor and Athabascan artist Rose Albert's painting of Jeff King Leaving Rainy Pass. See Rose Albert and Nowitna River Studios on Facebook. Photo front cover: Roxy Wright with lead dog, Penny, first place, Alpirod, 1990. Courtesy of Roxy Wright.

Back cover photos: mushers, left to right, top to bottom; Rose Albert, Ruby; Emmitt Peters, Ruby; Don Honea, Ruby; Gary Attla, Huslia/Fairbanks; Jerry Riley, Nenana; Ramy Brooks, Fairbanks; Rudy Demoski, Anvik; Ken Chase, Anvik; Henry Beatus, Hughes; Dean Painter, Grayling; Wes Henry, Huslia; Warner Vent, Huslia.

Produced in the United States of America

❦ Preface ❦

by the Yukon-Koyukuk School Board, Fairbanks

Why should our children try to make strangers their heroes, strangers they never knew or understood, when we have our own heroes walking among us that live our ways and in our times? There are individuals among us who are showing the way for our young people. Their accomplishments are the perfect examples of what happens when one is willing to put in the work and sacrifice for what he wants and believes in. Our hope is that this book will exemplify this and show our children that there are heroes among us who are just like they are.

These biographies are recordings of the amazing individuals whose lives have inspired us to create this book. Our hope is to portray the ups and downs that these dog mushers went through in working toward their goals. Our purpose is to show how their hard work paid off, and that when a person perseveres and accomplishes what he or she sets out to do, that individual becomes an example for everyone around him. Most importantly, we want our children to know, "No matter what it is that you set out to do, if you work hard and accomplish your goals, you are a hero to someone."

Dian Gurtler, Manley Hot Springs

It is important to document our people's history and write these biographies on our elders. It brings to light the many challenges, hard work, and self determination that these individuals had. They not only paved the road for the younger generations, but they gave a part of themselves to the people. It is our hope that through this book and sharing their stories, we can inspire our children to move forward, reach for their goals, and challenge themselves.

Shirley Kruger, Nulato

There is great value in this project that YKSD was a part of; a project that seeks to help maintain our Native values, strengths, stories, and achievements. These are stories from different villages; great stories of great people who overcame many obstacles to participate in this great race. My hope is that our youth read this book and see that our people from the villages can accomplish anything they set their mind to.

Wilma David, Minto

Our Native peoples have used dogs for thousands of years and these dogs were an integral part of our way of living. In the 1960s, technology advanced and brought us snow machines. We transitioned away from dogs to make a living and many of us gave up this part of our way of life. Those that had dogs kept them for racing; be it for sprints, middle-distance, or long distance racing. This book encourages our younger generation, our students, to read about our dog mushers who raced in the Iditarod and hopefully can increase our knowledge of our dog mushers while also encouraging some of our youth to raise their own dogs and help us maintain our traditions and culture.

Wilmer Beetus, Hughes

We older people see a problem with our younger generations. After high school a lot of them are afraid to go on and become lifelong learners. When we look at our forefathers and foremothers, they didn't have that problem. They got up and did whatever it took to dream, implement, and achieve. That's why I thought it was important to document our Iditarod mushers' accomplishments in hopes that our young people could emulate that blue print for their own lives, and be able to make their own way in life.

Our Native mushers were our mentors back in the day. When they went out and chased their own dreams, it gave us people on the sidelines hope, courage, and a tremendous sense of pride. We looked up to them and thought, "Someday that's what I'm going to do." They were larger than life, ten feet tall, and bulletproof. It's my hope that our younger generations will follow our old people, and also take a gamble."

Fred Bifelt, Huslia

Sled dog team positions, harness, and sled rigging. Working dogs of any breed termed "village dogs" were the eons-old dependable means of travel in winter and pack dogs, in summer.
Double tandem hitch, *War Department Field Manual.* 1944.

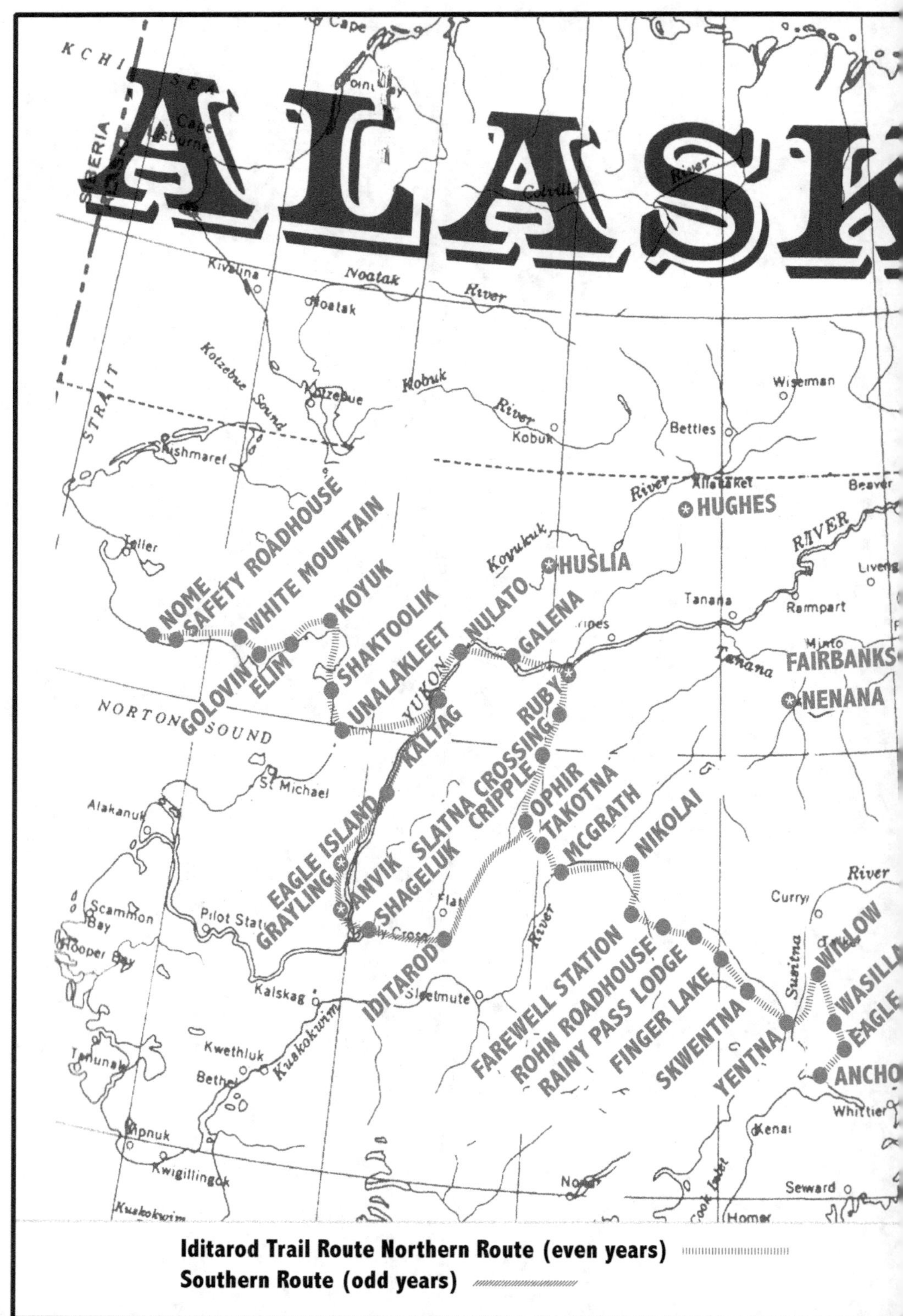

Iditarod Trail Route Northern Route (even years)
Southern Route (odd years)

Mushers' villages noted on map by *
1 Henry Beatus - Hughes
2 Warner Vent - Huslia
3 Jerry Riley - Nenana
4 Rudy Demoski - Anvik
5 Ramy Brooks - Fairbanks
6 Roxy Wright - Fairbanks
7 Wes Henry - Huslia
8 Dean Painter - Grayling/Nulato
9 Don Honea - Ruby
10 Emmitt Peters - Ruby
11 Ken Chase - Anvik
12 Rose Albert - Ruby
13 Gary Attla - Huslia

Introduction

There is much blood intra-connectedness among we Alaska Natives. Traditionally when we first meet, we may ask each other, "Where is your family from? Who were your parents?" Historically at potlatches, elders shared at length who was related to whom and in some areas, to which clan each one belonged. The point was to teach history, to orient the generations, and to eliminate marrying too close a relative. Not only are a person's cultural and familial origins key to who he is, but so are his ethnographic and historical roots. Knowing this, it was traditional in many villages, as it was in mine, for the men to gather often during the winter and share the stories of our survival throughout the eons. It was critical for the men and women who kept and retold our history to repeat it with great precision. How we'd survived throughout the millennia was important to our own continued survival both as providers and tenders of the home.

Moreover, our history included most, if not all, the mistakes made by those who went before us. The benefit was that when we encountered life-threatening situations, the knowledge of our forebears' mistakes gave us confidence that we could also overcome. We might not avoid the mistakes, but at least we were aware of the dangers. It gave us both a sense of and the knowledge of how we could make it through life. It was and is how we have survived.

George Yaska, Jr., Huslia

Historian, lay linguist, ethnographer, song-writer, and genealogist George Yaska, Jr., in conjunction with Susan Paskvan of YKSD, constructed the family trees for each musher in *Ten Feet Tall and Bulletproof: Alaska Natives Blazing the Iditarod Trail*.

As a child growing up, the oral tradition the men shared, George said, "Saved many a life, including mine." In his passion for his people, he has shared his research with the rest of us. He has also given countless hours to studying the records of Fr. Jules Jette, S.J., professor, ethnographer and missionary to the Yukon River (1864-1927), as well as the files of the Rev. John W. Chapman (1858-1939), 43-year Episcopal pastor to Anvik.

Not only is *Bulletproof* a long overdue story of the First People, who were among the originals of the Iditarod, but it is also a window into each musher's familial, historical, and cultural story. It is our privilege to hear their traditional "talking circle." There are many books on the Iditarod. *Bulletproof* is about the First People breaking trail in the Great Land and particularly in the Great Race.

Judy Ferguson, Big Delta

With great respect and thanks to all those featured and referred dogmen and dogwomen in *Ten Feet Tall and Bulletproof,* without whom historic, rural Alaska would not have had "ease" of travel, exploration, development, mail, and the serum run. We salute those souls who braved subzero temperatures, fierce wind, overflow, and ocean ice: yesterday and today's dogmen and dogwomen, who taught us how to survive.

Anatomical traits to look for in a top quality sled dog.
Drawing by Nikola Kocic, graphics by Justin Maple. ©Judy Ferguson.

Table of Contents

Chapter 1

Jerry Riley, Iditarod Icon

Prior to 1912, the local band of Tanana Athabascan people traveled through the Minto area to trade furs for goods. According to Jerry Riley, they were based at Cache and at Graveyard.

Once steamboats began to come up river, the stopping place known as Old Minto became more permanent. Old Minto village is located in interior Alaska, on the banks of the Tanana, a tributary of the Yukon River. The nearest town is Nenana.

Jerry Riley, 1976 Iditarod.
Photo by Marilyn Coghill Duggar

In 1971, many in Minto were tired of the repeated spring floods. The elders got together and selected three possible places with good fishing at the Minto lakes where they could move their village. In 1971 they moved from Old Minto to new Minto.

During the 1970s and early 1980s, Jerry Riley of Nenana was a big name in long-distance, competitive sled dog mushing. A carpenter by trade, Jerry was described in the Iditarod annual as "intense, quiet, unassuming," and saying, "on the trail, he is all business and doesn't indulge in liquid spirits." His wife, Marge, said, "Anything Jerry does, he does his best. He puts his whole being into raising dogs. He strives to keep them happy, but tough."

When I began writing children's books in 2004, I thought there should be a book dedicated to the early Alaska Native sled dog champions. In 2016 when the Yukon-Koyukuk School District asked me to write such a book, I was happy to agree.

It has been my privilege to hear these famous men's stories. While I was vending at the 2017 Festival of Native Arts in Fairbanks, I drove to Nenana during the morning to talk with Jerry and his wife, Marge, in their home.

In the course of the conversation, Jerry said that some Athabascans, including himself, are of Mongolian descent while others are related to a more Japanese-Chinese root. As Jerry described his experience in the Iditarod, he sometimes referred to "us Mongolians." As we sat at their kitchen table, Jerry began his story.

Jerry's father, Harry Riley, 1946, military sharpshooter, Tanana.
Courtesy of Jerry Riley.

The original Athabascan mushers were women. The men walked everywhere but the women had three to five dogs to haul their children. The women had the best dogs and knew how to raise them. Men got into dog racing because of the aspect of a contest. It began with the Sweepstakes race in Nome. Leonhard Seppala used to haul miners from Nome to Fairbanks by dog team. Our village dogs were absolutely bullet-proof: the cold didn't bother them, they never got sore feet, nothin'.

My dad, Harry Riley, was the second oldest of three children born to unmarried, eighteen-year-old Lucy Jr. Riley. Harry's father was a redheaded Russian. His younger half-brother was Lee Edwin. In the 1910 census, the family was with Lucy's sister, Annie Edwin and her husband, Koyukuk Edwin, and the girls' parents in Tanana. (Previously, Lucy, Jr. was asked to leave Huslia. She, her parents, and my five-year-old dad either mushed or walked to Tanana.) Lucy must've passed away sometime after Lee's birth because Dad and his younger half-brother Lee were raised by their Aunt Annie Edwin and her husband Koyukuk Edwin of Tanana. The Edwins also adopted other children including George Edwin, Sr. My dad and his brother became known as Harry Edwin and Lee Edwin.

My mother, Grace Smith, was born in 1910 to a Norwegian prospector Charles Smith and his half Athabascan wife, Sarah Grant. My mother was musically gifted and grew up playing the piano. Her father, Charlie, had a bar but some nut blew him away with a shotgun. My parents

Jerry's mother, Grace Smith Riley, ca. 1925, Tanana.
Courtesy of Jerry Riley.

had two older sons, Eugene, born in 1929, and Walter, born in 1930, both in Nenana.

Dad had a trapping cabin at the mouth of Montana Creek near Old Minto as well as a fish camp on the Tanana River. He hauled mail from Circle City on the Yukon, downstream to Tanana. In his life, he only ran one sled dog race: from Fairbanks to Livengood and back, but he used a dog team for trapping all his life. In those days they didn't use booties.

In early November 1936, while my parents were on their trapline, I was born by a hill in the north end of the Minto Flats, called *Bandudayi* [pronounced: "Bandoodieyee], eight miles southeast by dog trail of new Minto. As my dad was Harry Edwin then, I was called Gerald R. Edwin.

My mother died sometime after 1940. After her death and with the beginning of World War II, my dad, who was a sharpshooter, joined the army when I was six years old. He hauled me and my younger sister Flora, born in 1939, on a sled to Tanana.

This part of my childhood was difficult. I was sort of raised by my adopted uncle George Edwin. But no one really raised me so the village of Tanana passed me around—but nobody wanted me. I never ate for three days at a stretch. When I was born, I was big. My mother thought I'd grow up to be over six feet. But when I said to my relatives, "I'm hungry; would you give me a salmon strip," my uncle would said, "No." The only one who treated me good was Lester Erhart. Once when he got a goose, he gave it to me, which I gave to the family I was staying with. They cooked and ate it and threw me the bone. I got really good at cracking the bones open and eating the marrow. The village dogs became my friends. It was survival of the fittest. I became the leader of the pack and understood each dog's limits and capabilities. I learned to be inventive in order to eat. I learned not to be afraid, to make a fire, and to set snares for rabbits. Once I caught a lynx and walked round trip from Minto to Tolovana to sell the pelt to the trader, Mr. Burke, for ten dollars. That was my life for four years.

My father's second wife was Josephine Titus Riley, who, unlike my father's family, had been nomadic. Together, they had fifteen children.

In 1946 when I was ten, the BIA flew me to Juneau and then, on an amphibious plane, to Wrangell for school. On my arrival, a boy beat me up until I couldn't see. I cried for my mother. Nobody cared. If one of us did something wrong, we had to run a gauntlet of our fellow classmates while they beat us up. I said, "That won't happen again. I'll learn to box." I was there for three years. Then I was sent to Mount Edgecumbe boarding school where it was a little better. However, the local Tlingit and Haida students thought that we weren't as good as they were. We were also restricted to the

Jerry Riley, half-sister Lucille Riley and father, Harry Riley, ca. 1958, possibly Minto.
Courtesy Jerry Riley.

island as the school wouldn't allow us to cross a bridge to the local residential area.

After being hit so many times, I learned to be fast, to duck, and to hit back. When I was fifteen, I'd had enough. The school found my dad, Harry Riley, in Minto and sent me to him in 1951. That turned out to be a good move. He and I went trapping together.

In 1952 an Episcopal preacher named Dick Simmons came and told everyone that they were entitled to 160 acres under the Native Allotment Act of 1906. Dad researched what was available. He showed me a parcel of land, C.O.D. I call it, where gas was coming out of a hole in the ground and he told me to file on it. I liked it because there was a lot of timber there. I figured when I got the money, I could build a house on it. I wanted a home where no one could run me off ever again so I filed on it. It was my stake in the ground and my dream.

I stayed with my dad two years and trapped with him until I was sixteen. In those days we either had to snowshoe or mush. At the end of the trapping season every year, in the spring, we villagers would race our dogs on fourteen-mile runs.

My dad and I had nine dogs. I split wood to cook for them, and I fed and watered them. I cut grass for their beds. I first ran a team when I was seven. We couldn't afford many dogs. Driving them was my favorite but I sure didn't like losing the team, which meant I'd have to walk the twenty miles back home.

My mushing mentors included Charlie Titus, Sr. of Minto, Horace "Holy" Smoke, and Doc Lombard of Wayland, Massachusetts. I thought he was a people doctor, but I found out later that he was an animal doctor. I'd never heard of veterinarians. With that kind of job and knowledge of dogs, it was no wonder Lombard always won. Once in a while, however, we'd beat him.

There was a lot of drinking in the village. For some reason, it rubbed me the wrong way. I figured a person might be poor, but he could still be honorable. It hit me wrong for a person to destroy himself whether with alcohol, promiscuity, or smoking. Once when an obnoxious drunk was carrying on, I hit him. My dad figured I needed to get out of there. He told me to build a sled to take to Fairbanks to sell for pocket money. He gave Al Wright ten dollars to fly me and my sled to town, where I sold it for thirty-five dollars.

Jean Bertolocci, the woman who owned the Arctic Hotel on the south side of the Chena River, gave me a bunk in the basement in 1952. However, when I lay down and looked up at the ceiling, I saw a line of rats watching me sleep.

Jean told me that I smelled bad. I said, "Sure, I could take a shower but I have no other clothes." She gave me some money to go buy some and gave me $5.00 a day for meals. A year later, I finally got a job for a dollar an hour working at Edwin Reed's sawmill. At last, I got to eat three meals a day. I worked all summer. I didn't care how hard I had to work. Every day there was pie or cake! We went up and down the Salcha River, logging. When the floating logs got jammed up against the gravel bars, I'd jump in Reed's old boat and free them up from the gravel bars. I saved $500.

When I was going on nineteen, I trained Dick Kenison's dogs. Then I began helping Jim Lundgren's daughter learn to race dogs. I tried to get into the electrician's union but I couldn't do the math. I decided to join the navy and enlisted as Jerry Edwin for four years. When I was twenty-two, I returned to Alaska. When I arrived at Dad's, I discovered that he'd been bootlegging and had gone to jail. When he got out, he'd changed his name from his adopted surname of Edwin back to his mother's name of Riley, so I also corrected my name to our proper family name and became Jerry Riley.

During the next two years, I worked for Gareth Wright and then as a deckhand. I became a licensed pilot running the *Yutana* barge in Nenana. During the winter, I returned to Minto where I trapped with my dad. He gave me six dogs including a lead dog, Joker, who later became the father of Sugar.

Jerry Riley, racing in Anchorage, early 1970s.

Courtesy of Jerry Riley.

Lee Edwin, Tanana.
Courtesy of Jacqueline Edwin.

When an elderly friend of mine named Mr. Fritzlynn was dying, he willed me his lumberyard in Nenana. His relatives didn't want it. There was an old forklift and truck on his land near the railroad where he offloaded his lumber and paint.

I sent my Uncle Lee Edwin material for a 16- by 16-foot building. In return, he sent me eight village huskies. With what my dad and my uncle had given me, I had a dog team then. I decided to race dogs for two years. The sprint races I entered included the Open North American, the Rondy, the Minto spring carnival, and Nenana sprint races. Sometimes we went just to support the race. It was fun. When someone had an exceptional race, we honored them by saying, "Wow, I'd like to have a dog like yours." The response would be, "If you have a male, you can breed into the team." It was always the male, never the female dog, and then the male's owner could take the pick of the litter.

New Hampshire musher Keith Bryar, who helped preserve the Leonhard Seppala Siberian huskies, and Dr. Roland Lombard, of Massachusetts, seemed to know the secret of successful sled dog competition. In 1964, Doc Roland won three top sprint races: the Rondy, the North American and the Soldotna race. However that same year, when I was twenty-eight, I was running ten of Keith Bryar's dogs and two of mine against Doc Lombard at the Tok Race of Champions. My leaders were extremely fast. On the first day of the first race we were off at 22-23 mph and into a quick right-hand turn and then just as quickly into a quick left-hand turn. Everyone thought I had lost my dogs, but I hung on. On the return, I plunged down an embankment into a creek, but I still beat Lombard and won the race with nine minutes to spare.

A group headed by "Red" Olson wanted to bring the significance of Alaska mushers and races to the attention of the eastern states sled dog circuit. With the slogan of "Let's Send Jerry Away," their goal was to raise three thousand dollars and have me race in the Lower 48 sled dog race circuit. I wanted to learn what secrets I could from these veteran mushers.

In Nenana, a carpenter friend built dog boxes on top of an old Dodge truck bed of Red Olson's, that he'd donated to me to use. Charlie Ned of Allakaket had some good dogs and he also wanted to race. He wasn't immediately free to join me so Richard Frank, of Minto, agreed to go with me as far as Seattle, where Charlie would join me.

En route I saw that my dogs were wormy. I tried to find some wormer, but it seemed like no one would help me. The dogs must've only had a few parasites because they were all right otherwise so we drove on into Seattle where Richard left and Charlie took his place. Charlie and I went to Lake Tahoe and raced

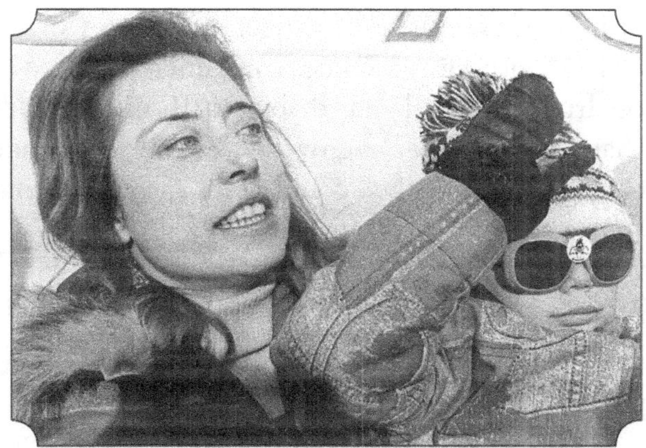

Margie Ann Gillispie Riley and their son, Gerald Roy Riley II, Anchorage, 1976.
Photographer Marilyn Coghill Duggar

against mushers from all over the states on a nearly vertical course. Mel Fishback, editor of *Team and Trail* magazine in Nevada City, California, was there. I asked him where I could get worm medicine, but he said he didn't know. In spite of my problems, I came in second at Tahoe with my great leaders Sharkie and Jasper.

In the midwest, I met Margie Ann Gillispie, my lifelong mate. She and I were married in January 1966. As soon as I could teach her to stay on a sled, we divided up my dogs and began mushing two teams on the sprint circuit. Sharkie and Jasper were my favorite dogs because they were competitive leaders and I beat Lombard with them. They never were wormed, but nonetheless, they won. They loved to race.

The next year was the big 100-year celebration of the purchase of Alaska from Russia. Alaska Centennial celebrations were going on all over the state. Wasilla historian Dorothy Page proposed a fifty-mile sled dog race from Knik to Big Lake, first called the Iditarod Trail Seppala Memorial Race, and referred to later as the Alaska Purchase Centennial race. It would comprise two twenty-five mile heats over two days including several miles on the Iditarod Trail. Joe Redington began fundraising; he and Dick Mackey blazed and reopened nine miles of the long overgrown Iditarod Trail. The purse was billed at an unprecedented $25,000, which drew well-known mushers including me. Other drivers included George Attla, Gareth Wright, Earl Norris, Orville Lake, Herbie Nayokpuk, Dick Mackey, Dr. Roland Lombard, and Dr. Charles Belford. I came in nineteenth of a field of fifty-four. Despite all of the celebrity entrants, a relatively unknown musher from Teller named Isaac Okleasik took the purse.

I'd spent my life pretty much finding my own way. I was strong and often walked without snowshoes in six inches of snow for fifty miles, never eating or drinking in all that distance. The Lord made me strong so I could do that. Due to how I'd grown up, I was independent and had strong convictions. Consequently, I could never agree on racing philosophy with potential sponsors so except for the 1975 and 1976 Iditarod races, I had to pretty much pay everything out of pocket. However in 1975, my sponsors included Jack Coghill, Coghill's store, Robert Coghill, Nenana Fuel, and "Ketch" Ketchum, and in 1976, the Coghills along with Ernie's Service at Anderson, and Elder Lebert of Fairbanks.

Our rural dogs were tough. I got them already developed out of the village. Puppy, out of Dean Painter's line in Grayling, had leather feet, much like the old-time mail carriers' dogs. In 1974 Rudy Demoski placed fourth in the Iditarod with Puppy in the lead. That summer I went to see Dean Painter, the owner of Puppy, and traded him an old Arctic Cat snowmachine for three dogs, which included Puppy, Sleeko, and Carlson.

I finally found a good vet from Seattle: Dr. Sachen of Mt. McKinley Animal Hospital. He cleaned my dogs of parasites using an IV. When I finally got them in harness, boy, were they good. My leaders were the pace-setting Sugar (out of my dad's bloodlines) and the go-getter, resilient Puppy.

When I first ran the Iditarod in 1974 and 1975, it was an absolute adventure. Some mushers like Warner Vent from Huslia understood long distance racing. He never lost a dog; how he kept all of his dogs healthy, I don't know.

I began to learn what a musher had to watch for. When dogs tire, they stop working and they stop eating. I, personally, could go a long time without eating and drinking and I figured the dogs could do the same, but that was a mistake. Initially the vets in the Iditarod didn't explain pulmonary edema to the Natives. Edema happens when the dogs' lungs get overstressed. As soon as dogs stop working and eating, a musher needs to drop them. If they stop drinking, they get dehydrated, succumb to pneumonia, and die.

That first year in 1974, I didn't read my dogs right and I had to scratch. Ken Chase taught us a lot. I'd say, "Ken, I didn't do this right. I lost dogs." He said, "Every four hours, feed. Four hours on and four hours off." He taught me how to win. I refined it and I finally learned how to read the dogs. They like to sleep during the heat of the day. I stopped between 11:30 and midnight every day. The dogs slept in their harness. We were up and going again at 5 AM. I tried to rest between midday to 3:30. As soon as we stopped, I fed them good warm meat and a lot of water; then they ate again at 3 PM. I'd crank them back up and run them two and half more hours.

I fed them again at 6 PM, followed by an hour off. At 9 PM, we fed and ran until midnight. They got at least eight hours of sleep in twenty-four. The dogs have to have two pounds of warm meat with two cups of water every twenty-five miles. I used ground meat, beef hearts, liver, and some fat.

In 1975, I came in second and might've won but my dogs didn't have the intense training that I gave to them the following year. During the winter of 1975 through 1976, I ran them six to ten miles per day and as the race neared, I trained them on runs up to seventy-five miles. My team was looking good and it

Jerry Riley repairing his sled, Unalakleet, 2001.
(Al Grillo.) Courtesy Jerry Riley.

was speculated that I could be a possible winner. My plan was to stay with the pack at the front, and when the time was right, to pour on the steam.

As we lined up at the starter gate of the 1976 Iditarod, people handed us sandwiches and pieces of pie. There were snowmachines at the ready in case our dogs got unruly. If need be, the handlers would catch them and hold them for the musher, so he could just walk up and take off again.

After the first part of the race, as we were coming up to Rainy Pass Lodge, the temperature began to drop to -50° with 50 mph wind. Bud Smyth had a frozen beard and had to hole up there to thaw it. (That's why you never see a Native with a beard; it holds the moisture as well as the cold. In the old days, Mongolians pulled their beard hairs out with a sharp knife.)

In Ptarmigan Pass where the wind was blowing a gale in the extreme cold, the trail became chaotic. My dogs made a U-turn and came back at me, flipping the sled and throwing me off. The team ran into a nightmare of willows and brush. When I caught up and began trying to separate the tangled harnesses and dogs, I busted my headlamp. Puppy had night blindness and needed my headlamp to see, but it was shattered. Warner Vent came along and at first, he toyed with me and held back about having a second headlamp. At -50° with a wind, it would've been impossible, without frostbiting our fingers or dropping the fragments, to find and piece together the tiny plastic pieces as stated in the book, Iditarod, *The First Ten Years*. After messing with me, Warner gave in and gave me his second head lamp.

Beyond Ptarmigan Pass was Dalzell Gorge, a steep, curving descent sliding down between big boulders! Sometimes a musher can't even see

"When I open my eyes, I'll be across the finish line," Jerry Riley, seconds after crossing the finish line as champion in 1976.
1976 Iditarod Trail Annual.

his leaders. Another hazard was a makeshift bridge with guardrail poles that spanned a rushing creek. I didn't dare slow down. The creek must've been running at 20 mph. One woman whose sled got hung up on the bridge got stuck down by the creek for sixteen hours. Another musher heard her hollering, stopped, threw her a line, and pulled her up.

When we came to the old Rohn Roadhouse, cold as we were, we piled in. Mike Williams, Sr. of Akiak said, "Get your sleep, man. Crawl under the bed, get a couple of hours. They'll run us off pretty soon. Too many come in here." Mushers always need to warm up.

Dogs need to warm up too because after frost collects heavily on their guard hairs, they can't get their body heat back up and pulmonary edema can set in. The vets knew that. At -70°, they should have a 70-foot long tent with heat for dogs so that all the frost can come off. (During the roadhouse days, they had dog barns.) Race officials got mad if we took a whole team into a cabin, but it only took an hour to get the frost off so their hair could work again.

After leaving Rohn Roadhouse, we headed down the old mail trail toward the FAA station. After the Post River Glacier, there was an incredibly steep hill that plunged to the valley below. There was no way to stop the dogs, not even by dragging a tree behind the sled. It was terrifying. Rudy and Warner helped me. At the top of the hill, Rudy would tie his dogs off, and wait for a couple more teams. Together, they would disconnect the back lines and hold them while someone else held the leaders, and the third person would ease the sled down. They'd tie them off down below on a drift log on a gravel bar. My dogs were frantic to get going and they were about to rip the log out of the ground.

I took my break at McGrath because Goog, Babe, and Eep Anderson were there. The town had a little restaurant, bar, and hotel. It was party time, especially for Rudy. For all of us, every checkpoint was a welcome sight.

From there to the coast, we had to break trail for days. Other mushers held back while we Mongolians snowshoed the seemingly bottomless trail at Poorman and beyond. We took a beating.

You only had to be concerned about ice conditions in the gorge, the south fork of the Kuskokwim, and when you got near the ocean ice. None of us knew what to look for on the coast. It was cold, windy, and there was no trail. I wouldn't go out on the ocean ice unless it was well marked. If the ice was soft, the water could be right underneath. Two of my friends died doing that. They were oldtimers looking for seal, but they hit that soft ice and they disappeared. I wouldn't go out on that ice unless I was following someone with experience. The Iditarod was going to disqualify me because I had someone from Koyuk lead me to Elim, but I got the trail put in! The Iditarod finally let it go. Today the race won't allow villagers to help. It should be about community. For the villages the Iditarod should be like a good movie coming to town.

People opened their doors and invited us to dinner. They had cardboard boxes for our dogs to lie on. No one had done a race like this before. Our arrivals broke up the winter for them. At Unalakleet they gave me some rabbits, which I cooked and boy, did my dogs perform. That's our Native tradition to help others, but historically, that kindness was taken for weakness by others.

Dr. Sachen also told me to give my dogs tetracycline hydrochloride to prevent infections for ten days straight, but I figured I'd break it up to stagger it throughout the race. I used it before the race, three days into the race, and

Jerry Riley with lead dogs Puppy and Sugar, Nome finish line, Iditarod champion, 1976.
Photo Rosemary Phillips. Courtesy Jerry Riley.

Jerry Riley into Eagle, Yukon Quest, 1981. "It took me four years to get those dogs," Jerry Riley.
Anchorage Daily News. Courtesy Jerry Riley.

then again outside of Unalakleet. I also fed them, gave them water, and let them rest. When dogs are healthy, they eat and drink really well. Boy, they started picking up! At Golovin, my position in the race could still have gone either way so I gave my dogs frozen meat to keep us moving. Marge and our friend Marilyn Coghill Duggar flew over and said I was running like there was no tomorrow. The pilot said, "There's the 1976 champion unless he takes a nap! We'll see him in Nome!" At 7:45 AM Nome's fire siren began blaring the message that a musher was in sight. People from all across town began making their way to the finish line. The dog catcher's truck came in sight first, its red light blaring. I arrived March 25 as the sun was rising. I paused before crossing the finish line, picked up my five-year-old son, "Guy," (Gerald Roy Riley II), put him in the sled and crossed the final line. I made it from Unalakleet to Nome in thirty-eight hours! We'd done it in eighteen days, twenty-two hours, fifty-eight minutes, twenty-two seconds and I was five hours ahead of Warner Vent. The dogs thought it would never end! I only had to drop three dogs and two were due to dog fights. Without a special leader like Puppy, the dogs would have lost interest. By the time they got to Nome, they were thin and in tough shape. We didn't use booties back then. A few had cuts in their frog (digital pads), but most didn't. Eighty-five pound Puppy got the Golden Harness as best leader.

In the celebratory mood of the race's finish, every gift shop gave us a Native handmade gift like slippers.

I don't remember much about the awards banquet. Nome was a very busy place and I was tired, hungry, and I wanted to go home. The Iditarod paid me and my dogs' passage to get back home. Nowadays, however, a musher has to pay his own way home.

I learned a lot on the first Iditarod and ended up running fourteen more, finishing nine of those. From the time I was thirty-nine until I was seventy,

I never got tired, just sleepy. I was durable and I had a lot of stamina. If I drank coffee or ate chocolate, it messed with my head.

I got another good team out of Grayling—even better than Puppy—but there was a lot of pressure from other mushers for those Grayling dogs. I let my team go to Bob Watson and that was a terrible mistake.

At the peak of my career, my kennel amounted to about eighteen to twenty-five dogs, but I always ran twelve. When I won the Iditarod, my dog lot only included twelve adult dogs and a couple of yearlings. We couldn't afford more. In those days, we could buy Kasco dog food for five dollars a bag; today the cost for the new standard of high quality food is way over the top.

To run the Iditarod it's necessary to have a good vet. It took a lot of years for me to get the vet help I needed. While Dr. Sachen did help me with advising me to use tetracycline hydrochoride to keep my dogs from getting pneumonia, no one told me that it had to be alternated with a different antibiotic or the dogs would become immune to the tetracycline. The next year I figured it out and I used Amoxi tabs but by then, I was out of the Iditarod.

Irritated at the lack of vet help in the Iditarod, in 1983 I talked with a lawyer, Mark Grover, and a late Juneau musher, who had a Samoyed-husky line of dogs. We came up with the idea of an alternate long distance race, one from Fairbanks to Whitehorse. We approached Leroy Shank of the *Fairbanks Daily News-Miner* for support, but as it turned out, he and three others were given the credit for the concept of the Quest.

I ran that race three times, placing seventh in 1984, scratching in 1985, and coming in second in 1988. I was the first musher to attempt to run both the Quest and the Iditarod in one year but due to a botched mandatory meeting, I had to scratch from the Quest.

What kept me going in the race was that I loved a challenge. We had fun doing it. For strategy we liked to mess with the wannabee mushers who'd let us break trail for them. Warner, Rudy, Emmitt, and I would see mushers coming. We'd drag up a ten-foot dry log, make a campfire, put a big pot of snow on the fire for everyone to eat. We'd tell them what a good team they had. After shooting the breeze, we'd say, "You got good dogs, you go on ahead." We knew that later on the trail, we could beat them.

When I was seventy-eight and ran my last race, I sold my dogs in 2014.

Today the race is too expensive. The cost of dog food and vet bills is prohibitive. Also sponsorships aren't what they used to be.

Trapping is a thing of the past and for some reason, youth love snowmachines more. They don't want to cook for dogs or shovel poop.

Today the Iditarod race is a highway to Nome; there are ten snowmachines out ahead of the mushers. The musher only has to stay awake. In my day, snowmachines were far from dependable, but our dogs could keep going, running hard.

I ran fifteen Iditarods and completed nine: winning in 1976, placed second twice in 1975 and 1977, and with only five dogs, fourth in 1979, fifteenth in 1986, thirteenth in 1987, seventeenth in 1989 and 2002, and eighth in 2001. My total prize money for the Iditarod was $77,586. My total for the Quest was $16,900. In between long distance races, I was competing in sprint races—like the Kuskokwim 300—where I placed well.

The real dogs started

Jerry Riley, 2003, Iditarod start first rerouted out of Fairbanks.

Time News Scoop Ed, 03/14/03. Vol. 8 #20

disappearing in the 1950s when well-known Lower 48 sprint sled dog champions like Keith Bryar, Doc Lombard, and Dr. Belford came from the east and started buying them. It bothers me because I was also selling our Alaska village dogs. After mushers got the most out of their dogs, they disposed of them. They didn't hang onto them. Also instead of making the dogs better, they inserted the hound into the bloodline and now, they've ruined them. Finally snowmachines came in and that was the end of village dogs. The racing dogs of today are not the same; their bloodlines and genetics have been altered so that it's not race it was. The old dogs are gone, gone, gone.

To today's young mushers, I would say: be well versed in the health care of your animals under stressful conditions and alternate cold and warm water. Never be blinded by over confidence or by fear. If you've got a weakness, you have to overcome it. Paying to be in the Iditarod is not an investment, but it is a total loss. Only enter if you have a good financial resource and have good vet care. You need to be a strong person. Don't go down the path of self-destruction: alcohol, cigarettes, and promiscuity. A man may be poor but he can walk in honor.

Chapter 2

Son of the Iditarod; Deg Xit'an Musher: Ken Chase

Ken Chase competed in the first Iditarod when it wasn't certain in 1973 if there'd even be a race. During his seventy-nine years, Ken has entered a total of sixteen Iditarods. Ken asked that the backdrop of the world into which he was born, Alaska's story as well as that of his family heritage, be presented as both contributed to the man he is. We begin with Russian America.

Ken Chase and Piper, eighth place in Iditarod.
Bill Devine photo. *Iditarod Runner*, 1980

In 1833, Russian governor Baron Von Wrangell appointed Andrei Glazunov, a man of Russian and Alaska Native heritage, to explore the Yukon and to establish trade. Ten years later, scientifically trained Russian naval officer Lavrenty Zagoskin explored and documented the Yukon River and its people extensively. However the arrival of the Russians also brought smallpox, which left devastation in its wake, resulting in many orphaned children.

During the late 1870s, Captain Michael Healy, in command of an American revenue cutter that was patrolling Alaska waters, witnessed the decimation of the whale and seal populations, food sources for the Alaska Native. In Siberia, Captain Healy had seen Natives successfully herding and utilizing reindeer. Out of pocket, he purchased some of the reindeer and transported them to the Natives in Alaska. Hearing of this innovative idea, missionary Dr. Sheldon Jackson proposed to the U.S. Congress the importation of reindeer to Alaska for Natives to cultivate for a food source. Additionally in 1884 Dr. Jackson invited churches to select regions of Alaska respectively for outreach to the Natives. Three years later, the Rev. John Chapman and the

A reindeer herder and pet, 1918.
John W. Chapman family papers.
UAF 2008-15-CO1

Rev. John W. Chapman, ca. 1918.
UAF-1985-72-145

Rev. Octavius Parker of the Domestic and Foreign Missionary Society of the American Episcopal Church opened one of the most important missions in Alaska, Christ Church at Anvik (Gitr'ingithchagg in the Deg Xinag Athabascan language). Chapman spent the next forty years in Anvik. He was able to get a land grant from the federal government across from Anvik Point village at the mouth of the Anvik River. The villagers lived mostly in underground houses, which were vulnerable to seasonal flooding. They were encouraged to move over to the mission side of the river, pay a dollar for rent per year, and to build cabins. At the mission school, both English and Deg Xinag languages were taught.

There were two flu epidemics, one in 1918 and one in 1927, which resulted in more orphans. Motherless children came to the Anvik mission from as far away as Fort Yukon.

A descendant of one of those orphans and a grandson of prospectors, Ken Chase is well known for his many roles in the Iditarod Trail Dogsled Race, including winning the Red Lantern, the prize for last place.

In his area of Anvik, Ken Chase helped define local Native land claims as well as found his area's regional corporation.

In 1975 when Ken was deeply involved in both Native politics and commercial fishing, my husband, my young son, and I canoed down the Yukon River. We dragged our canoe up the bank at Anvik where Iditarod mushers Ken Chase and Rudy Demoski were seining salmon. Ken's dad, William R. Chase, ran the

Cabin and dugout, Anvik Point village, ca. 1918.
John W. Chapman family papers, Album 2, 2008-15-105

Anvik mission, 1919.

John W. Chapman family papers, album 1.: UAF-2008-15-029

local store. During those years, the Japanese were buying fish roe; business on the Yukon River was hopping.

As my husband, Reb, talked firefighting and dog mushing with Ken and Rudy, I watched elder Priscilla Wood digging spruce roots, which she carefully split for basket weaving. The old Episcopalian mission stood nearby. I was in the middle of history.

Thirty-five years later, Ken and his daughter, Marilyn, met me and Reb in Fairbanks. Ken shared his story, which was first published in Windows to the Land, An Alaska Native Story Vol. Two: Iditarod and Alaska River Trails *in 2016. Three years later for the Yukon-Koyukuk School District book,* Ten Feet Tall and Bulletproof, Alaska Natives Blazing the Iditarod Trail, *Ken shared more in-depth about his sixteen Iditarods. In April 2019, we sat down together, and Ken told me about his family lineage and how he came to participate in so many Iditarods.*

My sixteen-year-old Bohemian-Dutch grandfather Jim Ebena (pronounced: Ebb′uhnuh) from Chicago climbed the Dyea Trail with his father to get to the Klondike.[1] About 1909, he showed up at the Iditarod–Flat gold rush. He married a Deg Xit'an Athabascan, Cecelia, *Neq'ot*, who my brother told me was from Koserefsky, across from Holy Cross, and was born in 1878. Cecelia had a son, Joe Frank, from an earlier marriage. Her previous husband had left her and her son to starve by locking them out of the family food cache. Jim Ebena found her and Joe on the riverbank and in essence rescued and married her. Jim and Cecelia Ebena then had five more children including my mother, Katherine, "Kate," Ebena born in 1914. When my mother was only

---

1   However, Ebena's close friend Margaret Mespelt wrote that at age eighteen, Jim Ebena, born in 1869, came to Alaska in 1887, nine years before the Klondike.

L-r: Ken Chase's paternal grandfather, William Charles Chase, with second wife, Agatha Deacon Chase holding Alta, Hazel, John, Mary, Catherine (later, Kruger), Ken's father, William Randolph, and Nellie ca. 1925, Anvik.
Liz Kruger Coll. Donna MacAlpine, *A Brief History of the Anvik Mission*

three, her mother died.[2] My grandfather Jim Ebena could not take care of his four young children as well as earn a living. He loaded up two sleds: one that he drove with four-year-old Emilia and eighteen-month-old Jimmy in the basket, pulled by five dogs. Behind him, Mother's nine-year-old sister, Florence, drove the second sled with Mother in the basket, pulled by three dogs. They mushed eighty to ninety miles from Iditarod to the mission at Anvik. My grandfather Ebena left Emilia, Jimmy, and my mother, Kate, at the mission. I don't know how Mother's half-brother, Joe Frank, got to Holy Cross, but he and Mother's older sister, Florence, grew up at the Catholic mission there in Holy Cross. Mother and her two younger siblings spent the next ten years at the Anvik mission. Grandpa Ebena returned to Iditarod, and settled ultimately in McGrath.

Not long after Jim Ebena was in the Klondike, my paternal grandfather, William Charles (W.C.) Chase, came north to the Nome gold rush. Born in Michigan in 1868, he must've followed the various gold strikes down the coast because when he was in Paimiut on the Kuskokwim, he saw an ad in the Nome newspaper for a handyman and carpenter at the Anvik Mission. The mission founder and pastor, Dr. Chapman, in Anvik needed help at the mission and had sent out a plea for "anyone who can drive a nail and saw a board straight" to come and help there. About 1902, W.C. Chase, my paternal grandfather, moved to Anvik and married a half-Deg Hit'an woman, Lucy Gitsiyuku. Before she died, they had two daughters, Mary

2   The November 1, 1917, *Iditarod Pioneer* newspaper, supplied by Anvik historian Donna MacAlpine, states that "after months of suffering, Mrs. Ebena passed away in Iditarod in October, leaving five children, the youngest being only a few months old."

and Catherine Chase.[3] When local trader Max Simel left for the new gold strike at Ganes Creek, he sold his store to my grandfather, W.C. Chase. That store was at the post below Anvik, where the steamboats used to land.

Sometime after W.C.'s first wife's death, he married Agatha Deacon. Born in 1879, Agatha was a young, pretty, full-blooded Alaska Native woman who had grown up at Holikachuk on the Innoko River. She was 28 years younger than her new husband. When they married, Agatha could not speak English, but she learned quickly. She could never read or write but she could speak well and played the harmonica like crazy: "*Yankee Doodle*" and such songs. They had two daughters and three sons, including my father, William (W.R.) Chase, born in 1911.

My grandfather's prospecting partner, Frederick Kruger, and others began placer mining at Stuyahok, northeast and inland from Russian Mission. My grandfather W.C. Chase joined Kruger and mined there from about 1922 to 1927. Three years later, Kruger and W.C. began a larger scale placer operation near Chase Mountain. That winter, they brought in pipe to build a hydraulic plant. For the next four years, they mined using the hydraulic lift and plant. The pay was reasonably good.

When Mother, Kate Ebena, was growing up at the mission, she would see my father, William R. Chase, helping his dad, W.C. Chase, with carpentry. When he was fourteen, Dad and Granddad built one of the largest buildings on the Yukon, a thirty-six foot by seventy-foot, two-story log and shingle roof building with a basement for the Anvik mission.

In about 1930, after forty years of ministry, Dr. Chapman, the founder of Christ Church mission and boarding school at Anvik, retired, which also resulted in the closure of the boarding school. With no place to stay any longer, my mother went to her father's in McGrath, but that didn't work out. The very hospitable Vanderpool family, which included children her own age, invited her to stay with them. In the spring, she returned to the Yukon River to work as a housekeeper at the Stuyahok mine. My dad, William R. Chase, was also working at the mine at the time, hydraulicking. In 1932, my father married my mother, Kate Ebena.

Four years later, Vance Hitt bought out Kruger, my sixty-eight-year-old grandfather, and their other partners.

When World War II began, the heavy equipment in Alaska was taken for the war effort and mining was shut down.

After the mine closed, Dad worked as a carpenter and a mechanic at the Episcopal mission. At that time, a man had to be able to do everything. He

---

3   Catherine Chase was born about 1899. Later Catherine married her father's mining partner, Frederick Kruger, twenty-two years her senior.

Ken's family: back, l-r: Gloria and Rudy; middle: William Randolph Chase, Ken, Kate Ebena Chase, Allan. Front: Calvin, ca. 1955, Anvik.
Courtesy of Donna MacAlpine.

mined in the local area as well as ran the sawmill for my great uncle John Deacon for two years. Like everyone else, he also trapped, hunted, and fished. The only time Dad worked out of town was for the FAA runway at the Farewell station near McGrath.

My oldest brother, Rudy, the first of seven, was born in 1935. He was followed by Allan, Gloria, me in 1941, Calvin, Ernie, and Leonard. My parents also adopted my sister, Gloria's son, Clinton Chase. My mother had no time for things like beading. She cooked, washed clothes, and cleaned all the time.

My mother kept our family together. She disciplined us, talked with us about our problems, and took over everything. Our dad was pretty nil on such matters. He was there but he never criticized us, spoke harshly, or spanked us. We honored that and we did not have to be disciplined by him.

Mom had a little trapline for pleasure, west of Anvik at Whitestone Creek drainage, and a registered fish camp allotment about three-fourths of a mile upstream.

My dad and grandfather were both pretty generous. I guess we were a little better off than most people. My grandfather had a friend who he looked out for and offered a meal to as needed. Likewise, my dad had a couple of friends he always helped out and who sometimes worked for him. It was a pretty close-knit community. Besides my parents being generous, they never had alcohol around. That was a blessing.

Anvik was the only territorial school in the area. Missions had the first schools in Alaska. Holy Cross had a Catholic mission school and Anvik had an Episcopal mission school. However, when the missions shut down, the Territory of Alaska took over their schools. Where there was no mission, the forerunner of the BIA, the Office of Indian Affairs, built schools, as they did at Holikachuk and Shageluk. The OIA schools seemed to have more resources and offer more opportunities than the territorial schools, since the OIA had better funding, but our school mandated that we take off two weeks each spring for practicing survival skills. That was really good.

My grandfather and dad had the local store in Anvik. He and Dad used to buy fur so there were lots of pelts lying around. I liked to roll in them, trying to bring them back to life I guess. My grandfather gave me the Athabascan name of *Tixgedr* (pronounced "Tugh gedge"), which means "mink."

As soon as we kids were old enough, our dad let us learn things on our own. He didn't show us anything. We weren't told not to do stuff. We had freedom and the camaraderie of our peers, but we had to find out pretty much everything on our own. For a few days of each year, we gathered berries, hunted small game, and put up smoked fish, some of my best memories. Despite these traditional activities with my family, I learned most of my Native subsistence skills from the Young family, Wilfred, Lucius, John, and Franklin. They were great dogmen too. Wilfred was a genius with training dogs and leaders, but it was never passed on to me. He was a dog whisperer, but I think it amounted to having patience and always speaking in a mellow tone of voice. Several in the village were like that, but I wasn't. I lost my temper pretty quickly.

I was always one to challenge things. I was told that I talked back but I was inquisitive. I asked why and I wanted to know answers, but I was told that I was "too young" regarding whatever it was I was asking. This lack of communication is still a hindrance in the Native community today: that of keep quiet and watch, but don't ask. Well, I asked and I learned. I had to 'cause no one was going to show me.

Our family had five eighty-pound dogs. When I was five, I got my first, Bibs, from Wilfred Young. I bred her to one of our family's dogs and eventu-

W.C. Chase's dog team, ca. 1918, Anvik.
Chapman Family Papers. Album 1, UAF-2008-15-CO1

ally, I had six or seven trapline dogs that I disciplined and trained. For six years, I won the local Yukon River sprint race championships including an 18-mile race near Anvik. I had really good dogs.

When I was nine I started running the fishwheel with my brother Allan, and later with brothers Ernie and Calvin. We put up 3,000 to 5,000 fish a year and built our own smokehouse.

Since our territorial school mandated a two-week spring break for practicing subsistence, when I was eleven in 1952, my cousin John Walker, my eighteen-year-old brother Rudy, and I went out beaver trapping. We covered thirty-five miles.

After I graduated from eighth grade in Anvik, I went on to high school at Mount Edgecumbe in Sitka. When I arrived there, I was pretty naïve. I didn't know anything about basketball and similar sports. However, in my junior year, I went out for cross-country and track and I was a pretty good athlete.

During the summer when I was sixteen, I began fighting fire. The following year after I graduated in 1958, I joined the Army National Guard and did a six-year stint, followed by three more years in the army reserves. I was supposed to go to aeronautical engineering mechanical school at Northrop Institute of Technology in Inglewood, California, but my dad got tuberculosis and had to be hospitalized. I began running his grocery store in Anvik. After working there for a year, I didn't want to return to school. When I was seventeen, I was put on the village council. At nineteen, I became chief, a position I held until I was fifty-six.

During the summer, I fought fire and during the winter, I trapped. For mink, we got between $20 and $60 per pelt and for a beaver hide, $30 to $40. During the early 1960s, Anvik's main fur was beaver and mink, but today there is also marten.

During three summers fighting fire, I pounded the ground, doing line work, chainsawing and clearing fuels. In 1963, I became a Bureau of Land Management (BLM) permanent seasonal, training crews and traveling around the state, teaching chainsaw use and running pump operations in places like Northway, Aniak, Kalskag, and Bethel. Five years later I got into smokejumping and worked my way up to foreman and got into the jumping loft. During my years in fire control, 1957–1972, I learned a lot of skills.

One day in 1968, my friend Dave Ames and I were sitting in an airplane, wearing parachutes and getting ready to jump. He said, "Ken, we jump out of these crazy things. Why don't we also learn to fly them?" The next week, we went to Merrill Field in Anchorage and began lessons. A year and half later, we each bought ourselves an airplane.

For two years until spring 1971, I enjoyed aerial wolf hunting. Every year, I'd get my limit of ten. Until 1970, the fifty-dollar bounty per wolf was also on. But in October 1972, the Airborne Hunting Act or Shooting from Aircraft Act went into effect. Aerial wolf hunting was no longer allowed.

In the early 1970s, a veritable fish gold rush began. The Japanese were buying salmon roe. As an agent for Chun King owners Kemp and Gino Palouche of Minnesota, who had a plant in Bethel, I bought fish eggs and shipped them to the coast. In 1972, deciding to double-dip, I also got my commercial fishing license.

As the fight for Alaska Native land claims began in the late 1960s, John Deacon and I traveled to Anchorage to attend some of the first Alaska Federation of Natives meetings. With other Alaska Natives statewide, we testified before a U.S. Senate subcommittee about the use of our land.

In 1972, just after the Alaska Native Claims Settlement Act (ANCSA) was passed, the elders began calling me home. They had no leader and wanted me to work for the village corporation. Finally, I quit my job and came home. I got a small salary from the corporation, but of course nothing like from smokejumping. The elders were in a panic. Not only did they have to have a land selection committee, but that body had to research and document the lands that the Anvik people had historically used. I was hired immediately. As president of our Native corporation, Ingalik, Inc. (later renamed Deloy Ges, Inc.), I had to consult the elders and map the boundaries of where they

Ken Chase operating his fish wheel near Anvik, ca. 2010.

Courtesy of Ken Chase.

hunted, fished, and trapped. At the same time, I had to assess mining, timber, and fisheries resources. With these guides, we selected our lands.

After I left BLM, I became a professional board member, serving Doyon, the regional corporation, Tanana Chiefs Conference, and the Iditarod Area School District. I was also chief and mayor. I was going in circles, constantly going to meetings. My second wife, Adele, didn't like it so I began flying home more often, but while I was home, I also trapped. One day in late 1972, I heard something on the radio about people starting a dog race from Anchorage to Nome. I jumped up and ran to the radio, crying, "What's going

Ken Chase, BLM smokejumper, 1969.
Courtesy of Ken Chase.

on?!" My wife said, "They are starting a dog race to Nome." I said, "I'm going. That's it!" I was in really good shape. I was told if I'd trained, I could have won, but right up to the start, most people didn't think the race was going to really happen anyway. I had only five or six dogs. One was so old that he could hardly get out of his doghouse. I borrowed three dogs including a lead from a friend, Hoover Howard, in Shageluk, and one from Wilfred Young and one from Marcus Maillelle in Anvik, making a total of ten dogs. These dogs, however, hadn't been off the chain for more than two weeks. No one had run them except for me once in a while. Worse, on my first day out of Anchorage, the lead dog from Hoover quit. With no other choice, I began using my eighteen-month-old pup, Piper, who became a fantastic lead dog.

That first year the army broke trail down the challenging Happy River Steps into Happy River, followed the river into the gorge, almost to Pontilla Lake. Another difficult place was between Rohn River and Farewell, after the Post River Glacier, where the water comes out of the mountain, making it really slick. The descent was really steep where we had to lower our team down on a rope and then, our sled. We had to help Joe Redington lower his twenty dogs. Bud Smyth of Wasilla and an Eskimo from Unalakleet, Victor "Duke" Kotongan, and I pretty well stayed together all the way to Nome.

My only strategy was not to quit, to go with the flow, and to try to adjust. I had no idea how long it was going to take. Camping out didn't bother me, but we weren't used to pushing our dogs that hard and that long. I dropped three of my team that year and finished with seven. From Rainy Pass to McGrath, we did a lot of trail breaking and walking. As we neared Nome, Bud Smyth and I were really racing. We were just minutes apart even though previously, he'd beaten me into Rohn. When I crossed the finish line, I kinda wanted to keep going. I was in really good shape as were the dogs. The race staff took care of them so I could rest. It was all really good. With Piper, I came in thirteenth and for the next eleven years, he led. The banquet was held in Breakers Bar.

Dick Mackey with Ken Chase, who was the fifteenth musher into Nome, 1976.
Rosemary Phillips. *Iditarod Trail Annual*

Those first two years, we had pretty good meals, made easier with coffee pots, frying pans, and white gas stoves. We ate bacon, steaks, juice, tea, and pilot bread, pretty good feed. This was before the race began going toward K-Rations and sealed frozen bags of food, like they do nowadays.

I began building up my kennel. When I was working, I paid my daughters, Carolyn and Marilyn, to cook for our thirty-three dogs and to run them. In the 1974 Iditarod, I ran a team of twelve to fourteen dogs. In 1975, I ran fifteen to sixteen dogs, which enabled me to shave off nine days from my 1973 and 1974 race times.

My brother Ernie had an air taxi out of Grayling. Some years, he flew dogs into Anchorage for me, but I also ferried my own dogs, which included some of the offspring of my first dog, Bibs.

The first years of the Iditarod, Native mushers included me, Emmitt Peters, Jerry Riley, Herbie Nayokpuk, Isaac Okleasik, and Sidney's son, Carl Huntington, who won the Rondy, the North American, and the George Attla races. Johnny Komak of Teller, Rudy Demoski of Anvik, Ralph "Babe" Anderson, and Allen "Eep" Anderson (who happened to live next door to my grandfather Ebena in McGrath) all raced with us. There were a lot of Natives. It was a good time of joking, sharing, camping, and having a lot of fun.

I never wore store-bought rubberized boots, but rather Native moosehide "boots." I waterproofed them by dipping them quickly into overflow water in sub-zero temperatures. I let them freeze so that water couldn't get through them. I used caribou hide on the inside and outside and dried grass for sole liners. One time at a rest stop at Farewell Lake Lodge, a bunch of soaked mushers began pulling their boots apart, hoping to dry their liners. They looked over at me and Rudy Demoski as we started outside to get some of our dogs' straw bedding. "What you guys doin'?" they asked. We returned with handfuls of dry grass; "Changing the straw in our boots," we said.

I always had beaver mitts, marten or beaver hat, and homemade socks. Handknit

Ken's sponsor Alaska Native Brotherhood thanking Ken Chase for his Iditarod 1974 sixth place and 1975 eighth place finishes.

Courtesy of Ken Chase.

socks have a lot of holes that hold the heat and are the best you can get. I carried a head lamp, an extra light, and the bulky heavy lantern batteries that last a long time, lots of rope, open dog snaps, and a couple of short chains for roughlocking.

In my first couple of races, I had a poor sleeping bag. One night, Victor Kotongan and I were camping out. It was forty-some below. His sleeping bag was only two caribou hides sewn together, which he laid directly on top of the snow. Wearing a caribou hat, leggings, and mittens, he crawled inside. In my sled, lying in my thin sleeping bag on a bear-hide mattress with a tarp pulled over the top, I was trying to get comfortable while he was already snoring. In the morning, he got up as fresh as a daisy while I was half frozen. The next race, I didn't resort to caribou hides but I got a Gerry Mountaineering duck down sleeping bag. Even at sixty-three below zero, I slept much better.

I'd been a smoke jumper since 1967, weighed 160 pounds and could climb up a rope like a monkey. During spring beaver trapping, I worked sets all day long. In 1976, I was in top shape. When we left Solomon that year, several of us, old Joe Redington, his sons Raymie and Joee, Ron Aldrich, Dick Mackey, and I, were racing together. Raymie took off first and mushed thirty-two miles out in the blowing snow and the dark. He got off the trail and was wandering around looking for the way. Quietly, with my light turned

Ken Chase, Iditarod eighth place finisher, 1975.

1975 Iditarod Trail Annual.

off and with my lead dog, Piper, I came up behind him. I said nothing, not a word. He knew I was out there, but he didn't know where. He kept hollering for me but I wouldn't answer while I passed him by. Determined to get the best time from Safety to Nome, but at the risk of freezing my lungs, I ran twenty-one miles in very cold temperatures to win the fastest. However, when I got into Nome after midnight, I thought I was having a heart attack. I went to the hospital, but it was only pleurisy.

In 1978, I made up my mind to train my dogs well and to try to be one of the frontrunners. All was going well with Rick Swenson in the lead, followed by Dick Mackey, then Emmitt Peters, and me in fourth. I had a strong showing at Ophir and they knew I was the one to beat. At White Mountain, seven of us got bunched up: Joe Redington, Dick Mackey, Rick Swenson, Emmitt Peters, Joe May, Eep Anderson, and me. I deliberately left last because I knew I could catch them and indeed, I began passing them. At the Blowhole, thirty-five miles out of Nome, a hellacious big storm hit. One of my beaver mitts blew out on the glare ice and hung up on a tree root. After I got my mitt, it took me twenty minutes on my hands and knees, crawling up glare ice, to get back to my dogs. I didn't know I had passed some of the guys, but I came on Joe who was all bunched up with his dogs in the howling wind. I began to go on by him but he asked, "Can you help me?" I kept going, but I soon came back. I straightened up his dogs and then, lined them out to follow me. We went a ways, but when I looked back, his dogs were all bundled up again. They wouldn't go, but again, I got him moving. He said, "Don't leave me. I don't think I'm going to make it. Stay with me." So I said, "Okay," but his dogs wouldn't follow me. The only way they would was if we snubbed his dogs into the back of my sled so I could pull them, which is illegal, but it was kind of an emergency. He asked me to get him to Solomon, which I did, but by then, the leaders were two hours out ahead of us so the delay essentially cost me the race. I said, "Joe, you may as well stay with me as far as 9-mile."

Ken Chase's sled in which he carried his Iditarod mail cachet to deliver to Nome.
Courtesy of Ken Chase.

Nine miles out of Nome, Joe was falling asleep in the sled. At that point, we untied our sleds and I went on in alone. I had told the checkers in Solomon and again, I told the staff in Nome that I'd had to tie Joe's sled to mine. They tried to disqualify us, but other mushers protested, saying it had been an emergency. The race marshal, Bud Smyth, saw the need and dropped the disqualification. My highest finish was that year in fourth place, which I ran in fifteen days and two minutes. I got $4,000; now fourth place is worth ten times that, almost $40,000!

The next year Jimmy Demientieff was flying my plane so that I'd have it available in Nome. Emmitt and I took our 24-hour layover in Skwentna. Jimmy was landing my plane there, but he didn't see a big ditch a Cat had just made across the runway. He knocked the landing gear off and bent my prop and strut. My brother Rudy flew in the necessary parts, but instead of resting, I spent my 24-hour rest fixing my plane. As soon as it was in the air, I took off with my team and caught the frontrunners in Farewell.

I had lots of adventures getting my team to Anchorage, but the worst was the transit of my handlers, Alvin Hoover and my son Falcon Chase, to Anchorage. The boys were flying my dogs by Woods Air Service to Aniak to catch Northern Air Cargo there down to Anchorage. However, there was a problem and the boys had to overnight in Aniak. That night, they were walking down the street when a youngster on a 4-wheeler hit them. He almost killed Alvin, breaking his legs and hip, and he messed up my son's back. I almost scratched. I was pretty upset and I didn't feel like racing.

Another time, a state senator from Juneau was piloting me and my team through the mountains in the dark. We were in a hurry and we were push-ing conditions when the weather began to change. We almost didn't make it.

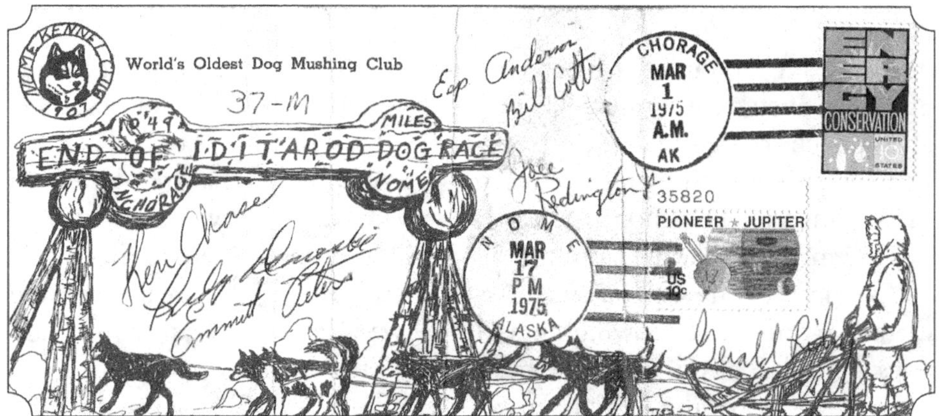

Ken Chase's official Iditarod envelope signed by other mushers, carried in his mail cachet to Nome, 1975.

Courtesy of Ken Chase.

With the extreme effort and lack of sleep, I hallucinated on the trail a lot. The worst time was between Koyuk and Elim when out on the ice, I sud-denly saw a huge cathedral all lit up, with its chimes ringing. Another time Carl Huntington and I were traveling outside of Farewell. I was so tired I saw a tree fall in front of my dogs and I stopped quickly, but there was no tree.

One year, Dick Mackey left Shaktoolik in an oncoming storm. Seeing the ferocity of the wind, Rudy Demoski, Babe and Eep Anderson, decided to return to the shelter cabin. Old timers at Shak said Dick Mackey was getting himself into trouble. Thinking that two are better than one, I left to check on him, out there on the ocean ice. Sure enough, he was there, struggling to get his tarp up. I helped get him get it secure, but we were eight miles out and by the time we were finished making a camp, I didn't feel like going back so we stayed there till morning. I laid in my sled all night, chewing on frozen cheese. In the morning, we pushed on to Koyuk.

On the other end of the temperature spectrum, there was a race when it was too warm and we mushed in pouring, blowing rain. Our clothes be-came frozen with ice. A musher can't always have it the way he wants. It's part of the game.

I may've started the tradition of leaving food at Old Woman. About 1980 between Ruby and Galena one year, I was traveling alone on a cold windy night. A driver had pulled off the trail. I asked, "What are you doing and who are you?" He said, "Camping and Martin Buser." It was Martin's first race and he was running Earl Norris' dogs. I said, "This is the coldest place on the river. C'mon with me to Whiskey Creek, about ten miles farther, where it's better. " Later in the race, when we got near Unalakleet at Old

Woman cabin. I told Martin, "There's a story that an old woman and her husband trapped out of this cabin on that mountain a long time ago. One day when they were separately checking their sets up on the mountainside, an avalanche came suddenly hurtling down. The woman was buried and her body was never found. Since then some people have said that they have seen unexplained phenomenon there, so we leave food to show the old woman that we mean no harm." I think Martin still leaves food there to this day.

The most dogs I ever had was forty-four. I was the only one really working them. My kids were growing up and they wouldn't let me cull out certain dogs. I think that was really the beginning of the end.

For seven years, the Alaska Native Brotherhood (ANB) sponsored me. In 1977, they decided to finance the Ken Chase Sportsmanship award, which the Iditarod approved and awarded me that year. (My leader, Piper, also received the Golden Harness award.) The sportsmanship award bore my name until 1982. However, ANB required for their financial support of the award that the Iditarod also recognize a certain number of other Native mushers. When that did not happen, ANB dropped out. The sportsmanship award became the Fred Meyer Sportsmanship award.

In the early years of the Iditarod, we Native mushers fed frozen fish, dried fish, and beaver meat—high-protein food. I didn't start sending commercial feed out until 1977. The Iditarod thought that not all mushers were bringing enough food so we were forced to provide three pounds per dog per drop, twice what was needed. To even the score a little, we packed extra dog food pans in our commercial feed to increase the weight of the food per bag. About 1983, I was flying to the Iditarod anyway so I flew my own feed out to the checkpoints, but in Anchorage, they told me they wouldn't allow it. They said I had to ship it to Anchorage and after the race, pick up any left-over feed. I had a big squabble with them over it. I was forced under protest to withdraw that year. Unfortunately, rural mushers are subject to the same rules as the urban mushers but they don't have the advantages of those living on the road system. Eventually dog food science became more systematized, but when it got to that point, I was no longer racing.

The first four to five years of the race, the Iditarod was made up of maybe fifty percent rural mushers, including many Natives. Now, except for the occasional person like John Baker of Kotzebue, it's pretty much roadside people running the race. The big expenses for rural Alaskans are the freight and having to buy dog food. Most modern teams cost $10,000 to $40,000 per year, and the top ten spend up to $80,000. The top finisher won at least $69,000, but that amount decreased when the 2010 winner received only $50,000. The race has become quite high tech and the rules require man-

Rudy Demoski, Ken Chase, and Warner Vent, Nome, 1974.
Photo by Richard Burmeister. Courtesy of Ken Chase.

datory meetings, which is not always possible with flying conditions in the Bush. The new rules and pressure have resulted in problems for the Bush mushers, but they can also affect everyone.

From Nicolai to White Mountain, I stayed with families most of the time: in McGrath with a teacher, Terry Chase, and in Ruby with George Kennedy, an older man who waited up a long time one year for me to come in. I stayed with him every year until he passed. Checkpoints were loose and fun with mushers helping each other bring their harnesses in to dry and hanging their wet outer garments. It was a good time. In those early days, everyone knew my lead dog, Piper, who I'd raised from a pup. Grayish yellow, weighing fifty-five pounds, Piper resembled a medium-sized wolf.

I was active in politics way too long. I took an interest in the traditional way of life because other village elders, the Youngs, took me out hunting, fishing, and camping. Also much later as a result of other elders, I served as our corporation president, executive director, and the head of our lands commission for thirty years. A lot of my top earning years were wasted, but I was not into making money.

Today I am chairman of the advisory fish and game board over four Yukon River villages: Grayling, Anvik, Shageluk, and Holy Cross. I also chair the Mid-Yukon Kuskokwim Soil and Water Conservation District, which serves twelve villages. We felt that bison could be another source of meat for us. In the fall of 2016, we moved about 123 woodland bison calves and adults from Portage to Shageluk to feed in the Innoko Flats. Over the last three winters, the herd has moved south toward Holy Cross. There are three pretty good size bunches and a few loners. They are still trying to find good pasture where they can settle in. They have to get better accustomed to survival in the Alaska wilderness. Last fall there were about 110 but I think the winter of 2018 to 2019 may've brought the numbers back up, but it's too early to tell yet.

I am also busy transporting hunters and guiding them as well as flying freight for a mine outside of McGrath.

Looking back, it's hard to figure how much running the Iditarod cost me due to the expense of flying and of staying home taking care of dogs, rather than having a career. Add to that, the incalculable hours of toil for our family putting up 5000 to 6000 fish per year for forty dogs, and a different method of analysis is needed to quantify my investment. A few times I got help with the entrance fee, but most of the time, it was all out of pocket.

Ken Chase, 2017.
Susan Paskvan photo

I have done many things in the Iditarod: raced in the first race, been in the top ten, placed fourth, been the fastest from Safety to Nome, taken the sportsmanship and Golden Harness awards, been a pilot, judge, trailbreaker, and checker, as well as sat on the board of directors. In 1997, I decided to go after the Red Lantern award. To do that, I hid from Jerome Longo for six hours in Unalakleet, to make sure I came in as the caboose.

Because I had to earn a living, I couldn't train like Rick Swenson and the other top runners. Due to subsistence fishing and the constraints of where I lived, in the off-season I couldn't do anything with my dogs. Beginning in November, I had only a few months to train before the Iditarod.

Over all, I have entered the Iditarod sixteen times, including its first eleven years. I finished twelve times, placing three times in the top ten, at fourth, sixth, and eighth positions. After 1983, I ran five more races with the last in 2002. From 1973 to 2002, I raced on and off for twenty-nine years. I might have one more Iditarod left in me, but I don't want to train dogs for only one race. If there were someone to mentor, to whom I could give the dogs afterward, that would make it worthwhile.

I am on the Iditarod Area School District board and talk often to kids. My message to the young is, "Put your mind and soul toward your goals. There are many vices out there today. You have to give up conflicting activities and entangling friends to achieve your dreams. You have to be willing to live outside your comfort zone." I've been trying to find someone motivated

Ken's mother, Kate Ebena, Anvik Episcopal mission. ca. 1925.
Donna MaAlpine, *A Brief History of the Anvik Mission.*

to commit to the race. I'll help them and even raise dogs for them but so far, only one guy showed interest but he's too involved with booze. I don't operate like that. The other day, a fourteen-year-old school drop-out kid told me that he wanted to learn to fly. I said, "That's the easy part but you have to pass the tests also. Hit the books, stay away from alcohol and drugs and make healthy commitments." I'm not preaching, but I'm talking from experience. Education is a necessity but even more so for the kids in the villages. They have to have it.

My Holikachuk paternal grandmother, Agatha Deacon, born before the gold rush, lived to see a helicopter fly in and circle Anvik. Completely amazed, she laughed and laughed. During the late 1940s and early 1950s, when we kids used to sit on the riverbank and watch the old Norseman airplanes come in on skis, we never dreamed that someday we'd be flying them ourselves. During one of the Iditarod races, my mother, Katherine Ebena Chase, who was born in Dikeman, near the Iditarod, wanted to go back and see it; my brother Ernie and I flew her there. In only three generations, we are not only in the space age, but also in cyber space. In a short time, our family has come over a difficult and winding trail, from the Iditarod River to the Iditarod Trail Dogsled Race, that may be monitored now moment by moment via the internet. It's a long way for a people to travel but we are up to the task.

Chapter 3

Warner Vent, Happy-Go-Lucky: Twice Second in Early Iditarod

Warner Vent, ca. 1980s.
Courtesy of Warner Vent.

In 1898 prospectors who couldn't find claims in the Klondike came over to the Koyukuk River. The influx of outsiders resulted in a deadly measles epidemic in 1902. Warner Vent's uncle, Edwin Simon, remembered, "Lot of people died. Some whole families just wipe out. Kids, old people. Everybody die."

Warner's father-in-law Joe Beetus said, "Around September 1911, my uncle Alfred Isaac went where Indian and Utopia creeks meet and found gold. After that Hughes City began." In 1920 Warner Vent's Scottish grandfather, Edward Vent, and his Athabascan wife, Mary Magdalena, were living in the mining area of Clear and Aloha creeks below the town of Hughes. Ten years later, they were cutting wood at Blackburn on the Yukon River where they lived with their second child, Bobby Vent, who, fifty-three years later, came close to winning the first Iditarod.

Bobby and his son Warner are among the handful of Alaska Athabascan Iditarod pioneer mushers. At twenty-seven, Warner, was already a veteran sprint musher. He ran in Joe Redington's 1967 Iditarod forerunner, the Centennial Race. Out of fifty-four finishers, Warner came in seventh.

In 1973 when reaching Nome was still very iffy because of hazardous trail conditions, and the prize money was chancy, sixty-year old Bobby beat men half his age in the Iditarod—and that was with a game leg. Bobby had one marginal dog that, had it gone down after the 1000 miles, Bobby would have been disqualified—but he alternated resting that dog and others in his sled and he came in second, just behind thirty-one year old Dick Wilmarth and before thirty-five-year-old Dan Seavey. With his $8000 prize money, Bobby started a much needed store, R & M Mercantile, in Huslia, first opening up with a counter top in his living room.

The following year, when the race was only two years old, Warner entered the Iditarod, the first of his four races. When Alaska Natives dominated the young race, Warner placed second both in 1974 and in 1976. At the 1976 Iditarod Trail Awards Banquet, Warner grinned, "I only owned one dog in my whole dog team!" Even though he did not own all of them, Warner trained them all on trails up the Koyukuk River. A man who lives up to his Athabascan name, K'esots'eeye', Happy Go Lucky Guy, Warner shared his story by phone during the 2017 sprint racing season.

Warner's parents, Mary and Bobby Vent, second place winner, 1973 Iditarod with Orville Lake, holding the mic and Joe Redington in background.
Courtesy of Iditarod annual and Warner Vent.

The son of Bobby Vent and Mary Olin Charlie Vent, I was born on a cold fall day in October 1940 out in camp. In those days, people lived in Cutoff, upstream from today's village of Huslia. Everyone lived in their family trapping or fish camps and there was no school. My dad had a cabin above the old town [Cutoff], where he trapped. Our whole family stayed there. For spiking out, he had an 8 x 10 wall tent with a Yukon stove (but even so, tents are cold). He also had a cabin at the mouth of Happy Slough and another one at the mouth of Nulitna (*Noolaaytne)* Slough twenty-one miles up the Huslia River. My parents raised seventeen children including five from my mom's first marriage and two whom they adopted. Dad trapped and hunted and Mom set snares for rabbit and ptarmigan. They worked hard to raise us kids.

The year I was born, people began moving slowly from Cutoff to Huslia. In 1950 when a school was built, I began first grade there and went on to the sixth.

My dad always had dogs: huskies and malamutes for both working and racing. I used to trap beaver with him.

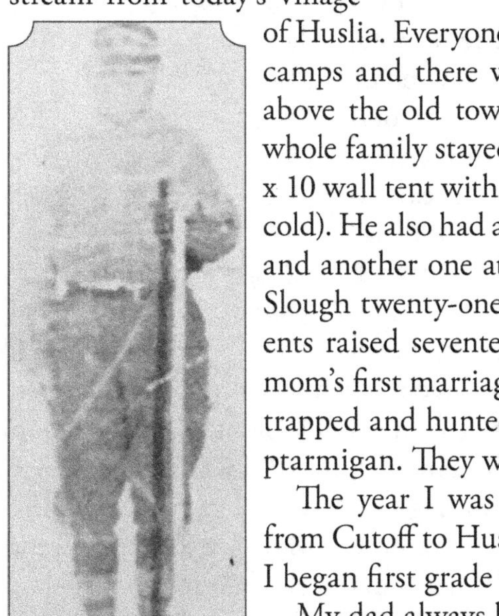

Hog River Johnny named Warner Vent K'esots'eeye', Happy-Go-Lucky Guy, because when Johnny was old and blind, young Warner visited him.
Courtesy Warner Vent.

No snow machine those days. Our village dogs had the best fur in cold weather and weighed about seventy pounds. We made our sleds of birch and later, put plastic on the runners that we got from Cutting Edge in Fairbanks. We used babiche (rawhide) to hold the stanchions [the uprights that connect the runners to the sled bed. *Ed.*]. Nowadays locals prefer toboggans that slide more easily over obstacles and aren't as likely to break up. For wood hauling, we used sleds with a seven-foot by four-foot basket, but for racing, we used a four-foot long sled. Dad's fur buyers were first Johnny Swagler, "Muskrat Johnny" and later on, Dean Wilson.

I looked up to my dad, to my uncle Steven Attla and to George Attla. Uncle Steven used to come by and visit me. He'd tell me what to look for in a dog. He and Tony Sam were a help to me. Grandpa Fred Bifelt used to read the weather. He'd say, "It looks like it's gonna get windy." I'd say, "How d'ya know that, Grandpa?" He'd reply, "If you see clouds like lines, it means that wind is coming." He used to live above old town on Duck Lake by Dakli River. There're no trees up there. On the way to the hot springs, there's that big Cone Mountain on the right, he'd point and say, "If you see blowing snow on top of that, get out, because a big wind is coming." I learned to watch the ice, look out for overflow, and pay attention if the temperature was about to drop.

When I was fourteen, I planned to quit school and trap like the older boys. I had three

Warner Vent, ca 1956.
Courtesy of Warner Vent and Sarah Malamute.

dogs at camp and I was trapping beaver. We'd just had really cold weather so my trap was iced in under three feet of glaciation. It took me all day to chop that trap out. That was my first night at camp by myself. I was so scared that I stayed awake all night. I tied my lead dog by the door but I still couldn't sleep. When morning came, I finally passed out. When I woke up, I went back home, thinking, "The heck with that," and I returned to school—but only until the end of sixth grade. Later I could've kicked myself for quitting school.

I worked here and there. I started out on the bull gang using a shovel, pick, and ax up at the Hog River mining camp for three or four years. The dredge was operated by Alaska Natives Cue Bifelt and Frank Sam. I began working as an oiler on the dredge and then, I learned how to operate it. They let me monkey around with the dredge but that's all history now.

Warner Vent racing Open North American, 1962.
Courtesy of Warner Vent and Sarah Malamute.

There's a smaller mining operation up there now, but long ago, everyone from Hughes, Allakaket, and Huslia—everyone—worked up there. I don't believe in living off food stamps, general assistance, subsidies for oil and wood; that's throwing my parents' lifestyle away.

I was always pretty strong. When I was eighteen in 1958, I used to run an almost five-minute mile four miles down and back to Richard's (Derendoff) Spring Camp. I always planned on running the Mount Marathon five-kilometer race on the Fourth of July in Seward, but I never quite made it. I won a lot of snowshoe races: the Huslia two-mile, Hughes, back and forth across the Koyukuk, and at Tanana across the Yukon River and back. I did pretty good that year.

I figured one way to please my dad was to take over mushing dogs. He drove them all his life so he understood them pretty good. When he and I got together and talked dogs, it was like two old buddies talking. I've been running dogs since I was able to hook them up. I started mushing competitively when I was eighteen. I won races here in Huslia several times. My record time stands: fifty-nine minutes on our seventeen-mile dogsled track, but there've been no dogsleds on that course in a long time. I raced in our Koyukuk village races in Allakaket, Huslia, and Hughes. However it was hard for the villages to raise money for three races so in the late 1970s, Alfred Attla, Beatus Moses, and I decided to have one race per year but rotate it between the three villages. The Koyukuk River Championship became very popular—but unfortunately, 2017 was its last year.

In 1959 I began training for the Open North American (ONAC). The champ, George Attla, Jr. and I used to talk for hours, trying to figure out dogs. For eight years, John Butrovich of Alaska Insurance Company in Fairbanks sponsored me. Four times I placed in the top five in the North American and twice in the top six of the Anchorage Fur Rondy.

May be Warner Vent who competed in the predecessor to the Iditarod, the Alaska Purchase Centennial race, Anchorage, 1967.
Photographer Harvey Sauder Courtesy of Randy Sauder.

My sponsors for the Iditarod in 1974, 1976, and 1977 included my dad and sister Mabel's store, R & M Mercantile, fur buyer Dean Wilson, and fur buyer Dave Stout. My dad blew a lot of money on me! Today dog food in Huslia costs $70 per bag. I can only afford a scraps-eating dog now.

When my wife, Alberta Beetus, and I got married in 1960, we had eighteen young dogs. Every other day, I'd turn them all loose and let them run the length of the sandbar and then, they'd jump in the river and swim across and back. Alberta would get mad because they would fly right through our—and my auntie's—fish camp tents. Running them on sand toughened up their feet so I never had foot problems with them. In the beginning of turning them loose, they'd get into a lot of fights. I'd wade right in there with them and discipline them. A few experiences like that made them afraid to fight. Then school began when I tied them back up to their posts. I'd have to pet them quite a bit before they'd forget their spanking. Dogs are really smart.

I had a young leader named Fanny in the 1960s, probably the best I ever owned. She was part husky and part collie and never got sore feet or became lame. When I walked along the sandbar with all my dogs, Fanny and another young teammate would wander away from me. I'd hide and whistle through my hands at them. Then all seventeen of my dogs would start looking for me and they'd find me. Once after the team was harnessed but before I got on the sled, they broke loose and took off on me. I climbed a ridge 500 feet up, cupped my hands, and whistled. Fanny turned the whole team around and began looking for me. I have had two other really good leaders: a part collie but mostly husky, Nellie, who I got from Joe Redington

Warner feeding his dogs, Iditarod Trail.

Courtesy of Warner Vent.

in the mid-1970s to mid-1980s. In the 1990s, I had my third good leader, Husky. He was George Attla's dog—part Aurora husky, part Siberian husky, and part village husky.

Every year as soon as there was snow, I'd start training dogs. I'd weed out the culls and begin looking for others. I trained and shopped by driving my dogs 100 miles to Hughes and then, on up, a little less than an hour, to Allakaket. My father-in-law, Joe Beetus, lived at Hughes where I frequently got dogs. On the way over, my son Leonard and I would stop at the halfway point, Bear Mountain, and have tea to rest for a half hour. Sometimes I come back around the middle of the night in the dark. That's just one thing you gotta learn. When I was out training, my dad would heat up a dog pot for me and have the team's food ready.

The first Iditarod, in which my dad placed second, was essentially a camping trip; nobody knew if they were going to make it all the way to Nome or not. In 1975 Dad tried again, but he got pneumonia and had to scratch.

When I entered the Iditarod in 1974, my dogs were good but I didn't have the right kind of food for them. We Native mushers fed dry dog food and didn't realize that dogs have to have water or they'll get dehydrated and quit. I didn't know hardly anything like what I know now. Now everybody has boots on their dogs from start to finish. If a paw gets sore, a dog is out of the race. In those days, we used boots but we thought it was only for certain kind of conditions. I had to learn on my own to buy booties and when to use them.

When I decided to run in 1974, my sisters pitched in making my clothing. I wore knee-high boots lined with caribou leg hide. I had rabbit-lined lynx mitts. On flat ground, I wore my bunny boots but in the hills, I wore the fur boots. I carried canvas boots for a backup. I had a down parka and down pants. I took a marten hat and carried an extra fox hat, which was good for windy days. I never wore a facemask. My buddy, a teacher in Tanana, Don Kratzer, gave me a good down sleeping bag.

Before we left, the Iditarod staff always checked our gear. All the food drops were mailed so the food had to be light, often dehydrated. I packed a lot of dried meat and fish for the dogs. I used salmon to flavor snow water to get the dogs to drink. Since I was working all the time, I carried a couple of Thermoses for myself because it seemed like all I wanted to do was drink. I boiled up dried food to eat.

Before I left for the Iditarod, Uncle Edwin Simon, my mom's sister's husband, an elder I always listened to, and who visited me every morning, stopped by. He told me, "Don't worry about NOTHING. You'll make it." That gave me a lot of hope.

I flew my team chained up in a Cessna 207 with my stuff into Fairbanks, then we trucked them to Anchorage. Sometimes we chained them in the back of the pickup going down because hardly anyone had dog boxes, them days.

So far as prerace gambling events, like Calcutta, I'm always a loser! I don't even want to talk about it!

We started at Fourth Avenue in Anchorage, where it was pretty crowded. I drew starting position twenty-one. When Herbie Nayokpuk, the Shishmaref Cannonball, took off in front of me, his dogs were going crazy and his parka fell off his sled. I picked it up and later, he sure was happy about it.

We mushed our sleds seventy-seven miles from Fourth Avenue to Willow, just to get out of town! We crossed the bridge with cars flying by! The dogs were scared so they stayed on the sidewalk and made sure not to crash. After the 1974 Iditarod, we drove our teams only twelve miles out of town and then, trucked them to Willow for the restart. There's no snow in that section now most of the time anyway.

The first two years of the Iditarod, the trail was pretty bad. I'd heard a lot about the steep, windy switchbacks dipping down into Happy River and back out again. I worried to the point of back flips but when I got there it wasn't so bad.

At the beginning of the race and through Rainy Pass and Rohn River, *Rudy Demoski, Ken Chase, Warner Vent, and Dan Seavey.*
Photo by Richard Burmeister. Courtesy of Sarah Malamute.

Carl Huntington and I traveled together, but after that, he got away and I hardly ever saw him again. He won that year but I came in second, arriving a day behind him.

When he could keep up, Rudy Demoski traveled with me a lot. We became good friends.

Past Rainy Pass, the trail went straight over a cliff. I knew that cliff was coming up but I didn't know where and thinking about it was giving me a fit. Uncle Edwin Simon had told me that before going off any steep drop-off, to cut a three-foot tree down and drag it behind the sled so I did. A poor Eskimo guy, who had a big load, and who didn't drag a tree behind, went down all right. Zheee, it was too steep, that hill, and it was dark. He went half-way over the bank and was stuck on a tree. His sled went two or three feet down and was busted up. I helped pull the sled up from the bottom. His front-end was busted up but his runners still had upturn. I felt sorry for the guy, but my buddy Rudy pointed and said, "Look, broke… !" I replied, "You don't talk English very good." He couldn't quit laughing.

It was windy as we approached the Rohn River. There was no dog trail, only glare ice. My leaders were blown around and they couldn't make it against that wind. I began walking with my leaders, looking for a ribbon marker to see where to cross the river; the water was only a little less than a foot deep, but it was swift. I had canvas boots so I had to walk on the bank's slippery rocks. I had a good leader I'd borrowed from Henry Beatus of Hughes. I told my leader Scotty to go through that swift water and he wasn't scared. Henry had trained him real good. An Eskimo musher was right behind me but his dogs were too scared to follow me across. He tried dragging his leader halfway across. My boots weren't waterproof so on the other side of the river I stood on my sled and threw him a rope to tie onto his leader and then, I dragged him across. That poor musher, his feet were soaked. I asked him if he had extra boots, "Nope," he said so I threw him mine but said, "At the next checkpoint, you gotta give them back." He was sure happy—but he wanted to buy my boots off of me. "Nope," I said, "that's my survival gear." You got to carry extra clothes with you all the time. You never know when you'll go for a cold swim. Rudy laughed when I told him that.

After leaving Rohn and then Post River Glacier, there was an incredibly steep hill where there was no way to slow a team, not even by dragging a tree. Rudy, Jerry Riley, and I had to take turns tying our dogs off and lowering our sleds down. Now, they don't use that section anymore.

Around Rabbit Lake I could hear someone yelling. A moose was standing right over Tim White's wheel dogs. He hollered, asking if I had a gun. I grabbed my pistol and yelled back, "Yes!" Every time his dogs moved, the moose kicked at them. He looked over at my dogs and then, I shot. The moose fell right on Tim's swing dogs. We managed to flip the moose off the dogs and it slid under a tree into a hole, but only its leg showed above the deep snow.

I took my twenty-four hour mandatory rest in McGrath, but I was actually there almost two days! I don't even remember McGrath! Rudy and I had a good time and that's one story you're not going to hear! When I finally got started, the other mushers were already on the Yukon. When I caught up to them in Kaltag, I said, "Nice trail, guys! Thanks!" Yeah, I had good dogs.

I had no race strategy and nothing figured out. I just had my dogs trained pretty well and I kept checking their feet. Good leaders should get a break now and then. They shouldn't be out in front all the time. The team should maintain a good steady fast trot. If they break into a gallop, I say, "Easy, boys" and drag my foot to slow them down, to maintain a good average speed.

One evening before the Iditarod checkpoint, I was crossing big open flats when the wind came up. I traveled as long as I could see the markers but it was getting dark and the dogs were tired. I lost the trail and came to six ten-foot-tall spruce trees. I cut them down and laid them on top of each other to make a windbreak for my dogs, then I snacked my team. I banked my gear inside my canvas bag against the windward side of my sled. I put my sleeping bag inside the sled bag and I climbed in. I could hear the wind howling.

My dogs were already covered up with snow. When I woke the next morning, it was calm and daylight. I fed the dogs and walked around looking for the trail without any idea which way to go. I finally found the markers, but I didn't know which direction to head. I stumbled over a hard drift and saw some dog tracks on it going in the right di-

Warner Vent, second place and Carl Huntington, first place, 1974 Iditarod.
Couresy of Warner Vent and Sarah Malamute.

rection so I got going. I traveled a couple of hours until I saw ol' man Joe Redington struggling in the distance. Snowmachines were coming to meet him and from there, the trail was clear.

At Old Woman Mountain and cabin, the race transitions from a protected inland run to one that cuts through the harsh, whistling winds along the Bering Sea coastline, the last leg before the finish line in Nome. I never stopped at Old Woman. Some say that they heard things there. I just go through there most of the time. [One story claims Old Woman is a form-changing person who can transform into a bear. Long ago she died in an avalanche on the nearby mountain now named after her, perhaps the result of being cursed for "doing a man's work" (the mountain was used by men as a hunting lookout in the old days, according to Kevin Keeler, administrator of the Iditarod National Historic Trail for the U.S. Bureau of Land Management.) *Ed.*]

Another time I lost the trail Rudy and I were at the bottom of a hill, where we were taking shelter from the wind. We were trying to get out on the ice to get to Shaktoolik, but in the blow, we couldn't find the trail. We left our teams, wandered around, found the way but then, we couldn't find our dogs! We were being blizzarded with snow and could barely see our own feet. Wearing headlamps, we crisscrossed the area looking for our teams. My leader had reflective cloth on his harness and finally my light flashed on it! It was snowing and blowing too hard, though, so we returned to the hill to make camp, but another musher was coming along. Rudy grinned, "Let's baloney this guy!" The musher stopped and asked where we were going. "Nome," we said, "where else . . .?" Perplexed, he said, "I must've gotten turned around at that glaciated creek

Warner's wife, Alberta Beetus Vent, son Warner Vent, Jr., and Warner Vent, Sr., 1976, Nome.

Courtesy of Warner Vent.

back there." We teased, "You better turn around and go back the right way." He began to turn his dogs around and we started laughing. He got pretty mad and began cussing us out. We told him it was too windy to go on but he went on down the trail and camped farther down. He wanted nothing more to do with us.

We Athabascans aren't used to mushing along the coast. You have to watch the weather and be ready to change your plan as needed. I go by how my dogs look. I watch them close. I don't push my dogs when they can't go any farther.

When Rudy and I were traveling on the ocean ice with Herbie Nayokpuk, we were nearing Moses Point, between Koyuk and Elim. It was snowing hard and the dogs were tired so we decided to rest out there on the ocean ice. Rudy announced, "I'm going to camp Eskimo-style." He dug a hole in the snow, nested his sled in, lined it with his sleeping bag and crawled in. He grinned, "Tomorrow is my birthday. I hope I get a good start!" Herbie was all smiles. The next morning Rudy woke up in four inches of melt water, cussing. I said, "Happy Birthday, Rudy! Looks like God baptized your rear-end!" I am sure old Cannonball knew what was going to happen, but Rudy had asked for it, saying he was going to nap Eskimo-style!

It had been a long mush from Shaktoolik to Elim. I'd already been on the trail five hours when I got into Elim. My dogs and I were tired; I had to rest. No matter what I did Carl Huntington was always five hours ahead of me. I

L: Rick Swenson, first place and rt: Warner Vent, third place, 1977 Iditarod, awards banquet.
Courtesy of Warner Vent and Sarah Malamute.

knew I couldn't win but I had held my own. I was surprised when I came in second.

After skipping the 1975 Iditarod, I traveled in 1976 to Anchorage to get back into the race. Rudy and I stayed in town with Ollie and Gladys Lord. I always call Rudy my hero dog man. We like to joke and say, "Some day, we may see prize money . . .!" He's half nuts like I am; that's why he's my favorite buddy. We traveled almost all the way to Nome together and really became friends. We did a lot of crazy things during the race and elsewhere. We'll die with those stories. It's good to have a close friend. When I am down, I always have him to talk to. I know he trusts me also.

From the Alaska Range divide, the trail is straight and steep through Dalzell Gorge. In five miles, it drops 1,000 feet. Mushers have little traction and can't zig and zag to slow our descent. We have to ride the brake most of the way down and use a snow hook for grip. Before the trail was made safer, there was a detour, but it went straight up and straight down for a little ways—but it was far enough for Jerry Riley to wreck his headlamp there. When I found him with the shattered light in his hand, he asked, "What am I going to do?!" I knew I had an extra headlamp, but I played it cool, "I guess you're just going to have to wait for daylight." He said, "Oh, no! Couldn't I just stay right behind you!?" After a little more give and take, I gave in and gave him my extra headlamp, poor guy . . . I guess he didn't want to wait for daylight. [According to the book, *Iditarod, The First Ten Years*, Jerry and Warner fixed the headlamp in the dark at -50 but Warner said, "Someone juiced that story up a bit." *Ed.*]

Another time, when I was traveling in deep snow between Rabbit Lake and Puntilla Lodge, my dogs winded something and lay down flat. A moose was coming right at them. The moose stepped on one of my swing dogs, but he didn't hurt him. The bull was suddenly right across from me, on the other side of my sled. His big eyes rolled around and my heart was going ninety miles an hour. I heard another team approaching. The moose swung around and took off after Jerry

Austin's team. Jerry stopped his sled and ran toward the moose as I shinnied up a tree like a wild cat. Jerry shot about five times and yelled out if I was okay. We reported the kill at the next checkpoint.

The first couple of years of the race we could stay with anybody in the village. Rudy lived in McGrath one year so in 1974, I stayed there with him.

Orville Lake interviewing Warner Vent, Nome, ca. 1976.
Courtesy of Warner Vent.

But in 1976 the checkpoint was no longer in the village of McGrath—it was down on the river ice, out of town. It seemed like it might've had something do with some of the mushers' partying in earlier years. Even though I needed a warm place to stay, I just checked in and checked out and kept on going.

At one point, Jerry Riley was right ahead of me, but I was gaining on him. I was tired, it was getting dark, and my dogs were starting to bunch up. I looked to see why the dogs were bunching. I was surprised to see that my swing dog had passed out so I had to haul him. It was a good thing I'd stopped. I quit trying to catch up to Jerry. He came in a day ahead of me, but I came in second.

In 1977 when we started the Iditarod, it was too cold. I saw blood on my dogs' feet so I stopped to put boots on their feet. At -50° it's hard to put booties on and to be careful not to put the booties on too tight. In those days, there were no Velcro booties.

This was the first year the southern route was included. Between Ophir and Cripple, the temperature dropped to -50° again. It was slow traveling so I decided to give the dogs a snack and rest them. I could hear trees cracking from the cold. I laid spruce branches for beds under each dog. I didn't take a stove but cooked over a campfire for me and the dogs. I made some tea. I remembered that elder Edwin Simon warned me about sleeping in extreme cold. I didn't want to take a chance, so I didn't get into my sleeping bag. There was an uncomfortable high spot on my sled, so I lay down on it knowing that if I went to sleep I'd roll off of my sled, and—after about an hour or so, I did! Wow! You talk about cold! My fire was out. I was shivering so bad that I couldn't make a fire. I started walking up and down the trail for half an hour until I finally warmed up. Good thing I fell off my sled, otherwise I might've frozen in my sleep. When you're tired, alone, and cold, it's not good to go to sleep. A 45-minute sleep in White Mountain once made me feel worse so I figured that when I got to a warm place, then I could sleep. One time I stayed awake for three days, all the way from Unalakleet to Nome. I rubbed my face with snow and that helped a little.

I did try to catch up. About three miles before the checkpoint at Safety, I stopped and fed my dogs early, figuring that the other guys would feed at Safety, twenty-one miles before Nome. When I signed in and signed out at the checkpoint and kept going, they were kind of mad—but I had to try something!

It cheers a guy up to see Nome off in the distance, but it can be seen for a long time before actually getting there. I came into Nome seventeen minutes behind rookie winner Rick Swenson and twelve minutes behind Jerry Riley. There was no steamed-up power left in any of us. I was happy with my race. I did the best I could. There were lots of friendly people to greet us including elders cheering us on. It was a tough race and we all did the best we could.

In 1980, I tried it one more time, but when we got to the Yukon, it was too cold to run my dogs and they lay down. I should've given them rest but I was anxious to push on and I had to scratch.

We didn't know nothing about dog food; we just cooked what we had and we fed dry dog food; the dogs got dehydrated and they fell out. We didn't know. We didn't have nothing. They got some fancy stuff nowadays. They cook while they're running. They put some kind of small insulated pot in the sled and it cooks itself. Lots of improvements now.

I play the guitar and violin. In my younger days, I went where the good times rolled. I drank, but I quit for about five years. I thank God I was able to do that. After I quit drinking, I got a job as the village water plant operator. My wife and six kids, Darrell Vent, Leonard Vent, Deborah Kokrine, Sarah Malamute, Warner Vent Jr., and Ava Crystal Vent were also very happy.

Upriver from Huslia above Halfway, I own 160 acres. At the first hill, I have two cabins, where we fish and trap. It was my parents' land but they gave it to me. In the spring sometimes my wife and I go there and overnight.

I can't race in the Iditarod anymore. Not only do I have a Pacemaker but I also froze half my foot one time when I was drinking. My scary stories aren't about the Iditarod but about when I used to drink. VERRRY SCARRYYY. Don't even want to talk about it.

Over the years, I borrowed dogs from at least thirty-two mushers. Once after George Attla, Jr. hurt his leg in a snowmachine race, he loaned me his whole team for the Huslia New Year's race, (where I won the 12-Mile Race). George should've stuck with dogs.

My dad died in 2006 at 93. I remember when he and I used to go trapping. I'd race him on the snowdrifts around the lake and get to the cabin

Raising and Training Pups

At two weeks old, pups need to go for walks. Keep an eye on those who fight or who are the fastest. Their hips should have a nice turn from their front to their rear and be a little lower than their shoulders. Their hind legs should be a little bowed and aligned with their foot, ankle, and toe. As soon as they can eat, pups should eat and drink water daily so they get used to drinking. Pups are susceptible at three months old to parvo. As soon as they might quit eating, give them an erythromycin pill morning and evening.

Up to one-year-old, feed commercial dog food with bone meal.

I start training when a pup is six months old. I take them on a crooked trail to teach them when they are running not to jump the towline but to stay on their side of the line. They have to learn to not be afraid of little banks in the trail. Some get over it but some don't.

When a pup is first hooked up to a sled, watch them because they can form bad habits like throwing themselves down, grabbing for snow, or stopping to defecate.

Feeding dogs

Worm them regularly.

If dogs get run down and use up their fat reserves, it takes a long time to bring them back up.

They won't give their all if they are not healthy.

Breed of Dogs

Looks aren't everything with a female and male dog a musher chooses to breed, but a cross between two breeds may be outstanding. Cross-breeding is the trick. Alaska huskies are the toughest dog, but they need some hound bred into them to have starting speed as well as contentment. Siberian Husky blood adds for a good coat and cosmetics. Smart breeding is still a process in the works

Sprint Race Training

I used to train my dogs to go three-25 mile heats, or two-20 milers or one 30-mile race, but that was over training. They got overrun and their feet gave out. They lost their stamina, their spirit, their interest and became slow. If a dog bolts at the start of a race or turns off the trail, it shows that he is not enjoying his training.

A musher has to know how to both drive a dog hard as well as make him happy. If you can figure this out, you're a dog musher.

I pick out twelve good dogs and take them out over and over for a 5-mile run until they can do that with no sweat. Then I run them hard for five miles until they can do that with no sweat. Every so often, I add a couple more miles to their racing regime until they can run hard for 20 miles. If they can run hard for twenty miles, they can do thirty pretty easy. They have to be good dogs and good dogs are hard to find. Judge a dog against the characteristics of your best dog.

A good dog will start and end going full blast. A dog that starts out slow and barely gets a musher back home needs to go.

Dog Positions: Neckline, Tugline, and Towline

A swing dog (the dog behind leader that, on a turn, keeps team going in the right direction) should spend a lot of time in that position because if he jumps over his neck line, he has to learn to untangle himself.

A wheel dog (the dog closest to the sled) has to be tough and light on his feet because a fast sled is right on his rear.

A neckline should be long enough so a dog can keep his eye on it and if he steps over it, he has a better chance of untangling himself.

Having a long enough tugline (the connecting line from the harness under the dog's tail to the towline) keeps a dog from being pulled around too much by the towline (the main line that the harness tug lines and necklines snap into).

Training a leader

This is tricky. I usually borrow a good leader, Lady, from Rudy Sommer. I used her a lot for training puppies. She is sharp on gee and haw, is happy, and a good teacher. She can jerk around a dog twice her size, but it's hard to find a dog like her. If I don't have an old leader to train a young one, I start from scratch. I pick a dog that's not lazy, not nervous, is smart, friendly, happy, and is the right shape. Size isn't too critical if the dog is good. I put him in harness and have him stand still in front of me. I hold his tugline while walking behind him and command him to "let's go!" I teach him that and "whoa!" I do this over and over until he knows it. Then I begin teaching him "gee" [right] and "haw" [left]. I say, "Gee" and pull his tugline to the right. As soon as he looks to the right, I say, "Go ahead!" If he does right, I praise him, "Good boy!" When I return him to his post, I give him a hug and say, "Good boy!" and give him a snack. A musher has to show his respect and appreciation each time they do good. However if they make a bad move, a musher better act mad because the dog has to understand his master.

Passing a Team

If I have a faster team, I let my dogs come up on the other team on their own. No yelling from me. If any dog makes a bad move, the next time I teach that dog to understand my command. For a dog to understand a driver's commands, he has to be around the dog a lot, talking to him, using his name a lot. If you have to spank a dog, be sure he understands why.

Command Sound: "Chirp"

Chirp is a double staccato tongue against the roof of mouth sound like a muskrat makes. It is useful in driving dogs; it can be heard by a dog from half mile away. While dogs are still in the beginning stages of training, I sweet talk and chirp them. I train them with chirping especially when we are going back home. While they are tender, if they don't respond to my chirp, I wait until they are toughened up. As long as they are working, I keep them happy so they feel secure. After I have given them lots of chances, if I can see that the dog is not going to make it, I weed him out. With the remaining core team, I chirp; if they don't respond, I discipline them. I raise my voice and chirp while I am spanking them so that they know why they are being disciplined and that I expect a response. When I have my core team toughened up, I run them hard—before the really tough training comes in. During the hardcore training, some dogs burn out. At this point, if a musher doesn't have enough dogs, he may have to buy, borrow, or lease a dog but in any case, he'll have to start the training all over again. Good dogs are hard to find.

Looking for Good Iditarod Dogs

Look for a tough, happy, dynamic, middle-sized dog that has a nice long swing while trotting. He should trot like a German shepherd, be as tough as an Alaskan husky, and be as frisky as an Irish setter.

Iditarod and Sprint Racing Training:

The best place to train any dog is in the wheel position. Sometimes I even put my lead dog there to break him of bad habits. To be in wheel, a dog has to be able to deal with a racing sled right behind his rear and two sets of lines: the towline from under the sled, his own tugline and the towline extending up to his neckline and beyond. He has to be alert, quickly adjust to conditions and be tough enough to stay ahead of the sled.

Use a dog's name a lot. Every day I go to each dog, call them by name and tell them to put their paw on my chest. I'd call, "Sharkey!" and tap my chest. I watched Grandpa George Attla Sr. do this and couldn't figure out why. It not only teaches them their name but it shows them love.

While out on a hard run, if the dogs start grabbing for snow, it means they are too heavy or not tough enough. I stop them, talk and pet them until they cool down to prevent them grabbing snow as a habit. Dogs have to be lean, mean, and tough so they can take hard trails and hot weather. If you have twenty good dogs, leaders who have a good diet and lots of water, you might stand a chance against the big boys.

Test runs

Before the Iditarod, I drive my dogs 100 miles to make sure they are tough enough, physically and mentally. Before sprint racing, I drive them hard for twenty miles. Dogs that haven't been trained enough will probably get hurt, but those dogs have no business going to a demanding race.

When a musher and team are ready, he is so worried that he can hardly eat or sleep before the race.

Iditarod Race

The key thing is to take care of your dogs through the whole race. From the start until close to the end, use booties on your dogs. About 50-100 miles from the end of the race, if you need to go faster, take the booties off. The dogs will feel better and have better traction. Check for dehydration by lifting their lip, push a finger on their gum. If it stays white a long time, they are dehydrated. Another test is to lift the neck skin, if it stays up, they need more water.

If a dog is limping, stop, and check him right away. Sometimes they get snow balled up in their pad which can cause a cut and make them lame.

In the old days, everyone in town used to be good dog mushers. [http://www.sleddogcentral.com/ONAC/nac_history.htm: "Teams from the Koyukuk region, driven by such notable mushers as Jimmy Huntington, Cue Bifelt, Bergman Sam, Warner Vent, and George Attla provided some of the best dogs and competition to be found anywhere. Other Interior villagers from places such as Minto, Tanana, Rampart, and Galena also continued to produce top contenders. *Ed.]*

Over the years, I borrowed dogs from at least thirty-two mushers: Steven, Alfred, and George Attla, Freddie Vent Sr., Cue Bifelt, Henry Beatus, Joe Beetus, Billy and Kenny Sam, David David, Jimmy Edwards, Pollack Simon, Sr., Marilyn Koyukuk Evans, Lester Sam, Bill Williams, George Frank, Alice Ambrose, Herbie, Floyd, Ricky, and Albert Vent, Rudy Sommer, Sam Billy of Galena, Gerald Esmailka, Barney Sam, Dave Stout, Leonard Huntington, Uncle Edwin Simon, James Williams, Attla Olin, and my dad Bobby Vent.

before him. He spent a lot of money on me, supplying me with dog food and dogs. He loved sports.

My advice to a young person considering competitively mushing dogs today is you gotta have about a million bucks! The first thing is to get a good sponsor. Maybe the musher could get a good job, but it's hard to find a job around here. Young mushers gotta know that it takes money, but it'll be fun. I could help them on that last part. You gotta buy six months of dog food: chicken, beef, and more . . . That new way of competing started about the time I ran my last race.

The Iditarod was one of my overcoming experiences. I thank all those who helped me with dog food and dogs. People once pulled for me, a racing hero from the Native people; now, I root for my Native people.

In 2015, the year that George Attla, Jr. passed away, the Iditarod went through Huslia for the first time. Warner remembered, "Both George and my dad Bobby ran in the first Iditarod race in 1973." Then grinning, he said, "Oh, yeah, the Iditarod went through all right; there's dog scat all over. No, just kidding. The boys in the village cleaned it up."

A year after Warner and I interviewed, I called him. Warner had just returned from the funeral of his good friend, Rudy Demoski. He said, "The family was all there and they were very glad that each of us came."

Warner Vent family: Leonard Vent, Darrell Vent, Warner Vent, Jr., Ava Crystal Vent, Sarah Vent Malamute, and Debbie Vent Kokrine. Front: Alberta Beetus Vent and Warner Vent, Sr., ca. 2001.

Courtesy of Sarah Malamute.

Chapter 4

Rudy Demoski, Holikachuk, Anvik

Rudy Demoski, Iditarod, 2013.
Photographer Bill Roth. Courtesy of
Rudy Demoski

In 1975 my husband, Reb, and I, along with our five-year-old son, Clint, took our 19-foot Grumman canoe down the Yukon River when fish wheels and fish camps were whirring with activity. In Anvik we met thirty-year-old Rudy Demoski. He and his brother-in-law Ken Chase, both Iditarod competitors, were busy catching fish for their families and dog teams. They chatted with us as they worked. Forty-two years later, Rudy shared his story with me by phone from his Wasilla home to docu-ment his part in the new book Ten Feet Tall and Bulletproof: Alaska Natives, Blazing the Iditarod Trail. *Rudy began his story:*

I was born on my mother's birthday in Holikachuk on the Innoko River off the Yukon on March 22, 1945 to Lina Stickman Demoski, born in 1927 in Holikachuk, and Edward Demoski, born in 1907 in Ophir, not far from McGrath. My father, an Athabascan-Russian, was thirty-eight when I was born. He was the fourth of eight children, a son of Leo Demoski, a Russian Creole, who was born in 1875 in Nulato. Leo had trading posts in Shageluk, Blackburn, and Anvik. He could read and write as could my father, Edward.

Until I was six, we lived in our cabin on the trapline; we never stayed in town. Our camps were 90 miles from Holikachuk and up the Innoko. The landscape encompassed rolling hills, Hammer Creek, and Lonesome, Dikeman, and Iditarod rivers that all drained into the Innoko. Dogs were part of our everyday life as we depended on them for transportation, wood, and water hauling. In the summer, we kids took turns taking care of them; Dad did it during the winter.

When I was six, I had to start at the BIA school in Holikachuk in a little log cabin which adjoined the teachers' quarters, built on the side of a slough. My teacher was Ms. Page. Highlights in the spring included celebrating Stickdance at the kazheem, the community hall.

Two years later when I was eight, I was shipped off to the Holy Cross Mission school in Holy Cross for a year. My family picked me up the follow-

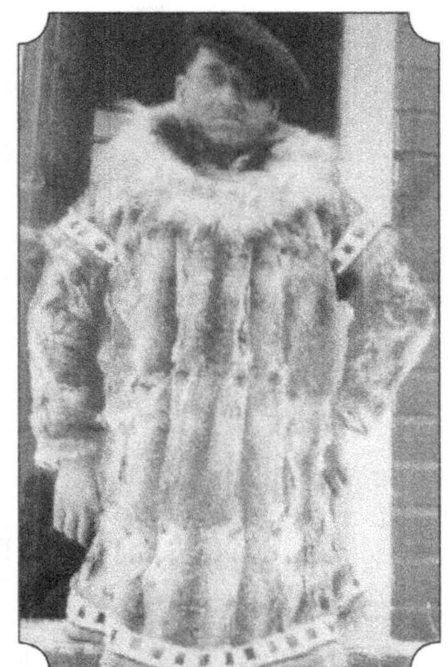

Rudy's father, Edward Demoski, ca. 1955.
Courtesy of Rudy Demoski.

ing year when they moved from Holikachuk to Anvik.

Five years later in 1959 when I was fourteen, I was sent to Mount Edgecumbe boarding school. I lasted there two years; when I was sixteen I got kicked out. The only means I had then of making money was to trap with my father.

Marten were so cheap that we focused on mink, beaver, wolverine, wolves, and otter. During the late 1950s to early 1960s mink were big money; a large male brought $60 while marten only got $12. We stretched a beaver pelt into a circle and measured it both across and vertically. At $1.00 an inch, a 70-inch beaver brought $70. Otters were $35 to $40 apiece. When Sam Applebaum from Seattle came through, we sold to him or to the local storeowner, Frank Walker in Holikachuk or Jack Wharton in Anvik. I trapped with my dad until I was twenty in 1965. Some of my best memories include checking the trapline at ten above and finding our traps full of fur.

My dad had ten Indian huskies. Some were part wolf and one was part German shepherd. They averaged about 70 pounds each and, although they were strong, hard-working dogs, they were slow. After beaver trapping, we had sprint races with our trapline dogs, sometimes going nineteen miles at a time. Once we had races every other day for ten days in a row. It gave us something to do.

From 1967 to 1973, I worked on a crab boat in the Aleutian Islands. When I returned to Anvik, there were only three or four dog teams. Ken Chase was the only one with a working team. Other dogs just sat on their chains. Snowmachines had replaced the working sled dog.

As I was growing up, mentors for me included my father, who was really good with dogs, and Wilfred Young, who was darned good at it—and George Attla, who was only twelve years older than I. I listened to what they said, but nobody taught me to how to run dogs. Every race in Anvik, Grayling, and Shageluk, I came in dead last until in 1974—when I ran my first Iditarod—I began to figure out how to

Rudy's mother, Lina Demoski, 2017.
Courtesy of Rudy and Ella Demoski.

put a good team together. I bought some dogs from sprint mushing champions in Koyukuk, Nulato, and Kaltag. I got three more from Leo Kriska, one from Justin Patsy, and borrowed one from Franklin Madros. I raised three that also turned out to be pretty fast. I had ten good core dogs.

My cousin Daniel Sawyer helped me take care of the dogs. We trained on the trapline, but we put in long miles. The farthest we went on one run was sixty to seventy miles. From November 10th to the start of the Iditarod, I walked be-

Rudy Demoski, ca. 1959.
Courtesy of Rudy Demoski.

hind my dog team or ran ahead on snowshoes to get in shape. When I left Anchorage at the Iditarod starting line in 1974, I was 153 pounds and when I arrived in Nome, I was 142. I was in really good shape.

When I first showed up with my team in Anchorage, I stayed with Dick Mackey and his wife. Lance and Jason were just little boys.

I had no way to cook during the race. I never even had a dog pot. I was green. I threw the dogs dried fish and sometimes, chopped up beaver meat. I don't remember how I even fed myself. Maybe I bummed off Warner Vent or Herbie Nayokpuk. I had a lot of Yukon king salmon strips, bread, butter, and ham. I must've made a lot of sandwiches. I had a coffee thermos so I guess I found a pot to boil cowboy coffee. I had no headlamp but rather, a hand-held, two-cell flashlight with enough batteries to make it to McGrath, where I had to buy more batteries.

In 1974, there were 43 musher entries and I drew number 42. My brother-in-law Ken Chase drew number 43. I was glad that there were a lot of mushers ahead of me. I didn't know where I was going. From Mulcahy Stadium to Knik, it was a long way through Anchorage. There were no trails. I let my dogs just keep going. From the first checkpoint in Knik to McGrath, we hoped we'd just survive.

In Rainy Pass, a 133-below chill factor was recorded. I had my parka over my snowmachine suit, pants, and long johns. My mother made me beaver fur and moosehide mitts with mouton liners, a marten hat, and a long woolen scarf, but still, it was too cold and windy. Warner had a pup tent so we put it up and crawled in for the night.

During the first two years of the Iditarod, we didn't go down Dalzell Gorge but descended through Hell's Gate. We went down the Happy River Steps where I rough-locked[1] but still, I tipped over a couple of times on the

------

1. wrapping ropes or chains around sled runners to slow progress.

Rudy Demoski, Iditarod, 2013.
Photographer Frank Kovalchek. Courtesy Rudy Demoski.

downhill plunge. [In 2012, the Iditarod decided to eliminate this treacherous portion of the trail, saying on Iditarod.com, "The Steps are found between Finger Lake and Rainy Pass. Mushers typically encounter the switchbacks on their second day. The trail will vanish over the edge of what looks like a cliff. It is a cliff. This is the Rudy entrance to the Happy River Steps. Stop the dogs at the top, say your prayers, revise your will, and then see how gently you can get the dogs to creep down the hill."]

When I finally made it to the river, it was not only 44 below zero, but there was also overflow[2], in some places up to our knees, all the way to the Rohn Roadhouse. I had dried grass under my felt liners in my mukluks, but my feet were packed in continually sodden and miserably cold liners.

From the Rohn, we zig-zagged down the glare ice of the Kuskokwim to Farewell. After escaping the perils of Hell's Gate, overflow, and glare ice, it was a matter of just going from village to village; it was like coming home. Sure, we had to snowshoe for miles on end, but a man could at least stay dry. It took us nine days to go from Anchorage to McGrath. At the checkpoints, we were happier than heck to see each other. It was very festive with mushers running all around.

In those early Iditarods, we got a lot of sleep because we camped all night. But we had no trail and had to break our own so—it was give and take. It was easier to focus on the dogs then because we were not so fatigued as in today's highly competitive race. There was no mandatory layover, but I took two and half days in McGrath anyway. At Kaltag, mushers began to get serious about strategy.

As we approached the coast, it was with trepidation. For us Interior guys, going out on the ocean ice was a nerve-wracking prospect.

I'd started out with ten dogs. We could only drop a dog at McGrath, Galena, and Unalakleet. I'd come a long way but in Unalakleet, I had to finally drop three dogs, who were just too tired.

On my birthday, five miles from Koyuk, it started snowing. We snow-shoed all day and then, I ran out of strength. I didn't want to overnight on

---

2. hydrostatically oozed water seepage on top of the river ice.

the ocean ice, but I dug a hole to nest my racing sled and I laid my sleeping bag in its basket. I was so tired. When I woke up the next morning, when I tried to get up, everything was heavy, heavy, heavy. There were four inches of water under me that had soaked into my sleeping bag. I was so tired that I never felt it. After I got my head up, I couldn't see Warner or Herbie. Nothing . . . We were buried under a blanket of snow. Warner knew it was my birthday, but after one look at me, he thought better of wishing me a "happy birthday"; he said I looked ugly—and a little mean—so he decided not to risk it!

At Koyuk I rested. From there to Elim, it snowed like a son of a gun. I snowshoed for fifteen hours. I kept lifting one foot after another, seemingly getting nowhere. Herbie, Warner, and I took turns breaking trail: slow, slow, slow. But by Golovin and White Mountain, we could take right off!

As we came around the cape and saw the bright lights of Nome, it was the longest fourteen miles ever. It seemed like we would never get there. I got in at 6 AM at 35 below, with six dogs out of my original ten. My family was there and it was a great feeling to finally get to Nome. Handlers in the chute took care of our teams. I wanted more than anything to rest. After a little reprieve, it was party time in Nome. I came in fourth; Warner was second and Herbie, third. The food at the awards banquet was great; the atmosphere was like Mardi Gras, people laughing, talking, telling stories.

My expenses included the $200 entrance fee and paying my friend and Ken's brother, Ernest Chase of Grayling Air Service, to get my dogs from Anvik to Anchorage. On the return, Larry Thompson loaded up my seven dogs, me, and my wife, and flew us in a Cessna 180 to Anvik. My winnings came to $1627 so I came out ahead plus I'd learned a lot about my dogs. Warner and I had also become darned good friends, having traveled together the whole time.

During the next couple of years, Kenny Chase and I were the only ones with dogs in Anvik but frequently fifteen teams would come over and compete with us in our sprint races, which were eight- and twenty-five-mile courses.

When my kennel was at its largest in 1975, I had thirty-six dogs. I trained on the snowmachine trails around Anvik and McGrath. I borrowed Puppy, a darned good lead-

Rudy Demoski, ca. 1977.
Courtesy of Rudy Demoski.

er, from my cousin Dean Painter. Puppy loved to go, was really smart and friendly and was a regular ol' Indian husky.

In November, we used to catch eels through the ice so the dogs ate fish, rice, and eels. In the spring I had meat from beaver trapping. Still, feeding that many dogs got so expensive that I had to downsize. By race time, I had only sixteen, the minimum required to enter the race.

In 1975 we loaded our dogs into the plane to go to Anchorage for the Iditarod, but it began snowing as soon as we were on our way. There was no way to get back to Anvik. It was a whiteout all the way to Anchorage. The only time I could see anything was when we almost flew into a mountain. I yelled at the pilot Hal Walch and he pulled up fast. I could have jumped out of the plane and been ten feet above the mountain. When we finally saw the Kuskokwim River, I said, "Follow it to McGrath," but we almost passed the town because it was so socked in.

In 1975 the Iditarod implemented the 24-hour layover so I took mine in McGrath. In Ruby I stayed in the community hall. In Galena, I was at my cousin Archie Thurmond's. In Nulato I overnighted at Rudolph Esmailka's. When I got to the coast, I stayed in the community hall in Unalakleet and in Koyuk, at the Army National Guard armory.

I didn't have to carry extra food because I had food drops at McGrath, seventeen miles down the trail at Takotna, and twenty-six miles later at Ophir. Unfortunately I didn't carry a repair kit because in 1982, I broke my back runners off so at the next checkpoint, I had to buy a $600 sled.

I never used vitamins either. We fed a lot of fish and meat and they got carbs in their cooked rice. When it was cold, we added seal oil and beaver fat. I put all types of dog and people food as well as dog booties in my food drops so I was prepared.

Rudy Demoski, 1980 Iditarod.
Courtesy of Rosetta Alcantra
and Rudy Demoski.

For some of us, the Iditarod was an extension of our ordinary life. In 1975 there was good weather, no big storms, but in 1976 it was 67 below. When it was really cold, Ken Chase and I built a fire and kept it going. I never carried a tent, but always slept in my sled. Normally I couldn't slow my dogs, but at that temperature coming out of Ophir, I had to slow them down so they didn't frost their lungs.

In 1980 I was crab fishing on the Kenai so the City of Homer sponsored me in the Iditarod. That year veterinarians also became intertwined more deeply in the race and began checking the dogs routinely. That year I was enjoying myself and not taking things too seriously, but when I got to Kaltag, I asked my relatives what place I was in. They said, "Oh, don't worry about it; just go on home to Anvik." It made me mad. I looked at the statistics and was surprised to see that I was 37th. As one ticked-off musher, I passed twenty-two teams and two days later, I arrived in Nome in fifteenth place. I jumped over the fence and went straight to the bar.

Mail cachet carried by Rudy Demoski, 1980 Iditarod.
Courtesy of Rosetta Alcantra and Rudy Demoski.

For work I carpentered. I can do whatever it takes to build a house from the foundation up as well as do all the inside finish work. I moved to Wasilla in 1989 where I could also train on the main Iditarod trail.

I've run seven Iditarods—and scratched three—including 1974 to 1977, 1980, 1985, and 2013. My total winnings were $3567. I kinda got set up to run the 2013 Iditarod. My cousin Louie Ambrose wanted me to run his distance dogs and he talked me into it. Suddenly I also had sponsors. I began training in the fall and went from a carpentry job to being on the back of the sled. The race was my fastest ever until I was forced to scratch in Unalakleet. I had a really good leader, Brock, as well as nine good dogs. The head vet said Brock was anemic and he pulled him. The dog was fine and he ate well. Many said I was doing really good. I thought it was unfair, but it's hard to say. All it takes is one bad guy to spoil it for everyone.

In my early Iditarods when I was younger; I could stay awake for the three and half days that it took to get to McGrath. Later when I did begin to get tired, I'd stop and regroup—before I fell off the sled.

During the year, it can be a problem for the village musher to come to Wasilla for the mandatory Iditarod meetings, which are mainly for rookies; most of the time I was able to talk my way out of them.

In between Iditarods, I sprint-raced. I got dogs from George Attla, Marvin Kokrine, Dennis Boyer, Bud Smyth, and a few others. With a good team, I won Wasilla's Aurora Dog Musher championship. In the Kenai-Soldotna Championship, I came in second. I raced regularly in Settlers Bay, Montana Creek, and the Open North American.

During all my years in the Iditarod, every time I finished, I was in the top twenty—but twice, I had to scratch due to sick dogs and then again

Rudy Demoski soaking dry dog food in hot water, Nikolai, 2013 Iditarod.
Photographer Bill Roth. Courtesy of Rudy Demoski.

in 2013 because of my leader. During the 1970s I had good dogs. For me, 1974 from Anchorage to Nome was a big party; I spent two and half days in McGrath, a couple of days in Nulato, and got beat into Nome by twenty-some hours. I was never really serious enough to make the money. In 1980 I had really good dogs, but I monkeyed around too much.

When my dad and I were trapping, dogs were tough and never had health issues. We got rid of the weak dogs and were left with nothing but the best. The only problem was dogs got torn up in dog fights, but we patched them up as best we could. Some guys had only four dogs but those four could bring in a moose. They were freight dogs, not racing dogs.

There was a lot of difference between what I wore in 1974 and in 2013. In my first Iditarod, I wore a $27 army-navy surplus parka and a $60 green vinyl snowsuit. I slept in doubled up army chicken feather mummy bags. In 2013 I had a $700 snowmachine suit and an R.E.I. down sleeping bag. I thought I'd died and gone to heaven.

In 1974 I paid $200 to enter the race and in 2013, my sponsors, Fort Knox and Fairbanks Justa Store, paid twenty thousand dollars for me to compete and I was still short on some things.

Today the Iditarod has so changed. Villagers are no longer allowed to help by breaking trail or hosting mushers. At the Iditarod's initial drawing for starting positions, there are so many mushers that there's no time for story telling anymore. In Nome at the banquet, it's too commercialized. Mushers tell their story and go home. There's no more Mardi Gras. When I think of the Iditarod, I remember a bunch of us dragging up a long log for a big campfire, laughing, joking, passing the bottle around, and having a regular ol' camping trip. I imagine alcohol is illegal in the race now. I doubt if anyone during the 1970s had race strategy until reaching Kaltag or Unalakleet, when we'd figure out who was behind us or who was ahead, what we'd have to do to catch the guy ahead or shake the guy behind us. Nobody had any strategy until Rick Swenson won the race in 1977 and then, people had to get serious. I never did.

Kenny Chase and I want to see a young person get involved and successfully compete in the Iditarod. The whole state of Alaska knows when a Native musher gets into the Iditarod. There would be so much attention on him that he'd really have to focus on his dogs to satisfy all those who'd be watching him. Today Natives have to look at what kind of sled Jeff King uses, what type of food the top mushers feed. If a musher has no money, he has to come up with a way to buy the high-class dog food. It's not an Iditarod anymore, but a sprint race to Nome. A NASCAR race, but it's still good to watch.

Rudy Demoski, hauling food drops, 2013 Iditarod.
Photographer Bill Roth. Courtesy of Rudy Demoski.

I was so happy when there was a cold start this year in 2017 because a couple of today's mushers called us old mushers a bunch of shuffle-along guys. It'd be good for them to experience 70 below, poor gear, and no trail made for them. Without the heritage of the trappers' dog teams, there would not be today's Iditarod. Yesterday's campers stuck it out and blazed the trail.

After approving his chapter in Bulletproof, *Rudy Demoski lost his battle with lung cancer at his home in Wasilla January 28, 2018.*

"War Department Field Manual, Dog Transportation, 1944.
Courtesy of Judy Ferguson

Chapter 5

Iditarod Record-Setter, Yukon Fox: Emmitt Peters

Emmitt Peters with his lead dog Nugget, three months after winning the Iditarod, setting a new record, at the family's Melozi fish camp, 1975.
Judy Ferguson photo.

In 2007, wearing the "lucky number thirteen bib," Lance Mackey won his first of four consecutive Iditarod championships. His father, Dick Mackey, his brother, Rick Mackey, and Rick Swenson also won wearing number thirteen. However, the rookie who set the record and was the first to win sporting the number thirteen was Emmitt Peters of Ruby in 1975. Emmitt changed the Iditarod into a competitive race; he credited much of his victory to his ten-year-old lead dog Nugget, the grandmother of his team. A few months after Emmitt's win, we met him in Ruby as we were canoeing down the Yukon River. He invited my husband, me, and our little boy to his parents' fish camp at Melozi. Fascinated from the beginning by his mother, Mary Peters, I listened intently to her stories over the next two days. One poignant moment was as Mary stood looking out her front door, remembering the tragic accident of her son, Heinie, and her other three lost children. She shared Heinie's story, as told below by Emmitt. Mary understood perfectly the people and time in which she lived. A beautiful, intelligent, and hospitable woman, she relished her work, moving fluidly from one task to the other.

Thirty-two years later, eight months after Emmitt's cardiac surgery and at the suggestion of his nephew, Aaron Peters, I had an appointment to interview Emmitt. As planned—sort of—I met his wife, Edna, and their sons at the Klondike Inn, but there was no Emmitt. They suggested I might check out the basketball game at University of Alaska Fairbanks (UAF). In the UAF gym, as I made a beeline for him where he sat in the front row of the bleachers, he grinned, "Well, congratulations, Ferguson. You caught me!" The Yukon Fox duly submitted and joined me for dinner, where I turned on the tape recorder and began listening to his story:

Mary Peters, ca. late 1970s.
Courtesy Emmitt Peters Jr.

My dad was the late Paul Peters, born around 1905 in Nulato, just after gold was discovered in Ruby. My mother, Mary, was born in 1915 also in Nulato. Her father died of tuberculosis and she was adopted by Pitka and Sarah Pavaloff. Pitka (born in 1853) and his brother John Minook (born in 1849 with the name of Ivan Pavaloff) were the sons of a Russian trader at St. Michael's and an Inupiaq woman.[1] Mary and her Pitka Pavaloff "sisters", Lucy, Lena, Madeline, and Florence were all raised together as siblings. Mary's adopted brothers included Timothy, Richard and Albert. No one referred to Mary as "adopted," however the following generations have made that reference."[2]

Both my parents were part Russian but my dad also had an interesting Iñupiaq lineage. During the Russian colonial period, Dad's ancestor was taken from Unalakleet as a Russian slave and brought up the Yukon River to the Russian outpost at Nulato.

During 1906 to 1910, the Ruby gold rush began. By 1911, the town was established. Before that, there wasn't much for wages in the area.

My dad used to market hunt for the miners, and in the winter he hauled freight for them. Two or three times a week, he

Mary Peters' adopted parents Pitka Pavaloff (1852–1932) and Sarah Pavaloff. (Sek'edzaaggoyh or Sekezakoiha Malasadak) (1863-1938), who lived at Pitka's Point on the left bank of the Yukon before its confluence with the Andreafsky River and before St. Mary's. From 1899, the point was a supply depot.

Courtesy of BreonnaNB, Ancestry.

---

1   The 1920 census shows four-year-old Mary living with Pitka and Sarah Pavaloff who had a daughter Mackline (Madeline) Pavaloff. The family surname was Pavaloff.

2   To attempt clarification why Mary and Madeline Pavaloff were not called by their father's surname of Pavaloff, but rather by his first name of Pitka. First Traditional Chief Don Honea said that in his area of Ruby his mother took her father's first name as her surname. Don assumed that it was the Native custom to take the father's first name and take it as the progeny's surname.

L-R: Bertha Demoski, Mary Peters holding toddler, Emmitt, Sarah; front: Mary and Joe. Ca. 1950, Melozi. Courtesy of Emmitt Peters.

brought in their mail. Using a one-man crosscut saw, he cut wood for the steamboats. After he and Mom married, they manned the saw together.

My mom was as tough as a mule and lived a clean, rugged life. She never drank or smoked. People were always welcome in our house. She had many skills, and she called a spade a spade.

Over the years, my parents had eleven children: Leonard, Lilli, Loretta, Heinie, me, Sarah, Bernard, Mary Antonia, Mary Rose called Peggy, Joe, and Debbie. We lost three: Leonard, Loretta, and Bernard. I have three living brothers and five living sisters.

I was born October 1, 1940, at our fish camp at the old Melozi telegraph station on the north side of the river. Altona Brown helped my mom with my birth. I was raised at fish camp, one mile below Ruby. While Dad was working on the cabin, we camped until December on the point of the island on Ruby slough where there was a lot of game.

My mother didn't do things at the last minute or waste time. In the mornings, she tended to her skin tanning. Then she helped Dad cut and smoke fish. At night, she knitted and sewed, because winter was always coming. She made all our outdoor gear from her own tanned hides and fur: boots, parkas, and mittens. At first she put straw for insoles in our moosehide mukluks and later, rabbit fur. For blankets, she twisted rabbit hides together. We lived in a fourteen-by-sixteen-foot log cabin with no phone. It was a tough life at that time.

In the 1940s, when I was about four, my dad cut twenty cords of firewood a year for the steamboats. Everybody worked for themselves back then.

During the summer, we got blueberries. Mom would layer them in sugar in five-gallon barrels. In the evenings, while she was busy knitting, Lenny, Lilli, and I, like camp robbers, would get into the berries and she'd get mad.

Every morning since I was four, I went with Mom to check our rabbit snares. She was always happy skinning rabbits. Over a couple of years, she also caught herself 150 squirrels, tanned all of them, and made herself a beautiful parka. She and Dad used to go down to Galena where Mom would sell her fur parkas at the air force base.

When I got a little older, I consulted a book on trapping. It said to bend a branch over, set a snare and when the rabbit got caught, the branch would whisk the rabbit up into the air in the snare. But when I tried it, it was too cold and the branch always broke. I thought, "That's baloney; this'll never work" and told that to Johnny Muskrat (John Swagler), a fur buyer my dad always sold to. He said, "You have to use a metal trap and a wire snare." I said, "I never have any money for that stuff." He said, "Bring me a rabbit skin and we'll make a deal." I asked, "How many do you want?" "As many as you can get," he said. So using my dad's number one traps, I began helping my dad. That way I was able to get us more traps and snares. Johnny Muskrat also helped my paternal cousin Harold Esmailka to buy his store on the riverfront. Then when Harold saved up enough from the store, he began his own aviation company, Harold's Air Service.

When he was eleven in 1949, my brother Heinie slid on a cardboard box from the top of Ruby's steep hill down to the river. He got going so fast that he couldn't control himself. He hit a chunk of ice, bounced hard, and hit squarely on his back. He not only broke his hip and shattered his leg but he did damage to his spinal nerves. He had paralysis. At the time, communication for medical help was bum. He was in unbelievable pain. He was first sent to the Alaska Native Hospital in Anchorage where they did a poor job of trying to set his leg. He spent two to three years there before he was sent to Mount Edgecumbe's renowned orthopedic department in Sitka. The hospital rebroke Heinie's leg and put in a new socket. They put a mold over his hip to immobilize him while he healed. He went through so much pain. Before the accident, Heinie could hear and talk like anyone else, but afterward he was never the same. While he was at Edgecumbe, he also attended four years of trade school. They taught him sign language and to read lips. During his stay, he became good friends with fellow patient George Attla, seven years his senior. However, after Heinie returned home, he fell down and broke his hip again. He went back to Edgecumbe where they did the best they could, but this time there was no hope. When he came back home he could at least move around. When he looked at you, he seemed to be able to read your mind. He knew his special people by name. He called Debbie "Deb," and me, "Emma." If someone didn't pay attention to him, he'd knock them over the head. When he called a name, that person had

Emmitt Peters' family: parents, Paul and Mary Peters with their grandchildren: Phillip, Nina, and Timmy. Melozi fish camp near Ruby, 1975.

Judy Ferguson photo.

better jump. Once some kid who thought he was a mechanic was working on a snowmachine. Heinie could tell right away that the kid was no mechanic. When the punk broke a nut, Heinie said to him with sign language, "That's enough." The kid thought Heinie didn't know what was going on, so he ignored him. Heinie banged him on the head to get his attention. After that the kid never forgot again that Heinie meant business.

Not long after Heinie returned, I went to Mt. Edgecumbe for school in 1956. I ran track and did well but I never won. After I graduated in 1961, I returned home because I missed my dad's dogs.

Before I ran dogs, Heinie used to drive a dog team. After I got into mushing, we began competing, using three dogs, to see who could get to Dad's wood yard first. Sometimes he won; sometimes I did.

When I was about five, Dad gave me his old retired lead dog, Red. One day after my dad and his eleven dogs headed fifteen miles down the trail, I told my mom I wanted to follow him. I didn't understand the difference then between him going fifteen miles or one mile. When Mom wasn't looking, I hooked up Red, harnessed and snapped him into the sled's tugline to follow him. But around the bend, a gigantic moose blocked the trail. He wouldn't get off the road for nobody. When I got home, Mom was putting on her snowshoes to come after me; I got the licking of my life. I said to her, "But aren't you glad I'm home?"

When I was little, I fell in love with my dad's dogs. I'd go out to what I called the dog barn—in reality, it was a big doghouse—and I'd pet the puppies. Dad once told me that the way to test a puppy's worth was to hold the puppy by the tail. If his head went to the right, it was a good dog; if it went to the left, it was a bum dog. Once while Dad was gone, I sat there with three females and three males. I decided to test the litter. Picking one up, I said, "Uh, huh, yep, that's a bum one," then I'd check another, "Yep, that's a good'un." When Dad returned two days later, he said, "Mom, what happened to half of the pups?" I said, "I killed 'em." I explained that I'd used his method and helped him weed them out. He said, "Oh well—less feed."

As a young child, I fed the dogs and they got accustomed to me. They're smarter than you think. They know when you're scared of them or when they're going to get fed or when they are going to get hooked up. Once I tried to sneak away without feeding them but they set up a racket with their "yap, yap, yap!" to let my folks know that I was trying to leave the yard. We used to feed them mostly fish, moose, and bear fat, whatever we had. When I was grown and landed my boat on the shore, even though they couldn't see my boat, they knew the sound of my outboard motor. When they heard that engine, they'd jump up and holler.

About the 1950s to 1960s, long-distance dog mushing stopped. Alden Williams, a pilot for Wien Consolidated Airlines, was the main bush pilot. He ferried people up and down the Yukon River to Fairbanks or Anchorage.

My dad still kept his dog team and took real pride in them. In the springtime, he always went by dog team to Nulato, Koyukuk, Galena, and back to Ruby. That's how I got into long-distance dog mushing.

One of Dad's male dogs from the litter I had thinned out as a kid, I bred to a fancy bird dog of Tim Pitka's. Out of that litter, I got a real smart lead dog, Nugget. Once with her pulling, I fell off my sled in a sprint race at 16 to 18 mph; my hat was in the back of the sled and I lost my glasses. I said, "Whoa!" and Nugget stopped. Bird dogs are loyal and smart. She stopped the whole team. They began rolling in the snow while I picked up my glasses and hat.

I built up a dog yard of twenty-some dogs, with the females averaging about forty to forty-five pounds and the males at least fifty-five pounds.

Once in Fairbanks at the North American Championship sled dog race, a musher told me, "Emmitt, you gotta get used to this commercial dog food. You can't just feed them frozen fish every day supplemented with cooked rice now and then." Later at the World Championship Fur Rondy sled dog race in Anchorage, Doc Lombard said, "Emmitt, you're in the wrong race. You should be in the Iditarod." That perked me up. Without knowing it, I was training at home for the Iditarod, not for sprint racing.

In Ruby, I watched the first Iditarod mushers coming in. I told a musher that his dogs were too shorthaired, that they didn't have a good undercoat. He sneered at me like I didn't know anything about dogs. Then I turned my atten-

Post card of Emmitt Peters racing in 1975 Iditarod, Ruby.

Courtesy of Emmitt Peters.

tion to watching Herbie Nayokpuk come in with his team.

In 1974, I loaned Nugget to Carl Huntington, who won the Iditarod that year. After that, I told my mom I was going to run the Iditarod. She said, "It's a long-distance race," but she started sewing dog booties and anything else I might need.

In 1975, I took Nugget back from Carl. At ten years old, she was the grandmother to most of the four-year-old pups in my team; they followed her every move. When other mushers' teams saw a moose, they charged it, but not Nugget. She would go around the animal.

That year while I was training for the Iditarod, we were running on our fifty-mile trail. The temperature was dropping to twenty below so I began zipping up my parka when the dogs winded a moose. They bolted and knocked me off the sled. I knew Nugget wouldn't let them go beyond the trail's end. For ten hours in the dark and cold, I kept walking until I found where she'd held them at the end of the trail. The next year, near Twelve Mile, I was mushing downhill when a moose crossed the trail in front of us. Sixteen dogs ran into the brush, thrashed around, and got really tangled up. I unhooked all but the lead dogs. When we got back on the trail, the leaders began jumping up and down, ready to go. The loose dogs came back, eager to get harnessed, all fourteen of them.

In 1987 at Twenty-two Mile, while out training, I ran into a pack of nine wolves, about a quarter of a mile from us. My fifteen dogs lay down; they never moved. The wolves kept their eyes on them but I kept moving around. I remembered that my dad told me if I were ever in such a situation, without a gun, to break off a willow branch and whip it through the air like a

Emmitt Peters' Iditarod racing card.
Courtesy Emmitt Peters

switch, making a whistling sound. I did, and one by one the wolves melted into the woods. I went five miles down to the old mining camp at Long Creek and told a miner about the wolves. He jumped on his Snogo and darned if he didn't get two of those wolves.

In the early days of the Iditarod, we cooked for our dogs over an open fire. I carried a jar of diesel along with a gunnysack soaked in the fuel. During its first three years, the Iditarod was more of a camping trip.

Ruby is on the route from Anchorage to Nome. I always used part of that trail for training dogs. It is thirty miles round trip, going south of Ruby to Long Creek on the Iditarod trail. In the 1975 race when my eight tired dogs hit the thirty-mile mark, I stopped, made a fire, melted a cup of snow water for them to drink, and cooked fish and rice for them. Afterward, they took off at a steady lope going about nine miles an hour up and down those hills. Even that far into the race, they were moving out! I was the third one into Ruby. I came up to the checkpoint at the community hall. I'd decided to take my mandatory twenty-four hour break there, at home. Despite the crowd, Nugget made a charge, knocking people down in her eagerness to get to my dad's house, down the hill.

However, as I tried to rest at the house, my mom wouldn't let me sleep. She'd look out the window and say, "Those guys are taking off!" My dad kept saying, "He's got to take his twenty-four; he's got to wait a while." She'd get mad at Dad, and say, "Aw, shut up! You don't know what you're talking about!" While I tried to sleep for twenty-four hours, they argued back and forth. I fell asleep but I really couldn't rest. At midnight when my twenty-four was up, I took off. Our fish camp was on the south side of the river. I was worried if Nugget would go there, to Melozi. But with the Iditarod trail on the north side, and since it was midnight, Nugget passed it on by.

Still tired, twelve miles out of Ruby, I made a nest in my sled, zipped up my parka, put on my beaver hat and my mittens, nice and warm, and I fell asleep. Nugget knew where to go; she followed Carl Huntington's path. (Thank God that in 1974 Carl didn't stop on that trail to feed his dogs.) So in 1975, Nugget never stopped. When I woke up, I was twelve miles out of

Emmitt Peters leaving Ruby as his family watches him continue the Iditarod. Rose Albert's late brother Howard Albert is walking across the ice, ca 1982.
Photographer Fran Durner. Courtesy of Emmitt Peters.

Galena. It was daylight; I told my dogs to stop. Nugget rolled in the snow to get rid of the frost. I fed my dogs and went on.

When I pulled into Galena, the checker was really amazed at my time. I'd left Ruby after midnight and arrived thirty-five miles later in Galena at ten minutes to six. The fastest time was over eight hours and my time was five hours and fifty minutes. I was number twenty-six coming out of Ruby and I arrived into Galena as number twenty-four. The checker asked me, "Where are the two mushers you passed?" I didn't know I had passed anyone. Apparently Nugget had gone past two teams without stopping and without any dog fights.

At Unalakleet, when I caught up to number five position, my mom got excited. She said to my dad, "Let's hook up the dogs and go!" In his gentle way, my dad negotiated, "Emmitt took all the tug lines and harnesses. We have no way to hook up dogs. No way at all." For twenty-four hours, Mary cried, "Let's get the dogs going…" Paul kept repeating, "Too bad. Too bad. Too bad."

Along the coast, Nugget stopped at every cabin where Carl Huntington had stopped in 1974. When she thought it was time to stop, I'd say, "No," and pet her to make her happy. However, in White Mountain and Golovin, she would go right up to cabin doors. An Eskimo would answer the door and ask, "Who is it?" "Emmitt Peters," I'd say. "Who the hell is Emmitt Peters?" he'd ask. I said, "Is this where Carl Huntington stayed last year?" "Yeh, yeh," he'd answer. "My leader just brought me here," I'd say. "How the hell did she know?" he'd ask.

When I was four miles out of Nome, Nugget saw drydocked fishing boats. Remembering riding in my boat at home, she made a beeline for the boat and jumped in. My team was tuckered out.

Thirty miles out of Nome at Safety, the last checkpoint, we had to cross the slough and come up the bank. The race marshall, Orville Lake, announced, "Ladies, and gentleman, we have the first musher coming up the bank, Jerry Riley." I said, "Nope. That's Jerry Riley back there, four to five miles behind me. I'm Emmitt Peters." "Ladies and gentlemen," he corrected, "I made a mistake; it's Emmitt Peters, the Yukon Fox!"

Along with mushers from the lower Yukon River villages, I became a part of the new cutting edge of long-distance racing. As a rookie, I changed the Iditarod into a speed race. Everyone up and down the river got excited. With Nugget, there was no mishap, no danger, no moose.

Once during the 1987 race, Joe Redington Sr. was all bruised up; I was tired and had frozen cheekbones. At the last checkpoint, at Solomon, he said, "Emmitt, we may as well go in together." I answered, "Yeahhh," but I wanted to beat him in the worst way because he was always ahead of me going into Nome. We sat down and had a cup of coffee. He sat next to me and asked, "Emmitt, when are you goin' to go?" I said, "Oh, let's give the dogs a rest. There's no hurry. We're out of the race anyway." We were both tired but we had twenty-two more miles to go. I wanted to beat him so bad. I was trying to sneak away from him but he caught on. When I tried to ease away, he said, "Where are you going?" I answered, "Oh, I'm just moving around." I stayed quiet for a while. While he tried to nap, he put his hand on my knee so that if I woke up and moved, I'd wake him up! When I fell asleep with Joe's hand on my knee, Joe's wife, Vi, later told my wife in Nome, "Our husbands are sleeping together!"

Since 1975, I have run the Iditarod thirteen times and had some pretty good years: seven in the top ten. In 1975, I won with a time of fourteen days, fourteen hours, forty-three minutes, and forty-five seconds and I also was named Rookie of the Year. The two previous races in 1973 and 1974 were slower. In 1975, I won in a close race. In the next five races, I placed in the top ten and in the sixth race, Nugget won the Golden Harness in 1979. In 1982, I took the GCI Halfway speed award. I earned a total of $54,149.00. I earned the "Yukon Fox" nickname, because even with five or six teams chasing me I could sneak away from all my competitors.

There are people, like inexperienced dog mushers from the Lower Forty-eight states, who don't belong in the race. Some of them expect outhouses at every checkpoint, and sometimes, they wait too long. Once in a hurry, one desperate musher accidentally hit his parka hood. When his dogs took

Emmitt leading his dogs into Nome.

Courtesy of Emmitt Peters.

off, he threw his hood up and grabbed his sled. The checker at the next stop asked what the odor was. Even with his hurried effort, scrubbing with snow had not been enough to clean the musher up.

I have always liked sports: mushing, basketball, and baseball. In April 2006, I was elected to the American Indian Athletic Hall of Fame at Haskell Indian Nations University in Lawrence, Kansas where I joined the ranks of some of the greatest Native American athletes, including Jim Thorpe. As the first Alaska Native to be inducted, I went to Arizona to receive the award. The audience couldn't believe it was possible to race in sub-zero temperatures across a thousand miles of frozen terrain, from Anchorage to Nome. While I explained, we showed movies of us running the race.

I have also been elected to the Knik Museum: Historic Iditarod Trail and Dog Mushers Hall of Fame near Wasilla and the *Anchorage Daily News* Iditarod Hall of Fame.

In 2000, twenty-five years after setting the Iditarod record, to celebrate the new millennium, I leased a dog team and mushed one more time to Nome. This time, my sons, eighteen-year-old Emmitt Junior and fifteen-year-old Emory, rode snowmachines toward Nome. When it became impassable, they returned to Ruby.

During the 2000 race, I got very tired. The last time I had had any sleep was in Old Woman, fifty miles out of Unalakleet. Every now and then, I'd get a catnap and I'd keep on going. Three days of little sleep and not moving due to the flats and the cold put me into a hallucinogenic stupor. I thought I saw my wife, Edna, and I asked her, "How much farther?" She said, "Oh,

Emmitt Peters interviewing, 2007.

Judy Ferguson photo.

just a couple more miles." I could see Emmitt Jr. jumping up and down, saying, "You're almost there, Dad!" But my family was only a chunk of ice on the coast.

When I came in forty out of sixty-eight, my last time crossing into Nome, I finished in twelve days, two hours, and forty-two minutes, my fastest time ever. I earned the Most Inspirational Musher award, based on the votes of the other finishers.

While I was on the trail, when I'd hit the hot air in a cabin, I'd fall right to sleep. Then during the night, I'd jump up and get back on the trail. After the race was over and we were in Nome, during the middle of the night, I jumped up once to rush to get back on the trail. My wife said, "No, Emmitt, the race is over." I told her, "No, I have to catch Herbert Nayokpuk!" According to my wife, I fell back asleep like a felled tree. After that 2000 race, I decided that no one was ever talking me into anything like that again.

In 2007, I had five-bypass cardiac surgery. All of my arteries were completely clogged except for two that were nearly shut. The doctor kept shaking his head amazed that I had pulled through. If I'd waited a little longer, this interview would never have happened. It was a rough recovery but I am coming back. I have only one dog now because for a year I have not been able to lift anything heavy.

I hate to see the traditional Native way of life evaporating so rapidly. Nobody is out there fishing, trapping, making the effort I did to get into the Iditarod.

Every year, I try to go see the Iditarod kick off. As I go, I carry with me two of the most remarkable parents anyone ever had: Paul and Mary Peters, the lady who wanted to hook up her team, get on the trail, and follow her son on into Nome.

As Bulletproof *readied to go to press, Emmitt Peters passed away at his home in Ruby April 3, 2020.*

In 1997 when Emmitt was inducted into the *Anchorage Daily News* Iditarod Hall of Fame, they quoted ADN reporter Scott Heiberger:

The [Emmitt Peters] victory was no fluke. For the next five years, Peters was never out of the top 10. His ability to stay among the leaders even in years when his team wasn't the strongest earned him the nickname "the Yukon River Fox." In 1975, Emmitt Peters brought speed to the Iditarod. For its first two years, the event could just as well have been called the Iditarod Trail Camping Trip with Dogs. The journey wasn't easy, but it wasn't fast, either. The mushers required twenty days to travel the thousand miles. Then the rookie from Ruby burst onto the trail, cutting six full days off the time and setting a speed record that stood for five years. An Athabascan, Peters grew up with sled dogs, and brought a lifetime of knowledge to the race. Peters was ahead of his time in the 1970s with his strategies for resting and running his team and in dog care and training.

However in 1986, he shattered a knee in a freak training accident. Although he ran the race a few more times, he did not finish near the top. As the years went on, top mushers got big-money sponsors, ran big dog lots, and bred faster dogs. Peters couldn't keep up.

None of this seems to have marred his reputation in the slightest.

But his fellow mushers remember more than his competitiveness. "He's never hesitated to offer volumes of valuable advice and encouragement to me and many other rookie mushers," wrote reader and Iditarod musher Don Bowers.

"Even after retiring from the race, Peters has served as the checker in Ruby," wrote nominating committee member John Tracy. "Probably the only checker more famous than the mushers. Most of the racers don't consider their race complete unless they've shaken hands with The Fox in Ruby."

The Hall of Fame wouldn't be complete without him, either.

In the late 1990s, Emmitt had to sell his dogs to cover his racing debts. He was only able to do his final race in 2000 because two friends donated $10,000 each, Dineega Native Corporation gave him about $3,000, and villagers held bake sales and raffles. He also leased a team from Rick Swenson.

Emmitt epitomized one of the Iditarod's original goals—to revive the then-dying art of dog sledding in rural Alaska. The Iditarod succeeded wildly. It launched a surge in mushing across Alaska and became the sport's premier event. Ironically, that success all but squeezed out rural competitors and Natives, who struggle with higher costs and poorer access to sponsors.

Chapter 6

Henry Beatus, Hughes, Koyukuk River

Henry Beatus said in his book Henry Beatus, Sr., *"It's not our way to show our greatest side but to speak better of other people." In this book published by the Yukon-Koyukuk School (YKSD) District in 1980, he spoke honestly about himself, often deferring credit to others.*

Almost forty years later in Fairbanks, when I met Henry at the home of Ryan McCarty, Henry's adopted son, Henry was mild-mannered and soft-spoken but his hearing was impaired. Due to these constraints as well as those of time, I asked him to speak mostly about his

Henry Beatus, Hughes, 1991.
Courtesy of Henry Beatus, Sr.

Iditarod race. I could rely on his book for his life story. Later at Project Jukebox online, I discovered short interviews with Henry at KIYU in Galena, by Raven's Story, recorded in 1997. These tools helped me to write Henry's updated story. Henry's daughter Cynthia kindly edited the chapter with her father.

In Bulletproof, *in the chapters relating to the upper Koyukuk, there are references both to the village of Dalby (Dolbi) and of the village of Dulbi, both seemingly located on Dulbi Slough, very near both Cutoff and Huslia. My guess is that Dalby and Dulbi were the same village because of the similarity of the root word of the Koyukon name of the old village* Dolbaakaakk'at. *In the YKSD biography of* Edwin Simon *of Huslia, he refers to* Dolbaakaakk'at. *He adds that the 1930s trader Sam Dubin had stores in Koyukuk Station, Dulbi, Hog River, Hughes, Allakaket, Bettles, and Wiseman.*

*Henry Beatus was raised by his grandmother, Ida, and her husband, Little Beatus (*Yaa'eeneeyo*), whom Henry referred to as Grandpa or "the Old Man." Raised by an older generation, Henry learned the ancient skills of a disappearing way of life. I asked him to sing me a song that his grandmother used to sing in Koyukon to him. As he did, he was immersed in an earlier time, an intimate memory. He then began sharing his story.*

Dalby trading post token, 25 cents.
http://alaskagoldrush.info/
Towns/Dalby.htm

I was born Jan 6, 1932 to Helen (*Ts'iyeelno*) and Fred Bifelt in Hughes. My oldest brother Lincoln died as a child. When I was about eighteen months old, my mother passed away. She left behind my siblings Annie and Cue, and of course, me. Annie didn't know that Dad was planning on only taking Cue with him to Cutoff, but still, she kept a close eye on him, watching to see if he was going to leave in his boat. A nice non-Native couple had taken my sister in. They gave her her own room as well as nice dresses. She didn't know that they planned on adopting her and taking her Outside with them. By late fall, when it was getting cold and the river would soon freeze over, Dad began preparing to get downstream to Cutoff. When my sister saw

Young Henry with Celia Beetus near 250 stretched muskrats that Celia and Joe Beetus hunted and trapped, 15-Mile camp, ca 1939
Joe Beetus photo, *Henry Beatus, Sr. Biography*

Dad shaking hands with the white couple and then turn and begin walking to Cue, who was sitting in Dad's boat, she ran straight out of the house and jumped in the boat as well. She had no winter clothes on but she was not getting out of the boat. Some old grandmas took pity on her and brought her their winter gear for the trip downstream. Annie said their loaned adult boots were really big. In Cutoff, which later became Huslia, my dad raised both Annie and Cue. During that time, he was first married to Cora and then, later to Edna.

My mother's mother, Ida (*Alahseey*), who was from Dalby (Dulbi) Slough, raised me. For many years she'd lived in Allakaket where she and her husband, Leon Bergman, had raised eight children. When three of their children were young, Leon died. Gramma then married "Little Beatus" (*EE EE Nee Yo*, Must Be Fast). They and her son Joe Beetus raised me. [1] Naturally I grew up speaking my language. I went everywhere with Grandpa. I watched everything he did and I learned the traditional way of life. Gramma wanted to raise me good; I was her baby. All I did was eat so I got pretty heavy. She used to call me *Nedoł* (pronounced "*Ndalsh*," "Heavy.")

---

1. Henry's daughter Cynthia Beatus wondered if the difference in the historic spelling of Beatus and Beetus was the result of an old spelling error. Those separate surnames have endured to the present.

*Celia Beetus, Ida, and young Henry
Beatus, holding two puppies, 15-Mile
spring camp, ca. 1940.*
Joe Beetus photo, *Henry Beatus, Sr. Bio.*

When I was very young, Hughes was more of a camp than it was a village. Gold was first discovered there at nearby Utopia Creek in 1906, but more active prospecting and mining didn't happen until about 1929. The year I was born in 1938, machinery came in and large-scale placer mining began. It continued until about 1952. Utopia may've been the largest gold producer on the Koyukuk River.

When I was about eight, the trader Mr. Les James and his wife, Esther James, and their son Johnny, who was a little older than I, came to Hughes. I learned a little English from Johnny. They either had health or financial issues but they had to leave our area.

There was no school in Hughes until the 1950s so I had no formal education. My grandpa wanted me to go to the mission school in Allakaket, but I didn't want to leave him. I paid close attention and learned my acquired skills in life through keen observation.

When I was very young, I went out every winter, from mid-January to March, with my grandparents to our Hog River trapline. Besides Gramma and Grandpa, there was Gramma's son, Joe Beetus, and two of her daughters, Martha and Maggie.

After Joe, Martha, and Maggie got on their own, only the Ol' Man and I went out trapping. We didn't have enough dogs to pull both us and our freight so we always walked, Grandpa in front of the sled and me behind. Every day, we went about as fast as I could walk so we didn't get very far; soon, it would be time to set up camp again. I was pretty young and it was all sort of hard for me. That was the year I caught my first mink and I got eight dollars for it! I never had eight dollars in my whole life! Also we got two more dogs. Grandpa always had warm clothes for me and every morning, he made us breakfast. When it was -50, we'd wake up in a frost-encrusted tent, but still, we'd hit the trail. One winter when I was twelve, there was really deep snow. A run that was only ten miles took us from early in the morning breaking trail until 10:30 that night. When we finally arrived, our tent was collapsed from the heavy snow load. Tired as we were, we shoveled the tent out with our snowshoes, got a fire going, ate, and four hours later, we got to bed. Some days I wondered why we couldn't take it easier, but I didn't know that Grandpa was preparing me for life, to not make excuses for myself, but to push through. When I was twelve years old, I began trapping by myself, but not too far away. At fourteen, I had my own line.

Grandpa taught me that the best muskrat were up in the hills in the deep lakes. The smaller rats were in the flats in the shallow lakes. I got paid about a dollar a rat but in 1950, the price went up to over $2 per rat.

In 1940, beaver trapping was opened up (but before that, we shot them). We caught and dried the rich meat and saved it to eat. There weren't many caribou around in those days. They came back much later.

Grandpa made fish traps from split spruce roots. There were two great spots at Four-Mile and Nine-Mile where the deep channel ran off the downstream end of the sand bar. In early December, I often run a wire fence along a riffle in swift water to corral loche (burbot) and white fish into a funnel, which leads them into a fish trap box with chicken wire over a hole at the far end. It's important to keep the water flowing. The trap catches fish during their six-week run.

Back in the 1960s Uncle Edwin Simon told me that the pike were multiplying so much that they were going to wipe us out by driving the muskrat from the shallow lakes and into the rivers.

Back then, our only summer transportation was by canoe. In 1948 or so, I made enough trapping to buy a canoe and a 5-horse kicker. As soon as the ice went out, Arthur Ambrose and I crossed the river. Normally, when crossing a river without a motor, a person drifts downstream about five miles and then has to paddle back up on the far side. But with that kicker, we landed in exactly the same spot on the other side! I had that motor quite a while.

My great-grandmother, Madeline[2], originally established our winter camp on a point in front of a hill on the river, the best one on the Koyukuk, eight miles below Hughes. The best times in my life were spent there. Some of Madeline's ("Old Mama's") children included Liza, who was George Attla's mother; Sophie Sam, Bessie Henry, Little Peter, Hog River Johnny, and my paternal grandmother, Anna Huntington of Huslia, (who was the mother of Sidney and Jimmy Huntington and my father, Fred Bifelt). My sister Annie was named for Grandma Anna Huntington.

At Twelve-Mile, my grandparents had their summer fish camp. I still have a camp there today.

____

2. *Yaghoyinaatlno*, referred to as "Old Mama" in *Shadows on the Koyukuk*.

Henry Beatus' grandparents, Little Beatus (Yaa'eeneeyo) and Ida.
Bertha Moses Collection UAF 1985-67-26

My grandpa taught me to hunt bear in the fall, how to look for just the right knoll for a potential bear den. He told me not to hunt in the hills close to town, but I didn't necessarily tell him when I went out there. When I got older, some of us went in a group. We'd camp and then split up, scouting out certain areas. I really enjoyed that.

The musher who first wanted to help me learn sprint racing was Bobby Vent, of Huslia. In 1942 when I was ten, I met him at Cutoff. I wanted to be with dogs, so I'd gone over to the old village for a potlatch. As soon as I got there, I began running around, looking at the animals. Pretty soon, I saw a guy hooking up six dogs. In those days, no one used an anchor to hold the sled. The sleigh itself wasn't even tied to a tree. To help the musher, I ran over to the sled and stepped on the brake to hold the dogs for him, but it turned out to be unnecessary. He hooked up his dogs, walked to the back of his sleigh, and took off. When I began training my own dogs, while I was harnessing them I never trained them to hold still. I couldn't anyway. When I was on the trapline, however, they learned to wait for fifteen minutes while I checked each of my fur sets.

In 1939 when I was seven, the first race I saw in Hughes was a five-miler, but the next year, they extended it to nine miles. In those days, there were a lot of mushers. In 1948 when I was fourteen, I got my first dog team, four dogs; my leader was Buster. We trapped out of a tent. A husky, Buster would do everything for me. With dogs, you won't break down, but with a snowmachine, you can. A musher might lose his team on the trail, but a good outfit will always come back to you. That spring of 1948 when I came in from trapping, Hughes was having their spring carnival. I wanted to race but I needed two more dogs, which I borrowed, and then I came in fourth.

After that first race, I continued racing pretty much every year. I ran the racetrack a lot up in the hills behind Hughes. The first Huslia race I ran was on a nineteen-mile track. I enjoyed racing there in the spring carnival. In 1959, I came in third and in 1961, second. I raced in many of the villages well into the 1970s. I had a pretty fair team with a pace of about 10 mph. Winning races was one way for us to get sure money. We pooled

Henry Beatus with wolf.
Courtesy of Henry Beatus.

our village dogs, and every year, one of us would go up to the spring carnival.

I also trapped beaver, mink, marten, lynx, fox, wolverine, otter, and some wolf. The first fur buyer I remember was Johnny Swagler who was called "Muskrat Johnny." After Johnny's time, there were quite a few more buyers. More recently, I used to sell to my good friend Dean Wilson of Kenny Lake. When Dean's health declined, he sold his business to Bill Wivoda, also my good friend, but today, I only trap a little.

My first job working for wages was in 1950 hauling freight for a contractor in the mining camp, Utopia, behind Hughes. I helped a little with "cleanup," handling the gold. After the first two weeks, I got on a Cat and started hauling freight behind the contractor, who was doing the same. I learned to use a blade, how to repair the Cat, and then, how to operate every piece of equipment they had. During the summers, I worked on Jimmy Huntington, Jr.'s freight boat, the *Galloping Goose*. When the barge closed down, I went back to work at the Hog River mining camp, where I worked for eight years on the Fairbanks Exploration Company's dredge.

In 1952 I married Sophie Koyukuk from Allakaket. I trapped in the wintertime and every chance I got, and I hunted and fished to supply food for us and our dogs. I learned carpentry and worked various construction jobs.

When I was out working, my wife Sophie took care of all our kids as well as doing the fishing by herself. We had eleven kids, but we lost Norman and Sandra and then, three to a boating accident in 1985: Ruth, Ray, and Henry, Jr. Once when I got hurt, we had to adopt our new son Gerald to the Oldmans. In 2019, our surviving children include Almira, Miranda, Hazel, Ron, Cynthia, and Gerald. We also raised Ryan, whose parents are Esther and Pat McCarty. Sophie also began working as a health aide. Unlike me, our children went to school. When I wanted to show them how to do some of the old skills, however, they weren't much interested. Later when I was busy working at the school and the kids had graduated, then they wanted to learn some of the old ways, but it was harder telling them than showing them like my old man had done with me when we were living the life together.

With my job experience, I got a permanent position at Hughes school in maintenance in 1969. I learned to work the furnace and the light plant. With the steady salary and the benefits from that job, I was able to eventually retire. Even though I can't read, I watch people. I see how they do things and I catch onto things pretty well.

In 1973, the year the Iditarod began, even though I was forty-one, I wanted to run it. For the next two years, I looked for support and for dogs. Jimmy Huntington and Alfred Attla gave me some money while

Henry Beatus, sixth in 1975 Iditarod.
1975 Iditarod Trail Annual.

Barney Sam, Fred Ned, Art Williams, Bill Williams, Joe Beetus, and Lester Sam loaned me dogs. My two leads were Fred Ned's dog Boozer from Allakaket and Barney Sam's dog Starr from Huslia. The dogs all came from Allakaket, Huslia, and Hughes.

In the fall right after the first snowfall, I always start my dogs out slow, pulling a load so they can't run fast. If they run fast before their muscles are hardened up, they'll get hurt. I begin by running them only five miles. I harden them up before I let them run fast for twenty miles. By the holidays, they are in pretty good shape.

Dogs get into mischief. I train pups by hooking them up with older well-behaved dogs. When pups act up, I give them a spanking to teach them. Whether chained up or in a harness, my dogs never get by with anything. I am always the master. That way in a race when I need them to pour it on, they'll listen to me. Both Raymond Paul of Galena and my brother Cue Bifelt taught me a lot.

For the Iditarod, I had a good store-bought, really warm Alaska sleeping bag filled with down. My wife made me mukluks[3] from wolf leggings and from moosehide. I also had heavier, warm, store-bought boots, lined with mouton and felt "sock" inserts. For cooler weather, I wore tall canvas, leather-soled, military mukluks with felt boot liner inserts. I wore military-issue, warm

3   *Kkaakene*: boots in Athabascan.

coveralls, and a down parka. Mostly I wore gloves, but for subzero temps, I had wolf skin arctic mitts insulated with a fur liner that I could pull out. I wore a beaver hat but never a facemask.

In 1975 running as a rookie, I started out at the back of the pack at the starting line in Anchorage. My fourteen dogs were straining to go but I held them back. Even though

Race marshall Dick Tozier and Henry Beatus.
1975 Iditarod Trail Annual. Courtesy Henry Beatus.

I'd trained the team in distance racing, I hadn't camped out with them. They were used to going all out during a one-day event and then getting their rest. At the Iditarod, the team took off, wide open. Unlike in sprint racing, there was no chance to rest. We had to keep going, going, going. A lot of dogs got hurt.

Going over Rainy Pass, it was a very cold all-night mush. I caught up with Ray Jackson's long string of dogs. After many hours, I found a snow-covered rest tent that, despite its snow load, was still standing. Ray and I were both able to crawl in. We built a fire in the stove, ate, spent the night, and we became good friends.

I had to keep dropping dogs and by the time, I reached the Rohn River, I had to leave the last of seven injured dogs. With half my team gone, I was pretty much walking and pushing the sled uphill, but still, we were doing all right.

It had been cold before reaching McGrath, but at 2 AM when I pulled into town, it was -48, the coldest yet. Some people offered to put me up so they waited for me to check in, and then I strung the dogs out on a chain in their yard. After leaving McGrath, it began to warm up.

I had food drops at all the checkpoints. Each of my packets had plenty of matches and food for one night and for the following day. I always carried a pot and cooked over an open fire but in Galena, I bought a gas stove and Blazo (white gas).

I ate dry fish and Indian ice cream,[4] same menu as when I was on the trapline at home. Everywhere I stopped, people served me cooked food and asked me what I needed. In Ruby, I spent an hour with my friend Harold Esmailka.

Herbie Nayokpuk and I had camped at Rohn River and traveled together the following day. Later when he pulled in at Long Creek behind Ruby, when I was putting my camp up, he said, "There's a place down there a little ways." I said, "This is all right. The firewood is handy here," so he parked his dogs and also made camp. He had a long string of eleven dogs. The next morning, I watched him take off, climb the hill and pull away with his big team. That's the last time I saw Herbie.

At Kaltag, a guy had a little beaver meat. I asked if he wanted to sell it. My dogs were so happy to eat that rich food.

First at Unalakleet and especially at Shaktoolik, the wind began to hit us. When we reached the bay, I couldn't see the hills for the storm. It began to rage and I couldn't see my wheel dog. When it cleared, my dogs looked back at me to make sure I was still hanging on.

As we mushed along, I kept an eye on the dogs to make sure their eyes didn't ice over. When a blizzard hits, frost can build up around their eyes. If they ice up, a musher has to melt the crust, crack it out and then, get going again.

With only seven dogs, it was walk, walk, walk. Time became a blur. I couldn't remember how long it had taken me to go the five or ten miles to Koyuk. Once in a while, I could see the hills and then, I knew I could make it. When we finally got to Koyuk, we spent the night. The dogs were weak from pushing for six hours through the blizzard.

*Henry Beatus, cook-
ies and coffee break,
Farewell Lake, 1975.*
Photographer Alice Puster.
Anchorage Times

---

4   *Akutaq* or in Denaakk'e, *nonaałdlode*: dried berries, tallow, snow, and sometimes fish, all whipped together)

My close friend Joe Redington, Sr. was stuck in Koyuk. His dogs had laid down on him. We talked and I told him that maybe his team could use me as a shield and follow me. Joe was happy (he was a lot older than I was). The next morning when I hooked up, Joe's dogs were right beside my sleigh. They were standing up, looking like they would go. As long as they could see me, they would go.

On the trail when I going through brush, they couldn't see me and I heard them lie down, but after a little while, Joe got them going again. Later when the dogs saw me, they were happy.

After spending the night in Elim, my swing dog wouldn't eat or even drink broth. I figured, "Well, I gotta keep going, but he'll never make it." But I had to try something, I'd never make it with just six dogs. I looked in my lunch box and got a spoon. I began ladling meat broth into his mouth and he swallowed it. I kept doing it until he'd eaten half the broth and then, he began to eat by himself. I was happy. Twice before, that dog had been in the race with George Attla. I had only twenty more miles to Nome and I knew he could make it.

During the race, I cooked mostly sheefish with rice, which was a little light for running long distances. Meat gives more strength and endurance, but with no experience in such a race, I hadn't known to bring meat. I was feeding them like I did on the trapline, but on the line, I don't run them steadily but only for so many hours a day. In the Iditarod, the dogs gotta go and go . . . and go, but it was fun.

When I got to Shaktoolik, I saw the wind was blowing again. I thought, "I gotta make it. I don't want to drop out." Every time I rested the dogs, I worked on their food and made sure I had it ready for them. There was no time to really sleep, but sometimes I rested in my sled.

I was so tired when I came into Nome that I was sleeping while standing on my runners. As we approached the finish line, I fell forward onto the cold tarp covering my sled. I woke up and my dogs stopped. I pushed the sleigh and got them going again. I came in sixth place and got $2500, but my total expenses came to $3600. Because I had no sponsor, it was too much. My close friend Joe Redington, whom I'd helped in Koyuk, came in fifth. He beat me in the end. I did the best I could. Joe and I were still friends; that's sports.

When I got to Nome about 3-4 AM, I was so tired. Even though I had a place to go, I couldn't sleep, so I called Harold's Air Service in Galena. I was only in Nome about eight hours. That afternoon Harold came for me and took me back home to Hughes, but it was expensive. I just wanted to sleep in my own bed. No Iditarod banquet for me. Darlene Billings from Galena

Henry Beatus, 2017.
Judy Ferguson photo.

picked up my prize money and my sixth place trophy.

The Iditarod was really work, but I met a lot of people. If I'd trained all winter by camping on the trail and used meat during the race, I probably would've been closer to the front.

There's a big difference between trapline dogs and racing dogs. They may be a different size and for sure, they have to be trained differently. Trapline dogs have to learn to trot steady a long ways. They have to stop and wait while a trapper checks his sets. You got to have a good leader in case the team gets away, the leader must be able to circle and come back. Sprint racing dogs just run straight out fast. They don't stop or rest. It's all about getting across the finish line fast. During the 1970s Iditarod, trapline dogs were more what was used for long distance mushing.

At the last minute before the race, I had asked Dick Hanks' wife to make me a bag of canvas boots, a real rush job. I used booties for all of my dogs except for two with good feet. For those two, I just kept checking their feet pretty often.

Three years later, I tried to run again. I had thirty-four running dogs but I couldn't find enough sponsors. Jimmy Huntington and Alfred Attla came up with some money because they wanted to help me, but more was needed.

In 1979, I won the Huslia New Year's Race three-year trophy. Before I turned sixty, I used to say I wouldn't quit until my dogs crossed the finish line without me, that as long as I could hang onto the handlebars, I was going to race.

I'd like to see local young people more involved in sled dog racing, but today it is not like when we were young. Now the price of everything is high. For some of us, money isn't easy to get. People who have businesses, they can do it more easily. Nowadays, there aren't too many Natives in the Iditarod. It's expensive and it's year-round work. When my nephew, Archie-Ray Beetus of Hughes, came back from the Iron Dog race, I called him and said, "Change your way of racing so I won't worry about you." He said he'd think about it. He might start dog racing locally. I'd like to see more young people with dogs but I don't know how that will go.

Chapter 7

Tanana Chiefs First Traditional Chief Don Honea, Seven-Time Iditarod Competitor

Don Honea, Sr., ca. 1976, used for race marshal photo.
Courtesy of Don Honea, Sr.

Before the 1914 construction of a telegraph station at Kokrines, there were family subsistence camps all up and down the Yukon River. Surrounded by hills, Kokrines was upstream from Ruby, a white mining camp that sprouted after a 1910 gold strike. When the Kokrines telegraph station started up, people began moving in from their camps, including including the family of Clara McCarty Honea, former wife of Don Honea, Sr., Iditarod musher and Tanana Chiefs Conference First Traditional Chief. The War Department promised to supply fuel and dog food to the forts and telegraph stations in the early 1900s. The Kokrines people cut firewood for the steamboats, the traders, the school, and the Northern Commercial Company at Ruby. Villagers sold dried fish, meat, berries, moccasins, boots, and furs. Some of those from Kokrines later moved to Tanana, near Fort Gibbon. Today there are people from Minto and

Kokrines, ca. 1911–1914, L-R: Paul Clarence, Frank Albert, Hardluck; Don Honea's maternal uncle, Harry Pitka.
History of Ruby, Alaska: the Gem of the Yukon. Basil Clemons, PCA 68-55, Alaska State Library

Don Honea's maternal grandfather Andrew Peter with his brother and Don's grandfather by marriage, Adamon, 1920s.
Alaska Diary by Dr. Ales Hrdlicka.

Stevens Village who say their ancestors came from Kokrines.

When I interviewed Don Honea, he opened A History of Ruby, Alaska: the Gem of the Yukon *to page fourteen, pointed to a photo, and said, "The fourth person from the left is my mother's brother Harry Pitka." Then picking up* Alaska Diary *by Dr. Ales Hrdlicka, he showed me a late 1920s photo of "Jacob and Andrew" on page 190 and said, "That photo is captioned wrong. On the left is my mother's father, 'Little Andrew,' (Andrew Peter) and on the right is Andrew's brother and Clara's grandfather, Adamon." Of the first man, Don pointed out, "Little Andrew looks exactly like his great-grandson, our son 'Rocky' Wayne Honea."*

Eighty-eight-year-old Chief Honea, a seven-time Iditarod competitor, began sharing his life's story.

The marriage of Don Honea's parents, Margaret Peter and Bill Honea, 1925.
Courtesy of Don Honea Sr.,

Don's father, Bill Honea, with son Jeb, 1935, Ruby.
Courtesy of Don Honea, Sr.

My dad John William Honea, "Bill," was born in 1885. He was an early Signal Corps operator at Kokrines. My father was born in Alabama and enlisted in the military and served various stints first as a telephone operator in the Lower 48 and then in Alaska as a telegraph operator at Fort Gibbon near Tanana and finally, at Kokrines. He was first married to a woman named Mary. Her little brother Johnny grew up to teach me a lot about dog mushing. Dad adopted Johnny and he became Johnny Honea. However when it became clear that Mary could bear Dad no children, he divorced her. After he was discharged, he re-upped and was stationed at Kokrines, where he met my mother, Margaret Peter. After his stint was over, he and Mom married and began trapping out of Kokrines. At the age of forty-two, my father and my seventeen-year-old mother started a family of fifteen children. Born in 1931, I was the sixth.

At the time in Kokrines, dogs were the only means of winter transportation so we had seven sled dogs, weighing about 60-70 pounds apiece.

My dad got a job working for the Civil Aeronautics Administration (CAA, forerunner to the FAA) in Ruby so we moved there in the early 1950s.

Siblings: Bella, Harry Pitka, and Don's mother, Margaret Honea, 1945.
Courtesy of Don Honea, Sr.

My mother's brother "Harry Pitka" (James Harry Pitka Andrew) used to haul mail from Kokrines to Ruby. When the old mail carriers would come into Ruby, we'd holler, "Wow, look at those BIG dogs!" Not only were they huge to us, but the mail carriers ran long strings of them. During the 1940s, Scotty Clark used to haul a thousand pounds of mail with twenty-two big dogs from Ruby to Poorman and out to Long Creek. Sled dog mail delivery ended as late as 1963.

At home, we had a pretty disciplined lifestyle. At 6 p.m., we had to be at the supper table or we didn't eat. Every day Dad assigned chores to us but he rotated them: hauling water, cutting wood, taking care of the dogs so I never got tired of any one thing.

In those days, it was tough to support a family. In 1943, we moved to Fairbanks where Dad found work as a jailer, a painter, and also as a laborer at Ladd Field. Due to too many city distractions, I couldn't make the transition from the village to an urban school, so five of my eleven brothers

Bill and Margaret Honea family, 1942: Arnold holding Roger, Harriet, Dexter, Wheeler, Clay (living), Don (living), Jeb, Margie, Leroy (living), and Bob.
Courtesy of Don Honea, Sr.

and I were sent off to boarding school at Eklutna. The students pretty much ran the system. We studied half of each day and then we worked on farm equipment, or with a carpenter, an electrician, or in the laundry room. The second year I was there, the school was moved to an old army camp in Seward. Then in the middle of the following winter, it was going to relocate at Mt. Edgecumbe in Sitka. My friend John Greenway and I decided that was too far from home so we both quit. After my training at the school, however, at age fourteen, I could do almost anything.

I got a job on the steamer *Nenana*. I spent the spring going up and down the Tanana. When I got to Ruby, I felt so at

Johnny Honea, Ruby, ca. 1976.
Courtesy of Don Honea, Sr.

home that I quit the boat and stayed there. I knew all the people. My uncle Harry Pitka had a house where I could live. Later I went a little farther down the Yukon to Blackburn where the Thurmond brothers, Clinton, Hughie, and Billy, had a camp. All summer, I went back and forth between my uncle's and the Thurmonds'.

I had no one to teach me the traditional way of life so I began learning subsistence by watching and doing. That fall I went trapping with my older and adopted brother, Johnny Honea. We went trapping with ten really nice, dogs. When we were finished for the season, he gave me a female dog who I named Darling after his dachshund.

John Honea was a good musher. He knew a lot and he always had a good team. An early renowned dog driver, Johnny Allen, used to run his dogs from Kokrines to Fairbanks to race in the North American, which he then won three times. But at home, Johnny Allen used to lose regularly to my brother John Honea.

In the spring of 1949, I went to Kokrines, where Clara, whom I'd known all my life, caught my eye. She was the oldest of the ten McCarty kids. Not only did I like Clara, but in that village of eighty people, everyone was Native with the exception of one white person. I'm not prejudiced but I feel more relaxed around Natives.

Clara and I moved to a fish camp owned by her father, Billy McCarty, Sr., three miles above Ruby. In 1949, we married and moved back to Kokrines,

Don and Clara Honea, ca. 1976.
Courtesy of Don Honea, Sr.

where her family lived. I used my father-in-law's dogs. I trapped and drank with Clara's brother, Billy, Jr. Clara and I soon had Rosemarie, the first of our fourteen children. We lost two when they were infants (Ronald and Marvin), but we still went on to raise twelve children.

Initially I got my dogs from trappers in Kokrines who wanted to cull their teams. I raised pups from my dog, Darling, and had part of my father-in-law's team. I used them every day hauling wood, water, and trapping. I wound up with a real good dog yard. When I was trapping beaver, I used my team for twenty-four straight days. They were good about waiting while I checked my sets. The most dogs I ever had was ten.

I only raced the fifteen-mile sprint races in Kokrines, Galena, and Ruby. My dogs, at about fifty pounds each, were too fat so we never won any of the races. Galena people would laugh when Ruby and Kokrines people came to the annual spring carnival. They'd say, "Here come those beaver-eating dogs again!" A lot of the top mushers got their start in the village races.

We lived in Kokrines about six years until our children needed to go to school. With our kids, Rose, Glenn, Don, Jr.; Billy (John William), Dale, and Rocky (Wayne), we moved to Ruby in about 1955 when Rose was six.

In those days, I worked as a laborer at Clear Air Force Base and on construction projects in Ruby.

Don's mother, Margaret Honea, after she and Bill moved to Tennessee, 1963.
Courtesy of Don Honea, Sr.

I learned how to operate a CAT working for Bill Carlo at his Ruby mine. I took any work I could get. Jobs were pretty scarce. In 1961, I began working part-time for the Department of Transportation (DOT), keeping the airfield open.

I'd fought fire where I met BLM smokejumper Bill Edlund of Minneapolis, a World War II paratrooper. I'd trapped all over, but in 1961, I bought a trapline from Uncle Harry at Moose Mountain, way up the Nowitna River (the Novi)[1]. My trapping partner was pilot Bill Edlund. During our ten years of flying that plane, we had some scary moments. Although I never had any formal training or

Don Honea with stack of beaver pelts, stringer of lynx, and river otter, 1964.
Courtesy of Don Honea, Sr.

a license, I took off and landed not only Bill's plane but also my friend Harold Esmailka's.

During the building of the pipeline and as a member of the Operating Engineers Local 302, I decided to go to Fairbanks in 1975, work construction, save my money, and get a good stake. One day as I was working on a light plant on South Cushman, I saw my buddy Emmitt Peters from Ruby on TV, who'd just won the Iditarod. I thought, "Hey, man, that's what I need to do!" but I only had two dogs including my wheel dog, Hickie. When I told Mitch Demientieff that I wanted to get a team together, he said, "Oh, yeah, I alternate years with Bill Vaudron running a team, but Bill used them last year so it's my turn this year." Later, he called me and said he couldn't run them after all and asked, "If you want them, I'll send the team to you." He paid to fly eighteen dogs from Nenana to Ruby. When they arrived, they were in rough, skinny shape, but I fed them up and worked them. I believe if a dog doesn't have the drive, don't try to beat it into him because he'll never learn through any other means. Only use dogs who have the instinct to run. Some of Vaudron's dogs were really good. One of them was Present, a great wheel dog, who'd been a gift to Bill from Nulato. Most of Bill's dogs I couldn't use, but later I picked up three good leaders: Reefer

---

1   Nowitna in Athabascan: *Nogheetno'*

Bill Edlund, ca. 1957.
Courtesy Don Honea, Sr.

from Henry Beatus' son Norman, Sweetie from Alfred Attla, and Candy from Warner Vent.

I went all over the state, picking up and renting dogs and I wound up with a good sixteen-dog team. In Ruby, there was a sled building class so I took it and learned to build one. In those days, I had my winters free so I could give the dogs the food and workout that they needed. (Later when my job became more demanding, I made time in the evenings and on weekends to train.) I was motivated, but if after extra care, a dog didn't work out, I paid his travel back to his owner, who got to keep both my rent money and the two-way travel I'd paid for. I had a lot of friends. I got dogs from up the Koyukuk, Rampart, Galena, Tanana, Fairbanks, from Gareth Wright, Henry Beatus, Cue Bifelt, and Wilson Sam in Huslia.

When I was training in the hills six miles outside of Ruby, I had a big heavy leader, a really good dog, but as I got ready to leave for the Iditarod, that guy got stove up so I had to leave him behind. I thought, "Well, if nothing else, I'll have to take Sweetie." But that turned out to be a godsend. Usually after pausing at a checkpoint, it's hard to get a team going again, but not with Sweetie. I'd just whistle and she'd jump up and start jerking, jerking at her tug line. She always got the team going again, a really nice little dog.

To pay for renting dogs, flying them, and for the essentials to run that first race, I raised $2500 from my sponsors, mostly from my construction contacts and from Harold's Air Service.

During the year, I fed my dogs fish that we caught and commercial dog food, but as the Iditarod approached, I began putting them on meat.

Some guys cooked, bagged, and froze their own food ahead of time. On the trail then when they were boiling dried fish for their dogs, they'd drop their own bagged, frozen food into the water to thaw but for me, the fishy water always seeped inside and I couldn't stand it. I always had trail mix and candy in my pocket. I didn't cook much on the trail. Before the race, I made ground meat sandwiches, packed salmon strips and pilot bread, and I cooked steaks, which I shipped out in my food drops. I'd thaw my frozen fish strips inside my parka, which got me a little greasy, but they sure tasted good.

For temperate weather, I took shoepacs but for when it got cooler, I had caribou legging boots with moosehide bottoms. Some Hughes women made me caribou liners with the hair turned outside, which were really warm. Over my Carhartts, I wore Eddie Bauer down pants. I had a goose down parka and marten skin cap. I never wore a facemask because they frost up, get wet, and then freeze. With a good ruff on my parky, I'd pull it forward and I'd be fine. I had a pair of mitts Clara made for me. A family in Galena tanned their own rabbit skins and made mitt liners, which Uncle Harry Pitka gave me. I had a top-of-the-line Eddie Bauer bag with a light down liner inside. I got a caribou skin sleeping pad through Mitch Demientieff's wife's family in Barrow. Even at -50, I never had trouble with getting cold in the Iditarod.

Don Honea, Ruby, ca. 1976.
Courtesy of Don Honea, Sr.

After I began training, one time when I was putting on my shoes, I got winded. I thought, "How in the world am I ever going to run the Iditarod?!" And thought, "And, gee, three years ago, I quit drinking," but clearly, I needed to do more. I managed to get myself in good shape, but my real hardening up happened on the Iditarod itself.

I routinely ran my dogs six miles outside of Ruby in the hills of my wife's Native allotment. However during training, I didn't camp out with my dogs. My first year, 1976, I wound up with such a good team that had it only been up to them, we might have won on our first time out. However not only does stuff happen but all summer, I had been operating heavy equipment. I was in good enough shape but when unexpectedly, during the race, I was suddenly reduced to six dogs, I wasn't in top shape to make up for that loss.

I had enough leave time built up from my job at D.O.T. so that I could take off for the race. Two weeks before, I headed down to Anchorage so just in case my dogs got sick, they'd get it out of their system beforehand. From Ruby, Harold Esmailka flew me, my son Rocky, and the team to Nenana. Once on the road system, Charlie Stevens loaned me a truck to get to Anchorage.

There were a number of mandatory items each musher had to have at the beginning of the race, at checkpoints, and in Nome. Since the Iditarod was founded on the tradition of a mail courier trail, each musher had to always have his mail cachet of envelopes, each of which he signed, "Cachet carried by (the musher's name" and were postmarked in Anchorage. At the race's end, the envelopes were postmarked in Nome and all the letters, except the five that the musher kept, were then auctioned off at the banquet.

I began in #17 position. I wasn't nervous. I was looking forward to seeing what my dogs had. As each musher left the starting line, the crowd clapped, cheered, and hollered. Initially, I had to slow my dogs down by dragging my foot, using the brake, and talking softly to them.

Figuring the race would differ each time due to trail conditions, weather, and the dogs' energy, I had no fixed race strategy. I tried to pace it so that I'd get to a location by a certain time so I could rest there. It didn't always work out so I had to take my breaks on the trail in between. A musher has to flex according to the situation.

Rohn River was a good place to camp, but it was also tough because most people took their 24-hour rest there. There were not only a lot of mushers and teams there, but when everyone took off with that many rested dogs, they went crashing out like bats out of hell over bare muskeg and ice strewn with tree stubs.

All of the country was new to me, so racing sixteen dogs over those terrible trails was both awful and wonderful. Awful because of places like Ptarmigan Pass where the descent required that sled and team be lowered down separately by a rope. At the bottom, the team was tied off while the sled was let down. However there were many awesome moments like coming up into Rainy Pass where the view was spectacular.

Before the 1978 fire, Farewell was a straight shot through trees, but after, that charred maze became a good place to lose the trail. A musher had to stay alert, looking for red tape markers on burned out trees as he worked his way through the aftermath of that incineration.

Due to the dogs' fatigue, I'd dropped five of them at various checkpoints. When I came into Ruby, I had eleven good strong dogs. My brother-in-law helped me bootie. I told him, "Be careful, don't put those on too tight." "Oh, no," he said, "I know what I'm doing."

Don Honea's sled and team, Iditarod.
Courtesy of Don Honea, Sr.

The next day when I pulled into Galena, those dogs' feet were frozen, which left me with only six good working dogs. But even with them, I maintained fifth position and was passing mushers who had ten or twelve dogs.

At dark near Kaltag, I lost the trail. I decided to wait until daylight, turned my dogs around, and camped in the protection of some trees. Soon other lost teams showed up and camped in that grove as well. In the morning I led out, but for five hours I had to walk ahead of my team, feeling for the base trail.

Don Honea's team.
Courtesy of Don Honea, Sr.

On the last hill near Unalakleet and before dropping down to the coast, Terry Adkins with his twelve dogs came up behind me. I said, "You wanna go by me?" "Nope, he said, "I'll wait because I'd just have to pass you again going up the next hill." That annoyed me so I ran all the way up to the top of that hill and looked down. He was still there at the bottom, looking about the size of an ant.

As I came into Shaktoolik, a blizzard was kicking up. Many teams were stranded so we decided to have a basketball game. They beat us by one point. When the wind died down, Billy Demoski and I took off. On the way to Koyuk, one of my dogs got tangled up so Billy began to pass me. I told him not to because as soon as I untangled the dog, I'd just have to pass him again. He got mad because he had eight dogs and I had only six. To prove my point, I decided not to ride but to push, push, push my sled so that my dogs only had to run ahead of the sled. After twenty miles, I turned around but I couldn't see Billy. I was too far ahead. However at Golovin, I had to drop another dog, but with only five dogs, I still came in twelfth and almost won Rookie of the Year. Rick Swenson at tenth place barely beat me out. Rudy came in eighteenth. Everyone pushes hard before coming into Nome. When a musher comes in, the officials check all his mandatory gear including his mail cachet, which is then postmarked Nome. A handler takes the musher's dogs, ties them up, and puts the sled away. The musher is given a packet with gifts and cards from various businesses. The winner signs all the mail cachet envelopes, the bulk of which are then bid on as a fundraiser at the banquet.

When I arrived in Nome, I'd lost eighteen pounds and had gone from being in good to excellent shape. I only wanted to rest. I hadn't slept for thirty-eight hours. My hostess had made me a turkey, but I was too tired to eat. I took a bath where I fell asleep in the tub. It was good she knocked on the door to wake me, but I didn't eat then either, I went straight to bed.

The awards banquet was a lot of fun. The mushers were rested and having a few beers.

I flew home, but was back in the race again in 1979. Once more, I had a really good team. That year, I was the first into Kaltag, first into Unalakleet, where I still had fifteen dogs but suddenly, my team started slowing down.

The following story is my account of the version of the same incidents as recited by Joe May in *Iditarod, the First Ten Years*. Between Shaktoolik and Koyuk, Emmitt Peters and Sonny Lindner caught up with me but still, I was in fourth place. After Elim, it's all hills. The worst is a climb of 1000 feet over a space of three miles. To avoid getting sweaty, I hung my down parka and heavy mittens on my sled's handlebars but up ahead, my team suddenly heard other dogs. That team had gone around a curve in the trail and headed straight down into Golovin. My dogs left the trail in a dash to catch the other team and began crashing through a thicket of brush. I hit a tree and my brush bow and runner hit hard and snapped in two. I looked down at my demolished, caved-in sled and thought, "Oh, crap! What am I going to do?" I anchored the wreck and in the twilight, I began trying to see both what kind of terrain lay ahead and how to get back on the trail. My headlamp was growing dim. I finally found the trail, but when I turned back to get my dogs they'd blended in completely into the deep dusk. With no outer parka or heavy gloves, I wandered for hours, looking for my team. I wouldn't let myself lay down and I kept repeating Psalms 23: "Yea, though I walk through the valley of the shadow of death, I will fear no evil: for Thou art with me." I was becoming hypothermic when a headlamp appeared in the distance. It turned out to be Joe May. I told him about my accident and that I wasn't sure I could survive the night with no parka or gloves. After talking, he loaned me a pair of beaver mittens. I didn't want to go to sleep because I might freeze. A couple of hours later as daylight began to dawn, I stumbled over my team.

I cut willows and poles and wedged them into each side of my sled and wired and taped them into place. It got me into Golovin where I looked for a sled but there was none to be found. I pushed on to White Mountain where I got a wooden sled with iron runners. In spite of my heavy sled and few dogs, I was still doing pretty well, but as I began descending Topkok hill, the wind began ripping really hard. Thirty miles beyond White Mountain, between Topkok and Safety, on the north shore of Norton Sound, there is the infamous "Blowhole," where the wind does squirrelly things and drives blinding buckshot snow into a musher's face, reducing visibility to nil.

I began seeing pieces of someone's headlamp, a coffee pot, and other stuff strewn along the trail. I wondered what was going on. Pretty soon I saw sled handlebars and sled runner tails sticking up above drifted powder but there was no driver! I began hollering and suddenly, Joe May, with his face all wet from blowing snow, reared up and said, "Huh, huh?" He was in his sleeping bag with his sled canvas pulled over him. I said, "Joe, are you okay?" He said, "Yeah, yeah," but he was totally out of it. He was in no state to take care of himself. I said, "C'mon, Joe, I'll help you get out of there." I walked him in circles until his circulation in his limbs returned. Both of us could've been the first fatalities on the Iditarod. After he was more with it, we loaded up his dogsled, lined his dogs out, and then he followed me in. Before we got to Safety, the last checkpoint before Nome, he said, "I'm really thankful, Don, that you came along and helped me. I was in big trouble back there." I agreed. We ate and rested about an hour at Safety. We knew four teams were ahead of us. He said, "You go on in first. If it weren't for you, I wouldn't be here." I said, "No that's okay" (because he had a good team that the next year he won with) "you'd be holding your team back. You go on ahead." I had fewer dogs, and worse, I was weighted down with the heavy wooden sled. There was no way I could race him. He came in fifth and I came in sixth. Later people asked me what happened back there with my team. I said, "Well, you know how it is when you get old. First you lose your gloves, and then your cap and . . . then, your dog team!"

I raced seven times in the Iditarod and finished four times. I experienced a variety of weather and trail conditions. Twice my dogs got sick and on my last race I had to scratch because I lacerated my leg on the ice and I couldn't bend my knee to bootie my dogs. One year, it was so warm that it was raining. The lakes had eighteen inches of meltwater on top. There was no choice but to mush through it and get soaked. On the other hand, at the high elevation of Finger Lake, there could be ten feet of snow. Many years, it was fifty below. The wind could also be merciless. There might also be no snow on the frozen rivers or ocean, which left us completely vulnerable to the wind. We'd skid wildly, zig-zagging and leaning on the brake, dragging a foot for steerage. Going into Shaktoolik, there was often a fierce gale that would blow us off the trail. We'd have to keep walking up ahead to bring our leader and team back onto the course, over and over and over.

The first year, we cooked on open fires, then we used white gas, and finally, Sterno fuel. I always carried wire and tape for repair and tools to change my plastic runners.

We got so tired we couldn't think straight. When I thought the horizon was a tree limb under which to duck, I knew that I was hallucinating but there

Don Honea, Sr. leaving Ruby on Iditarod, 1976.
Courtesy of Don Honea, Sr.

was nothing I could do about it. On those long mushes, I prayed and I forced myself to stay awake.

Sometimes I traveled with Rudy Demoski (1975 to 1985 era), with Warner Vent (mid-seventies) and in the late 1970s to early 1980s, with Sonny Lindner. But most of the time, I mushed with that crazy Rudy, quite a guy.

Most of the checkpoints had food for the mushers, but Takotna was famous for its hospitality. They cooked for the mushers, made sandwiches, had pie and cake, and handed the musher a sack lunch when he left. One family in Nikolai used to meet us every year up the Salmon River. They'd give chicken sandwiches to the non-Natives and beaver ones to the Native mushers. Warner Vent got a beaver sandwich, but I got a chicken. Disappointed, I said to Warner, "How come they gave you beaver and me, chicken." He laughed and said, "They think you're white." I sure wanted that boiled beaver meat.

In my drops for my dogs, I not only sent out meat and booties, but also vitamins. If a dog quit eating, I'd give him a vitamin shot and in an hour, he'd be back up and okay. I was one of the only mushers who used vitamins.

When the race still allowed villagers to put the drivers up, I overnighted at Ann Egrass' in McGrath, at Nick Alexie's in Nikolai, with a teacher-friend in Kaltag, and at Duke Katongan's in Unalakleet.

My first year in the Iditarod, I raised $2500 through sponsors, but ten years later, I solicited $25,000 from people like Charlie Stevens, owner of a Nenana dirt company, as well as through Anchorage's first TV cable subscription owner, Bob Uchitel. Legislators including John Sackett also contributed. I needed that much money because I didn't have my own dogs and had to keep renting them. One year, I trained twenty-four two-year-old pups and out of them, I only got one good dog. Sure, it didn't cost me a lot to feed them because I fished for them and fed them Friskies, but it cost to pay for their transportation and rental fees. Two months ahead of the race, I began feeding

One of three top ten finishers from Ruby, Don Honea with his lead dog, Iditarod, 1976.
Courtesy of Don Honea, Sr.

the dogs meat. It was critical to ease them into their horsemeat, liver, and beaver diet before the race began.

After I quit racing in 1986, I served on the Iditarod board and in 1996, I was the race marshal. I had to make all the judgment calls. My motto was, "We're not here to be liked, but only respected." I have really bad arthritis. For two weeks, I was crammed into the back of a narrow Super Cub, and supervised at every checkpoint. I also got a dangerous hernia, which was topped off by catching the flu in Nome. I couldn't hang around the finish line to make judgment calls or go to the banquet, but I had to fly out right away and get the hernia taken care of.

As one of fifteen children of a white father and a Native mother, I am the only one who took an interest in Native culture. We were mostly raised in white society. When I was born, Ruby was a white man's mining town. We went from there to Fairbanks and then on to Eklutna boarding school, and back to Fairbanks again. Ever since I can remember, however, I felt defensive when whites talked negatively about Natives. Even into the 1970s, Fairbanks was a very prejudiced town. Natives were

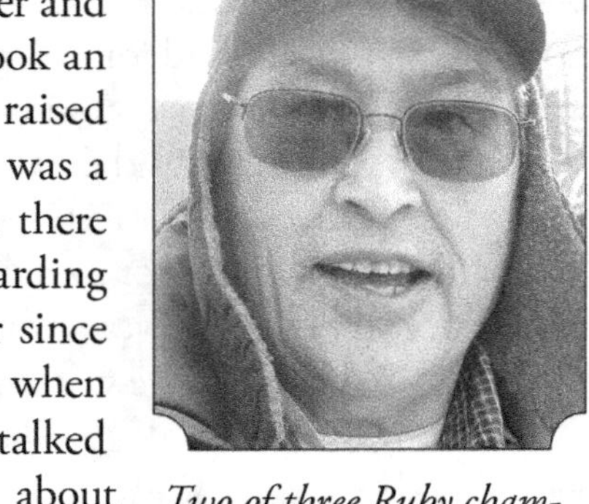

Two of three Ruby champion dog mushers, Emmitt Peters, winner of 1975 Iditarod.
Courtesy of Rose Albert.

Three of three top ten Iditarod finishers from Ruby, Howard Albert, placed seventh in 1978 and 1979 Iditarods.
Courtesy of Rose Albert.

really looked down upon. Various businesses, bars, and restaurants had signs, "Whites Only" or "No Natives." About three years after my wife and I married, we took our first baby and went into Hills Bar, owned by Polaris Hotel owner Wally Burnett. We sat at a table waiting to order. When the waiter approached, he announced that the bar was for whites only.

When I go to Alaska Federation of Natives' annual elders and youth conference, *Denakkanaaga,* various seniors will say my grandpa taught me to do this and to do that. Notwithstanding being Tanana Chiefs Conference First Traditional Chief, I feel funny because I didn't grow up that way. What I learned of Native culture was after I was fourteen when I began living with the Native people. When the third First Traditional Chief David Salmon was dying in Chalkyitsik, I stayed there for a week both to be with David and because I was comfortable there, like when I first went to Kokrines.

The Iditarod taught me to persevere. For example when I couldn't find my sled and my team for eight hours, I figured God had a plan for me in life so I wasn't afraid. Additionally I persevered with scraggly untrained pups, pouring time and money into them so that they might become a world class Iditarod team. It takes training, good feed, a little love, vision, and patience. To the young I would say that running the Iditarod is not a short-term investment. It requires planning for the long haul.

Tanana Chiefs Conference First Traditional Chief, Don Honea, 2007.
Judy Ferguson photo.

The biggest change in today's Iditarod is that the dogs' nutrition has been resolved and systematized such that mushers can begin the race with animals who are not too fat but whose weight and diet will carry them through the long, demanding pace of the race. Today's large kennels employ vets who regularly check the dogs, but villagers can't afford that. They have to ask others how to supplement their dogs, but it can be done and it's a matter of just beginning and staying with it. Ruby, has produced three mushers the top ten: Emmitt Peters, It can be done again. the gem of the Yukon, who, in 1979, finished in Howard Albert, and me.

Chapter 8

Iditarod to Art: First Alaska Native Woman to Race: Rose Albert

Rose Albert.
Courtesy of Rose Albert.

Rose Albert is a survivor. In 1982 she was the first Alaska Native woman to race in the Iditarod. It was one of the many challenges she's faced in her lifetime.

She was also always interested in art and began painting when she was fourteen. One day, a friend took her to the Anchorage Museum, where she saw paintings by Sidney Lawrence. On the way home, her friend bought Rose a small oil painting kit and she was on her way.

In 2008 after reading my published story in the Anchorage Daily News *about fellow Ruby resident Don Honea, Sr., Rose contacted me. We collaborated and in 2016, I published her own story in* Windows to the Land, An Alaska Native Story Vol. Two: Iditarod and Alaska River Trails.

A year later, the Yukon-Koyukuk School District contacted me asking me to write Ten Feet Tall and Bulletproof, Alaska Natives Blazing the Iditarod Trail. *They selected thirteen living Athabascan, Iditarod mushers to present in their new book and they included Rose. She and I revisited her earlier presentation of her life story and of her Iditarod experience.*

Rose is an accomplished artist. She specializes in painting both the Iditarod and her people. She is the sister of the late Iditarod competitor Howard Albert and grew up mushing sled dogs. Her paintings have the majesty of the light bathing the peaks of the Alaska Range and showing sled dogs at their best, in every mood on the trail. We are grateful to Rose for doing the cover of Ten Feet Tall and Bulletproof, Alaska Natives Blazing the Iditarod Trail. *Who better to illustrate life on the trapline than the daughter of those for whom it has been a way of life for a millennia.*

In the comfort of her home, Rose began remembering.

In May 1956, my family was spring camping up the Nowitna River[1] near the confluence of the Titna[2]. When we were ready to leave, Grandpa Frank Albert picked us up in his houseboat to return to our home at Kokrines on the Yukon River. As we headed downstream and ap-

1   *Nogheetno'* in Athabascan.
2   *Tetno'* in Athabascan.

Albert family, l-r: Rose, Barbara, mother Justine holding Howard, Phillip Jr., and George Albert at Edward Clarence's camp, nephew of Rose's paternal grandmother, left bank of Sulatna River (Soolaahno'), 1958.

Courtesy of Rose Albert.

proached Henry Titus' downstream tent, Dad stopped to tell Agnes Titus, "Justine is about to have her baby." Agnes was happy to help Mom and she delivered me May 22 on a plywood bed over the inboard engine in our houseboat.

My early years were spent in Kokrines but when I was three, Dad boated all of us to Ruby so we kids could go to school. Ruby had begun in 1911 as a mining town but as its population decreased, the Native village of Kokrines began to migrate into Ruby. By 1975, Josephine Corning, whose Koyukon name was *Koda*, was one of the last living at Kokrines, along with her man, Frank Titus. She was a cute, small woman who was hard of hearing and who spoke no English.

Our parents instilled good values in us and taught us to work hard. Dad only went to school as far as the third grade, but he continued to teach himself to read and to write. He always carried a little spiral pad in which he wrote down words that he didn't know: verbs, and nouns as well as brand names. When the itinerant public health nurse came through, he would ask her the meaning of the words he had noted. When Dad was gone on construction jobs, it became my brothers' job then to bring home our meat. My mother, who had deep dimples and a hearty laugh, worked hard to clothe and feed us. She was beautiful inside and out. Her door was always open to homeless friends. If someone ran out of food, a family could borrow from neighbors to tide them over. My mother washed her diapers in the Yukon River. As a subsistence fisherman, she tore nylon feed sacks apart and tied the strands into her fishnets to strengthen them. She used cottonwood bark for her seine net floats and loaded rocks into old jeans for sinkers.

After the Head Start program began in Ruby in 1967, she became one of the original teachers, followed by work at RurAL CAP, and then at Tanana Chiefs Conference.

Mother made us go to the Catholic Church, but I didn't grasp what they were trying to teach us. I always came out of the confessional, crying. We were also allowed to attend Russell Arnold's Arctic Mission at the Presbyterian church, so I learned a lot of Bible there.

Growing up, I loved to draw, to be outside with the dogs, and to be in the woods—they provided an escape from the problems at home. In 1970 when I was fourteen, my thirty-seven-year old Mother moved to Anchorage, where she had a job waiting for her. Even though he was against living in the city, Dad tried to live there with her for a month, but he returned home with my brother Howard. Mom remarried and took my youngest brothers, James and Harvey, with her to Florida, but later, Dad got custody of both boys.

After our mother left, Grandma Zeta Cleaver, originally from Kokrines, became a surrogate mother to us. We'd grown up with her children, and she was always there for me and my siblings.

Through the boarding home program, my dad sent me to school in Tanana, but it didn't work well for me. Through the same program, I was transferred then to Robert Service High School in Anchorage, where I lived with Gary and his Christian author wife Ina Olson and their children, Tami and Ronnie. In 1974 during the second Iditarod, I was out skiing with the family at Knik Lake Christian camp. As the sled dog teams departed

Anchorage, I saw Sidney Huntington's son Carl mush by, racing with his dog team. The previous year, he had won the Fur Rondy. After I saw him, he went on to win the Iditarod, later followed by winning the Rondy, followed by taking the Open North American in 1977. He became the only triple-crown winner in dog-racing history. The image of his perfect Yukon dogs mushing quietly past me stayed in my mind, and planted the thought, "Someday I want to race in the Iditarod."

At eighteen I felt too old to still be in high school, so I crammed to finish. After I graduated in January, I returned home to Ruby but none of my family was there. I knew that my siblings Barbara and Howard

Carl Huntington defending his Iditarod championship in 1975.
Anchorage Daily Times.

were at our family's trapping cabin at Bering Slough above Ruby, Kokrines, and the Novi so I flew there with Harold Esmailka. Later George joined us as well, but Dad was still gone, working on the construction of the Trans-Alaska Pipeline. However Dad came down sick and had to quit his job, so he came home to Bering Slough. When his plane landed on the ice, he looked up at the riverbank and saw all of us standing on the bank, waiting for him. Later he said, "When I saw all my big kids standing there, I wondered what they were all doing at trapping camp." I told him, "We didn't, any of us, know what else to do." Much later, after a kidney operation, when he was barely coherent, Dad remembered, "That time when all of you were standing on the bank waiting for me was one of the happiest moments of my life." Speaking for myself, my heart is still at Bering Slough.

While I was there, I drove my brother Howard's dogs up the creek for miles and just forgot about everything. When it would start to get dark, I'd finally come back home to camp.

In March, we went into Ruby to see Emmitt Peters as he came through, running the Iditarod. His lead dog was Nugget, the same leader with whom Carl Huntington had won the previous year. That year, 1975, Emmitt set the record time, which held for the next seven years.

My brother Howard had a leader named Darky who was a pup of Nugget's and was also a good leader. When Howard first started to breed race dogs, he moved to Bering Slough with Dad. One day after Darky had pups, Howard and Dad left on their sleds to check traps without Darky. At dusk on Howard's return, he thought there was a wolf up ahead on the trail. When he realized it was actually Darky, he hooked her into the team but up the trail, he saw some wiggling dots. When he was almost on top of them, Howard realized the dots were Darky's pups. He scooped them up into the sled basket and took them home, to camp.

During the summer of 1976, I was the first woman to get hired out of the Pipeliners Union 798 as a welder's helper. That year, Howard decided to run the Iditarod, so I gave him $2,000 for his entry fee while Dad built his sled. Howard

Rose's paternal great-great grandfather Big Albert with his father Ivan Hardluck in doorway, Kokrines, ca. 1914.
Jules Jette photo, Oregon Province Jesuit archives. Courtesy of Eileen McGlynn.

trained the puppies that had followed Darky up the river that night. In March 1977, Howard did well as a rookie and he finished sixteenth.

One time when I was in Fairbanks at my cousin Poldine Carlo's house, I saw an oil painting of my great-grandfather, Big William Demoski, which inspired me to begin portrait painting. My friend the late Merreline Kangas encouraged me to go to Santa Fe, New Mexico, for art school.

While I was gone, Howard ran the Iditarod again in 1978 and 1979, placing seventh both times. Discouraged with seventh the second time, he sold all his best dogs to Rick Swenson and to Sonny Lindner, keeping only a few for himself.

After receiving my associate degree from the Institute of American Indian Arts in Santa Fe in May 1981, I spent part of the summer working for Icicle Seafoods on a floating fish processor in Bristol Bay. The fishing season was poor, so I returned home without a lot of money. I began thinking about my earlier dream of running the Iditarod. I asked Howard if I could use his dogs to run it. He said no at first but later he relented.

Rose's graduation from Institute of American Indian Arts, 1981. Rose's dress and slippers by Altona Brown. Courtesy Rose Albert.

By that time, I had only five months left to train. Howard's dogs were tough village dogs; at first, I didn't have much control over them. As I ran into trees or crashed at the bottom of a steep hill, I kept Dad busy repairing my wrecked sleds.

My life with my dad was a little awkward but when it came to sports, he was very supportive of each of his kids. When I broke Howard's first sled, fearful, I ran to George's house. However in his soft-spoken voice Dad said to me, "You don't have to run away. You only have to go out there and try again." What he said resonated with me. Now every time I feel like quitting, I think about that.

Early that fall when Howard was out setting traps, a willow skewered him in the nose. He sat up a few hours at Junior's house with his nose bleeding uncontrollably. Later after running the dogs, I went to see him. Junior had just returned from hunting. Howard stood up but he collapsed. Junior picked him up and put him on the bed and then, he went to town. Howard was looking pale to me. I said, "I'm taking you to the clinic." There, the health aide did all she could to stop the bleeding, but it only got worse. I started to panic, and he whispered, "Don't get excited, Sis, I'm okay." We kept calling for an airplane, but none came. Finally, some friends of Howard's called and said to have him ready to take to the hospital in Tanana. At one point, Howard squeezed my hand and said, "If I don't make it, go through with the race." In Tanana, they were finally able to stabilize Howard, but he was still not out of danger. After we returned home, Howard was medevacked to Fairbanks Memorial Hospital. On the way to Fairbanks, they almost lost him twice. At the hospital, they cauterized his nose to stop the bleeding, and followed that up with a transfusion.

Howard Albert under the Iditarod burl arch, Nome, 1983.
Courtesy of Rose Albert.

As Howard had encouraged me to prep for the race, I began saving money for the Iditarod. I was commissioned by the Ruby area district to paint a picture of the late Merreline Kangas, the namesake of the local school. Gil and Sophie Gutierrez, my friends from Anchorage, also sent me two hundred dollars. Our village corporation, *Dineega* (moose in Koyukon) gave me thirty dollars. Dean Wilson, a fur buyer from Kenny Lake, donated a tanned moosehide that I raffled off in Ruby and Galena. While out selling raffle tickets at forty-below in Galena, I stopped at Sidney Huntington's house. He handed me fifty dollars and said, "I like what you're doing; maybe this will help." In response to my friend Raine Hall's letter to the *Anchorage Daily News*, I received another thousand dollars. With my grubstake and a new sled, I was ready to run the 1982 Iditarod.

After spending weeks in the hospital, Howard finally returned home. We were waiting for him when his ride stopped above Dad's house. In late January after he started feeling better, he and his trapping buddy, the late Ernie Cleaver, and I decided to go out to the trapping camp. On a little Élan snowmachine, I pulled a sled of supplies in while Howard drove the dogs. Then he and I took turns driving the dogs while Ernie ran the snowmachine. We reached camp about 1 a.m. Over the next days when Howard and Ernie were out checking their traps, I drove the dogs over the trails. I loved being out there.

Ruby had a mixed response about me running the Iditarod, but I was determined. It was a dream, a necessary exploration to see what I was capable of, and where my limitations were. The whole family pitched in preparing race food for me and for the dogs. At 4 a.m. one night, Dad was outside chopping frozen beaver carcasses while I was inside cooking the meat. My

Rose Albert, first Alaska Native female to run Iditarod, 1982.

Courtesy of Rose Albert.

good friend Kenny Harding and his family sewed dog booties for me by the bundle. George built me a sled that wouldn't break. And Barbara raised money with her bake sales.

Harold and Florence Esmailka were my biggest sponsors. Owners of Ruby Trading Company and Harold's Air Service in Galena, they helped everyone from Ruby who ran the Iditarod. When the day came for me to leave for Anchorage, the Esmailkas sent a young pilot from their air service to fly me, Howard, and twelve dogs to Galena, where we caught an Alaska Airlines flight to Anchorage. In town, we stayed with our friends Mark and Terry Rosevear, who are like family to me.

Before the start of the race, Howard asked, "Aren't you nervous?" "No," I said. Susan Butcher, Sue Firmin (who later scratched), and I were the only women running in the all-male race.

As I went flying out of the chute with twelve dogs, Howard rode with me. When he jumped off, he said, "You'll be okay." However, at the bottom of the big hill up ahead, I could see bunched up dogs. I wondered if a racer had stopped to untangle his team. As other teams were approaching, chaos would soon ensue, but my leader Pepper knew what to do. He pulled my team around the other racers and he would not look at them.

At Skwentna Lodge, the owner was offensive to me, so I chose to stay outside and visited with Alex Sheldon. During a heavy snowstorm when I reached Gene Leonard's cabin, which was filled with dog racers hanging up their snow-laden, wet gear, he told me, despite the bad weather, that it would be best for me to keep going. I was really tired, so I slept a few hours in my sled.

No one had warned me about the descent off the mountain, the notorious Happy River Steps. We slid down one cliff, then down onto another.

The dogs came to a small ledge, circling, looking for the best descent, only to drop off onto another ledge, which went straight down, sliding to the next drop off until we reached the bottom. I said, "Oh, crap!" as we went airborne.

It wasn't easy for me to get my overloaded sled up the mountain and through Rainy Pass. Then on the way down through the plunge of Dalzell Gorge, I broke my brake and lost my snow hook. At the bottom, we skidded sideways over the slick river ice. The dogs scented Rohn Roadhouse and picked up speed. In the mad run my second leader, Rae Rae, snapped her foot on the glare ice. I managed to stop the dogs, unhooked her and put her in my sled. We arrived so fast going into Rohn that it took several bystanders to stop my sled. Because my dog was injured, the press started coming after me, accusing me of abuse. I thought about scratching, but Joe Redington talked me out of it, saying, "Keep going." He said that he was proud of me for running the Iditarod. Since he was the father of the race, his words made me feel almost as good as if I had won. Rick Swenson said that I should travel with him, but I was too shy. The press apologized for accusing me of hurting my leader; they offered to take her to a veterinarian in Anchorage. (When Rae Rae was flown to the clinic, a member of the staff fell in love with her. She called my brother to see if she could adopt the dog. Although Howard hated to lose his favorite dog, she could never race again, so he was happy she was going to a good home.)

I should have left Rohn Roadhouse with Rick Swenson and Susan Butcher, who had eighteen very strong-looking dogs. (I thought, "How can that petite woman handle all those dogs when I, at five feet, eight inches, and 125 pounds, can barely handle twelve?")

During the night, I mushed alone across the Farewell Burn. In the quiet hours, I thought about a dear friend who had been reported missing in a downed airplane. Once when I told him I was going to run the Iditarod, he'd promised me, "No matter what, Rose, I am going to look after you while you are on the trail." About thirty miles out of Nikolai at three in the morning, I heard a plane flying above us. Every time I started drifting off to sleep, the drone of the plane woke me up. It bothered the dogs. I decided that somehow my missing friend was keeping his promise to me.

At Nikolai, Joe May, the 1980 champion of the Iditarod, had left a toboggan for me there, which made it much easier for me to get over the trail. After I switched sleds, I took my layover there.

During the race, I got a flu bug. I was thankful because Alex Sheldon, a Yupik racer and a friend of Howard's, thoughtfully left me packages of *akutaq* (ah-goo-duck,

Eskimo ice cream)—caribou tallow and cranberries[3]—at various checkpoints. For a while, I couldn't keep anything but *akutaq* down.

Rose Albert painting of Jeff King Leaving Rainy Pass, *used for cover of* Ten Feet Tall and Bulletproof.

Courtesy of Rose Albert.

Although I preferred to be alone, I ended up traveling with a group of young rookies, which turned out to be good. One night after leaving Takotna late, I was alone and with no headlamp. As the dogs trotted happily down the trail, I could see a beacon far off in the dark. That was a moment frozen in time to me of trail magic. I loved the Iditarod, being out alone with the dogs on the trail.

When I reached Ruby at 3 a.m., only the late Zeta Cleaver was up to meet me. She ran up the road, saying, "Rose, Rose, you made it!" The next morning, Dad had a new birch sled waiting for me.

With stormy weather obliterating the trail, it was a long, rugged trip to Galena. Needing a rest, I stopped in to visit my Uncle Peter's family in Koyukuk. At Bishop Rock, somehow, I got turned around. I was heading back upriver when some people on the trail told me that I was going in the wrong direction.

Going overland to Unalakleet, there was one storm after another. Late one night, as I was getting close to the village, there were so many trails that my dogs wound up in a deep creek. In the dark, I could see my lead dog on the other bank, looking down at me, while the other dogs were below, in the water. I called, "Pepper, come around!" and he did! I pulled the other dogs by their tugline out of the creek. Even though he was wet, I hugged Pepper with joy. Teenagers appeared on their snowmachines, calling, "Here, doggy, here, doggy," and I followed them on into Unalakleet.

I mushed on to Shaktoolik, Koyuk, Elim, and White Mountain. In every village, the folks were good to me.

When I left for Safety, the traveling was okay, but it got stormy and cold. With other racers, I was forced to camp on Topkok Hill. While I was getting settled, I realized that I had lost one of Dad's wolverine mittens, so I tied up my team to a sapling and walked around until I found it. Then I began to think that I was lost when I felt a nudging on my leg in the dark.

---

3   *Nonaałdlode* Athabascan for ice cream.

My leader had broken loose and come after me. I hugged him, then we all bedded down for the night.

As soon as it started getting light, we blasted down the mountain to Safety. I stayed there to feed my dogs and wash up. I tried to cover the frostbite on my face with makeup and braided my hair. But when I came out of the restroom, my fellow travelers were all gone.

I sprinted to Nome. It was almost as if the dogs knew that Howard was at the end of the race, waiting for them. When Pepper finally saw Howard, he flew into his arms! We finished thirty-second; it was a good last leg of the trip. I was sad, knowing that I had done something that I would never again do. Later I fantasized about racing again. I envied Howard when he got back into the 1983 Iditarod. As he prepared for that year's race, our family pitched in to help him, but he seemed withdrawn and quiet.

When Howard almost bled to death, he had stopped drinking. But after the 1983 Iditarod, when he finished sixteenth, he started in again. There were signs that he was crying out for help when he said, "If there were an Alcoholics Anonymous in Ruby, I'd be the first one to join because I'd like to learn to fly or go to medical school." But every day we lost a little more of him. On August 14, two weeks before his twenty-sixth birthday, he shot himself in the head. He was mourned across the whole state. Junior (Phillip) took Howard's death the hardest because not only had they been trapping partners, but they were also very close.

Like some of my brothers, my other brother Harvey was a musician. Before he left for the trapline, he sang to his daughter, Melanie, on a tape, which along with a card, he had intended to give to her. After he died in a tragic accident in subzero temperatures, I wanted to send those mementos to her but over time, they vanished. After the death of my two brothers, Howard and Harvey, I stayed home for a year taking care of dogs, fishing, painting, writing, hauling water, cutting wood, and of course, drinking too much. I realized that I had to move on. If I hadn't been drinking, perhaps things would have been different. I felt bad that I was leaving my dad. After losing his two sons, he was doing what he could to keep his family together, but I knew that he could not continue to support me. When I moved to Anchorage, I had plans to return to school, but between my drinking and my new job working for one of the airlines, it never happened.

Harvey Albert, Ruby, '83.
Courtesy of Rose Albert.

In 1985, I did the cover for *Women on the Trail.* Five years later, I was painting Southeast Alaska designs on deerskin drums for the owner of Alaska Fur Exchange for beer money. Drinking had taken over my life.

By 1991 alcohol was defeating me and I asked Jesus into my heart, to be my personal savior. I was thirty-five when I met my soulmate,

Painted, carved yellow cedar box featuring two-time Iditarod winner Mitch Seavey by Rose Albert.
Courtesy of Rose Albert.

Roy Westfall, who had a ten-year-old son, Austin. His child said to me, "If I were to ask you to give up something, it would be beer." That was enough; I never picked up alcohol again. In 1993 Roy and I married.

Five years later, I started drawing, carving, and painting Southeast designs on boxes that I found in thrift stores. They sold like hot cakes, so Roy and I figured how to build boxes. Roy ordered a jig and we made a few. Roy taught me how to use woodworking tools, to build cedar boxes. My life as an artist began to take off.

Today, I work in my studio painting wildlife, portraits, and the Iditarod as well as carving and painting cedar boxes for my three annual shows at the Alaska Native Heritage Center Holiday Bazaar, annual NUKA conference at South Central Foundation and at the Alaska Federation of Natives bazaar. In 2009 I began collecting beautiful beads for making necklaces to sell to tourists at bazaars. To save time, I hired Carl Hartvigson and his father, Vern, to build boxes for me out of yellow cedar, the traditional Tlingit carving wood.

Since 1998 I have been working nonstop as a painter and box carver. Over the years, I had to recreate myself through my faith in God and through my art. I believe some of the pain I have gone through has helped me to grow through Christ. It's a daily struggle but I have come a long way.

It took me far too long to devote myself to my artwork. At nineteen after I saw the oil painting of my great-grandfather, Big William Demoski, I began painting portraits of people of different races because they reflect the beauty of different cultures. I feel like I'm keeping them alive through my oil paintings. Before I paint, I pray, and I rely on images in my dreams. Photos help with the hard parts.

Rose Albert, Anchorage, 2010.
Courtesy of Rose Albert.

In my early twenties, I had a vivid dream. I was with Chief Big Albert during the gold rush of 1912. I was wearing his furs, walking down Front Street in Ruby. He was holding my hand, pointing out where Indians were allowed and where they weren't. Someone threw a dishpan of water out of a door and the water droplets turned into sparkling diamonds. Emmitt Peters' grandfather drove by on a dog team. At that point, Great-grandpa Chief Big Albert let go of my hand and turned to walk back to Kokrines. I begged him not to go. As he was turning away, he said, "I am not supposed to be here, but I came to protect you from what looms ahead." After Howard died, I had a couple of similar dreams about him, protecting me. I felt that, in the end, love conquers all.

In portraits, landscapes, and wildlife, I try to capture the vitality and mood of the subject, to communicate the natural essence to the viewer. I let it sink deeply into me. One review said of my work, "Her rich northern colors capture the vastness and magnificence of the Alaskan wilderness. Her canvases bring the dogs and mushers to life in a cold but romantic setting as they race to Nome." My new line of boxes consists of only realistic wildlife images and of famous Iditarod racers and their dogs. My work may be seen by searching "Rose Albert" on the Internet and by Googling "Nowitna River Studios."

I no longer dream about running the Iditarod, which today is prohibitively expensive. But coming from Ruby, the halfway point on the Iditarod's northern route, and as the first Native female to run the race, I enjoy painting that window of time I had on the trail. I ran, wanting to encourage other women to follow their dreams. Through my experience in the Iditarod and in my art, I am living my dream.

In 2011 Rose had a show, "An Artist's Rendition of the Last Great Race," at the Alaska Native Arts Gallery.

"Over the years, painting our centuries-old wilderness life and the Iditarod has brought me joy," she said. "It is my record of my heritage, a history of life along the Yukon, and a testimony of overcoming addiction through Christ."

Chapter 9

THE MISERABLEST RACE: THE IDITAROD! Dean Painter of Holikachuk/Grayling

Dean Painter, ca. 1982.
Courtesy of Margie Walker.

During 1842 to 1843, Russian naval officer Lavrenty Zagoskin explored the Yukon, Innoko, Koyukuk, and Kuskokwim rivers. He reported finding six villages including seasonal camps in the Innoko River area including Khuligichagat (Holikachuk). The inhabitants of the upper Innoko spoke a different language than those living in the nearby Deg Hit'an villages of Shageluk and Anvik. The Holikachuk were culturally aligned with their neighbors, but were a separate culture and language.

The village of Holikachuk was on a large, flat lip of land below where a branch of Shageluk Slough, called Holikachuk Slough, joined the Innoko River. The village was about four or five feet above the river and frequently flooded. In 2013 a friend of Dean Painter's, Thomas Maillelle of Holikachuk, said, "Only four or five of us speak the language fluently. Less than hundred full-blood Holikachuk Natives remain." He continued, "Our neighbors included Dishkaket, Dikeman, Flat, and Iditarod. Shageluk was part of the Anvik and Holy Cross culture, Deg Hit'an, the last downriver Athabascans." He continued, "Before 15,000 people came to Flat and Iditarod with the Gold Rush, I have been told that we were 1,500 people strong. The story came down to me that before the big sickness [the late 1830s smallpox epidemic that devastated Natives in the Kuskokwim and Yukon areas, Ed.], that there were the six villages with a strong tribal society."

Born ten years after Thomas Maillelle, Dean Painter was a young child in Holikachuk and became a strong contributor to the Iditarod Trail Sled Dog Race. When Jerry Riley won the Iditarod in 1976, his lead dog was Puppy, a dog he'd horsetraded from Dean Painter's kennel. Myron Angstman, a musher whose dogs Dean has often trained, said in an interview that when he first met Dean in 1979 he was a young guy with a wealth of dog driving experience, and he had trained Puppy before the dog was traded to Jerry Riley for a used snow machine.

In many of my interviews with the mushers, particularly with Dean Painter and Warner Vent, they told their stories with honesty, transpar-

ency, and reality, seasoned with a warm humor. In the fall of 2018, Dean began his story.

Dean's mother, Delia Rock Painter, Grayling, (born 1928), 1994.
Courtesy of Margie Walker.

I was only fourteen when the first Iditarod happened. When I was growing up, times were tough in Holikachuk. When I was a little boy, Native land claims were not on anyone's mind. My youth was mostly before President Johnson's Great Society began distributing assistance to the Alaska Bush and long before the oil pipeline. Nine of us lived in a one-room log cabin lit by a gas lantern and heated by a wood barrel stove, for which I helped my mother get firewood. We got an occasional subsistence moose from neighbors but mostly, we kids raised ourselves. When my mother married Billy Painter, he brought a son, Clarence, to the marriage. He and my older brothers helped Mom until I was old enough to help out.

My mom, who was born in 1928, grew up in hard times. Her father, *Qui-yi-dat-l-kie* ("Rock") whose name evolved into Peter Rock, was born in 1888, probably near our village of Hologachakat, twenty-one years after Alaska was ceded to the United States and eight years before the gold rush.

I loved dogs ever since I was young. In the fall after the ground froze, our people trapped white fish. We blocked off the Holikachuk Slough with willow and bone fences and set our nets. Every day, we caught hundreds of white fish to feed ourselves and our dogs.

When I was three, the people of Holikachuk moved to the main Yukon River to the new site of Grayling. One reason was flooding, but after we moved, Holikachuk never flooded again. However, freighting into Holikachuk was difficult. Yutana Barge had to drop goods off at Holy Cross until someone could get the freight up to our village. I think the state wanted to get us located more conveniently. Henry Deacon had a saw-

Dean's older siblings, Margie (Walker) and William Painter, Holikachuk, ca. 1959.
Courtesy of Margie Walker.

Dean's maternal uncle Edgar Rock, Holikachuk, 1940s.
Courtesy of Marvin Deacon.

mill and cut logs to build twelve houses at the new site. We kids—Steve and Archie Deacon and me—shoveled sawdust.

My mom's brother John Rock and my older brother Roy both had dogs. All summer at our camp three miles above Grayling, we cut fish and during the winter we trapped beaver. When we cooked oats and cornmeal for the team, we threw in fish, moose scraps, or beaver. In the days before Friskies were used very much, Davy Walker of Holy Cross mushed up to Shageluk one day. When he arrived, he reported that "Hamil" (Hamilton Hamilton), an early user of Friskies, was on the trail. Someone asked, "Did you see him?" "No," Davy grinned, "but I saw a pile of Friskie poop on the trail."

When I was about nine, my uncle John gave me three pups: Puppy, who became a big black and white dog with sloppy ears, Seoko, and Carlson, a well-built, brown, smooth-trotting dog. The pups and I were both young and green. I used to drag them with a sled down to the riverbank, then I'd have them run me back home. They really trained me. When I was

Grayling elders: back, l-r: Belle Deacon, (slightly in front, grey-haired, in kerchief) Lena Dementi, (dark-haired young lady in back) Marcia John, Sarah John, David Maillelle, Dean's godmother Hannah Maillelle, Lucy Charlie, Dolly Deacon, Henry Deacon, Mary (aka Selma) Deacon, Mountain Deacon, Virginia Maillelle, Walter Maillelle. Front: Margaret King Alexander, unidentified child, Jimmy Alexander, Marvin Deacon's parents Bede Deacon, and Jobia Deacon. Ca. 1972, Grayling. Identification by Marvin Deacon.
Courtesy of Shirley Deacon Clark.

ten or eleven, every Friday night, I used to mush my dogs down to Anvik to stay with Hughie (Rudy's younger brother, Hugh Demoski) and his mom, Lina Stickman Demoski. Those three dogs got me there pretty good. On Sunday I usually started back, but in an attempt to try to get me to stay longer, the Demoskis used to like to scare me with the story of the Four-Miler woodswoman. Sometimes it worked. The story was that this bushwoman had become so bushy that it took nine men to grab her

Dean Painter with his leader, black dog named Doo Dad, Grayling, ca. 1983.
Courtesy Margie Walker, Andrean Madros.

and bring her in to Anvik. The Anvik people cleaned her up and she began going to church and became normal, but I still didn't like Four-Mile. When I finally would mush upstream, Four-Mile still gave me the willies as I went by.

Once when Hughie, my cousin Edgar "Larry" Rock, and I were in Grayling, I loaned each of them a dog to pull their little snowboat (sled). I was pretty tough in those days. The wind was blowing hard so we were leaned forward in our individual sleds. Unbeknownst to me, the dog behind me pooped on my back but Huey and Larry didn't want to tell me because they were afraid I'd rub the mess on them! Two hours and eighteen miles later, we'd made a round trip to Anvik and back! Pretty good dogs!

When I was thirteen, the men were having a seven-dog, sixteen-mile race from Grayling toward the Shageluk Trail, uphill seven miles and back. I had only five dogs but I asked if I could race anyway. They laughed at me but I talked them into it and then, I beat them all. After that, they wouldn't let me race again until I got older.

We had races like the Yukon 200 that typically went from Grayling to Anvik, on to Holikachuk, Shageluk, back to Anvik, down to Holy Cross, and back to Grayling. Each year, villages alternated where the race would begin. Also we had 16-miler sprint races at our spring carnival every year. I used to win the kids' sprint races, but when I was fifteen, I left home for school, first going to Dimond in Anchorage and then, to Bethel. While I was gone, Hughie's older brother Rudy Demoski borrowed my dog Puppy and ran the Iditarod in 1974. Two years later Rudy and I were on our way to Grayling to get my dogs, but before we arrived, my older brother William traded my dogs Puppy, Seoko, and Carlson to Jerry Riley for a used snowmachine. Puppy won the Iditarod for Jerry that year.

I began training dogs for a Bethel lawyer, Myron Angstman. I picked up some dogs from Myron as well as a big female from Lizzie Kruger's kennel in Anvik. I got Goldie and Blue from Ed Foran that came from the Morgans' line out of Kalskag. I began messing around with long distance

Joe Petruska of Nikolai Mushers Association presents first place to Dean Painter, 1985.
Kuskokwim Courier. Courtesy of Margie Walker and Andrean Madros.

racing, beginning with the Yukon 200, which I won several times. I also raced in McGrath's Mail Trail 202 and twice in the Kuskokwim 300.

Once when I was in Anvik with Rudy, a commercial fisherman, Ed Foran, gestured to his dog and said, "I'm going to kill this one." I asked, "How come?" He said, "He's good for fourteen miles and then, he drops, every time." His name was Patches and he was a big dog from the Losonsky racing line. I said, "Well, let me have him." "What you want him for?" he asked. I kept saying, "Give him to me." He really didn't want to, but he finally gave in. Sure enough, as I was heading upstream to Grayling, at fourteen miles, all of a sudden, the dog flipped over. I disciplined the dog. He got the message and jumped up. We flew all the way home to Grayling.

Two weeks later at the Yukon 200, I beat Ed Foran with his dog Patches in the lead. He got mad and said that I didn't thank him. I said, "Why would I thank you? You were going to kill him."

For years, I supported my dogs by working construction all summer and in the winter, I trapped beaver partly to feed my dogs their rich meat.

Since the beginning of the Iditarod in 1973, I'd watched Ken Chase, eighteen years my senior, and Rudy Demoski, fourteen years older, both of Anvik, run the Iditarod. I helped Rudy train. At twenty-three and in excellent condition, I was ready to try myself but I had three strikes against me. In 1982, it was exceptionally cold but more importantly, I had little experience with long distance racing and worse, I had a drinking problem.

Every winter as soon as it snowed, we started running the road behind Grayling, but it only went three miles. We had to wait till November when the Yukon froze to go longer distances, but still, Shageluk was only thirty-five miles away and Anvik, just eighteen. Sometimes I'd go from Grayling to Shageluk to Anvik and back to Grayling, seventy-some miles.

To run the Iditarod, I got two sponsors, Arirang Restaurant in Anchorage and Walt's Air Service out of Anvik. Walt Walton's company flew my team to Anchorage and he paid my entry fee. I kept my dogs at Connie Curan's place

Dean's cousin Rudy Demoski running Iditarod, 1980, Wasilla restart. Dean in basket.
Margie Walker and Andrean Madros.

in Anchorage. The day before the race, my main lead dog, Sally, got in a fight and wound up with a hole in her leg. I had to leave her behind, but I had three other good leaders: Goldie, Puppy Two, and Blue; however, I was down to thirteen dogs. I had no particular strategy, but I was eager to race, to get from one village to the next, and I let the dogs go at their own pace.

For gear, I had an Eddie Bauer sleeping bag, but I did get cold. I had a red headlamp with four big D batteries and for tools: pliers, screwdriver, wrench, and a knife. I could splice towlines pretty fast with that knife.

The weather got really cold, fifty-some below. I had a good marten hat, winter pants and parka, beaver mitts, Sorel boots, and bearskin mukluks. Going over Rainy Pass, the wind chill factor was like -108° and I got frostbit. It was really windy and of course, I never wear a facemask.

Mostly I ate dried red and king salmon fishstrips, crackers, and candy bars. In the villages we ate but I didn't unless I stopped. I burned fish strips over the campfire until the oil dripped and ate them with crackers. I had a lot of fruit juices, but they were frozen, so to thaw the cans, I threw them in my boiling dog pot.

Before the race, I'd shipped a beaver carcass, white fish, silver salmon, a little dried fish, some beef, dried dog food, and tallow to each of the twenty-five checkpoints. However at Shaktoolik, someone dug in my sled bag and took my beaver meat. The checker told me there was only one person who went in that building when he, the checker, wasn't around, so I knew who did it.

In those days, I used to drink coffee to try and stay awake, but when I was about to nod off, I'd start hollering and screaming to try and stay awake. After a day and half of no sleep, between Rohn and Nikolai, I started hallucinating. I saw dead people laying around, men with big beards, and an old white man standing in the middle of the road. I slammed on the brake so I wouldn't hit him but as it turned out, nobody was there. That day, I traveled quite a way and it was really cold.

I took my 24-hour rest in McGrath where I got bombed out in the bar. In Galena, I stayed with Hobo Benson, the owner of Hobo's Bar at the Yukon Inn. He told me I could help myself to anything in the refrigerator, but when I opened it, the fridge was plumb full of booze. I stayed there for more than twenty-four hours.

In Nulato, I rested at Glenn and Ida Demoski's (Glenn was my sponsor's brother), but when I got hung up there, imbibing, they told me to get going. After that, I stayed in checkpoints, where the staff was always happy and waiting for us.

Somewhere near the coast, I started traveling with Ken Chase and another musher. At one checkpoint, they said they'd wake me up before they left, but when I woke six hours later, they'd been gone for five. I'd been goofing off the whole race, but I was determined to catch them. Outside of Safety, I passed them and beat them into Nome. One thing that helped was that at Unalakleet, I ran out of booze.

Dean Painter with his cousin Rudy Demoski in sled basket, Big Lake, 1982, Dean's Iditarod race.
Courtesy Margie Walker and Andrean Madros.

If I'd prepared, I could've done a lot better. I've done the Yukon 200 in less than thirty hours. I used to drive eleven 60-70-pound dogs from Grayling, Shageluk, Anvik, and back to Grayling —75 miles in little more than five hours. My dogs could've made two villages a day, but I got booze in Ruby,

Galena, Nulato, and Kaltag. I was drunk all the way. From Unalakleet on, I sobered up and I picked up speed. But unlike Rudy and Warner, I did pass up Leo Kriska's Last Chance liquor store, twelve miles above Nulato. They went by it, turned around, and picked up booze. For me, alcohol has been a life-long battle. I've been in and out of three rehab centers. My favorite part of the Iditarod was finishing. That was the miserablest race I've ever been on in my life. A musher is always tired, every darned day: get up, tired; feed dogs, tired; stop, you're tired. It's amazing that I found time to drink.

After a little less than three weeks, I came in twenty-ninth in Nome. I had a little money and went into Breakers Bar where I plopped down on a recliner. Someone informed me that I was sitting in Cowboy Smith's chair. I wouldn't get off. Pretty soon Cowboy came in and was standing right beside me. He said, "That's my chair you're sitting on." I said, "I guess it is." We laughed and the two of us drank for about the next four to five days. After a while, I said, "I'm going home." He asked, "How come?" I said, "I'm broke." He dug in his wallet and handed me three hundred dollar bills. He told me, "Stick around." I asked, "How am I supposed to get it back to you?" He said, "Don't worry about it." (He never told me had a couple of gold mines.) He wanted me to go on to Dawson with him and train dogs.

The banquet was a good party. Oly was sponsoring the Iditarod so we drank a lot of beer.

Sprint musher Dean Painter.
Courtesy Margie Walker and Andrean Madros.

After the Iditarod, I began racing dogs again for my lawyer friend Myron Angstman, also the founder of the Kuskokwim 300, who ran the Iditarod in 1979 and 1981. Myron wanted me to race his team in the Norton Sound 200. It was a twelve-dog limit race and I had only ten. We began in Unalakleet, went to Kaltag and back to Unalakleet. (Middy Johnson of Unalakleet who'd run the Iditarod was my main competitor.) I beat them all to Kaltag. There was a mandatory four-hour rest during which I fed my dogs

Martin Buser, Dean Painter (Iditarod checker) with son, Dean II. Phillip Nickoli and Dave Burkett, behind, Grayling, ca. 1995.
Courtesy of Margie Walker and Andrean Madros.

and rested some, but I got no sleep. On the return to Unalakleet, one of my ten dogs quit so I had to stop and throw him in the sled, which allowed Middy to pass me. The press got wind of it so Myron heard and thought it was all over. After I passed the "Twenty miles to Unalakleet" sign, Middy stopped his team, saying he was going to snack his dogs. He added, "We're still quite a ways out," but I'd just seen the sign saying that it was only twenty miles farther. Middy gave each of his dogs a big hunk of meat the size of a fist. I gave my dogs some beaver belly fat, but only half the size of a Sailor Boy Pilot Bread cracker. He wanted to rest his dogs. I said, "Well, I'm going to go." All of a sudden my dogs picked up and began loping. I'd put my 'ol stupid leader, a Jeff King dog, in wheel because he's usually only good for about nine mph, but he began barking so I put him back in the lead. I beat Middy by two hours in a twenty-mile race into Unalakleet. (I think Middy put his dogs to sleep with all that meat.) I called Myron and said, "I won the race!" Since he'd heard that Middy had passed me, he asked me how that happened. I said, "I got him!" (I thought for sure I was going to lose that race.)

The last time I raced for Myron, about six years ago, was in the Aniak 150 from Aniak to Georgetown. He called and asked if I could bring his dogs up to speed in two to three weeks. I told him, "I think I got a chance." He said, "You can't beat that Pete Kaiser, he's kinda crafty." I said, "Heck, I got him." I was pretty confidant. Nathan Underwood was really fast. I didn't really know what Richie Diehl had. When I left Aniak, it was getting dark. In the moonlight, I thought I'd passed everyone but I heard planes flying over and knew we must be getting close to Georgetown. Suddenly I saw something ahead of me and I slapped my sled hard to get the dogs to pick up and they went into a dead gallop. I sailed around Pete Kaiser on the snow crust. I passed him so fast that he didn't have a chance to hit the brake. Three miles later at

Georgetown, he pulled up behind me and said, "I'm going to call you Dean Streeper." Then I beat him back to Aniak, 75 miles, in a little bit over an hour. I'd trained those dogs to lope-lope-lope. I wouldn't let them quit on me. It doesn't take much disciplining, but it takes some.

In January this year, Myron called me to come train his dogs but I was still working construction.

My wife Rita has family upriver so in 2000 we moved to Nulato where she works for the city and I continue to work construction.

Racing for a lifetime has taught me to be persistent. Whatever I do, I try to get an early start. If I have to be at work at eight, I'm there at seven. Pretty soon, I'm in sync, working twelve hours a day, just by being persistent. My advice to young people is to be prepared

Rudy Demoski and Dean Painter.
Rudy's last Iditarod, Grayling, 2013.
Courtesy of Margie Walker.

and to start early. Train hard and know how long you can stay up and how fast you can get to sleep. I have no idea what it costs to keep a kennel because, in my day, we fed from cooking and from fishing and trapping. But why race dogs? You'll be broke the rest of your life!

I volunteered a lot, helping the Iditarod. Lots of times I've gone to Eagle Island, stayed in a tent and froze out. (But now they have Arctic Oven tents, which with a stove, heat up great!) I've also gone to Kaltag a lot to help the main checker Richard Burnham. The last time the Iditarod came through

Dean Painter and grandson Trevon Madros, 2012.
Courtesy of Andrean Madros and Rita Painter.

Nulato, I let the racing staff use my truck. Sometimes I even help out at Shageluk.

Here in Nulato, the school district has a sprint racing dog team [A-Chill program, *Ed.*]. I never bothered with the sprint breed. My wife's uncle, Henry Agnes, ran the Rondy a long time ago as did Justin Patsy. Everybody used to have dogs, but now no one does. However I want my grandsons to grow up like I did: seeing the land from the back of a sled. I picked up three dogs from my buddy Davy Walker. One of them is from Doug Swingley's line.

Dean Painter, Nulato, 2017.
Susan Paskvan photo.

Just before my lifelong friend and cousin, Rudy Demoski, died, he told me I could trap his line. This winter I plan to trap my area and then, Rudy's. With the fur money, I want to get more sled dogs for my grandchildren. I talked to Mitch Seavey and Jeff King. Jeff said I could get a pregnant female for $1500.00 so it depends on how I do trapping in early winter and then later, on Rudy's line.

I'm never going to run the Iditarod again, but Rudy did in 2013. He got me to thinking about it, but now, even he's gone. If I get two pregnant females next year, and I work with the kids and the dogs . . . well, who knows. Norman Vaughn was 84 the last time he ran the Iditarod!

Chapter 10

Roxy Wright, Oldest Musher to Win Rondy and ONAC: Forty Years Championship Racing

Winner of 1990 Alpirod, Roxy Wright-Champaine with lead dog Penny.
Courtesy of Roxy Wright.

Roxy Wright is the descendant of one of Alaska's most prestigious dog mushing families. Her half-Athabascan grandfather Arthur Wright traveled across Alaska by dogsled with Episcopal Archdeacon Hudson Stuck in the early 1900s. Arthur Wright went on to have seven outstanding sons including Don Wright, whose indispensable negotiations between Alaska Natives and the White House led to President Nixon signing the Alaska Native Claims Settlement Act in 1971, Al Wright, the owner of Wright Air Service, and Roxy's father, Gareth Wright. Gareth and his brother Don—along with Don Peterson—founded the Alaska Dog Mushers Association. For years, Gareth dominated the sprint mushing circuit. In 1950 and 1983, he won the Open North American (ONAC) Sled Dog Race in Fairbanks, and in 1950, 1952, and 1957, he won the Fur Rendezvous Open World Championship Sled Dog Race in Anchorage. In 1967 Gareth raced in the Alaska Purchase Centennial race, the forerunner of the Iditarod. When Roxy's time came, her racing genes proved true. Roxy was a queen of the Rondy and the North American circuits as well as of the European Alpirod at the height of sprint racing history — the 1970s and 1980s. After a twenty-one-year hiatus, at age sixty-six Roxy returned to racing and swept both the Rondy and the Open North American in 2017[1] On March 5th, 2017, Roxy shared her story.

I'm not only the first and only woman to win the Anchorage Fur Rondy, but at sixty-six, I am also the oldest person to have won both it and the Open North American. Doc Lombard was sixty-one when he last won the Rondy. I was also the first, but not the only, woman to win the North American.

1   *Mushers refer to the Open North American Championship (ONAC) as the "North American" or the "Open". They refer to the Fur Rendezvous Open World Championship Sled Dog Race (OWC) as the "Rondy" and the "Rendezvous".*

Co-founder of Alaska Dog Mushers Association, Gareth Wright, winner of Open North American, 1983 and below, in 1950 with lead dog, Venus.

Alaska Dog Mushers Association.

It takes an entire family to race dogs, but many women did not have the time or the resources to compete in the open class races. The first Women's North American was started in 1952. Effie Kokrine won the first three. Rosie Losonsky won four times, and Jean Bryar six times. The Women's World Championship (the Fur Rondy in Anchorage) was begun in 1953. My mom, Vera Carter Wright, won both of these women's sled dog races in 1958.

Eight years earlier, in 1950, I was born in Fairbanks to Vera and Gareth Wright. I was the fourth of my mother's seven girls.

My dad was born in 1928 in Old Minto. The third of seven sons, he was one-quarter Athabascan. His large family lived in the big mission house in Old Minto, but moved to Nenana for continued mission work when he was very young. The family earned money in a variety of ways ranging from emptying the community's honey buckets to trapping. My dad ran a trap line with his dog team. He liked to visit one of the old mushers Bobby Bruce, from whom he learned a lot.

When they were teenagers, Dad and his brother Don went to Fairbanks for high school. They stayed at a place in Graehl. They drove their dogs to school as well as to the movie theatre. By 1947, Dad was mushing competitively and did into the early 1990s. He got one of his first dogs from Johnny Allen, a top racer from Ruby during the 1920s to 1930s.

My mother's side of the family was also Alaska Native, either Aleut or Yup'ik. Her mother, Stephanita Lucille Hansen, married Henry "Harry" Carter from California and together, they ran the trading post first in McGrath and then, in Fort Yukon. They had twelve children including my mother Vera, who was born in 1924. Mom married Frank Brown and they had three daughters, Pam, Polly, and Sandy. When that marriage ended, my mother married my father, Gareth Wright. Pam and Polly went with their father while Sandy stayed with my mom. Dad and Mom had two more girls, me and Lynette.

I remember riding in my parents' dogsleds. I always liked riding in Dad's because he didn't make us keep our hands tucked into the sleeping bag. He would run behind

Vera Carter Wright, ca.1940.
Courtesy of Roxy Wright.

and sing, but if he got too far behind, he had to run hard to catch up.

We had a house on the Old Steese Highway across from today's Fred Meyer East. There used to be a gravel pit there with a dirt speedway where my dad and his friends used to race cars. Dad was called the Phantom. He and his brothers owned and operated Wright Truck and Tractor.

When I was six, my parents split up. We three girls and Mom moved to the state of Washington, where we lived for two years. In January 1960 we finally came home. That spring, Mom got a job as a gardener at Circle Hot Springs, the resort at the end of the Steese Highway at Circle City. There she met and married Bill Strack; they had two more daughters, Donna and Yvonne. Bill ran a barge from Circle downstream to Fort Yukon and upstream to Coal Creek below Eagle. In Circle, he ran a power plant and sold electricity to the town. For five years, from my fourth to eighth grades, I went to a one-room school in Circle.

At that age, I didn't have any sled dogs. During the late 1950s to early 1960s, the dog mushers were people's heroes and those who couldn't go to the races listened closely to them on the radio. During the winter, the road to Circle was not maintained from mid-October till spring. We listened with rapt attention to the minute-by-minute accounts of our dad racing against Doc Lombard and George Attla.

When I was eleven, I had a pet dog, Lady, who was half German shepherd, half MacKenzie River husky. In Fairbanks she was too good of a watchdog, so her owners gave her to us, figuring she'd do better in our rural setting. I taught her to pull my sled. I borrowed dogs wherever I could find them. A friend in Central who had malamutes was moving to Fairbanks so he gave

L-r: Roxy's sister Lynette Wright (Holt), Lady, and cousin Jack Wright, Roxy Wright, ca. 1961, Circle.

Courtesy of Roxy Wright.

me his dogs. Running dogs was natural to me. In the spring, Circle had junior races. I raced in the two-mile, two-dog event on the frozen Yukon.

Because there were no high schools in the villages, I attended Sheldon Jackson Presbyterian boarding school in Sitka. That winter my mother and Bill moved to Fairbanks, but my sister Sandy and I finished our year at Sheldon Jackson.

The following fall when I was sixteen, I went to live with my dad who gave me Sam, a crazy dog. I had to wrestle him for five minutes to get his harness on, but I taught him to be a lead dog. He was a character. After I trained him, the first time that my dad ran him, I asked him how Sam had done for him. Evidently Sam kept looking back to see who this was who was driving him. With other people, Sam would circle back, try to get into the sled, pee on the snowbank, but he didn't do that to me. I'd trained him. Dad let me use other dogs to run as well. My friend Sally Clark and I began racing in the seven-dog class in the junior races. A lot of times Dad would be gone running the Rondy or at other races, so we weren't always using the best dogs. That was good experience for us, learning to train them on our own. Nothing replaces hands-on teaching and learning with the animal. Taking care of dogs is a part of being able to run them. I never minded the chores. It's an important part of spending time with the animals. If someone else does the menial work, then the musher is not spending time with his dogs. When the owner scoops poop, waters, and feeds, he stops and pets them. At sixteen when I finally got to be with dogs, I was hungry to take care of them.

In 1967, my dad married Miranda Hildebrand and soon I had another sister, Shannon, making a total of eight daughters in my family. In 1968 I married Mike Brooks. We had two children, Ramy and Tammy. I was able to continue training, but waited until the kids got a little bigger to race full-time.

When Ramy was four and was going to run in the one-dog race, I let him use my leader Sam. Most dogs slow up as they get near the end of the

L, Gareth Wright; far right, Roxy Wright Woods, 1974.
(Maxine Vehlow) *The World of Sled Dogs* Courtesy of Roxy Wright.

track—but not Sam. He'd speed up and flash past the finish line. Someone had to be ready to catch the dog because he was going to bolt right past, taking the kid with him. He also won three one-dog races with Ramy and one with Tammy.

When Ramy was four in 1972, Mike and I divorced.

Throughout my life, the longest I ever worked for someone was nine months, as a secretary for the Tanana Chiefs Conference boarding home program. It takes a lot more work to be self-employed, but as a dog driver, I did what I loved.

In 1972, I married Al Woods of Rampart. We moved above Rampart, where we lived seasonally. I commercial fished and we trapped until 1983. We built a log house in Fairbanks. In the fall or before each racing season, I'd enroll the children in school in town and compete in dog racing. I won the Women's North American Championship in 1972 and 1975.

One year after the race season when we were moving back to our camp on the river, we had to go through open water in the creek. My kids had the older dogs and I had the puppies. I was the slowest but when we hit the open water, I had to get my children and then my pups through the open water. Of course I got cold wet feet but I got the kids down the trail. My feet were sheathed in ice. I had to stop and build a fire to get my boots off and put dry socks on or I'd have frozen my feet. Back-country people always carry dry clothes and matches.

In 1976 I won the last Women's NAC and I also entered my first open Rondy and ONAC and placed eighth in both. I thought, "I like this. I want to continue racing the guys in the Open (ONAC) as well." Over the years, women had occasionally entered either the open Rondy or the North American, however I was the first woman to race annually in both open

Roxy Wright Brooks, second win of Fur Rendezvous' Women's Sled Dog Race, 1974.
Photo by Alice Puster. *Anchorage Daily Times*

races. For the next twenty years then I became a perennial competitor in the open sled dog racing circuit. I might have missed a race or two depending on what was happening with my dogs or in my life, but not too often.

I usually entered the Rondy and the North American with at least sixteen dogs. In 1982 I entered the Rondy with only twelve dogs, but I still came in third and never dropped a dog. George Attla was first and Clyde Mayo was second, but I won the last day's heat by a bit! I never finished lower than eighth place in either the North American or the Rondy so I was one of the top competitors—maybe not always in the top three, but I was a strong competitor—one to be reckoned with.

In 1983, I decided I wanted to do the Iditarod. It had nothing to do with my dog racing career; it was something I personally wanted to do. I'd have to get past my discomfort of being alone in the dark. Since childhood, I had often dreamed of a bear chasing me. As I was falling and the bear was about to pounce, I'd try to scream but I couldn't and I'd wake up. When we went hunting in the fall, I was not comfortable being alone in the dark. I didn't venture very far from the tent. During the Iditarod, I told myself, "The bears aren't out so there's nothing in the dark to fear." Doing the Iditarod was a way of not only facing a simple fear, but it also became a door for me to resolve some much larger problems.

In the fall living at our cabin above Rampart, I began training all nineteen of my dogs. I was also homeschooling Ramy and Tammy. In December, we got ready to move to the Manley-Eureka area to train. There was a mining trail from Eureka twenty-five miles outside of Manley that goes into the gold mines near Rampart. Mom was living in Manley and would take care of the children while I ran the Iditarod. We hooked up all of my dogs into two teams. Tammy was riding in her brother Ramy's sled. Only a few miles out of Rampart, Ramy complained that her weight was causing his sled to keep running off the trail into the snowbank. I said, "Okay, give me one of your dogs. She can ride with me." He took off and I never saw him again un-

Roxy's daughter, Tammy Brooks (Holland), in North American 3-dog class, ca. 1981.
Courtesy of Roxy Wright.

til we got to Eureka. Most kids steal the keys to the car but he took off with the dog team and had them parked by the time I arrived.

To prepare for the Iditarod, we cooked rice and fish in huge tubs and froze it. We sawed the solid dog food on a bandsaw into chunks and shipped it out.

My leader, Burner, born in November, was just over two years old and had never raced. About a month before the Iditarod, I thought, "I've never done this long-distance mushing before. I don't want this to be my only race this year." I took some weight off the dogs and speeded them up. I leased a leader from Bill Taylor to run with Burner and we ran the Gold Run in Fairbanks and the Rondy's Women's World Championship in Anchorage. The Taylors were also doing the Rondy so I ran Burner in that race as a single lead. Most mushers would not use a single inexperienced lead in the urban mushing of the Rendezvous. The race begins on Fourth Avenue, turns onto Cordova, goes one and half miles on the street before dropping down onto bike paths, over overpasses, and through tunnels. Pretty daunting for a single young dog. Leading on his third time ever, Burner did an awesome job. On the last day to help Burner, I put Penny in, a one-year-old who hadn't raced much either. Those two youngsters did great and we came in sixth! Ten days later with the same dogs, I headed out to begin the Iditarod.

I drew #69 and we were the last team out. We passed twenty teams going from Anchorage to Eagle River. At the Knik restart, we passed another twenty teams or so and were close to the front of the pack. Had we remained there, I might have learned the cycle of mushing and sleeping a bit faster, but I got off the trail. Someone had moved the markers. My dogs were on the right trail, but in the dark, I saw the markers stuck on a different trail. I had to go with what I saw and we went in that direction. We ran about seven miles up that trail, but it got very bad. Probably fifteen teams went down the wrong trail, and I had led the way. I was going to camp but my team was pretty wound up and they weren't going to rest (I had not done as much camp-

Roxy Wright Woods at Iditarod restart, Knik, 1983.
Courtesy of Roxy Wright.

ing with the dogs as I should have). On the way back I passed Ken Chase. He said, "Man, you missed a big tangle with those other fifteen teams." In both going and coming back, I was enough ahead so that I wasn't part of the chaos.

One of the things I was worried about was sleeping. I was afraid I'd sleep too long, but I didn't. After four hours, I'd get chilled and wake up. It took me five days to begin to have a good established rhythm of sleeping and waking. In fact I hardly slept. I was drinking coffee and began to realize it wasn't settling well. When I arrived in Nikolai for my twenty-four rest, I ate a good meal and went to sleep, but then I woke and threw up. I realized that too little sleep and too much coffee weren't working for me. I decided to quit coffee.

The food drops for my diet included meat, dried foods, and frozen food in Ziploc bags. The race was not nearly as high-tech then as it is now. Mushers used Coleman stoves, not the alcohol stoves of today. We took extra C batteries for headlamps. I had a tiny bag of tools: wrench, screwdriver—but no sewing kit. Just before the Iditarod my mom helped me finish my first marten hat. I had no high-tech clothing. My mom cut down her down parka for me. I wore Carhartt pants, long johns, and mukluks. I was young and tough. I had a decent sleeping bag—not like the fancy ones of today. I tried sleeping on the ground but it was too cold; my pad wasn't enough so I slept in my sled. I had a little pot to heat my frozen food. I had salmon strips and dry meat—food that doesn't freeze hard, is high-protein, and gives lots of energy.

When I left McGrath, it was thirty below with fresh snow. At that point, I should have bootied to prevent splits between my dogs' pads, but because they had awesome feet, I didn't know to bootie in those conditions. From Takotna to Ophir, they developed splits between their pads. The rolling hills near Iditarod were deep in sugar snow, which irritated my dogs' splits even more. I bootied my dogs, but as we were leaving Shageluk, one of my dogs was limping so I took the bootie off and she quit limping.

Since our kennel focused on sprint mushing, not long-distance racing, my dogs still had their dewclaws. On a long-distance race musher's bootie, however, the Velcro on the socks can rub and inflame dewclaws, leading to infection, something I had no experience with. (A dewclaw is on the inside of a dog's leg, positioned analogously to a human thumb. It can protrude slightly and become irritated. Many distance mushers have them removed.)

Roxy and Pluto, 1989.

Courtesy of Roxy Wright.

That was a low point for me. I said to my dogs, "I am so sorry." They could've done much better if I'd known how to take better care of them. My strengths, however, are to keep going, to try to do my best, and to learn from my mistakes.

When we pulled into a village, someone would always bring a musher to his house, feed him, and treat him like a celebrity. At each checkpoint, there was a big drum of snow water boiling for the mushers.

After we reached the coast and were crossing that vast expanse of sea ice, I began hallucinating. The horizon seemed to be a cable in front of me. I kept ducking to avoid being knocked off the sled. I knew the "cable" wasn't really there, but it looked real so I ducked anyway. The sky became a sheet of Styrofoam and I dunked my head so it didn't knock me off of my sled. I was getting very tired.

Since I was in 19th to 23rd place, I started resting longer, six to seven hours at each checkpoint. I just wanted to make it to Nome. When I left White Mountain, I dropped down from the hills and onto the sea ice. It was a nice sunny day so I stopped and gave my dogs a break under a bridge.

An Eskimo couple asked me to come in and have coffee. I protested, "My dogs…" and the woman reassured me, "Oh, they'll be fine." They were.

Nome can be seen for a long way before you actually arrive. I wanted us to look good as we entered Nome so I whistled my team up into a lope, but we kept going and going; it wasn't as close as it first appeared. I came in number 23 and did it in fourteen days, fifteen hours, fifty-six minutes, and sixteen seconds. I'd accomplished my goal.

Arriving in Nome that night was exhilarating. I had a delicious meal and was thankful for it and a warm bed. That night I slept, but I kept waking and thinking, "I have to take care of my dogs," and then, I'd remember, "Oh, no . . . that's right—it's okay."

At about the same time, Dad had just won the North American for the second time. Since Rick Mackey had won the Iditarod, his father, Dick Mackey, the 1978 winner of the Iditarod, and my Open North American champion father, were both in Nome for the banquet to support their kids.

I'd overcome my discomfort with two types of darkness: natural and that of a home life that was not good for me or for my children. I pushed through another door and left what had been a bad marriage.

Weather-wise, 1983 was an awesome year to run the Iditarod. There was no blizzard and no super cold. My dogs could've done better if I had had more experience. My challenges were not knowing when to bootie and the effect of a long-distance race on dewclaws. I also didn't do enough long-distance runs prior to the Iditarod but—it was what it was. I have a belt buckle with the year on it that all finishers get, as well as my Iditarod bib. It probably cost me ten thousand dollars to run the Iditarod. That doesn't count what it cost to feed the dogs all year long, but then we also always fished for our dogs.

I prefer sprint racing. I like going around corners fast, getting a shower, and sleeping in a bed at night.

I had no aspirations to run the Iditarod again. Every now and then, I dream I am running it again and always have the awful realization, "Oh my gosh, I never packed ahead of time," so I begin scrambling to find gloves and meat. A musher has to have everything ready before the Iditarod; in my dream, I don't have anything ready.

In the fall of 1984 I moved in with fellow competitor Charlie Champaine, but we maintained separate kennels. Two years later we married and combined our dog yards in Salcha. We became a pretty indomitable force.

In those days, there were a lot more races. Starting in December through end of March, there was a race nearly every weekend. We were on the road all the time going to races. The season peaked with Rondy in February and

Roxy rounds corner in her 1992 ONAC win, third ONAC win for the Wright-Champaine kennels. (In 1989 Roxy won and Charlie Champaine won in 1990.)
(Mike Mathers) 1992-93 Alaska Dogmushers Association Annual Program

with the North American in March. The Tok Race of Champions was the week after the North American and was the last main race on the road system. As the snow began to deteriorate in the central Interior, we stretched the season by going north. We loaded a sled and sixteen to eighteen dogs in a little airplane, along with food, gear, hay for the dogs and went to Venetie, Fort Yukon, Arctic Village, and to Allakaket. Originally Hughes, Huslia, and Allakaket each had their own spring races, but the children missed too much school and it took a lot to raise the money for three races. These villages consolidated their races into the Koyukuk River Championship and

Koyukuk River Championship, Roxy Wright-Champaine, 1984.
Courtesy of Roxy Wright.

rotated it among the three villages. When I ran in Allakaket, I won the first Koyukuk River Championship they held. I also raced in Noorvik and Kotzebue. People put us up. We brought in hay and cut spruce boughs to crib in the dogs' hay beds and tied the dogs in the yards where we stayed. Sometimes I raced the whole month of April in the villages. Then in early May I'd go back home to Salcha.

The most tense race I ever ran was in Kotzebue. The wind was hitting us broadside. Race officials had stuck frozen willows into the ice to mark the trail. The leaders stayed on the trail, but the wheel dog section and the sled were getting blown fifteen to twenty feet off the trail. When the sled hit the willows, it made the sled roll 360s. I was rolling with the sled, trying to hang

Charlie Champaine, Gareth and Miranda Wright listening to the radio for musher check -in times, Open North American Championship, 1992.
Courtesy of Roxy Wright.

Roxy, winner of the 1992 Open North American Championship, with Longnose and Austin in the lead.

Courtesy of Roxy Wright.

on. My body got so tense and so fatigued from hanging on. That was the first third of a twenty-five-mile race. Those first eight miles were horrendous.

Before I joined forces with Charlie, he won the Rondy in 1984. After we got together, he won the Rondy again in 1988. In 1990, he won both the Rondy and the North American. After winning the Rondy one final time in 1991, he retired.

Roxy, winner of 1992 Fur Rondy, running up Cordova hill.

Anchorage Daily News

In 1989, 1992, and 1993, I won both the Rondy and the North American. I was the first woman to win both races and the only woman to win the Rondy. I was one of five mushers who ever won the Triple Crown, which includes the Rondy, the North American, and the Tok Race of Champions. When I won the Rondy, I beat George Attla, a ten-time world champion. He said, "I gave it everything I got. She had a stronger dog team.

For six consecutive years the Wright-Champaine team won all three heats of the Rondy.

In 1990, there were a lot of long-distance mushers going to Europe to race in the Alpirod, a series of multiple races over twelve days through the Alps including several countries: Italy, Switzerland, Austria, France, and Italy and covering about 500 miles. Each day or stage of the race is a certain number of miles, each musher's race is timed, and the winner is the one with the shortest cumulative time. It was the largest sled dog race outside of North America and it promoted conquering the wild. Like the Iditarod, it intrigued me. I thought, "I think I want to do the Alpirod." I began corresponding with the Alpirod staff and they found sponsors for me.

Since Charlie was using our main team in both 1990 and 1991, I began building my Alpirod team. I took Penny, one of my leaders who was eight and too old to run in the sprint team. I also took the dogs that were slightly old as well as a few young ones I'd trained. I put my dogs, sled, and gear on a pallet on our flight to Europe. When my dad found out I was going—even though I was forty—he asked my stepmother, Miranda, "Is she going by herself?" so the two of them flew over to support me.

On my first Alpirod in 1990, I won. The race was totally insane: high speeds on mountain trails with hairpin turns. Tim White went off a cliff with his team and crashed, but recovered and finished the race. After I won the Alpirod, I didn't plan on returning. Later I sold some of those dogs and the special sled Ed Salter built for me for the Alpirod. However, the race yielded substantial prize money and I'd done very well, so that summer we decided that I'd return in 1991. My leader Penny was too old so I needed two new leaders. There was a risk in taking young leaders rather than an older dog who is able to handle many different types of trails. Nonetheless I took Elroy and Dudley, two-year-old leaders who proved their mettle. The route went uphill on a downhill ski run, which is hard enough, but the descent followed a traversing course. On one sharp turn, my sled dropped off the lip of the trail and rolled while my dogs were still uphill on the trail. My young leaders thought, "She must want us to go down." I dug my (front bumper) brush bow into the scant snow cover and—it held; the ice hook definitely wasn't going to stop them. If I'd let the sled go, it would've been a disaster. While I was trying to command my leaders and get them back on the trail, some non-English speaking skiers came by. Since my dogs' harnesses were badly tangled, I used tone and sign language to direct the skiers not to unsnap hooks on the dogs' collars, but to undo the snaps near their butts. They helped me get the team back on the trail. Other people had al-

Roxy, winner of 1990 Alpirod with her leader Penny. In second, Joe Runyan is to her right and in third, Tim White, is to her left.

Courtesy of Roxy Wright.

ready rolled downhill and lost their gear and well-meaning bystanders tried handing their stuff to me. People complain about trails in Alaska, but they don't know what bad trails are. Later, Elroy and Dudley both proved to be great dogs for two other top competitors as well.

In 1994 I took the main team for the first time to the Alpirod, and again in 1995. When I returned home, I continued doing quite well at the Rondy. However, in retrospect, it would have been better to focus on one type of race and train for it, not try for two very different races.

In 1996 due to lack of snow, the Rondy was cancelled. Over-burdened by the demands of the Alpirod, the owners of that race shut it down permanently. There were beginning to be fewer races and it was getting harder to make a go of it. I decided that year to retire. I was a grandma and I wanted to spend time with my grandchildren. During my racing years, I couldn't be at family functions. When competitively training dogs, a racer has to remain focused: training and caring for dogs. In 1998, Charlie and I also parted ways.

During the last twenty years, I've been able to be with my family a lot more, which is very important to me. In 2000 I married Dave Freedle; between us, we have nine grandchildren and three great-grands.

I racked up a record eight wins at the women's Fur Rondy race. Kathy Frost tied that win record there. My niece Carey Rose Erhart-Roberts won the final women's Fur Rondy race in 2006.

For years, sprint musher and veterinarian Dr. Arleigh Reynolds and I have been friends. Arleigh always considered me as one of his main mentors.

I have a good eye for pups. When developing a team, a breeder must decide which pups to keep and which to find a good home for. Dogs, like humans, are not all elite athletes and they are born that way. To compete in the Rondy and in the North American, a dog must be both fast and have endurance. Those qualities don't always happen in one dog.

Roxy retires

Legendary Alaska musher trades in dog team for time with her grandkids

By TIM MURRAY
Daily News reporter

When there's no 401(k) to liquidate, no company stock to sell and no gold watch from the CEO, how do you know when a dog musher has retired?

If the musher is Roxy Wright Champaine, you know it when she sells her dog team and announces it's time to become a full-time grandmother. Goodbye Fur Rendezvous, hello Toys 'R Us.

Wright Champaine officially ended a stellar 30-year mushing career April 14, when she won the Arctic Circle Championship in Kotzebue.

Since then, Wright Champaine and her husband, Charlie Champaine, have sold 38 of their 62 dogs, including every husky off their 1996 race team.

Several dogs stayed in the family by going to Ramy Brooks and Curtis Erhart. Brooks, a distance musher, is Roxy's son; Erhart, a sprint musher, is her brother-in-law. Four-time Iditarod champion Susan Butcher also bought several hounds.

Three more dogs are still for sale, but because the demand for Champaine sled dogs is the Alaska equivalent of a Kennedy family auction, they won't last long.

When the sale is complete, 21 dogs — a mix of yearlings and retired lead dogs — will remain in the Champaine kennel in Salcha. "If we sold all our dogs, I'd have acute withdrawals," said Wright Champaine.

As dog sales go, the Champaines' liquidation sale is a rare one. Seldom

Please see Page A-7, **ROXY**

BILL ROTH / Daily News
Roxy Wright Champaine at the 199 Rendezvous sled dog race

Roxy retires in 1996. Anchorage Daily News *article by Tim Murray and photo by Bill Roth.*

Courtesy of Roxy Wright.

compete in the Rondy and in the North American, a dog must be both fast and have endurance. Those qualities don't always happen in one dog.

I have also helped Arleigh train. I was at the Rondy helping handle his team both times he won in 2013 and 2014. We're similar in the way we interact with and train dogs.

As the associate dean of UAF's Department of Veterinary Medicine, Arleigh is developing a vet program that dovetails with the vet program of Colorado State University, which enables returning Alaska students to pay less tuition in Alaska than their out-of-state counterparts. To focus on his work, Arleigh retired from competitive mushing, but that left his kennel without a trainer.

At the same time, my husband, Dave, had gone back to work so in 2015 when Arleigh asked me to train his dogs, I agreed. My husband and I weren't willing to live in Salcha to train dogs so I commuted from Fairbanks. Luckily, Arleigh has a lot of good people working at his kennel. Without them, none of this would've worked. It's a big learning curve for dogs when they have to work with a different musher, but not with Arleigh and me. The transition was nearly seamless for the dogs to adjust to either me or Arleigh. After each training run, I would call and give Arleigh a report.

Dr. Arleigh Reynolds and Kyle, the father or grandfather of the championship teams with whom Arleigh and Roxy won the Rondy and ONAC in 2013, 2014, and 2017. 2015. Courtesy of Arleigh Reynolds.

Arleigh's main leader, Guts, had retired because of age. The summer of 2015, Arleigh bought four young dogs from Joee Redington. We had intended to just try to train those dogs, but by November, they were looking good. Arleigh asked if I'd consider racing them. I said, "Well, if these young leaders are ready, I suppose I could, if it would be a positive experience for them." However by the time of the race, we had only twelve dogs who were okay to race and only one of them was only a year old. The Streepers had eighteen dogs. I ran two-year-old Cloud and five-year-old Anya in lead. Even with our disadvantage, we still finished second, only two minutes behind Buddy Streeper. A week later, I met Arleigh for lunch and said, "Let's start training and planning and try to win!" We decided to build up our kennel. From Joee, we picked up two more dogs, including a female, Pale, who wound up as my lead. I was going to give my best for the dogs and for me—regardless of where we placed but—we had set our sights set on winning.

Before running the Rondy in February 2017, I had a lot of congestion in my chest from a cold. I had trouble breathing and seized up with coughing

Roxy crossing the finish line with wheel dogs Rondy and Storm, winning the Fur Rendezvous Open World Championship Sled Dog Race, 2017.
Photo by Britt Coon. Courtesy Roxy Wright.

fits. In all my years of running the Rondy and helping Ramy at the Iditarod, at the start I always ran the leaders up to the front, often through knee-deep snow. But at the 2017 Rondy I had Arleigh run the leaders, Cloud and Anya, up to the front because I knew I had only so much running in me. I had to save it to run up Cordova Hill. (Someone who was at Cordova Hill later said that I was one of the few mushers who ran up the hill . . . but I thought everyone did.) The first day I got almost a five-minute lead on everyone else—incredible. There was no radio coverage so Buddy Streeper got a surprise when I came in that first day. I knew he couldn't outrun me by five minutes so I kept my dogs going steadily. My goal was to win the race but I wouldn't be pressured into pushing my dogs unnecessarily. On Saturday Buddy beat me by forty-five seconds and on the last day, he beat me by a minute, forty-nine, but I still beat him by two minutes, twelve seconds over all. On both days, he was running full out, but to make up five minutes is pretty tough. My team, with two swing dogs in heat, ran within thirty seconds of its own time. I was slightly faster on Saturday and even faster on Sunday. The team was running beautifully. Buddy had not had a loss in years. When I beat him, other mushers said, "You just gave the mushers in North America hope." Years ago, I used to race against Buddy's dad, Terry.

In the North American in March, I used Pale, a leader I'd tested the last day of Rondy. Pale and Cloud swept us to a second victory in Fairbanks. All the dogs on Arleigh's team—including those from Joee—were out of Arleigh's main stud Kyle.

Twenty-one years after I retired, winning the Rondy and the North American again in 2017 was like a fairy tale. My grandchildren, who'd either been too young or who weren't yet born, didn't remember my racing career.

Winner of Open North American Championship, Roxy Wright with second place, Buddy Streeper to her right, 2017.

Photo by Sasha Housley. Courtesy of Roxy Wright.

It was really special for them to get to see me race, for us to share that. My winning was also a symbol to many Alaskans that the golden age of Alaska sprint racing is still alive and that we can push past the limits of age. It was an instant hurrah, "We can do this!!" It was very special for me and Arleigh because of all we had poured into it. Five of the dogs with whom I won the Rondy were also on his winning team in 2014. This victory was a way of giving back to those who have supported me throughout four decades.

A lot of the top dogs in sprint racing and distance mushing—including Arleigh's—go back to my leader, Burner, to my dad's line of dogs. My dad's breed had good feet, unlike many today, and an exceptional undercoat. I could sell them to both sprint and to long-distance mushers.

I stay in shape by remaining active, living the traditional subsistence life: hunting, fishing, berrying, gardening, getting firewood.

There's a lot more technology now: composite metal sleds, rubber tracks for braking, GPSs, Go Pro cameras. A lot of things have changed, but it still comes down to having good dogs and good dog sense. The outcome of long-distance races tends to depend more on the musher than on just the dogs. Being efficient and being a good dog person are critical for successful long-distance mushing.

I have had so many awesome dogs: Oly, Bony, Pluto, Mustang, Cordova, Long Nose, Penny, so many wonderful dogs. There is a photo of me with Pluto, in which he seems to be saying, "Mom, hold me." He loved me lots. My dogs and I have a very close bond. I was very blessed. I don't think the good dogs are all gone.

> On the first day of the 2017 North American, I predicted Roxy's winning time would be 64:19. Even though her GPS didn't work, she still calculated perfectly and won in 64:16. (She's that good.) On the third day I told her I thought that the heat would be won in 94 minutes and her time was within 3 seconds of that. She beat Buddy by 6 seconds and overall by 23 seconds. She became the oldest person to win either race and she remains the only female Rondy Champion. At the time, she was (and is) a great grandmother.
>
> **Dr. Arleigh Reynolds**

Mushing dogs is an awesome way to connect with animals, with nature, with our Alaskan way of life. Whether a young musher sticks with it or not, mushing can teach a person about his weaknesses and strengths, giving him invaluable life lessons. The simple process of putting one foot in front of the other—for hours and hours in the dark and the cold—until one reaches a cabin is an important lesson. Both of my parents raised me to stick with something even when it is hard. That commitment made a difference for me in the Iditarod and in my many other races. Do your best and learn by your mistakes. In 2017 we Alaskans broke through and swept Rondy and the North American. Dare to dream. Your dreams, like mine, can come true.

Roxy Wright with granddaughter Molly Brooks, in 1999, when Roxy's son, Ramy Brooks, won the Yukon Quest.
Courtesy of Roxy Wright.

Chapter 11

Ramy Brooks, Overcomer, Winner of the Quest

Ramy Brooks, 2017.
Judy Ferguson photograph.

During the Gold Rush, prospectors got any dog off the streets of Seattle and brought them north to pull their sleds. To get hardier dogs, they were bred then to Alaskan huskies. The grandson of one of Alaska's most prestigious sled dog mushing families, Ramy Brooks said, "Today the Alaskan husky is considered one of the healthiest breeds due to his genetically diverse background. Diseases like hip dysplasia, found in purebred dogs, are not common in the husky. Sixty years ago, my grandfather Gareth Wright bred Irish setters to the husky line to develop his breed, which became Wright's Aurora Husky."

In fact Ramy looks very much like his grandfather, Gareth Wright, who helped establish the Alaska Dog Mushers Association in the late 1940s. Gareth developed the Wright's Aurora Husky and was not only a legend in Alaska sprint mushing but also ran in the precursor to the Iditarod, the Alaska Centennial race in 1967. Ramy's grandmother, Vera Carter Wright Strack, and his mother, Roxy Wright, were also both champion dog mushers.

When Ramy was four, he won the One-Dog Junior North American Championship, and went on win the race three times in a row. By the time he was fourteen, he had won every junior class, from the one-dog to the seven-dog.

He first ran the Yukon Quest in 1993. As a rookie in 1994, he placed number seventeen in the Iditarod and was also named Rookie of the Year. He took second twice in the Iditarod and in 1999 he won the Yukon Quest. Ramy, like many youths growing up in Alaska's small villages, faced difficulties. When he was sixteen, Ramy experienced profound depression and attempted suicide. His close call as a teen inspired him as an adult to work with the Alaska Mental Health Trust Authority. As a young man, Ramy left Alaska for several years and spent time in the U.S. Navy's nuclear power program. He was selected for an officer program, which led to his attending the University of Washington in Seattle. He never forgot his childhood dream of winning the Iditarod, however, so when the opportunity came for him to return home to Alaska to pursue that dream, he took it. At home, Ramy also joined forces with his sponsors and the Alaska Mental Trust to fight the epidemic of mental illness in Alaska, knowing that if you can make the difference in just one person's life it is worth the effort. In 2002, Doyon ltd. named Ramy Doyon's Citizen of the Year, the fourth generation of a world-renowned dog sled mushing heritage.

In March 2017 in Fairbanks, Ramy shared his story:

I was born in Fairbanks in 1968, the first child of Roxy Wright and Mike Brooks, followed two years later my sister, Tammy. My Native heritage is through my mom's side of the family. My mom's mother is Yup'ik-Aleut and my mom's father is Athabascan.

Since I was young, hunting, fishing, berry picking, and dog mushing have been part of my life. A traditional indigenous lifestyle, by nature, involves hard work, tenacity, and determination. I have always enjoyed calling moose. For many years I hunted with one of my uncles and a close family friend. When we didn't readily see a moose from the boat, as the youngest, I was often tasked with going into the woods and calling in a moose. After several years, they began joking that all they had to do was to drop off their little wolverine and a moose would come in, so my nickname, Little Wolverine, stuck. Later when I was competing in the Kusko 300, Mike Williams Sr. heard this story. He began calling me *Tre'gan-naq*, Yup'ik for "the Little Wolverine."

My earliest memories are of dogs. We lived near Peger Road, in Fairbanks, where my grandpa Gareth had his kennel. I remember going into his Quonset hut with its fragrant smells of dog food and dried fish. I liked to play with the puppies and race in the Junior North American. I won three or four one-dog championships with Mom's leader Sam and then continued racing in the juniors. I got good dogs from Mom and Grandpa, but I had to work to earn the right to race. During junior high and high school,

Roxy Wright mushing with Ramy, ca. 1974.
Courtesy of Roxy Wright.

I got up early to run pups before school. I liked the long runs in the dark, but scooping dog poop was not my favorite. Mom said, "If you're going to race dogs, you have to be dedicated to all aspects of it. Come race time then, you'll have good dogs who depend on you and who will be willing to give more than they might otherwise." If I worked hard, Mom gave me good dogs from her team to run in the Junior North American and the Junior Rondy. I liked the long runs, but I also enjoyed going fast in the sprint races. After Mom ran in the 1983 Iditarod, I daydreamed about winning that big race.

When I was four, my parents got a divorce. My mom remarried and we moved to Rampart. We lived 18 miles upriver in fish camp most of the time. From the age of four to thirteen, I helped train dogs, do chores, and fish in the summer. We either wintered at our fish camp or in Rampart while Mom trained for races during the early winter.

Ramy Brooks and Roxy Wright, ca. 1974.
Courtesy of Roxy Wright.

When we were at camp, my sister and I did school through correspondence, but when we were in the village, we attended the one-room classroom. In January when the races started, we went to Fairbanks where we attended went to public school. We stayed there until after breakup and then returned to camp. I remember the correspondence school teacher traveling from Fort Yukon to bring us books and give us tests. Depending on conditions, he would either come to fish camp in a ski plane or fly to Rampart and travel upriver to us by snowmachine.

In camp we had no electricity, no running water, and of course, no TV. We listened to KJNP for the news. I had no idea about sports icons; my heroes were dog mushers like my mom, my Grandpa Wright, Carl Huntington, and George Attla. Periodically Carl or George would stop by in a boat, sit around the kitchen table or by the campfire, and for hours they'd talk dogs. Those were the people I looked up to. As a little boy, I imagined myself racing in the North American or in the Iditarod.

When I was fourteen, however, I decided I didn't want anything more to do with dogs. As a typical teenager, I saw only the work they required and I felt that they controlled our lives. While others were talking about what TV shows they were watching, I was scooping poop. With other kids, I felt like I didn't belong. Now, looking back, I know that those dog chores were teaching me the importance of hard work. They were an indispensable preparation for when I returned to Alaska to begin racing as an adult. I realized long after scooping all of that poop that cleanliness in a kennel is essential to the health of the dogs. Shoveling the yard is important to maintain the competitiveness of the team because it reduces the spread of disease and worms.

Keeping the yard clean also discourages visits by disease-carrying ravens. In the world of dog racing, winning comes down to attention to detail and to hard work, the latter which is not of particular interest to most teenagers.

When I was seventeen, I moved in with my dad who was living in Fairbanks. When he got a job at a sign shop in Colorado, I went with him and finished my senior year. His work took him to California, where after a few months, I followed him. For several months, I worked a couple of jobs trying to decide what direction I was going in life. I wanted to go to college, but I didn't have the money. I visited the navy recruiter to see if I could get an ROTC scholarship, but instead, I enlisted in the navy's nuclear power program. I was one of the first in my group to qualify for the Broadened Opportunity Officer Selection Training (BOOST) in San Diego. After I finished the program, I went on to attend the University of Washington.

While I was at UW, Mom helped me return to Alaska for the holidays. I had not been back in over six years. She was busy running in the Alpirod, the North American, and the Rondy. While I was home, I helped her run a few puppy teams. Over Christmas dinner, Grandpa Wright said that he wanted someone to run his dogs in the Iditarod. My dream of winning the race was rekindled and I realized how much I missed Alaska. I'd been in Colorado, Florida, Idaho, California, and Washington where the population is more concentrated, a great contrast to rural Alaska. Alaska's vast wilderness provides opportunities that overshadow where I had been. I realized how much I belonged in Alaska. Coming from a village of less than sixty, I didn't fit in those big cities. I was better off in the woods than with hundreds of thousands of people all around me; I was ready to come home.

After I returned to Seattle, I shared my dream of winning the Iditarod with my commanding officer and I asked the navy if I could get a sports leave of absence to run the Iditarod. My commanding officer said that the chances were slim to none but he added, "You have a good record. We'll consider it. Write an application and I'll give my recommendation of approval." About two months later, I got a letter from the Secretary of the Navy that my application had been approved. As I wrapped up the semester and prepared to return home to run dogs spring of 1992, President Clinton was downsizing the military. I was given a choice of staying in and completing the NROTC program or I could leave the navy, but I would not be able to take the sports leave of absence. One of the officers counseling me said, "Serving your country isn't limited to the military. There are other ways to give back: by being a good citizen and also a good role model." What he said stuck with me and helped me decide. I returned to Alaska to pursue my dreams.

L-r: Ramy's grandfather Gareth Wright, unidentified, and Ramy Brooks, Alaska sled dog symposium.

Courtesy of Roxy Wright.

After I got home in 1992, I trained for the Yukon Quest. Initially I started racing dogs from my grandpa's kennel. By 1994 I had my own kennel with dogs largely from Grandpa's and Mom's kennels.

I began my mushing career with a used 1980s dog truck. It was in pretty good shape, or so I thought, but the body was peeling so we painted it. Once on a racing trip, the heater quit working and the windows iced up. Another time, just after the ceremonial start of the Iditarod, the brakes gave out. The next day we had to be in Willow. We pulled into an Eagle River garage for repairs with the dogs still in their boxes. Instead of wasting time fixing bad brakes, I should have been in Willow going through my gear, making sure I was ready to race. Finally, once when we stopped at a gas station, the engine caught fire. My cousin, who was exiting the gas station with a cup of coffee, threw it on the fire and managed to put it out. That old truck became a symbol to me as I focused on not just becoming a musher, but on becoming a successful musher—one who could afford a dependable vehicle.

After I first returned to Alaska, friends told me, "You don't want to run dogs. You'll be broke all the time." But racing is more than running dogs. It must be approached as a business. I had to figure how to make my passion support itself. Long distance mushing has a lot more potential financial reward and public exposure than does sprint racing. I am a big NASCAR fan so I used that example as my business model as drivers not only have to compete, but also be mechanics and balance the books. To compete seriously, I must be able to function as a veterinarian as well as a business manager. Further, I couldn't approach sponsors in a dirty pair of Carhartt pants and expect to be chosen as a spokesperson for their enterprise. To learn more, I went to a seminar in Chicago where I talked to sports marketing people.

As a former machinist mate in the navy's nuclear power program, I was able to get a job in the Prudhoe Bay oil field. From 1993 to 2000, I worked up north, from May through October. During the summers, I focused on making money so I could have my winters free to race. I depended on my wife, Cathy, to take care of the dogs at home. One year, I could not get home for almost five months.

During one of my first Kusko 300s, Jeff King flew by me like I was standing still. That was discouraging, which made me analyze my training program so that my team could be more competitive. I ran the Copper Basin and the Yukon Quest races to learn where and how I needed to improve. Togie Wiehl, a friend from Rampart, handled for me at the Copper Basin. He said it took me forty-five minutes to an hour to bootie my twelve-dog team. The top mushers like Susan Butcher, Martin Buser, and Rick Mackey booted their dogs in fifteen minutes. I began to practice with my dogs, getting them to sit still and not pull at their feet as I put booties on them. I got so I could go through the team, back to front, and have them sitting still, not barking, jumping, or chewing on the line, not making any distractions. Anything done well requires consistency and patience. I asked my competitors questions like, "How do you pack your booties?" They said to fold the Velcro so it was a snap to get the bootie onto the dog. From the Copper Basin race in 1993, when it took me an hour to bootie, fast-forward to a couple of years later when I was able to bootie a sixteen-dog team and pull the snow hook in just twelve minutes.

Training with mushers of my mom's and my uncle Curtis Erhart's caliber helped me a lot. They both not only put in long training runs with me, but they traded off teams with me as well. I read running books on how marathoners did marathons and used those tips to develop my training regimen of run-and-rest to maximize the speed and endurance of my team. Mom emphasized how important it is for a musher to be completely honest with himself so that he can find his weaknesses and improve. He has to analyze a dog's performance and ask, "Is my favorite dog a help or will I go faster by dropping him from the team?" I had good dog people teaching me how to identify weak links. I ran 200- to 300-mile races including the Kuskokwim 300, Copper Basin 300, Tour de Minto, Fire Plug, Sheep Creek Classic, and Henry Hahn 200. Eventually I quit going to the Copper because it didn't fit into my training plan. The Kusko 300 fit better with building the team up to the Iditarod as well as offering good prize money. It served as a training run for me while its prize also covered my expenses of getting there. I really enjoyed being out in the villages again. My first really long-distance race was

Ramy Brooks at Iditarod restart, 1995.

Courtesy of Roxy Wright.

the Yukon Quest in 1993. I used that to qualify me the following year for the Iditarod.

Top long-distance mushers like Susan Butcher, Dee Dee Jonrowe, Martin Buser, and Charlie Boulding, who'd gotten dogs from Mom and Grandpa, let me train with them as I figured the intricacies of distance mushing. As I planned my race strategy, I pondered how much time to allow from one checkpoint to the other to make my scheduled plan. My goal was to win, not to go for a camping trip. I was working with dogs, carrying five-gallon buckets, shoveling the dog yard, cleaning, hooking and unhooking dogs, dragging the trail, in short, putting in long hours—a demanding lifestyle.

In 1993, the first year I ran the Yukon Quest, I weighed about 155 to 160 pounds. To pass a fitness test while in the navy, I ran several miles per day so I was still in pretty good shape. However, in that first Quest, I didn't know how to eat, drink, or rest while competing in a long-distance sled dog race. I lost almost forty pounds in that race because I wasn't eating right. When I crossed the finish line, my clothes were falling off of me. I was down to 130 to 135 pounds.

Before that first Quest, one of the most important things Martin shared with me was to keep the dogs hydrated. After my first 1,000-mile race, I realized that the advice also applied to the musher. I learned to make myself drink and eat even when I was tired and I was not hungry. In order to

Ramy Brooks, 1994 Iditarod Rookie of the Year.
Courtesy of Roxy Wright.

care for the dogs, I had to be at the top of my game, both physically and mentally, which meant I had to have good nutrition and rest just like the rest of the team. A musher is an integral part of the team and if he doesn't take care of himself, he becomes a weak link in the team. A team is only as fast as the slowest dog in the string. I found that traditional foods like salmon strips and moose jerky with fat helped me maintain energy and stay warm.

When I ran the Iditarod as a rookie in 1994, I watched what others did and learned a lot of good lessons that helped me improve over the next several years. At the halfway point in Cripple, I was in ninth or tenth place, not far behind the leaders. Because I was watching the veteran mushers as well as trying to stay on my schedule, I wasn't resting well at checkpoints. By Cripple, I was overly tired and I overslept a couple of hours; a bunch of mushers caught up and passed me. Between Cripple and the finish line in Nome, I dropped several spots, but I managed to get Rookie of the Year and I came in seventeenth. Over the next few years, I learned to race the dogs in front of me—not to worry about the other teams, but to focus on the task at hand.

Looking back on my early years, I am not sure how I made it with some of my gear. Lighter isn't always better. My cold weather gear was lightweight ski clothing. While it looked good, it was not ideal for extreme cold. Somehow I toughed it out, but I ran a lot to stay warm. My sleeping bag met the race regulations' requirements, but I would not use it now. Later I upgraded to a Feathered Friends bag, rated to -50°, which meant that during the dogs' regular rests, I could sleep rather than pace to keep warm. I wore the fur mitts that Mom made because they are warmer than what's available in the store. Depending on conditions, I wore shoepacks or bunny boots. I had a back-up pair of mukluks in my sled since they are lightweight and also warm in extreme cold. I wore custom-made musher hats with Velcro for attaching a headlamp. I carried an extra set of dry gloves, dry socks, booties, wind shell pants, and an overcoat so that if my long johns got wet, I could keep in my body heat while I dried my clothes. I carried spare bolts, electrical tape, hose clamps, pins, a tiny coffee can cooker, and a stock pot for making snow water for dogs (which I kept clean so I could drink water from it also). I kept my load fairly light, clean, and organized. I learned by racing against top mushers, observing and noting what they did.

At the outset of the 1997 Iditarod, my dogs got sick. Only 400 miles into the race at Nikolai, I was down to eight dogs. Trying to make up the difference in the last 600 miles, I was off the sled running. By the time I got to Nome, the bottoms of my feet were black and blue. Even though I finished with only five dogs, I still came in eighth place. That race taught me how to choose dogs. I realized I wanted a team that was fast, but also had endurance. I learned to look a lot closer at the dogs' gaits—to match their pace and their strides so that the animals were evenly matched so the slowest dog could keep up without injury or fatigue. When Mom retired, I got several dogs from her. I decided that a dog that has the stamina to run the required speeds of three days of the Open North American or the Open Fur Rendezvous is the dog I want on my team.

Growing up on the river, I learned how to deal with adverse conditions, from overflow to an extreme temperature drop. During the winter of 1997 to 1998, Dave Monson and Susan Butcher let Cathy, the girls, and me to stay at one of their cabins in Eureka near Manley Hot Springs. On one round-trip training run to Tanana (*Noochu Loghoyet*) and back, I stopped at Joee and Pam Redington's house in Manley. I told Joee my plans so he'd know when to expect my return. When I got out on Fish Lake that night, the wind was blowing so hard I could not stay on the trail. I saw what looked like a light inside of a tent on the far side of the lake. Since it looked like it was about where the trail left the lake, I made for it. We skirted around the southern edge of the lake with the wind continually blowing the team off the trail. By the time we reached the other side the light was gone, but I was still able to find the trail.

At about three in the morning, I arrived at Lester Erhart's home in Tanana. I fed and bedded the dogs down before going inside. We'd had a tough run so I gave all of us a good rest. The next day I called Joee so that no one would come looking for me. Lester sent a snowmachine ahead of me to make sure I got back through Hay Slough okay. Assuming I was all right, he returned to Tanana. However, when I got to Fish Lake, the winds were blowing even harder than the night before.

For almost three hours, the team and I struggled to get across, but to no avail. I managed to get the dogs up onto a small peninsular spit where there were willows and hard-pack snow. I chopped chunks of snow out to build a small snow cave. The dogs and I crawled in and barricaded the mouth with my sled to keep the wind out and to weather the storm. For almost thirteen hours, the wind howled around us. About 3 a.m. it finally quit. I hooked the dogs up and in about ten minutes we were across the lake. Three hours later, we pulled into Joee and Pam's. He said that in another hour he was going to send out a search party. That was one of the worst trail weather situations I have ever seen. Over the years, however, I have raced in conditions that one can't necessarily rehearse: -70°, snowstorms, and ferocious winds on the coast, however with a well-trained dog team, the animals will trust the musher and get him through the tough conditions.

There is a fine line when it comes to having enough gear or not enough. When a musher is miles from the nearest help, he needs to be prepared for whatever he might face. Without proper gear, he could have a life or death situation. Sometimes I have carried more gear than might seem necessary, but given certain situations without it, I could have been in trouble. When crossing frozen water, there is the potential for overflow, so I always carry a backup set of dry clothes. On one of my early Iditarods, I got off the trail and onto some glaciated overflow ice. I managed to stop my dogs and get in front of them but I inadvertently hit a weak spot in the ice and punched through! I caught myself and was able to get out, but I was thoroughly wet. However, I had the necessary gear so I could keep on going. One year when two leaders in the Quest packed light, they got caught in both overflow and extreme cold. They had to scratch because they didn't have a change of clothes.

Competitive sports test an athlete to the core and cause him to dig to find the strength to overcome and to possibly become a champion. During the 1999 Yukon Quest, less than 200 miles from the finish and going into Carmacks, I was in the lead. In town, I was going to give my dogs a full eight-hour rest. Mark May, who had a different philosophy regarding resting his dogs, came in sometime behind me. After a brief respite, Mark went out to bootie his dogs. My dogs had had seven hours' rest, but with the race close to the finish I knew that I could not give May the advantage of another hour of rest for my dogs. A few minutes later I gathered my stuff and went out. When I arrived at my still-loaded sled, but with only eight dogs left, all I had to do was bootie and say, "Let's go!" In eight minutes, after a seven-hour rest, we were off while May still had four or five dogs left to bootie. Practicing booting has paid off. Unfortunately, though, as I left Carmacks

Ramy Brooks.
Courtesy of Roxy Wright.

across a chain of lakes, I could see May gaining on me. With most of the 1000-mile race behind us, I was tired. I began to despair, "I might not have the team; he might have me beat after all." Still, there was enough time for me to regroup and dig within. I reminded myself that I had a special team. Together we'd been leading the majority of the Quest. Most of the race, Pretty Boy had been running as a single lead. I realized I had two aces in the hole. I had a leader, Dillon, who, when he heard his name, would start charging. My other strong suit was that I had not yet asked the team to pick up their pace. I stopped and walked up the line. I snacked the dogs while I moved Dillon up with Pretty Boy. As I walked back to the sled May was within a couple hundred yards of catching me. I pulled my snow hook, whistled to my dogs, and called Dillon by name. He hit his harness hard and I began pulling away from May. Between where he almost caught me and Braeburn, I gained a 45-minute lead on him. All the hard work and training came together that day and I learned how to win.

It takes a lot more to be successful at dog racing than the public may see: a musher must know how to financially support the team, to be more prepared than the next guy, to grab a little rest for musher and the team when rest seems impossible. A musher may say he is willing to sacrifice, but does he want to work sixteen to twenty hours a day, for weeks on end as well as develop relationships with the dog? I only had to ask my dogs to pick up the pace one more time. I pulled away from Mark May and got a lead on him. The last part of the race I let my dogs run at a nice steady pace, but I knew that if he got back within visual range, all I had to do was pick up the pace again. I won the Quest by fifteen minutes.

When I won I remembered what my naval commanding officer had told me, "There are other ways to serve your country: by being a good citizen and by giving back to the community." A couple of friends knew of the struggles that I had had as a teen as well as of my attempted suicide. They asked me if I would consider sharing my story, saying that they felt that there was a lack of male Native role models. They felt I could help make a difference. I struggled with sharing my story because, although years had passed, it was still very raw. I made the decision, with my family, to go public, because what I would share would also affect them. They gave me the okay so I wrote my story, "One Boy's Walk Along the Yukon" and I did a lot of public service announcements (PSAs) for suicide prevention. Since I was affected by alcoholics and also suffered friends and family members committing suicide, I had a platform to share with kids. I worked with the Alaska Mental Health Trust and served on the Children's Trust Board for several years at the request of Gov. Frank Murkowski and two years under Gov. Sarah Palin. The work that I did with my sponsor to speak to kids and the PSAs that I did for the Alaska Mental Health Trust were some of the most rewarding work that I have ever done.

The year after I won the Quest we returned to the Iditarod with a strong team and with Pretty Boy in the lead, but as it turned out, I was the weak link in the team. As the Iditarod began, I had a bad cold but it kept getting worse. Early on, the team was one of the fastest, but due to my condition, my time-proven run-rest template got altered, resulting in undesirable pushes that ultimately slowed my team down. I took my twenty-four-hour layover earlier than desirable so I could see a doctor in Takotna. I got a shot of prednisone so I could breathe better. When I left, I was feeling pretty good, but my sled broke just out of Ophir. I had to make an unscheduled stop there to do repairs, which threw me off the schedule. I saw the health aides in several more villages and each time, I was given a different antibiotic. Considering all the problems I had, it was a pretty incredible team because we came in fourth. At the banquet, I received the Most Improved Musher and the Sportsmanship awards. However after I crossed the finish line in Nome, I went straight to the emergency room where I was diagnosed with pneumonia. Since then, I have had it two more times. Due to prolonged exposure to the cold air and from pushing myself too hard, I have sports-induced asthma, which is triggered by cold air.

In 2001, Pretty Boy developed a thyroid problem, which I treated with medication. I see now that he was my "security blanket" even though I knew he probably couldn't keep up. Sure enough on the Iditarod, forty miles out of Willow, I had to carry him into the first checkpoint at Yentna, where I had to send him home. I took a dog that I shouldn't have when I could have taken a stronger dog. Right off, I was down a dog. A musher must be totally honest and choose the dogs that during training have demonstrated their abilities. As we left the Iditarod's halfway point, weather moved in. The wind was blowing and a couple of inches of snow was falling per hour. Visibility was poor as we traveled down the Yukon and around the coast. Sometimes we couldn't even see our leaders. Vern Halter, Hans Gatt, Charlie Boulding, and I took turns breaking trail. We were pushed to our limits, but our hardships as well as our dreams forged us into a front to be reckoned with. When

Ramy Brooks, 2001 Iditarod.

Courtesy of Roxy Wright.

I thought I had nothing left to give, my aspirations kept me going. When we got to Koyuk, the weather improved.

With every race, I learned more how to improve.

After I came in second in the 2002 Iditarod, I knew the mistakes I'd made. The next year, as the race began in Fairbanks, I was more determined than ever. I entered the race with a team of dogs I felt was my best ever. I felt my goal of winning was within my grasp. As we left Fairbanks, I sensed the team was coming together at the right time, however on the run from Manley to Tanana, the team seemed a little bit off. As we left Tanana, the dogs began coming down with a virus. Poor trail conditions south of the Alaska Range had caused the race to be on the northern route that year, hence Ruby was still early in the race. I dropped off two sick dogs in Ruby, but I was able to keep to my planned schedule of a five and a half hour rest. I left the village in fourth place and headed down the trail to Galena. That run was tough. I had more dogs come down with the stomach bug. I loaded one of my strongest dogs into the sled, but he was so sick he threw up all over my gear.

As I neared Galena, I decided to stop for my 24-hour layover. Before the race started, our vet said he'd seen a bad bug going around, but he didn't think it would last long. I treated the dogs for the gut flu and got them bedded in a quiet spot, and then I began cleaning my gear so it would be dry when we woke. I got some good sleep and then started to hash out a couple of different plans of how to best run the rest of the race. I bounced ideas off Paul Gebhardt, and told him it all depended on how the team came out of the layover. As I left Galena in fifty-fourth place, I thought, "We'll see how this run goes. If it takes over four hours to get to Nulato, I'll stop and rest but if it's only four, I'll go to Kaltag where I'll take my eight-hour layover." It usually takes four and half to five hours to get to Nulato so I set my goal at four hours, but I made it there in two hours, fifty minutes. All of a sudden, I went from thinking, "I am totally out of this race" to "We still have a shot to get back in."

That year the trail went down the Yukon River and turned around in Anvik, then back up the river on the normal southern route to the finish in Nome. As I returned upriver, we started passing teams head-on in the dark, a couple of the teams called out to me, "Go get 'em, Jeff!" I answered back, "This ain't Jeff!" (They thought I was Jeff King chasing Robert Sorlie.) I went from fifty-fourth place to second. I kept the dogs on a regimented run-rest schedule. At Koyuk, Robert Sorlie was resting, but I caught him and passed. However, his lead was a little too much for me, but I gave it my all. There were other teams that hadn't been that far behind Sorlie, but essentially, they gave up. I finished two-and-half hours behind Sorlie and I took second for the second year in a row. A musher can't give up. He has to really want what he's going after, whether it's the satisfaction of running the race or of winning. He has to keep his goal in sight, work hard, and his dreams can come true.

A couple of years later, Sorlie had a slight lead on me, but leaving Takotna, we both had a six-hour lead on the rest of the field. We stopped at Don's Cabin en route to the race's halfway point, Iditarod, where we planned to take our 24-hour layover. I was going to rest briefly at the cabin since it was only five and half hours to Iditarod. To maintain my team's speed, it was important to not do super long runs and to follow each one with rest. While napping at the cabin, a group of snowmachiners with paddle tracks went through and destroyed the top crust of the trail. Since that section does not regularly see a lot of traffic, there was no base. When we got back on the trail, the dogs were swimming in sugar snow up to their bellies. It was very discouraging. A run that should've taken five hours took over ten. Our six-hour lead evaporated. My young team looked back at me like, "What are you doing to us?" We persevered while I adjusted on the fly and we managed to salvage a fourth-place finish. When a musher thinks he has it all figured out, Mother Nature throws a wrench in the plans. The team that adapts best wins. Sorlie managed to stay out in front and he won by thirty minutes.

The next year when we trained, I made the team break trail on really tough, long runs. My team always had speed. I ran them fast, but rested them long so that they could maintain their pace. However as I trained them to break trail, it became a real struggle. Their strength of speed was suddenly gone; they were a different team. It's critical for a musher to know and preserve his team's strengths while trying to eliminate the weaknesses. After I realized I didn't want to sacrifice my team's strong point, it was a while before I could retrain speed back into them. I wanted my dogs to travel at least as fast as they'd shown they could.

I ran the Iditarod thirteen times; I only skipped 1999 when I won the Yukon Quest. Each year when one race finished, I began preparations for the next one. We spent the spring and summer working with sponsors and planning how to improve our training and breeding programs. In the fall as temperatures dropped, we alternated training with fishing to get our dog food in for the winter. As snow began to fly, we focused on getting miles on the dogs so they'd be ready for the Iditarod. I planned my food drops and packed carefully so I could quickly find what I needed at checkpoints. As I filled my drop bags, I made a master list that I kept in a book. In it I also had my prospective schedule that I'd consult at each checkpoint. If an item was at the top of my food list it meant it was in the top of the bag and if at the bottom of the list, it was at the bottom of the bag. At each checkpoint, I could quickly cut into a bag and find what I needed in seconds.

To be competitive requires veterinary care, quality dog food, proven bloodlines, and good gear. We maintained a kennel of fifty to seventy-five dogs. Some of my favorite leaders over the years included Bean, Risk, Pretty Boy, Speckles, and Bruce; they were exceptional dogs who had incredible personalities. We kept older retired dogs for breeding and for training young dogs, as well as a core of race dogs, yearlings, and puppies. In the years when I was finishing in the top ten, the kennel cost us about $200,000.00 per year. As dogs aged, it was essential to maintain our bloodlines by developing young dogs. Sometimes there were lag periods of a couple of years as we waited for puppies to mature. Maintaining a continuous core dog team could be a struggle. Typically, teams will go on a winning streak for several years and then fall off because they didn't, or couldn't, replace the aging dogs.

After I ran the 100-year anniversary race of the All Alaska Sweepstakes from Nome to Candle in 2008 I decided to go to school for Geological Engineering and Geology. I was looking for a less demanding physical lifestyle as well as for a retirement. However the demanding rigor of what lay ahead of me in returning to college made me joke later and say I'd run the Quest and the Iditarod to prepare me for college. Going after an engineering and geology degree turned out to mean six years of a nonstop demanding schedule, working long hours, and getting very little sleep to complete projects and papers. I had to study hard and budget my time. At the outset

Ramy Brooks with his lead dog talking with school children.
Courtesy of Roxy Brooks.

a double degree seemed like an impossible dream, but I'd gone from being a rookie to winning the Quest, so I knew that anything was possible. Looking too far ahead can be so overwhelming that a person may quit. Focus on one simple task, then the next, and soon, a goal can be realized.

Even though I was in school, we still maintained our kennel. We figured I'd return to racing once I finished school. Some friends used some of our dogs in their teams. Ramey Smyth had a couple when he came in second in the 2011 Iditarod. Our oldest daughter, Abby, wanted to run the Junior Iditarod in 2012 and 2013. After Abby finished the Junior Iditarod in 2013, Mom speeded the dogs up and took them to Yellowknife where she again had a strong showing.

In 2014, I was almost finished with my degrees in geological engineering and geology and was thinking of returning to racing. John Dixon and I talked about us alternating, taking turns racing every other year. However as the Iditarod neared, I was overwhelmed by helping John train, going to school, working as an operator at Usibelli Coal Mine, and trying to maintain my family life. I realized I couldn't do everything; I had to prioritize my life. I was tired of being tired. My priority was my family and I knew that after graduation, I'd have a full-time job. As much as I wanted to race, I realized that I couldn't hold a job and be a competitive musher as well as give preeminence to my family. It wouldn't have been fair to my family or to my dogs. After John finished the Iditarod, Cathy and I sold the team to Grant Beck, a family friend, with the understanding that if we ever wanted to get back into dogs, we only had to call him.

My advice to a young musher today is that, like me, you may come from a village, but if you approach your dream with focus and dedication, you can achieve your goal. It won't be easy but nothing is and everything worth having comes down to hard work and attention to detail. I would also encourage a young musher to pursue an education so that he has the necessary tools to achieve his dreams. An education is one of the athlete's rungs on a ladder toward achieving his goal. Each step is another rung on that ladder.

Like other professional athletes, mushers have to dedicate the required time to train to be competitive. Many mushers get sponsorships and endorsements from businesses that expect to see a return on their investment. Often they will require a written contract and spell out their expectations. Success for a musher requires a team of people to put these essential parts together, to create and market an image to sell to a sponsor.

Racing isn't ten days out of the year; it's 365 days, year after year. During the few days of the race, the musher is in the spotlight. After the race, the company may require speaking tours, personal appearances at company promotions, and production of TV and radio commercials, which can become demanding and a job in itself, taking too much time away from the kennel. It is critical to find a balance.

There are other ways to consider how to support one's mushing dreams. Does he or she want to get into tourism or to offer camping trip tours?

A dog person has to love it and love requires commitment, vision, and innovation. The sled dog circuit is big business. In approaching a sponsor, a musher is saying, "Help me get down the trail," but the musher needs to be thinking, "What can I do to help my sponsor get a return on his investment?" It's a full-circle system. Each player's role must be understood and respected by the other but the reward is attainable.

Two days before the 2019 Alaska Federation of Natives convention, Ramy's legendary grandfather, Gareth Wright, passed away October 14, a man who helped found Alaska sled dog racing and who also ran in the precursor to the Iditarod, the Alaska Centennial Race of 1967. Above all, Gareth Wright was a devoted husband, father, and grandfather, and served as a loving mentor to young Ramy Brooks.

Chapter 12

THERE'S AN ATTLA RUNNING THE IDITAROD AND HIS NAME ISN'T GEORGE!

Gary Attla, Iditarod, 1981.
Courtesy of Gary Attla.

In 1958 when the two sprint dogsled championships, the Fur Rondy World Championship Sled Dog Race in Anchorage and the Open North American Championship in Fairbanks, were at their height, when hundreds of fans thronged the streets, an unknown Athabascan with a fused leg, George Attla of Huslia came to town. Despite having grown up isolated with tuberculosis in hospitals and far from home, George Attla, the Huslia Husler, found his way in life by taking on competitive sled dog mushing, which he dominated then for decades.

The year before George Attla caught the attention of the sprint racing circuit, his oldest son, Gary Stanley Attla, was born to him and to George's wife Shirley Oldman Vent in Hughes on the Koyukuk River. Gary's maternal grandparents were Abraham and Martha Oldman of Hughes and his paternal grandparents were George, Sr. (1901 to 1969) and Eliza Ragan Attla (1909 to 1990). "In that time, no one went to the hospital, they just had their kids in the village." Gary said. "When I was born, my dad got himself one heck of a dog handler!"

Before Gary Attla shared his story, family historian, George Yaska, Jr. set the stage of how life was in the Koyukuk and Kobuk river valleys before the gold rush. Later in the narrative, George shared the story of prospectors Ragan and Bifelt as told by grandmother Madeline. He began:

George Yaska on Koyukuk River history

Our great grandfather, Old Man Attla, had the proper name of *Taahts'etseghonh*, but he was usually called, *No'etł*. He was born in 1861 and grew up on the Kobuk River[1]. We know nothing about his parents, which is strange, but we do know the name of his mother, *Yendzehtl*, and his maternal aunt, *Yaanohodaało'*.

---

1   which, in modern times, is mostly Inupiaq

"Old Man Attla," No'etł, and his wife Annie, may be Hughes, ca. 1920.
Courtesy of George and Marie Yaska.

Well before *No'etł's* time, half of the Kobuk River was Athabascan, from the headwaters to Ambler. There was a good deal of trading back and forth. Men from the Kobuk River had kids on the Koyukuk River and vice versa so it wasn't unheard of for a person to be both Inupiaq and Athabascan, which *No'etł* may've been. There were also Athabascans in the Brooks Range at the head of the Noatak and Colville rivers, but after many battles, they were almost totally vanquished, resulting in the Kobuk Athabascans returning to the Koyukuk River. When he was only two, *No'etł's* mother and siblings drowned so he was raised by his grandfather. His grandfather was already raising a child *Yaghoyinaatlno* or Madeline. *No'etł* had a habit of hanging onto his adopted father's pant legs, causing his grandfather to have to keep stepping over him, like crossing a beaver dam. His "dad" nicknamed him *No'etł*, beaver dam. His name may have sounded to the 1909 U.S. Census recorder like "Attla" so his name was documented as Attla. *No'etł* had a big build and a beard, more like an Inupiaq than an Athabascan. His wife was *Seenlot'eyh* or Annie Attla, but we refer to her as Mrs. Old Man Attla; she was born in 1864. Together they had eight children including George Attla, Sr. who was born in 1901 as documented by Jesuit missionary and ethnographer Jules Jetté.

About 1894 the Koyukuk people began to migrate to Old Man River (off the Koyukuk River) just below Allakaket and Arctic City, following the game. As the people traveled looking for caribou or fish, they lived in half-subterranean sod and pole houses. For the most part, they did not live in settled villages, but there was a big one at Dulbi[2] and they also sometimes

---

2   Dulbi *Denaakk'e* name was *Dulbaakkaakk'et.*

congregated around an 1899-1901 military post at Rampart, built to protect a supply cache for gold miners.

In 1913, Kobuk Inupiat came down to Arctic City to celebrate the coming of the new year. Old Man Attla, who was the local chief of the Koyukon Athabascan, could see things were starting to get heated between Eskimos and Indians so he called for wrestling matches. That particular sport relied on little action, but rather on one burst of movement. The winner of each match advanced while losers would drop out. The men began getting rougher and rougher; it looked like a battle might soon erupt. The youth didn't realize it, but the elders did. One older gentleman was aware that there were ten loaded .22s pointed at his back. Great Grandpa threw a curve ball and called out, "Women's turn!" Great Aunt Bessie, a sister of Eliza Ragan, who later became George Attla, Jr.'s mother, was seventeen and she was in the best shape of her life. She jumped up; she wanted to beat everyone! She began wiping out opponents and everyone thought she'd be the grand champion, but someone pointed to an old Athabascan woman, *Neegedzoos*, who, in her day, had been pretty strong. Onlookers called out, "She hasn't wrestled yet." Aunt Bessie could've ignored this challenge, but she thought, "She's old; I can beat her." She grabbed the woman, but discovered it was like grabbing iron. Suddenly she was on her back and looking up at the sky. The old woman, *Neegedzoos*, became the reigning champ, but more importantly, a tense situation had been defused and a battle averted.

During his lifetime, *No'etł* saw monumental changes. Between 1887 and 1906, 1500 prospectors and miners arrived in the Koyukuk on seventy small steamers. They brought unknown diseases to us. The summer of 1902 became *K'enaalnonh de saanh*, "People Die That Summer." The influx of outsiders brought other kinds of trouble as well.

At that time two prospectors, Ned Ragan and Victor Bifelt [3], were in the same area, competing for firewood for the steamboats and for fur. A medicine man had told our great-grandma Madeline (*Yeghoyenaatlno*), who'd been married before, (and who was referred to as "Old Mama" in *Shadows on the Koyukuk* by Sidney Huntington) that she could not marry again, a warning she chose to ignore. For five years, she lived then with Ned Ragan in their cabin across the Hog River (Hogatza River off the Koyukuk).

In 1909, Madeline gave birth to her youngest daughter, Eliza Ragan, who later became George Attla, Jr.'s mother.

Madeline's oldest daughter Anna was married to Victor Bifelt. Later great grandma Madeline told the following story to her younger daughter Sophie Sam:

---

3   Spelled "Karl Viktor Bifaldt" in the census record

Potlatch George Attla, Sr. gave for his father, Old Man Attla at Hughes: Sammy Sam, Mary John, Chief John, Johnny Oldman, Neeneeyo *(Little Beatus),* Chief Henry, *George Attla, Sr., 1925, Koyukuk River.*

Courtesy of George Yaska, Jr.

Both Ned Ragan and Victor Bifelt had stores. Bifelt's was upriver and had high prices. Ragan's was at the mouth of the Koyukuk and had reasonable prices. It was said that Bifelt was greedy and wanted "it all." Bifelt made repeated assertions that he was going to kill Ragan. Finally, he left his cabin even though his wife, Anna, tried to stop him. He arrived at Ragan's cabin, who saw Bifelt reach for a rifle, and then say, "I'm going to kill you." Bifelt looked through Ragan's windows, saying, over and over, "I'm going to kill you". Ragan had enough and he went out and shot Bifelt. Madeline's son, Frank and Anna, Bifelt's wife, as well as an important Iñupiaq Kobuk River trader, *Silaayuk,* were witnesses to the murder. Later that fall, a marshall came upriver. He arrested Ragan and took him and the three witnesses, Anna Bifelt (and her children), Madeline's son Frank and *Silaayuk,* to Nome, where the three were questioned in a trial that lasted most of the winter. Throughout that time, the court paid the witnesses. Finally, before spring, Ragan was acquitted. According to this very detailed account by Grandma Madeline to her younger daughter Sophie Sam, Madeline's oldest daughter, Anna, Bifelt's wife, did not walk home from Nome to the Koyukuk River (contrary to *Shadows on the Koyukuk*). The court bought four dogs for Anna and her children, Edith and Fred, and her brother Frank to return home.

At home on the Koyukuk, Sophie remembered that throughout the winter the family didn't know what was going on. They waited throughout the long months for brother Frank and sister Anna Bifelt and her children, Edith and Fred (nickname for Alfred), to return home. One night, Madeline (Anna and Sophie's mother) had a dream that they were coming home. In the morning, she looked out and saw her granddaughter Edith running down the trail to her, ahead of the team and the rest of the family. The four dogs lived with the family for many years. One of them, Jack, who was white with black markings, was Sophie's favorite and became hers.

According to *Shadows on the Koyukuk*, Ragan later returned to the Koyukuk where he tried to reconnect with Madeline, but she was not inter-ested. For a short time, Ragan had a store on the Yukon River, at 22 mile below Kaltag. Madeline Solomon, born in 1905, said she and her parents once stopped at Ragan's Kaltag store, where her parents bought her a wide ribbon. Ragan's grandniece, the late June Dietrich, recalled that Ragan used to walk the beach in California and remember his daughter Eliza Ragan (Attla) in Alaska.

Nine years after the trial in Nome, Anna Bifelt became the mother of Sidney and Jimmy Huntington.

As the daughter of Ned Ragan, growing up with no father in the community of Dulbi (near Huslia) was hard on Madeline's youngest daughter, Eliza. However as a good athlete, at sixteen, she set her sights on winning a .22 special, the first place prize for the women's local sled dog race. As soon as she was eligible, she entered, and raced from Dulbi east along the Dulbi River to its confluence with the Koyukuk River, which she crossed and then returned to Dulbi village. She handily won the race and for the rest of her life, treasured her .22 rifle.

Chief Billy McCarty, Jr. once told me that his dad, Billy McCarty, Sr., wanted to marry Eliza, but his cousin George Attla, Sr. advised him,

Eliza Ragan Attla and George Attla, Sr., ca. 1938, Koyukuk River.
Courtesy of George Yaska, Jr.

"Cousin, don't marry her. She's lazy." That fall Eliza, nineteen years old, married George Attla, Sr., who'd outfoxed his cousin Billy McCarty! Together George and Eliza raised nine children including George Attla, Jr., born in 1933.

There's an Attla Running the Iditarod and It's Not George: Gary Attla

George Attla, Jr.'s son, Gary Attla, picked up the narrative, sharing his life as an early Iditarod dog musher and the oldest of seven children of world-renowned George Attla, Jr., whom Gary affectionately calls "the ol' man." Gary remembered:

Grandpa was a good trapper who relied on his dog team. After he and Eliza married, they took their boat

April 29th is George Attla Jr. Day

If there was a word to describe the late George Attla Jr. it would be "champion." He was known across Alaska as just that; a champion of Dog mushing, of the traditional lifestyle, and for Native Alaskans.

Born in 1933 at a fish camp just below Koyukuk on the Yukon River, George was raised in a subsistence lifestyle, fishing and hunting off of the land with his family. By the 1950s George had already became a legendary open-class sprint dog racer. His name was known and respected throughout the world. Known as the "Huslia Hustler" Attla Jr. won countless races and was even inducted into the first Alaska Sports Hall of Fame and later named the Best Musher of the 20th Century.

Governor Steve Cowper proclaimed April 29, 1988 as "George Attla Day" and Tanana Chiefs Conference felt it was important to also recognize his multiple accomplishments and

TANANA CHIEFS CONFERENCE • THE COUNCIL NEWSLETTER

Tanana Chiefs Conference honored the late George Attla on George Attla Day, April 29, 2015.

Courtesy of Gary Attla.

up Dulbi Slough where they built "First Cabin." After the local trader Joe Notti moved to Cutoff, the Attlas followed in 1927. Grandpa's trapline camps included Upper Cabin near Bear Mountain, which was fifty miles from Huslia and Lumber Cabin, mid-way down, and First Cabin, fifteen miles from Huslia. During the summers, my grandparents set up fish camp. At that time, boats were 35 feet long with 3-foot sides. My grandpa made his own boats, which he ran with a steamboat motor. They were slow, but they never broke down. He liked to have a drink now and then. When my cousin Vincent Yaska Jr. was a kid at fish camp with Grandma and Grandpa, Grandpa decided to go socialize one evening in Nulato. After a few hours when he didn't return, Grandma got worried. She sent young Vincent in his boat downstream to look for Grandpa. He saw Grandpa's boat floating on the current. Naturally he was alarmed. He pulled up alongside and saw Grandpa lying inside his boat. Grandpa then popped up, looked around, and asked, "Which way is upstream?" All three of us like to joke, Grandpa, Dad, and I. Sure, he knew which way was upstream.

During the summer when I was older, we lived at a fish camp twenty miles below Huslia on a rock bluff on the north bank. We stayed there for a couple of years, but the banks were steep. Grandpa made a fish compacter to make transporting his dried fish easier at the end of every season. With that device, he could squeeze his dried fish into a tight bundle that he lashed then on his boat rack. As he slowly chugged his load of fish back up the river, his dogs would run alongside the beach. Every two or three years, my grandparents would move their fish camp, which was strange because it was a lot of work.

Gary's mother, Shirley Attla Vent.
Courtesy of Gary Attla.

When I was about eleven, my parents divorced. A few years later, I went trapping between Huslia and Galena with my uncles Barney Attla, who was sixteen years older, and Vincent Yaska Sr., who was in his mid-seventies.

In the late fall after we'd built a trap cabin, Vincent, Barney, and I went bear hunting up the Koyukuk with Barney's small boat and 50 h.p. motor. We walked the ridges above the sandbars. He found a hole where he knew there was a bear inside getting ready to den. Uncle Barney said he'd show me how to trick the bear to come out. He pumped his feet on the ground like he was walking away. The bear jumped up and at five feet, Barney shot it with his .22 pistol between the eyes. Since it was fall, the bear was nice and fat. Unfortunately, we'd left our rope in the boat so we had nothing to pull the bear out with but my new leather belt, which snapped in half. We walked back to the boat, got the rope and dragged the bear out. After we gutted, skinned, and quartered it, and we packed meat and skin to camp. Uncle Barney drove his boat onto the shore ice where we drydocked it for the winter. We had a new cabin and fresh meat so we were set. Uncle Vincent said, "I'll show you how to make cheese." He cut out a one-foot section of bear gut and stuffed it with belly fat. He wrapped it around a spit and turned it slowly over the fire all night till all the grease dripped off. When it was cold, then he sliced it thinly and put it on Sailor Boy Pilot Bread. It was like eating cheese, only better.

I learned a lot that winter from late Uncle Vincent including how to read the weather. If I saw a ring around the moon, it meant cold weather was coming. Growing up, I learned to always be on the look out for overflow, a particular threat in the cold. He told me that if my dogs went through water to get their booties off immediately or their paws could become encased in ice.

The summer I was sixteen I fought fire. That fall, Mom and I bought a 12 h.p. snowmachine and a .30-06 and we went trapping.

During the building of the Alyeska Pipeline, Dad married Karen Manook. When I was seventeen in 1974, he began working on the construction of the Yukon River Bridge. He got a six-and-half acre homestead in North Pole where we kept our sixty Alaska huskies that weighed 45 to 50 pounds each and were strong. At that time, it cost us about $7,000 a year to feed Kasco commercial dog food, horsemeat, and fish.

Yeah, Dad knew he had a darned good dog handler in me. In Judy

Foreground: George Attla, Jr., followed by son Gary Attla, Fur Rondy, ca. 1978.

Courtesy of Gary Attla.

Ferguson's *Windows to the Land, Vol. Two,* the ol' man said, "In those days, we took my brothers' and sisters' kids in. At one time, I had twelve boys out at North Pole but I never had any problem with any of them. This went on for years. I couldn't take all those boys with me on the road so I left my oldest son, sixteen-year-old Gary, in charge. I left them a truck and a Greer tank with five hundred gallons of gas and grocery money. When I came back, they always had some gas and money left. They never got into any trouble. They were taking care of my dog kennel, particularly the young pups. That couldn't be done with youngsters today." Some of those kids included Wayne Attla, Glen Sam, and Ralph Bifelt.

A mile below the Yukon River Bridge on a friend's Native allotment, we set up fish camp so that while the ol' man was working, we could get dog food for the winter. One early summer day, dressed in their best clothes, my sisters flew in from Huslia to Fairbanks. The ol' man picked them up and took them directly to fish camp where they spent all summer in their city slicker clothes. They still laugh about that. We caught a lot of fish that summer. We had two fishwheels, that the ol' man and I built, and three boats. With the dogs and family there, it was crazy fun.

After I finished high school, I lived all winter with my Uncle Alfred Attla and my Aunt Helen in Hughes. I trapped with Alfred between Hughes and Huslia. In March when my uncle went to Fairbanks to race, my cousin Harold and I stayed in camp fifty miles below Hughes for three weeks where we checked traps.

That spring, Dad asked me to handle for him at the Rondy. The race began on 4th Avenue in downtown Anchorage. I was twenty and it was finally legal for me to go in bars, which were calling my name, but I could never get away from the ol' man. He kept an eye out. However Saturday night I sneaked away and went home with a lady friend. The next morning, I woke up to the radio announcing,

Making the movie Spirit of the Wind, *Ely, Mn., 1978.*
Courtesy of Amanda Attla.

"George Attla just left the starting line!" Oh, no, I was his main handler. I asked the lady, "Do you have any money?" "No," she answered. I went outside, trying to figure out where I was: 68th Avenue, a long way from downtown Anchorage! Worse, it was the last and most important day of the race and it was a Sunday. I began walking and running all the way downtown. When I got there I heard the PA system say that George Attla was just turning from Cordova onto 4th. I ran to the finish line, jumped onto one runner and he was on the other. As we crossed the finish line, the ol' man looked down at his watch, then looked at me and said, "You're goldurned lucky I won." Later I told him, I'd run sixty-eight blocks and he'd done only 30 miles!

In the spring when the ol' man and I went on the race circuit, we were working on his movie, *Spirit of the Wind* (SOW). He thought that Ely, Minnesota was the right place to film the reenactment of the Fur Rendezvous because Ely looked the most like 1958 Anchorage. For the movie, we set up trails, hooked up dogs, and on demand, I turned the team around. We made a circular racetrack, but in the movie, the audience couldn't tell it was not a straight course. Trot, the lead dog, who played Dad's winner Jarvie, was smart. We only had to tell her a thing once and every time, she did what she was told. We raced in Ely for a month, had a great time, and met wonderful people whom I'll never forget. Later when the movie was shown at France's Cannes Film Festival, Dad and the producers rode around in a Cadillac with a giant moose horn mounted on the front!

Gary Attla with lead dog Trot, Iditarod, 1981.

Courtesy of Gary Attla.

In 1980 my dad asked me to come to Fairbanks to help him. He asked if I'd be interested in running the Iditarod. He had a lot of dogs and many of them weren't being used.

I was twenty-three, strong, and I ran every day. There wasn't a thing wrong with me. I bet my dad I could run the Fairbanks Equinox race, which was over twenty-six miles and climbed 3285-feet, one of the world's most difficult marathons. Giving me incentive, he said, "I'll bet you fifty dollars you can't!" Without really training for it, I signed up. For the last two miles, my stepmother, Karen, and my little sister Dooby (Amanda) drove along beside me, asking, "Don't you want a ride back to the university?" "No way!" I told them. I wasn't about to give up and I won fifty bucks off the 'ol man!

In 1980 I had about twenty dogs, some from sprint mushers Don Andon and the late Bernie Turner; the rest were the ol' man's. My lead dog, Trot, had once been Uncle Alfred's dog, but during the 1970s the 'ol man bought her for the record amount of $2750. She won a bunch of races for him. When she went with me on the Iditarod, she was about six or seven years old and she made it all the way to Safety, almost to Nome. She was smart, real smart, and could stay up in front of the team. In 1981 when I began training for the race, I ran two teams a day. I'd take the first one forty miles down and then, forty miles back. I'd leave from eight-mile Badger, go down to the flood control project, on to the Tanana River, and then to over to Dennis Krisman's house in the Salcha, where they gave me tea and lunch. When I got home, I'd gone eighty miles in eight hours. After a brief rest, I hooked up my second team and ran twenty-five more miles in two hours. I did this every day, five times a week. We always worked as a team. Dad did the planning and I did the training. My main dog handler was my cousin Alfred Attla, Jr. aka "Duna." He and my other handler Bob

McAlpine cooked all the dog food, kept the dog yard clean, trimmed the dogs' nails and put booties on them. I assembled food both for me and for the dogs. Preparing for the Iditarod took every minute of every day. After the race I learned that potatoes should not be packed with ready-to-cook steaks. The spuds froze and they got black and soft. I learned a lot of things. My maternal grandmother Martha Oldman gave me wolf mitts and my paternal grandmother Eliza gave me mukluks[4] and a beaver skin hat. Ron Yatlin's mother-in-law, Elsie Pitka of Beaver, said she didn't want to see her Native people running the Iditarod with Sorel boots patched with duct tape so she gave me a brand new pair of size 10 Sorels.

In Willow before the race, I stayed with the former announcer for the Rondy, Earl Norris and his wife, Natalie Norris. They had over 100 mala-mutes and a lot of dog handlers. He suggested I lash and screw a one-inch thick by two-foot plastic runner around the front of my wooden bumper to protect my sled from smashing into trees.

I ran sixteen dogs with a double lead: Trot and Dandy, a former dog of Alfred Attla's used by Warner Vent in the Iditarod. That year, the race went through Knik. I was nervous about the upcoming nine-mile hill that had a steep plunge. As we flew downhill, I dug my foot into the brake with its two prongs digging into the snow but it wasn't enough. I wanted desperately to let go, but we were going too fast. I was banging into trees so to avoid them I began dragging my foot on the far side where there were no trees so we made it down okay. My shoulders and legs were strong, but with sixteen dogs pulling forward, it was all I could do to pull the buried snow hook out of the hardpack trail.

Out of Knik, the dogs ran steadily all the way to Yentna. I'd started pretty far in the back so I didn't know yet who was ahead of me. As we caught up, I began to identify mushers. As I came up on Bud Smyth, his part-wolf dog kept trying to get my dogs or me. It was legal then to haul a second sled with rested dogs for back up. A musher could swap his tired dogs for rested ones, and if needed, have an extra sled available. However this meant that every night, the musher had to take booties off of sixteen plus nine back up dogs, totaling 100 feet to take care of. Then the musher had to feed himself and his dogs. Maybe he got an hour or two of sleep. For a while I traveled with Emmitt Peters and Susan Butcher, but the latter soon left me in the dust.

A day and half later, we approached the Alaska Range: eighteen miles up a gradual climb and five miles down into Dalzell Gorge, where lots of water was running under deceptive shell ice, masking a deep bowl a musher wanted desperately to avoid. My brake had four little stove bolts holding it

---

4   Mukluk in *Denaakk'e* "*kkaakene.*"

Gary Attla, Rainy Pass check-point, Iditarod, 1981.
Courtesy of Gary Attla.

together and as we skidded down the gorge, my brake broke completely. I didn't wind up in the deep bowl, but with a shot brake, I barely made it to Rohn River. My new Sorels had a hole in them from riding the brake so long and so hard.

Right before dark, I arrived at the Rohn, where many including Susan and Emmitt were taking their break. I found some minimal stove bolts and did a temporary jury-rig job on my brake but I needed better bolts. After taking a 24-hour rest at Rohn, my dogs were crazy to go. While I was hooking up my fourteen dogs, my wheel dog chewed the three-quarter-inch nylon towline in half. Not realizing it when I took off, all became chaos. Mushers grabbed my sled and held it while others grabbed the towline and dug in to hold the loose dogs. I found my splicer and wove the towline back together while my forward dogs were screaming to go and others behind me were doing the same, but all the dogs were finally connected back to the sled. They took off then like a bat out of hell. To slow them down, I was dragging my snow hook, but it caught a tree root, and that thick line snapped in half! Again when I mashed my brake, everyone grabbed my sled and this time, I spliced my snowhook line back together, but by then, it was getting dark. I was a little worried because I'd be crossing the river with no light, and in some places, there was open water. As I went, I thought, "Man, I must've gone twenty miles on the east side of the river. The trail has to cross the river somewhere around here." It seemed to turn left but the one I was on, a snowmachine trail, went straight. I told Trot, my primary lead dog, "haw!" [left] My headlamp was getting dim and I could hear water running. I held the brake but Trot wouldn't turn left like I told her to. She could hear the running water and she stayed straight on the trail. I let her have her head and we safely crossed the Rohn. I realized then that she'd known it was the right path all along. That dog was so smart and she wouldn't listen to me. She knew where the trail was even if I didn't.

For the next sixty miles, I was on glare ice and bare ground, slamming and skidding all over. To slow my team down, I unhooked twelve of my fourteen dogs' tuglines so they were pulling only by their necklines, but then, we slammed into willows and tree staubs (stubs) on curves and ricocheted off them like a ball in a runaway pinball machine. The dogs ran like that for forty miles and they wouldn't slow down.

Six hours after crossing the Rohn, frontrunners Emmitt Peters and Susan Butcher had taken the wrong trail. Unknowingly, they'd gone

George Attla waiting Gary, McGrath, 1981.
Courtesy of Gary Attla.

down someone's trapline corridor for four hours, which cost them eight hours round-trip! At the intersection of the trapper's trail and the correct one that I was on, they took a hard right turn and unintentionally ran my dogs off into the woods. As a rookie, I only had two dog chains. I wondered how I was going to get that long string of dogs with each one wrapped around the wrong side of a tree, and pulling forward, out and back on the trail. Slowly, I began straightening the team forward, going two feet at a time. I dug the snowhook in, untangled each couple and moved one pair at a time ahead; then, I secured the snowhook and repeated the whole process. I finally led the whole team out of the tree thicket.

We hit the Farewell Burn. My dogs still weren't slowing down; they were so strong. I was the only weak link in the team because I really needed some sleep. Worse, my brake broke again.

Sometimes I saw wolves, but I had no rifle. Every now and then, I'd see a big pile of buffalo dung and I'd feel a little intimidated, knowing that wolves could be close by. I was getting really tired. Every night as I took booties off the dogs, I also cooked for them with the result that I only got a couple of hours of sleep each night. By the time I got to Nikolai, I was very tired. As I mushed, I thought, "I am pretty sure they said it was only fifty miles from Nikolai to McGrath but it sure seems a lot longer..." All night long, I kept seeing McGrath airport's lights but by 7 AM, I still wasn't there. I kept stopping my dogs, thinking I was going to have to take a 24-hour break, but in McGrath, my dad met me. He took care of the dogs and I slept eleven hours. I fell quite a bit behind in the race, but the dogs rested and so did I. Once I got out of McGrath, I went on to Takotna and then to Ophir, but after five hours of driving, I was already tired again. I kept going but I snatched a

Emmitt Peters and Gary Attla, Iditarod, 1981.
Courtesy of Gary Attla.

little rest here and there. I left Bud Smyth behind and caught up to other mushers.

When I slept, I hardly ever crawled inside my sleeping bag, but just threw it over me. Near Shageluk, it began getting much colder, dropping to -35. By 3 AM, way the heck out by myself, I was getting the chills. I didn't know how far the next village was. The chills told me I needed to stop and make a fire, but I didn't. I knew if I let it go too long, I'd be sorry, so I kept piling on more gear. Really tired, I got to Shageluk early in the morning. I knew people would soon be up, running snowmachines and making noise, so I went on past town, but stopped twenty miles out on a lake. I ran into Emmitt Peters of Ruby, Jerry Austin from St. Michael, and Dewey Halverson of Trapper Creek who had their teams straightened out and lying in the sun. After I got comfortable, Emmitt asked, "If you see those other guys wake up and get ready to go, wake me." I said, "Sure. No problem," but when I woke, I was alone. "Where the hell was Emmitt?" They had taken off when it was hot, in the middle of the day. When my dogs were more rested, I took off in the evening. I caught up with them, fed my dogs, then we four mushers continued twenty miles downriver to Anvik. When I pulled up, Emmitt was inside a cabin sitting in an easy chair I could tell by the look in his eyes that he was getting more and more comfortable. Pretty soon, he passed out so I left him there. With three hundred miles yet to go, he only had six dogs. I had twelve with lots of dog power. My team made a big push and we went a hundred miles in ten hours, going all night until noon the next day. At Bear Creek at 1 PM, I rested my dogs. Along came Emmitt Peters with his six dogs. He asked, "How come you didn't wake me up? I thought we were buddies." I said, "Yeah, how about last time? You didn't wake me either." So we were even. We took off and traveled a hundred miles over rivers, lakes, and portages, but there weren't many hills. My dogs had been running so fast that I was afraid that they might run themselves out so I rested them before reaching the next village.

There used to be two trails out of Unalakleet to Shaktoolik: a longer inland trail that followed the hills and a shorter coastal one that went direct.

A rookie, I decided to try the shorter one, but soon big breakers were slamming into the shore. I was mushing on a fifty-foot apron of beach littered with bare rocks. I decided it was too icy and there was too much rubble. I turned my team around. The dogs looked at me like, "This guy don't know what he's doing," and they slacked their pace into a dispirited walk. As we turned inland, I began dropping freight, trying to pick up speed. Fifteen miles out of Shaktoolik, I saw that others had also dropped gear: cook stoves and anything they could make do without. Today I don't think mushers are allowed to do that.

After I left Shaktoolik, I began to realize that Koyuk was too far, plus the wind was beating us up and I had to give my dogs a rest. Even though I was out on the sea ice, I pulled my sled canvas over me and bedded down in my sleeping bag nestled into my sled. As I slept, the wind puffed the white canvas up and down. When musher Donna Gentry approached me on the ice, at first she thought I was a polar bear. Later she said, "Gary, you're lucky I didn't have a gun!" After that, Donna and I began traveling together.

My dogs still figured I didn't know what I was doing and they wouldn't run so after Koyuk, I started running behind my sled. They began to get more energized and pretty soon they were back, running again. As we passed Elim, we saw whale rib bones sticking up, like big fingers arching over their cemetery as is traditional.

Late that night when we were having dinner on the trail, Donna and I heard a noise. She asked, "What's that?" and added, "Are you sure you heard wolves?" Encouraged, I told her a story about when two guys were out hunting wolves once near Huslia. One guy shot the wolf but it was still able to bite onto the guy's snowmachine's side rails. Even with the snowmachine revving forward, the wolf's teeth slid down the rail, stopping just before the guy's foot. Donna was afraid of wolves so, I thought she might stick closer after that story but it didn't seem to work quite like that.

Ninety miles before the finish, we took our eight-hour break, but Donna got an hour jump on me and beat me going into White Mountain.

My dogs were perking up. My second lead, Warner Vent's former dog, Dandy, was awesome. He knew he was getting close to the end of the race. The team picked up their pace. We ran full blast up and down every hill. On a hill outside of Safety, I saw a sled below but no one was driving it. On a closer look, I could see Donna was riding in the sled basket. By then, I had nine dogs left. At Safety, I caught up to her. I needed to rest my dogs so I tried to buy time by feeding her a beer and telling her stories. She told me she had two secret weapons, two dogs that had not yet worked all the way from McGrath. She thought that "with proper motivation" that they might kick in during the last twenty miles. I laughed, "If they never worked for 500 miles, what makes you think they're going to work during the last twenty?" Still trying to buy rest time, I said, "Before we take a break, let's leave our mittens on the freezer by the door. If one of us gets his mitts and takes off, we'll know that the other one has already left." She went outside but knowing that my dogs needed rest I kept drinking beer. When I finished my second one, I saw that her mitts were gone. Trot couldn't keep up, but I didn't need him to finish so I dropped him before going on. In the dark, I could hear Donna's dogs up ahead yapping so my dogs sped up. I passed her and kept thinking she'd catch up and pass me but to my surprise, she soon became a little speck. (I had sprint dogs while hers were all long distance.) (Nowadays, the Iditarod uses mostly sprint dogs, not the 'ol tough Alaska huskies.)

I knew this was my one and only Iditarod. It had to be. I had children. I had to start a career so my family would have a good economic base. I wanted to finish the best that I could so for the last four miles, I began running. When I crossed the finish line about 8:30 AM, there was a big crowd. As a rookie, after thirteen days and twenty-two minutes, I finished in seventeenth place, winning $1400 as well as $500 as Rookie of the Year with a trophy donated by Jerry Austin and his wife. My cousin Ron Yatlin paid his way to Nome, met me at the finish, and began taking care of my dogs. I didn't have to do nothing. I looked down the coast. It was clear and I could see a long way but there was no Donna in sight. I ordered a hamburger but I kept checking because I wanted to "greet" her when she came in. As soon as she crossed the finish line, she grinned, "Gary, you rotten kid!" Yeah, I beat her.

Gary Attla and George Attla, Jr., ca. 2014.
Courtesy of Gary Attla.

I went to all the Iditarod festivities. Cowboy Larry Smith rented a bar for the mushers and the handlers. Susan Butcher, my cousin Ronnie, and a bunch of others were all celebrating. I told Susan Butcher that I could "break people's arms," an arm wrestling term for winning. "Nobody can hardly beat me," I said. Susan challenged me, "Okay, let's do it." We sat at a solid, immoveable cable spool table. Everyone gathered around, but I could barely budge her arm. I decided I'm not gonna use any of my "wilies," suckering my opponent's arm to my chest, twisting my wrist and forcing her arm down. I played it straight, but I still couldn't break her arm. I had her arm right in the zone but I could barely move it even a little. I gave it everything I had, but I still couldn't break her arm. We were both leaning over the deadlock of our arms. I looked at my cousin Ron Yatlin, who had a big grin all over his face. I knew if I didn't beat Susan Butcher, I'd never hear the end of it. I really began to pour it on. Finally, she started giving a little, then I had her about three inches above the table when she stopped me. My arm was getting tired and everybody was holler-

George Attla's sister Rose Ambrose and nephew Gary Attla at the Huslia cemetery, ca. 2015.
Courtesy of Gary Attla.

ing. Finally I got her down to the table but I couldn't do nothing afterward so I said, "Let's try your other arm." She said, "No, un, uh, I only have one good arm." I don't know I could have taken her on that side but I can break using both my arms.

After the Iditarod, I had Wien Airlines send my dogs back home on credit while I went to work on the North Slope for a month. When I returned, I had a $2500 bill for shipping my dogs, but I had an unforgettable experience. It's a good thing I went to work right away though.

After the Iditarod I started a career in the oil field, working on a drill rig. Most of my job, however, entailed using my brain, not wearing out my body. I bought a house in North Pole where I raised my five kids. Working two weeks on and two weeks off, I was up north until 2014. With all that traveling, I didn't have much of a life, but my kids turned out great. Once they grew up, I didn't need all that money. I didn't want to waste a half-year of my life, year after year, anymore. It's my ambition now to do as many different things as possible without turning any one thing into a career.

This spring, I saw Jeff King and I reminded him, "Remember when I beat you and Martin Buser in the Iditarod?!" (In 1981, while I came in seventeeth, Jeff was twenty-eighth, and Martin was nineteenth.) "Yep, yep, go ahead and remind me!" he said and we both laughed. I understand why the Iditarod is so addictive. Once you do it, you want to keep on. It is the adventure of a lifetime.

Chapter 13

Following in the Steps of the Original Dogman: Wes Henry and A-CHILL

Wes Henry, Huslia A-CHILL.
Courtesy of Jessie Henry.

Sled dog champion George Attla and other Huslia mushers were trailblazers, a force to reckon with. They paved the way into championship sprint racing. Every spring many villages welcomed the return of the sun with sled dog races. To compete outside of the local area, it was no small thing for a musher to get his team to Fairbanks or Anchorage where championships were won and purses claimed. These early mushers trained hard and pushed forward, carrying the torch of Alaska's ancestral mode of travel, the dependable sled dog.

Those championships didn't just happen. George Attla worked hard, and elders who noticed his gifts shared their knowledge with him. George's intuition with dogs resulted in a training protocol that broke trail for dogmen who followed.

One of those who learned sled dog care first-hand from George and who has become a mentor himself is Wes Henry, also of Huslia.

In the following chapter, I present trailbreaker George Attla, his era, and the impact of today's vicissitudes on Alaska Native village life. With the changing times, I introduce Huslia musher Wes Henry and his family who today are carrying the beacon for the traditional use of sled dogs in village life. The Henry children and their parents are all deeply involved in their kennel and with the passing on of indigenous ancient skills to the new generation.

At the time when George Attla was mastering sled dog racing, the commonly accepted training for sled dogs often included force and was usually from a man's point of view, not from that of the dog's. In his book, *Everything I Know about*

A-CHILL logo.

Courtesy of Kathy Turco.

Training and Racing Sled Dogs, George pointed out, "The dog never makes a mistake, he is just a dog and he does what he does because he is a dog and thinks like a dog. It is you who make the mistakes because you haven't trained him to do what you want him to do when you want him to do it."

Wes Henry and George Attla coaching Wes' son Trevor Henry at Arctic Winter Games, Fairbanks, 2014.
Courtesy of Jessie Henry.

In the decades that followed the height of George's career, the use of the village husky began to wane, replaced by snow machines. Later television and the Internet began displacing time-honored village activities. Elders died and a way of life went with them. George began to see the need for young people to learn traditional skills including the immemorial use of sled dog mushing, however, little by little, popular culture began encroaching on regional values.

Since its introduction in the north, western education didn't seem relevant to traditional Alaska Native lifestyle. Public schools didn't address education from an indigenous point of view and rural teaching positions were often staffed by people from the Lower Forty-eight, who were not only unfamiliar with Alaska, but who also felt uncomfortable in the Bush.

With the late 1960s social revolution, family principles began to break down in America, even in the most remote villages. Increased drug and alcohol use weakened and diminished traditions. The erosion of the family unit and of the work ethic began to further impact conventional domestic life. Children felt the lack of security, pride, and cultural identity.

Due to his childhood tuberculosis, George Attla had been raised in western hospitals and was comfortable both in mainstream America and in rural Alaska societies. As an adult when in Huslia, he was frequently asked to join the classroom, where he could act as a bridge. He had a gift for understanding children and he also understood both western and Native values; he respected both. He wanted teachers to become active in the village so that they might learn the ancestral ways and break down the wall between expected academic goals and Native ways of learning. A means of doing this was the study of the Alaska sled dog, which was part of Alaska's history, and a window into how we as Alaskans have evolved. The biology of dogs was also a way to usher students into a study of science. George proposed that both western and Native values as well as culture and science could be studied through twice-weekly field trips to the local sled dog kennels where, during school hours, students would learn from both academic and dog musher teachers. The village could take pride in the program and would see to its being sustained.

As a youth, George had been rescued both through the elders and through his own interest in dogs. He felt that because dogs offer unconditional acceptance, today's children might also find themselves through "man's best friend."George wanted to give back to the youth what the elders had given to him.

In 2007, George Attla was inducted as the first member of the Alaska Sports Hall of Fame. He strongly supported healthy mentoring.

In 2010 George's twenty-one-year old son, Frank Attla, died during an asthma attack. George's grief was a catalyst that helped him focus educational ideas into a program he'd long been contemplating and also served as a means to honor his late son. At the time, there were a lot of suicides in rural Alaska. Huslia teacher Peggy Bruno was trying to find how best to reach her students. She remembered how happy she had been as a child watching cattle graze in a pasture. She and George began brainstorming. George suggested that students study sled dogs, an animal to which Alaska rural students could easily relate. Peggy was certified in animal husbandry and suggested teaching dog care. Students could do lab work with her and field trips to the local kennels. The principal of Huslia's Jimmy Huntington School (JHS), Teresa Cox, fully endorsed animal husbandry

George Attla's late son Frank Attla, for whom George designed the Frank Attla Youth and Sled Dog Program, died at age 21 in 2010.
Courtesy of http://attlamakingofachampion.com

as a vehicle for teaching science and culture. However in the after school hours in Alaska, it would be too dark to visit the kennels, so the new animal husbandry Frank Attla Youth and Sled Dog Program (FAYSDP) was embedded twice a week during school hours. The community-driven program gave students hands-on experience with sled dogs led by elders and experienced dogmen, such as Wes Henry in Huslia. The FAYSDP pilot program became part of the JHS school curriculum for three academic years (2012 to 2015). Approved by the Yukon-Koyukuk School District (YKSD), it involved a middle and high school teacher

Jimmy Huntington, Huslia, won 1956 Open North American Championship.
Courtesy of Jessie Henry.

and more than thirty high school and middle school students.

After George passed away in 2015, his partner Kathy Turco worked on a proposal with YKSD to continue the program. Although the proposal scored high, the grant was not awarded. George had told Kathy that to become a champion, a person had to be willing to go the distance. He coached, "Get the vision out there; give everything we've learned away. The vision will eventually materialize." While she was grieving his loss, Kathy wrote the essentials of FAYSDP in a manual, *How to Start and Run a Youth and Sled Dog Program* and with the intention of giving it to the schools in Alaska. She shared it with Alaska Gateway School District (AGSD) superintendent and dog musher Scott MacManus, who studied the manual. He understood George's vision and its potential for students in the village and told Kathy, "This is an idea I think we can do something with." Scott began the long process that resulted in his partnering with YKSD to compete nationally for a grant to

George Attla's grandnephew Joe Bifelt.
www.pbs.org/independentlens

start a program in both districts. Scott was motivated by both the passions of dog mushing and of education. He grew up with sled dogs and had known George since childhood. Scott's father, educator Pete MacManus, had competed in the 1977 and 1978 Iditarods and the 1983 All Alaska Sweepstakes sled dog races.

Graduation rates for Alaska Native students were below fifty percent; when they left school, they often had a lack of career readiness, minimal exposure to higher education

George Attla's partner, Kathy Turco, presenting A-CHILL, founded on George's principles of the making of a champion.

Courtesy of Jessie Henry.

opportunities, as well as a deficit of cultural heritage education. Scott was working hard already to provide high school courses that would give university credit to students and also act as a bridge to higher education, resulting in students being employed in their own communities. He felt that the FAYSDP model might particularly be a help to rural Alaskans by providing a cultural context for classroom learning. He had already developed a suite of programs that were pathways to careers: computer science which might lead to a career in information technology; small engines, which could help a student become a mechanic or a heavy equipment or power plant operator; welding which could lead to apprenticing as a pipefitter. There was also an introduction to medical terminology, which dovetailed with the FAYSDP animal husbandry class, both of which fit into health careers, the fastest growing fields in the state and nation.

In the late fall of 2016, in a nationwide competition, the U.S. Department of Indian Education awarded a four-year grant to AGSD in partnership with YKSD, for a community-based project called A-CHILL or Alaska–Care and Husbandry Instruction for Lifelong Living. The grant served the Alaska Gateway and Yukon-Koyukuk school districts, which included Dot Lake, Tanacross, Tok, Mentasta, Northway, Tetlin, Eagle, and Allakaket, Hughes, Huslia, Ruby, Koyukuk, Nulato, Kaltag, Manley Hot Springs, Minto, and Rampart. The grant began in fall of 2016 and will conclude the spring of 2020. If the program is working well, there may be a possibility

Mentasta student mushing Tok track, 2017.
Photo Roni J. Noonan-Agre. Courtesy A-CHILL.

of applying to renew. (https://www2.ed.gov/programs/indiandemo/16awards.html)

A-CHILL is ground-breaking as a true collaboration of academic instruction and traditional culture teaching. Last fall A-CHILL offered a total of five classes. An Alaska Culture-Dog Mushing class was developed from FAYSDP material and taught to both middle and high school students. These classes taught animal husbandry and depended on the working relationship between a local dog musher instructor and a public school teacher. The schoolteacher accompanied the students on all of their excursions and thus learned with them. These classes teach life and culture skills by local indigenous experts, who use their own lesson plans. For more advanced middle school students, an animal science class was available. For high school students, long distance instructor Peggy Bruno taught Veterinary Technology as well as Veterinary 100. Other high school students frequently joined the in-kennel classes taught by the local dog musher teachers of the Alaska Culture-Dog Mushing class. In December 2017 ten high school students from both districts enrolled in the Veterinary Technology class and earned both high school and University of Alaska Fairbanks credits, which was an encouragement to these students to continue

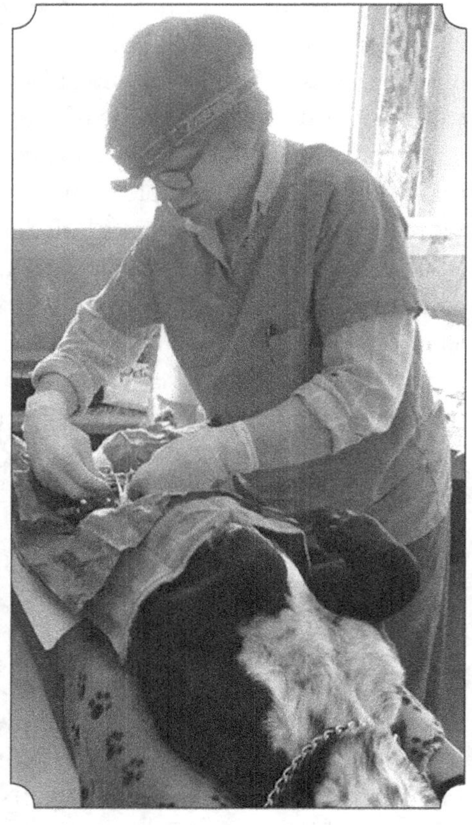

High school students shadowing Tok veterinarian Jeanne Olson, 2017.
Photo Jolene Kinsland. A-CHILL.

their education. Kathy Turco, A-CHILL's Musher Coordinator, is the liaison between each community, its dog musher teachers, its schools, and the grant administrators. Throughout the school year she sends necessary sled dog care supplies and equipment to each school and also verifies the local dog musher teachers' hours.

From the spring of 2017 through the summer of 2018, A-CHILL hosted two spring institutes and two summer camps for professional development of school-teachers, dog musher instructors, and for local culture expert teachers from all seventeen villages. In the spring of 2018, three pilot programs launched for trials in both districts. Visiting professional instructors taught middle and high school students: Native Youth Olympics and Beading by

Amanda Attla, teaching beading to A-CHILL students, 2017.
Courtesy of A-CHILL.

George's daughter, Amanda Attla, Skijoring and Dog Handling by Mari Hoe-Raitto, and Media Digital Story-telling by Ira Hardy. A fourth pilot project was tried in YKSD and AGSD schools. Six Fairbanks and Tok area veterinarians volunteered to teach vet science to dog musher instructors, school-teachers, students, and community members, gathered from ten villages.

Unlike many village public schools, A-CHILL has been successful in the returning rate of their teachers for the next academic year.

Mari Hoe Raitto was hired spring of 2018 to work with A-CHILL's Musher Coordinator Kathy Turco and will merge the kennel owners' goals with those of the academicians into A-CHILL's final refined lesson plans.

Wes Henry: Passing the Sled Dog Torch

To help readers understand how the dog kennel and subsistence skills classes work in the village, kennel owner James Westley "Wes" Henry gave the following interview from Huslia in the spring of 2017.

I have been around dogs ever since I was little. The son of Darlene Henry of Chilliwack, Washington and Thomas Henry of Allakaket and Dulbi (or the latter, *Dulbaakkaakk'et*, a village that preceded Huslia), I moved back to Huslia with my family in early 1975. Huslia was known for its outstanding

L-R: Wes and Jessie Henry's second son A-CHILL and FAYSDP participant Jeremiah Henry, Jessie Henry's father, Don Ernst, Wes Henry, Henrys' oldest son FAYSDP participant and staff of Henry kennel Trevor Henry, FAYSDP and A-CHILL participant daughter Talia Henry, Jessie's mother, Brenda Ernst.

Courtesy of Jessie Henry.

sled dogs and mushers including Jimmy Huntington and George Attla, the original Huslia Huslers.

When I was six, my late Uncle Roger gave me a 45-pound dog, Judy, from Cue Bifelt's line, part of the Allakaket-Huslia lineage. With the support of my grandfather Mathew Henry, I've been involved with dogs all my life. Judy was bred to one of Cue's dogs from whom we got pups. Every year, Grandpa and I cut fish for our small kennel of six to nine dogs. During the late 1970s through the early 1980s, there were about eleven dog kennels in Huslia.

After I married and had a family, I wanted my five children, Trevor, Jeremiah, Talia, Jared, and Trent to experience the life I had known: raising, caring for, and racing sled dogs.

About seven years ago, George Attla, Jackie Wholecheese (who doesn't race dogs anymore) and I were talking about sled dogs. George was trying to find a common interest for the youth. He said there's no dog future with the older men because they've made up their minds not to raise dogs either because they can't afford it or from a lack of interest. I told them, "I'm raising dogs for my kids." (Ever since Talia was little, she's been into sprint racing.) When I was growing up, I learned by taking care of dogs: drying fish and cutting firewood to cook for them. To me, it wasn't work. I wanted my children to also experience the way of life I had known.

In 2012, besides George's there were three kennels in Huslia: Floyd Vent's, Wilson Sam's, and mine. Wilson and Floyd were raised with dogs. Now in his early sixties, Floyd Vent has driven dogs since he was young. He trapped with and raced his five sled dogs. The brother of renowned dogman Bergman Sam, Wilson Sam, is seventy-eight and is the elder of the program.

George suggested starting a sled dog youth program that was run through 4-H because at the time a group in Tanana was using the umbrella of 4-H. As it turned out both

Wes Henry teaching students sled building, Huslia.
Photo Mickey Kenny. Courtesy of A-CHILL.

for them and for us, 4-H looked like it was only going to gum up the works. George said to us, "Hey, you guys want to volunteer your time working with the kids?" As George, Floyd, Wilson, and I began familiarizing the youngsters with the kennels, George got busy seeking private companies for support. Companies like Annamaet Pet Foods donated dog food and Ruby Marine provided shipping. Other companies and individuals donated funds for dog care supplies, equipment to work with youth, and generally helped out.

Some of the kids, not all, got excited about learning the dogs' different personalities and about subsistence skills like setting a gill net under the ice and hanging beaver snares. I taught the children how to be savvy walking on the ice, how to chisel an ice hole to catch beaver, and where to place the bait and the snares under the ice. Elders came and shared stories of sprint and mid-distance racing, as well as of the Iditarod. It took a little time to figure out how and what to offer the kids, but the program began to take off and other villages became interested in starting something similar.

Hanging fish, Ruby summer community youth pilot program.
Photo by Melvin Captain. Courtesy of A-CHILL.

A couple of years ago, I had twenty-one dogs, but I gave some of the older ones to families who wanted an experienced dog for doing the one- and two-dog races. I have sixteen now and am looking for pups to maintain the kennel's competitive edge.

Kennel owners Floyd Vent and Wes Henry teaching students how to vaccinate, Huslia.
Photo Mickey Kenny. Courtesy A-CHILL.

I feed the dogs good quality dried dog food, which I alternate with fish, cooked rice, and various oils. I use supplements, which contain powdered eggs and vitamins to keep them from dehydrating as well as to keep up their energy.

Initially we familiarize the children with each dog and with the yard. In winter, we dig snow out from the doghouses and in summer, we clean up the grass and cart the scat away. We showed the kids how to give the dogs the four-way vaccine, how to take care of their feet and nails, and we also do trail maintenance. Last year I began learning GPS training for teaching. I also made a sled parts pattern. When it was too cold to take the students out, we went over to the school where I cut out the sled parts. The kids sanded and oiled them and then we put the sled together.

Our teaching isn't limited to dog care but it also includes village issues: alcohol and drug abuse as well as challenges in getting along. We talk about resolving problems by working as a team. Carpenters, plumbers, engineers, all of them, have to work together to make a building. In a community we have to do the same for a healthy outcome.

We kennel owners, Wilson Sam, Floyd Vent, and I, don't keep any aggressive dogs—those that have a tendency to grab or bite. We don't allow the kids to run in the dog yard, throw sticks, or be in the livelier parts of the kennel. The dogs have to be comfortable in their homes. My five kids are always with our dogs so they welcome children into their yard.

Dogs will accept children whether they have mental or physical problems. Children who grow up in the village are fairly acclimated to dogs, but kids from the road system need more time to get used to them. When the children are comfortable with the animals, they put har-

Mentasta student mushing Tok race track, 2017.
Photo Roni J. Noonan-Agre. Courtesy A-CHILL.

nesses on them. Once after the kids had harnessed the dogs at Wilson Sam's kennel, he let the students run the dogs out to the lake. On another occasion, Floyd Vent had the children help hook up dogs to a snowmachine that would pull a sled. Then he ran the snowmachine slowly and let the dogs run behind at a comfortable pace. The kids rode in the sled and watched how the dogs performed.

Like the dogs, some students are more focused, have more intuition, and have more ability than others do in driving a team. We depend on these children to help show others how to take the corners, how to get the sled stopped and back upright if they tip the sled over.

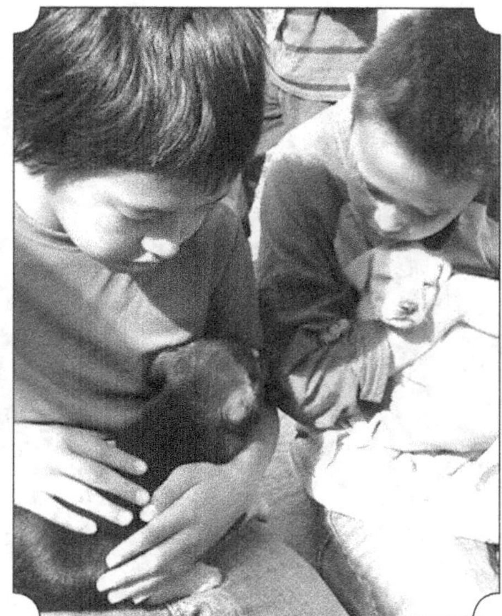

Ruby summer youth pilot program, handling pups.
Melvin Captain. Courtesy A-CHILL.

In 2013, Tim and Lorraine Pavlick's high school daughter, Jazmyn, was one of the first children that George trained to race in the Junior North American. The next year my nephew Thomas Henry as well as Wilson Sam's granddaughter, Courtney Agnes, entered the race. They took fourth and first place in the Junior North American.

My son Trevor learned a great deal from the late George and from Kathy. Trevor spent six weeks with them, taking care of the dogs, racing after school and on week-ends. In 2014 when Fairbanks hosted the Arctic Winter Games (AWG), Trevor represented Alaska. The first day he came in second by two-tenths of a second and won a silver medal. On the second day, he won a gold medal. The following year, he and Andrew Noble represented Alaska in the 2015 AWG, where, on

Huslia kennel owner and elder Wilson Sam sharing stories with students.
Photo Mickey Kenny. Courtesy A-CHILL.

Veterinarian Arleigh Reynolds and Mike Williams, Sr., Akiak, Iditarod musher.
Courtesy of Dr. Arleigh Reynolds.

the third day, the team came in second.

While George trained his grand-nephew Joe Bifelt, Kathy helped Joe with online college classes. When George had to go to Fairbanks for medical trips, Joe sent videotapes of his race to George to critique. Joe raced in the Open North American but, due to lack of snow, not in the Rondy.

Annually we race in Huslia and Hughes and sometimes, we loan dogs to race in Allakaket. Trevor came in third in the Huslia races and fourth in the Hughes spring carnival. Now one of our sons Jared is starting to become interested. We talked about Floyd Vent taking some of the kids to the North American, but round-trip air-fare to Fairbanks for the group and their dogs is $3600. Add another $2500 for living expenses.

In January 2017, we started working with A-CHILL. My wife keeps tabs on the hours our dog mushers teach, on how the students are doing: who is struggling and who isn't. We usually teach thirteen students and have a teacher present at all times. They come twice a week for an hour and half on Mondays and on Fridays. We rotate between Floyd's yard, Wilson's yard, and my yard. Now through A-CHILL, we get paid. The junior high kids, who are doing it just for educational purposes, have been great, joining in. Peggy Bruno, our former Huslia English teacher who has an animal husbandry certification, wrote a vet science course and is overseeing the high school students taking the course. They receive both high school and University of Alaska-Fairbanks (UAF) credits.

In 2015, three students traveled to Fairbanks to attend a vet science class taught by veterinarian Arleigh Reynolds at the UAF Veterinary Medicine Department. These students stayed on campus for five days while helping mushers and learning about the health of sled dogs running in the Open North American Championship. Purina donated dog food to our mushers.

Each year before school starts, I figure what basic skills I want to teach the children about the dogs and about traditional subsistence skills. So far there has only been one year out of three when I have been able to get through the entire program and finish with a child mushing with no problems. There is a lot involved in mushing both in coordination, steering by leaning and dragging a foot, balancing as well as anticipating trail conditions and dogs' responses. It takes a lot of time on the trail. I don't write lesson plans down, but what I've taught my own kids, I try to teach the students.

At the end of the year, there's a quiz. I ask the kids to itemize each part of a sled. For a reward, we go on a special outing and eat cookies my wife made. That's their A+.

When I was in school I had a hard time reading and writing. I had no patience with being cooped up inside. I wanted to be outside working with my hands. I am a carpenter and I enjoy making furniture and sleds.

I tell the kids, "Not all of us can go to college." I encourage them to stay in school but for those who learn less from books and more by using their hands, I tell them to learn a trade, a marketable skill.

Through A-CHILL, George's original vision for the children is continuing. Competitive dog mushing that originated in the villages is being rejuvenated. George's former partner and A-CHILL Mushing Coordinator, Kathy, shoulders the burden of expediting the needed dog food, rice, and bedding straw to each of the villages' kennels. She also sends the necessary supplies and safety equipment for students which include sleds, ganglines, skijor harnesses, helmets, and supplies for culture experts teaching the children.

After George's grand-nephew Joe Bifelt finished the Frank Attla Youth and Sled Dog Program (FAYSDP) at the Jimmy Huntington School in Huslia, George asked him why he thought the program was important. Joe replied, "Grandpa, when I see public school teachers putting harnesses on sled dogs and willing to scoop dog poop, I respect my teachers that much more." It takes a village and a school in mutual cooperation to raise a child.

A thank you to all the men and women who are mentoring the children and keeping alive the Alaska way of life.

For more, see: https://www.achill.life

Little musher Trent Henry.
Courtesy Jessie Henry.

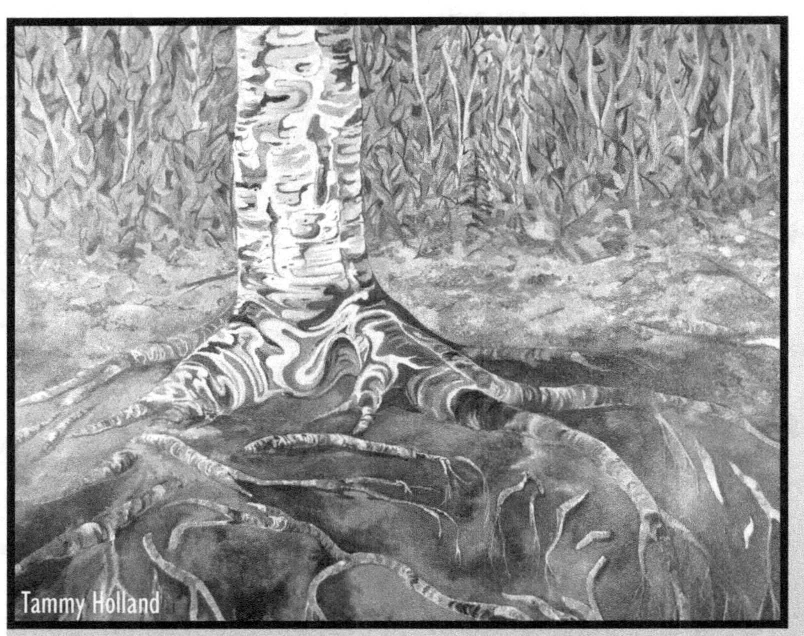

Our Elders, the roots from which we sprang, and we, the branches, reaching for the Light.

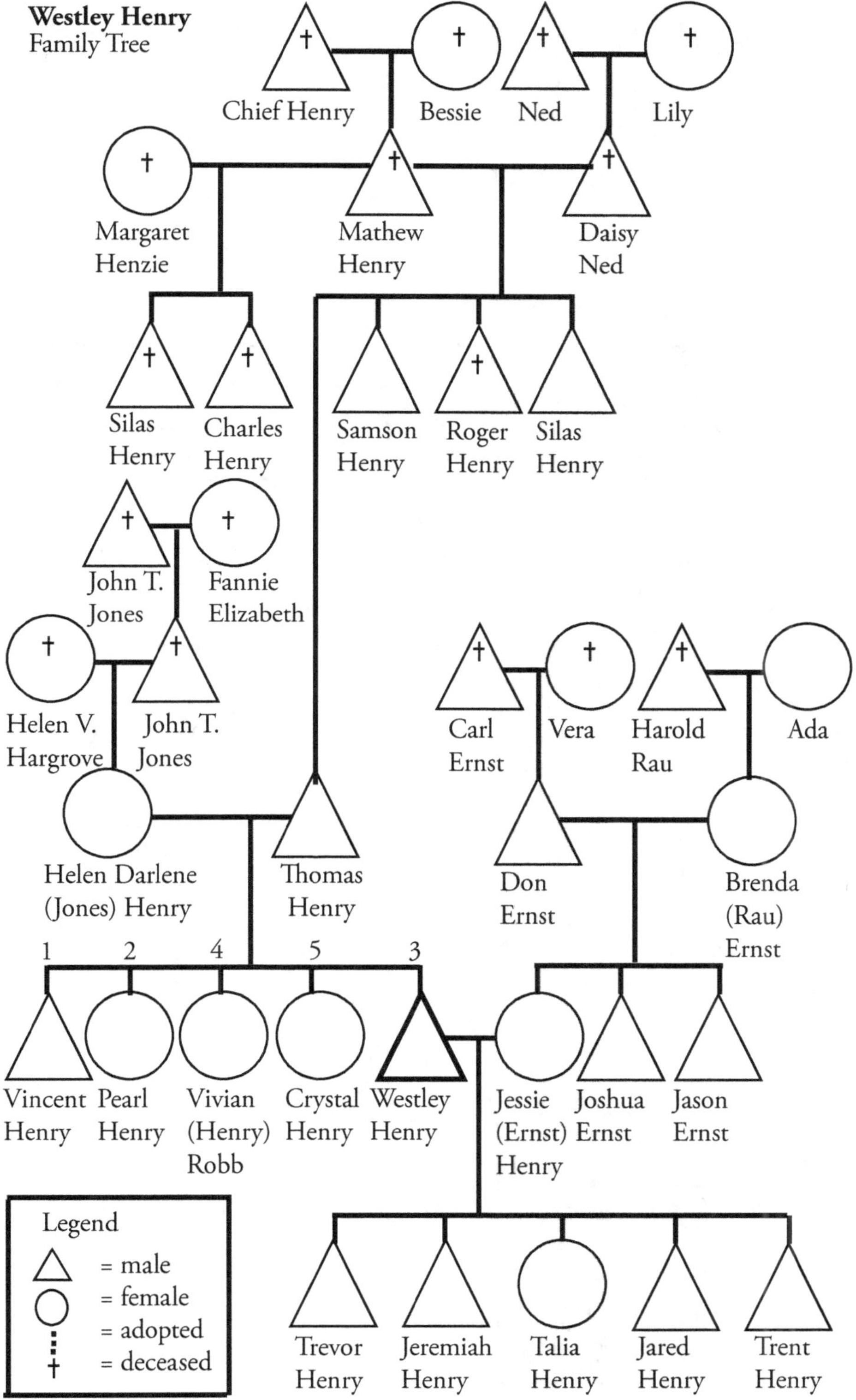

Westley Henry
Family Tree

Chief Henry
Bessie
Ned
Lily

Margaret
Henzie
Mathew
Henry
Daisy
Ned

Silas
Henry
Charles
Henry
Samson
Henry
Roger
Henry
Silas
Henry

John T.
Jones
Fannie
Elizabeth

Helen V.
Hargrove
John T.
Jones

Carl
Ernst
Vera
Harold
Rau
Ada

Helen Darlene
(Jones) Henry
Thomas
Henry
Don
Ernst
Brenda
(Rau)
Ernst

1
2
4
5
3

Vincent
Henry
Pearl
Henry
Vivian
(Henry)
Robb
Crystal
Henry
Westley
Henry
Jessie
(Ernst)
Henry
Joshua
Ernst
Jason
Ernst

Trevor
Henry
Jeremiah
Henry
Talia
Henry
Jared
Henry
Trent
Henry

Legend
= male
= female
= adopted
= deceased

Jerry Riley
Family Tree

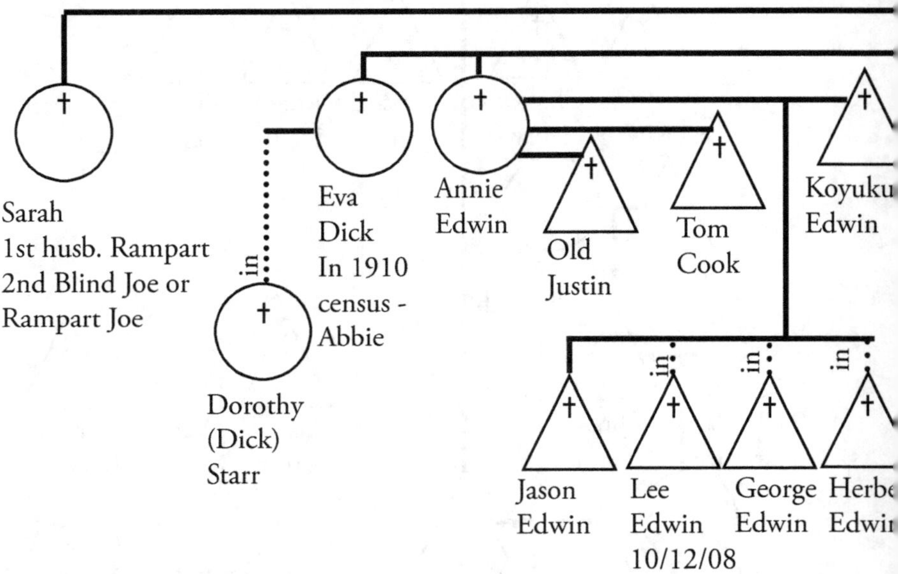

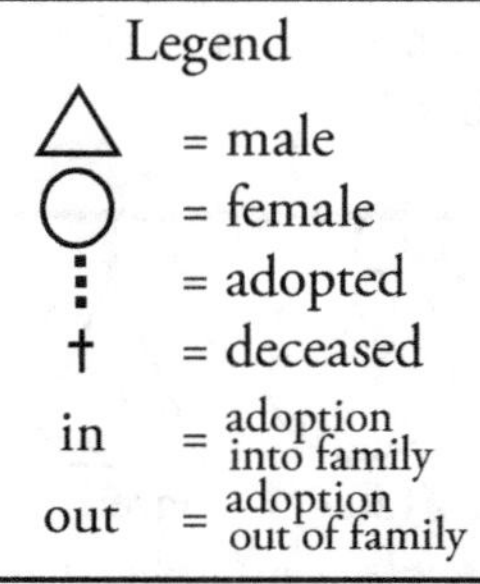

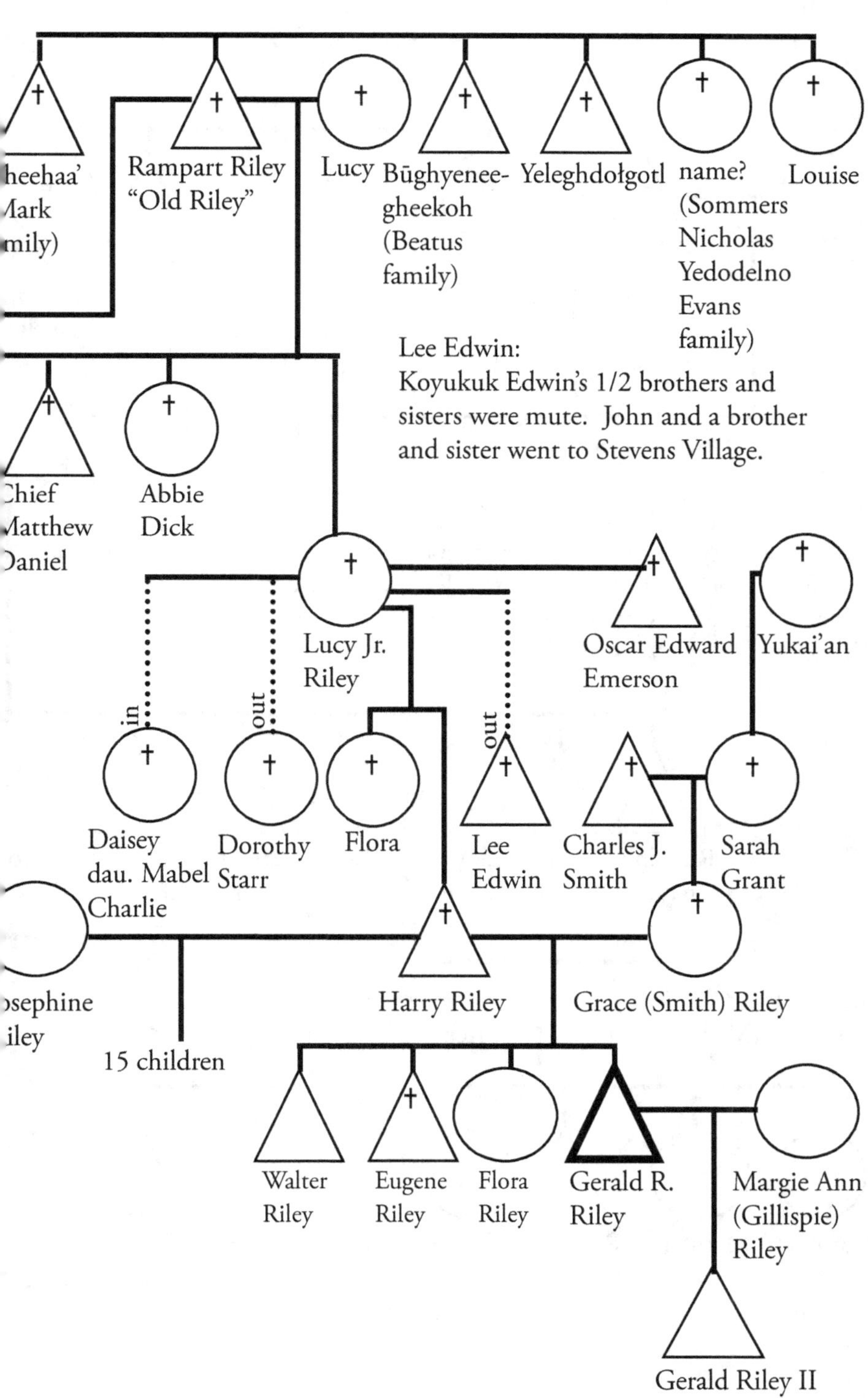

heehaa'
Mark
mily)
Rampart Riley
"Old Riley"
Lucy
Būghyenee-
gheekoh
(Beatus
family)
Yeleghdołgotl
name?
(Sommers
Nicholas
Yedodelno
Evans
family)
Louise
Lee Edwin:
Koyukuk Edwin's 1/2 brothers and
sisters were mute. John and a brother
and sister went to Stevens Village.
Chief
Matthew
Daniel
Abbie
Dick
Oscar Edward
Emerson
Yukai'an
Lucy Jr.
Riley
in
out
out
Daisey
dau. Mabel
Charlie
Dorothy
Starr
Flora
Lee
Edwin
Charles J.
Smith
Sarah
Grant
osephine
iley
15 children
Harry Riley
Grace (Smith) Riley
Walter
Riley
Eugene
Riley
Flora
Riley
Gerald R.
Riley
Margie Ann
(Gillispie)
Riley
Gerald Riley II

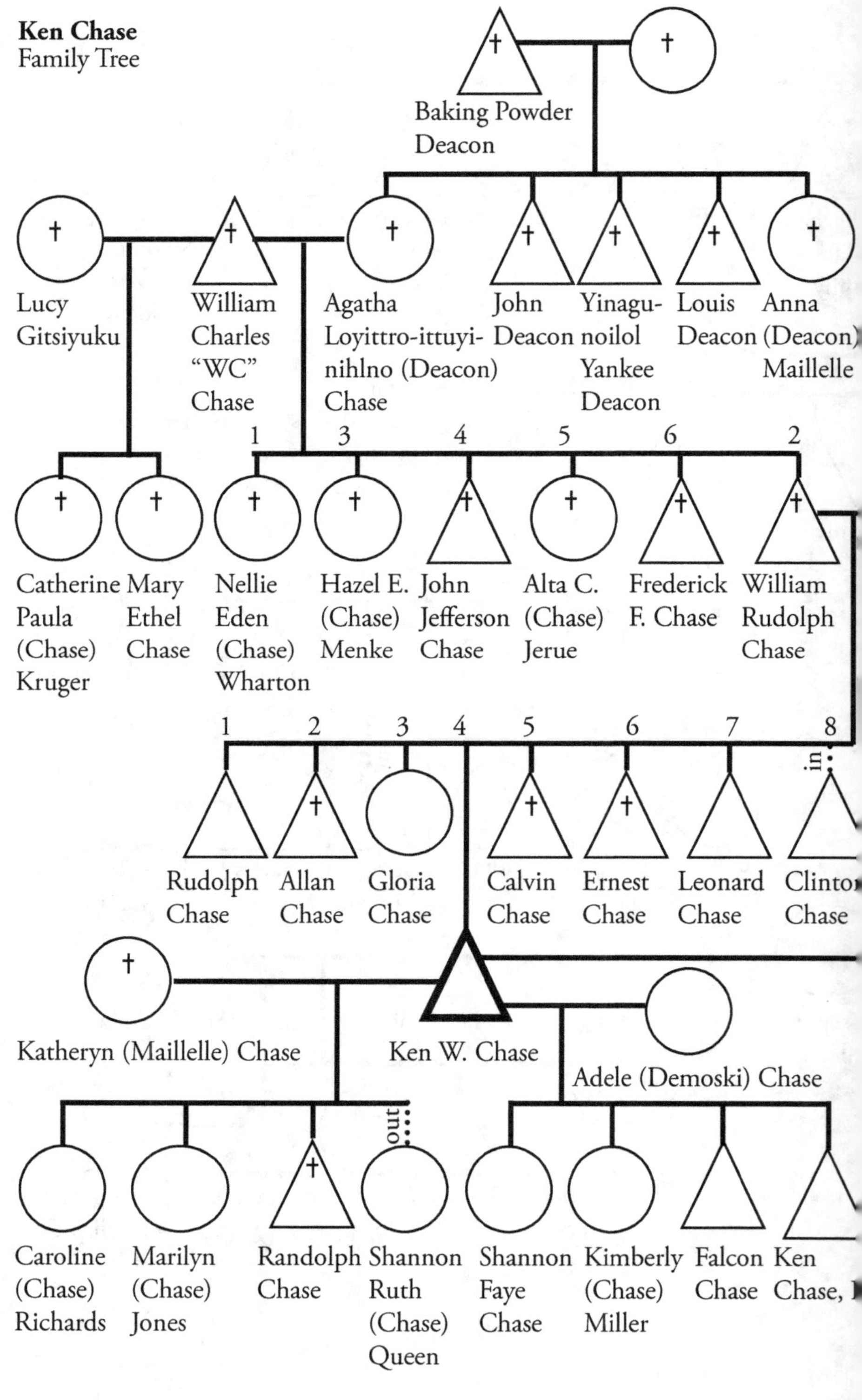

Ken Chase
Family Tree

Baking Powder Deacon

Lucy Gitsiyuku
William Charles "WC" Chase
Agatha Loyittro-ittuyi-nihlno (Deacon) Chase
John Deacon
Yinagu-noilol Yankee Deacon
Louis Deacon
Anna (Deacon) Maillelle

1
3
4
5
6
2

Catherine Paula (Chase) Kruger
Mary Ethel Chase
Nellie Eden (Chase) Wharton
Hazel E. (Chase) Menke
John Jefferson Chase
Alta C. (Chase) Jerue
Frederick F. Chase
William Rudolph Chase

1
2
3
4
5
6
7
8

Rudolph Chase
Allan Chase
Gloria Chase
Calvin Chase
Ernest Chase
Leonard Chase
Clinton Chase

in

Katheryn (Maillelle) Chase
Ken W. Chase
Adele (Demoski) Chase

out

Caroline (Chase) Richards
Marilyn (Chase) Jones
Randolph Chase
Shannon Ruth (Chase) Queen
Shannon Faye Chase
Kimberly (Chase) Miller
Falcon Chase
Ken Chase,

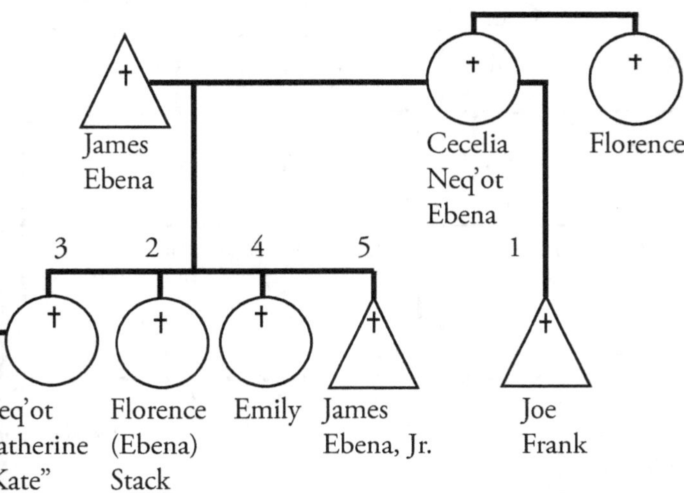

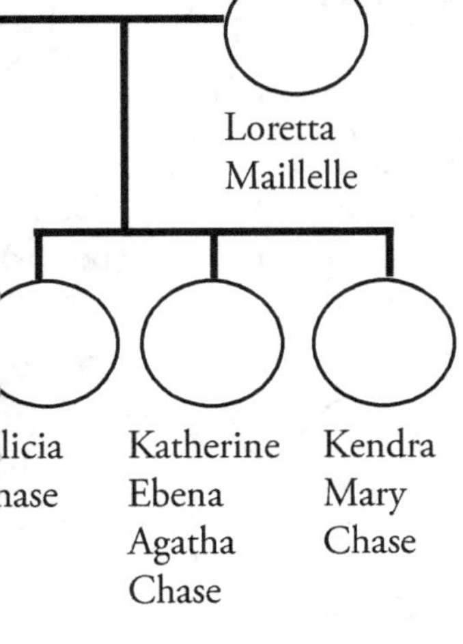

Legend	
△	= male
○	= female
⋮	= adopted
†	= deceased
in	= adoption into family
out	= adoption out of family

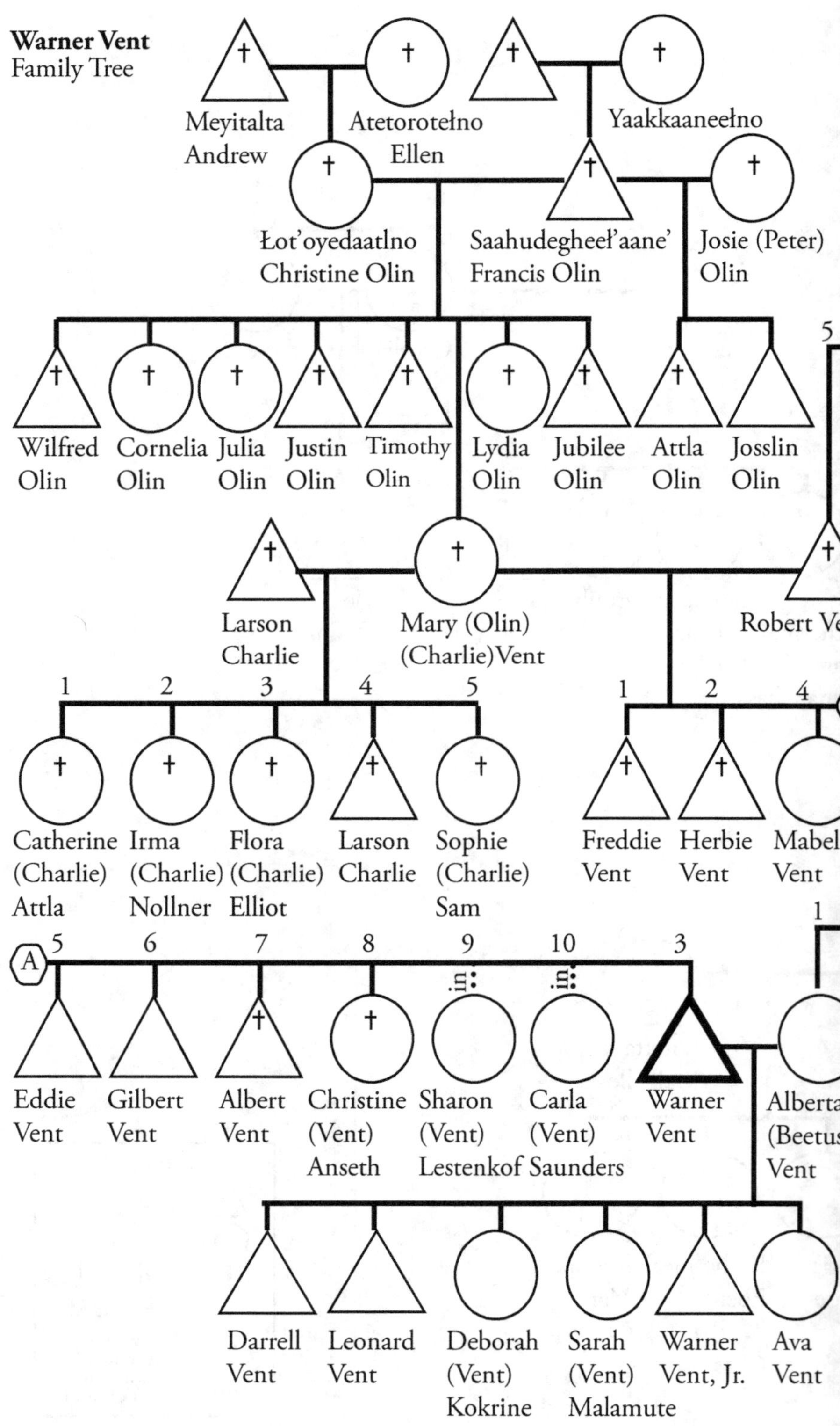

Warner Vent
Family Tree

Meyitalta Andrew
Atetorotełno Ellen
Yaakkaaneełno
Łot'oyedaatlno Christine Olin
Saahudegheeł'aane' Francis Olin
Josie (Peter) Olin
5
Wilfred Olin
Cornelia Olin
Julia Olin
Justin Olin
Timothy Olin
Lydia Olin
Jubilee Olin
Attla Olin
Josslin Olin
Larson Charlie
Mary (Olin) (Charlie)Vent
Robert Ver
1
2
3
4
5
1
2
4
A
Catherine (Charlie) Attla
Irma (Charlie) Nollner
Flora (Charlie) Elliot
Larson Charlie
Sophie (Charlie) Sam
Freddie Vent
Herbie Vent
Mabel Vent
1
A
5
6
7
8
9
10
3
Eddie Vent
Gilbert Vent
Albert Vent
Christine (Vent) Anseth
Sharon (Vent) Lestenkof
Carla (Vent) Saunders
Warner Vent
Alberta (Beetus) Vent
Darrell Vent
Leonard Vent
Deborah (Vent) Kokrine
Sarah (Vent) Malamute
Warner Vent, Jr.
Ava Vent

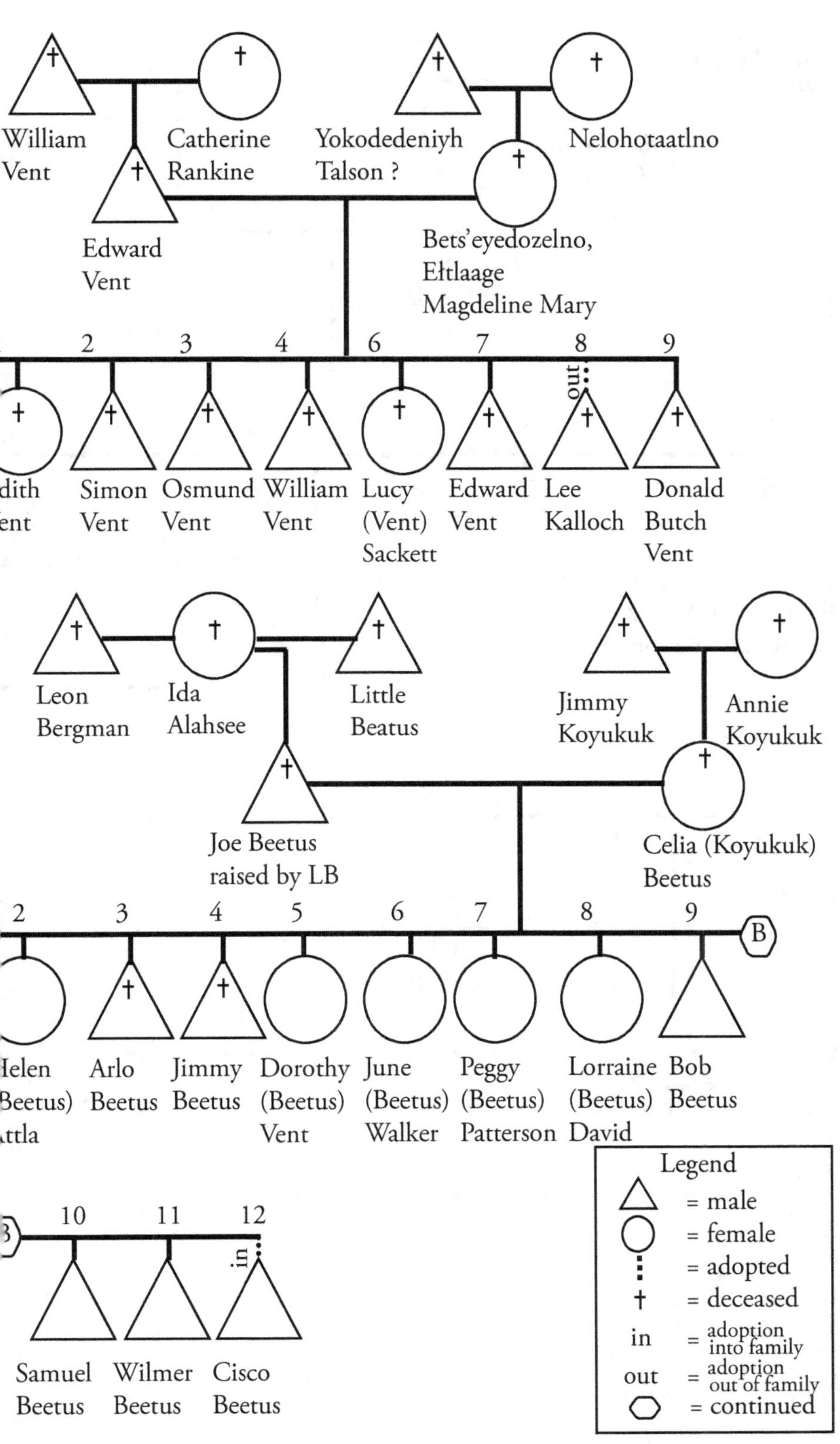

William
Vent
Catherine
Rankine
Yokodedeniyh
Talson ?
Nelohotaatlno
Edward
Vent
Bets'eyedozelno,
Ełtlaage
Magdeline Mary
2
3
4
6
7
8
9
out
dith
ent
Simon
Vent
Osmund
Vent
William
Vent
Lucy
(Vent)
Sackett
Edward
Vent
Lee
Kalloch
Donald
Butch
Vent
Leon
Bergman
Ida
Alahsee
Little
Beatus
Jimmy
Koyukuk
Annie
Koyukuk
Joe Beetus
raised by LB
Celia (Koyukuk)
Beetus
2
3
4
5
6
7
8
9
B
Ielen
Beetus)
ttla
Arlo
Beetus
Jimmy
Beetus
Dorothy
(Beetus)
Vent
June
(Beetus)
Walker
Peggy
(Beetus)
Patterson
Lorraine
(Beetus)
David
Bob
Beetus
3
10
11
12
in
Samuel
Beetus
Wilmer
Beetus
Cisco
Beetus
Legend
= male
= female
= adopted
= deceased
in = adoption into family
out = adoption out of family
= continued

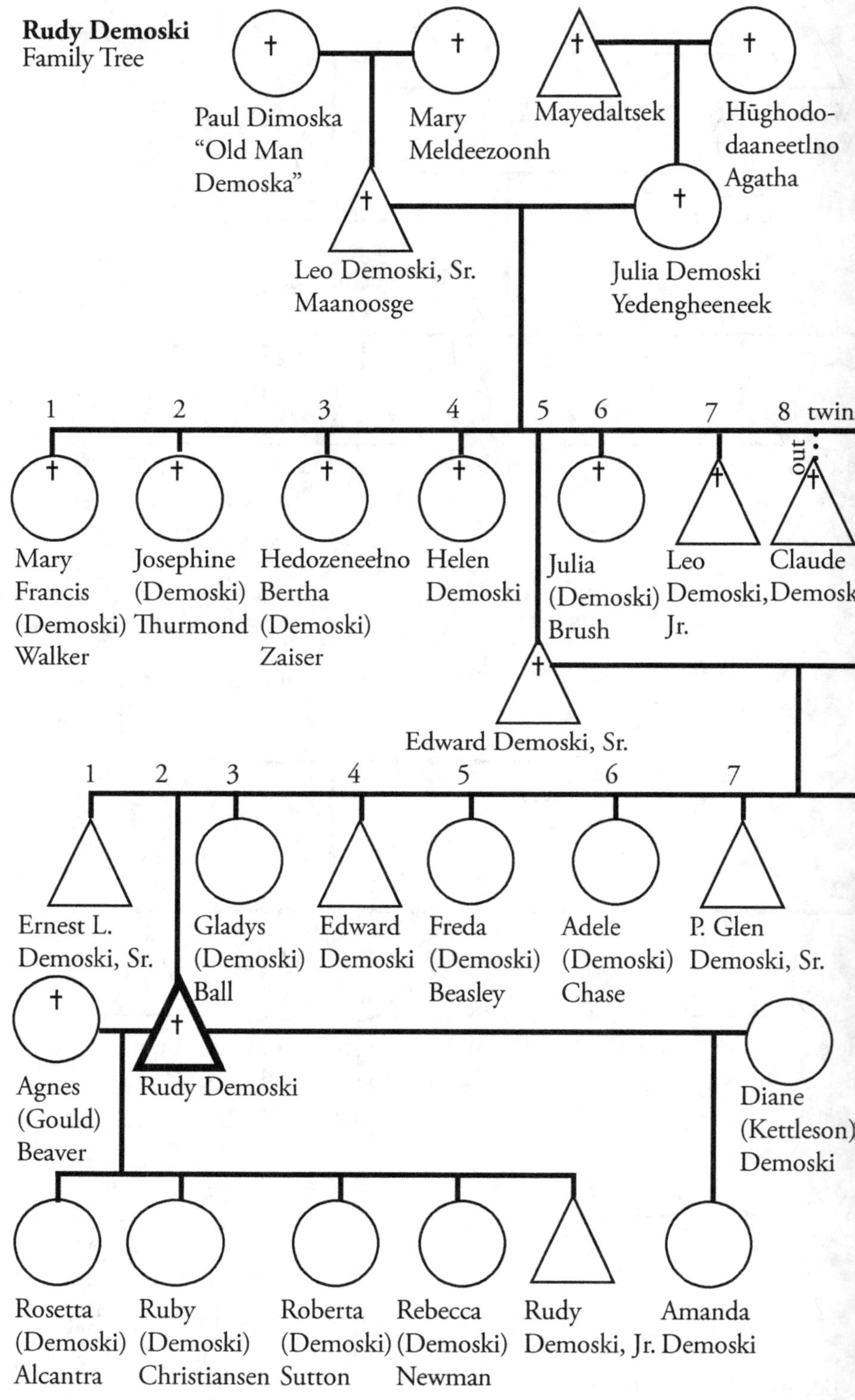

Rudy Demoski
Family Tree

Paul Dimoska "Old Man Demoska"
Mary Meldeezoonh
Mayedaltsek
Hūghododaaneetlno Agatha

Leo Demoski, Sr. Maanoosge
Julia Demoski Yedengheeneek

1 2 3 4 5 6 7 8 twin

1 Mary Francis (Demoski) Walker
2 Josephine (Demoski) Thurmond
3 Hedozeneełno Bertha (Demoski) Zaiser
4 Helen Demoski
5 Julia (Demoski) Brush
6 Julia (Demoski) Brush
7 Leo Demoski, Jr.
8 Claude Demosk

out

Edward Demoski, Sr.

1 2 3 4 5 6 7

1 Ernest L. Demoski, Sr.
3 Gladys (Demoski) Ball
4 Edward Demoski
5 Freda (Demoski) Beasley
6 Adele (Demoski) Chase
7 P. Glen Demoski, Sr.

Agnes (Gould) Beaver
Rudy Demoski
Diane (Kettleson) Demoski

Rosetta (Demoski) Alcantra
Ruby (Demoski) Christiansen
Roberta (Demoski) Sutton
Rebecca (Demoski) Newman
Rudy Demoski, Jr.
Amanda Demoski

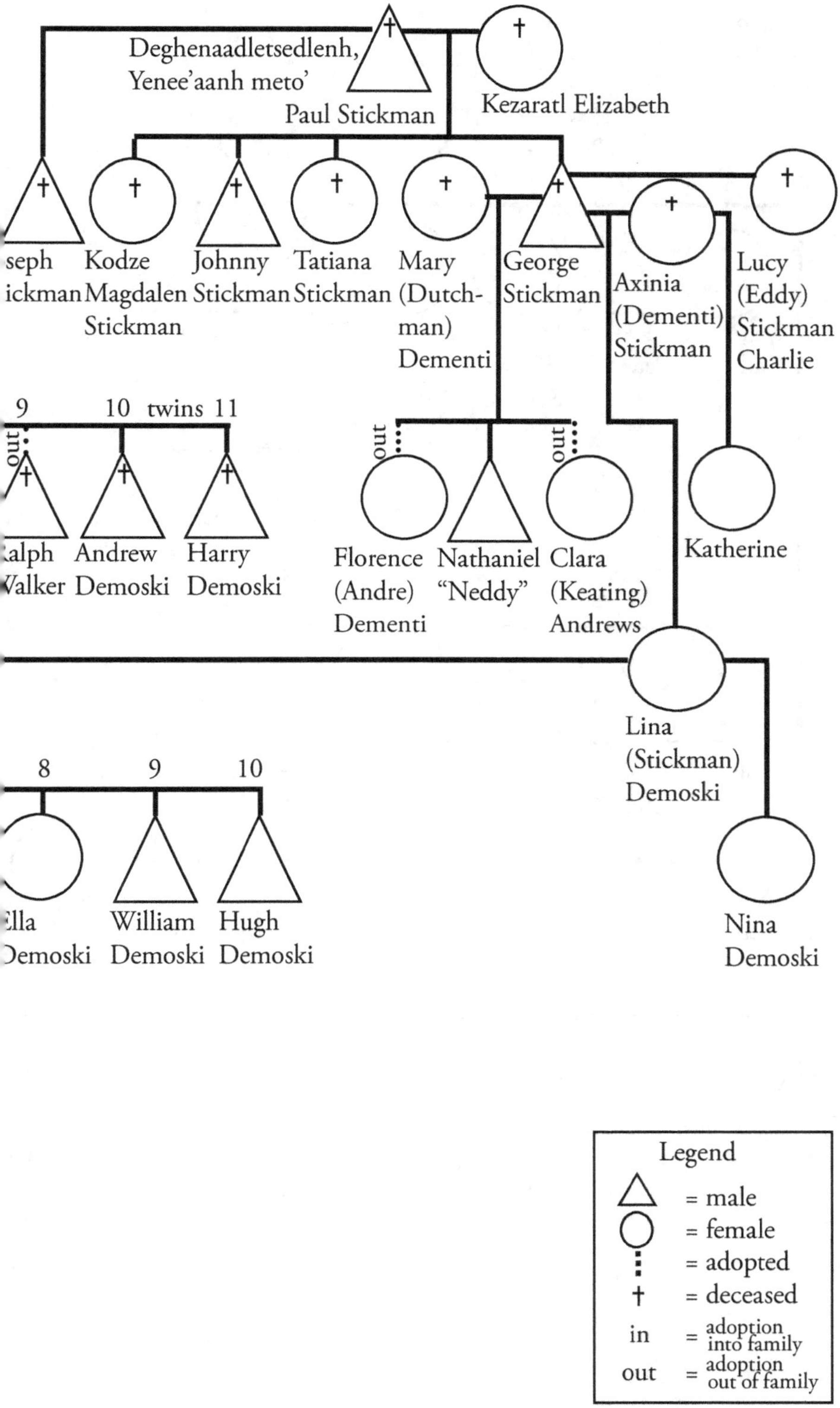

Deghenaadletsedlenh, Yenee'aanh meto'
Paul Stickman — Kezaratl Elizabeth

seph ickman | Kodze Magdalen Stickman | Johnny Stickman | Tatiana Stickman | Mary (Dutchman) Dementi | George Stickman | Axinia (Dementi) Stickman | Lucy (Eddy) Stickman Charlie

9   10 twins 11

out

Ralph Walker | Andrew Demoski | Harry Demoski

Florence (Andre) Dementi | Nathaniel "Neddy" | Clara (Keating) Andrews | Katherine

out

Lina (Stickman) Demoski

8   9   10

Ella Demoski | William Demoski | Hugh Demoski

Nina Demoski

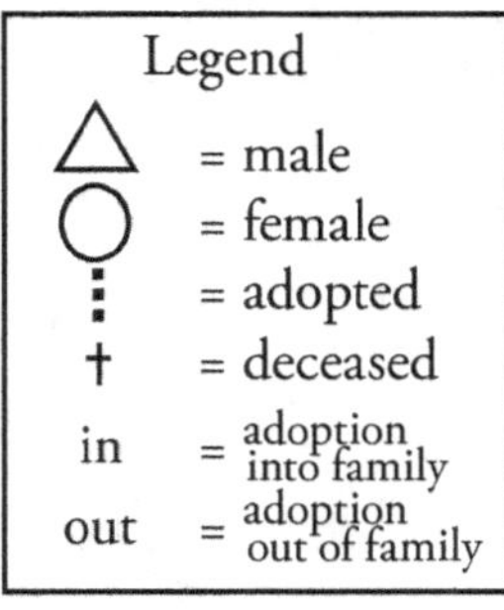

Emmitt Peters
Family Tree

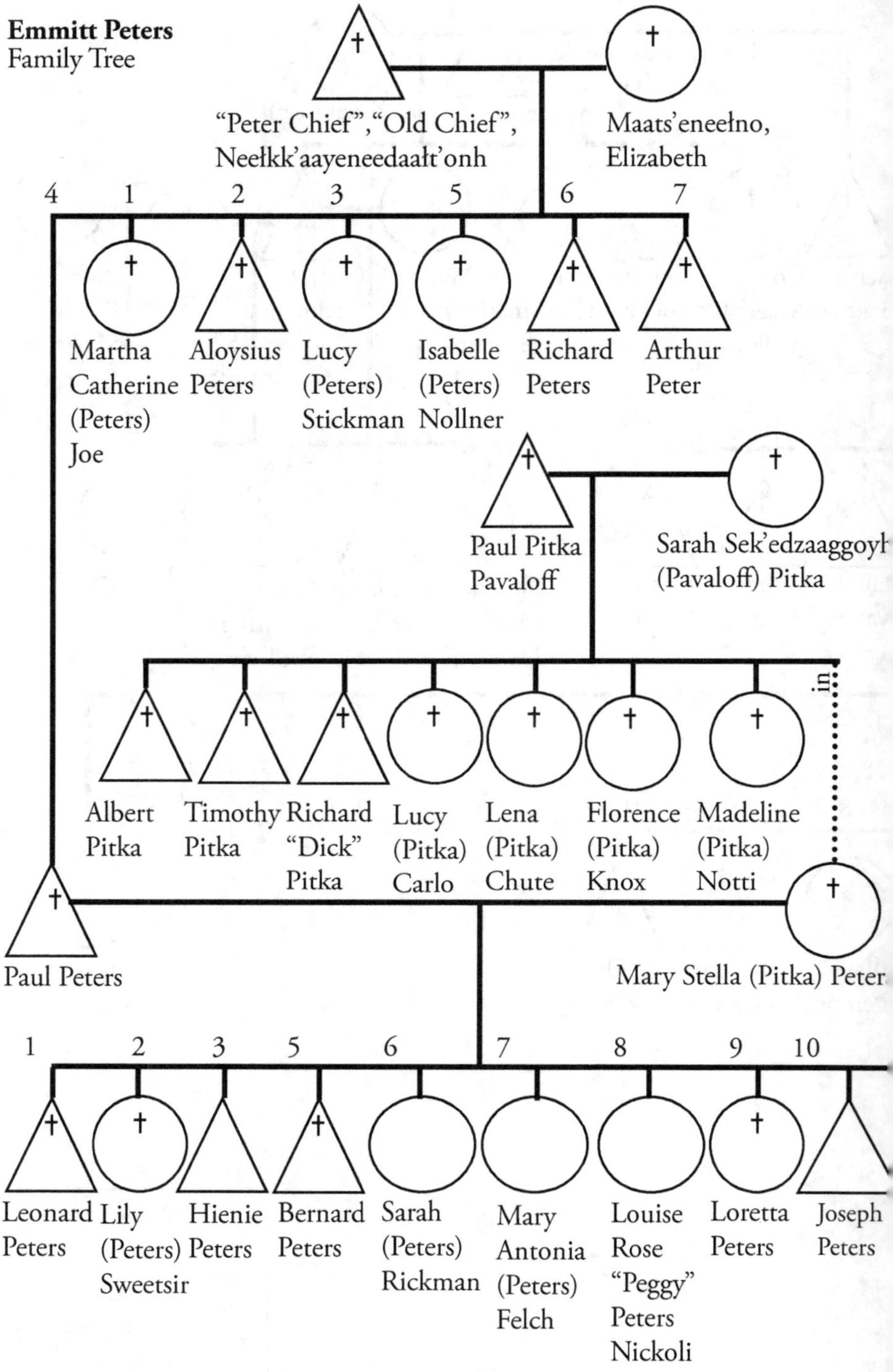

"Peter Chief", "Old Chief", Neełkk'aayeneedaałt'onh
Maats'eneełno, Elizabeth

4 1 2 3 5 6 7

Martha Catherine (Peters) Joe
Aloysius Peters
Lucy (Peters) Stickman
Isabelle (Peters) Nollner
Richard Peters
Arthur Peter

Paul Pitka Pavaloff
Sarah Sek'edzaaggoył (Pavaloff) Pitka

Albert Pitka
Timothy Pitka
Richard "Dick" Pitka
Lucy (Pitka) Carlo
Lena (Pitka) Chute
Florence (Pitka) Knox
Madeline (Pitka) Notti

Paul Peters
Mary Stella (Pitka) Peter

1 2 3 5 6 7 8 9 10

Leonard Peters
Lily (Peters) Sweetsir
Hienie Peters
Bernard Peters
Sarah (Peters) Rickman
Mary Antonia (Peters) Felch
Louise Rose "Peggy" Peters Nickoli
Loretta Peters
Joseph Peters

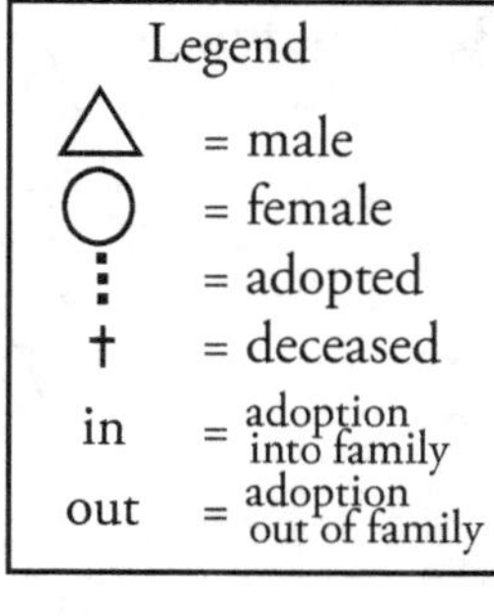

Legend
= male
= female
= adopted
= deceased
in = adoption into family
out = adoption out of family

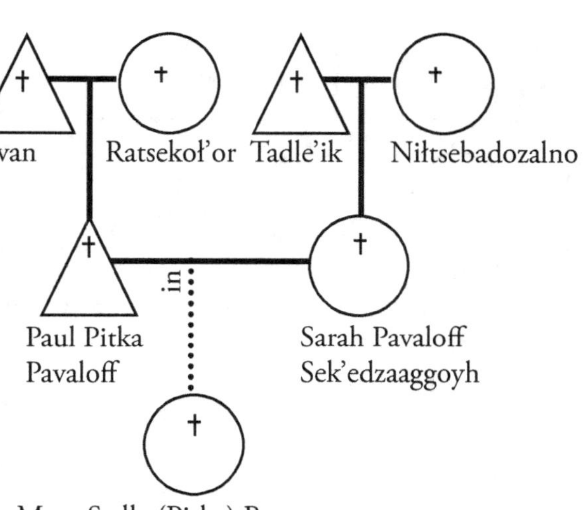

Ivan
Ratsekoł'or
Tadle'ik
Niłtsebadozalno
in
Paul Pitka
Pavaloff
Sarah Pavaloff
Sek'edzaaggoyh
Mary Stella (Pitka) Peters

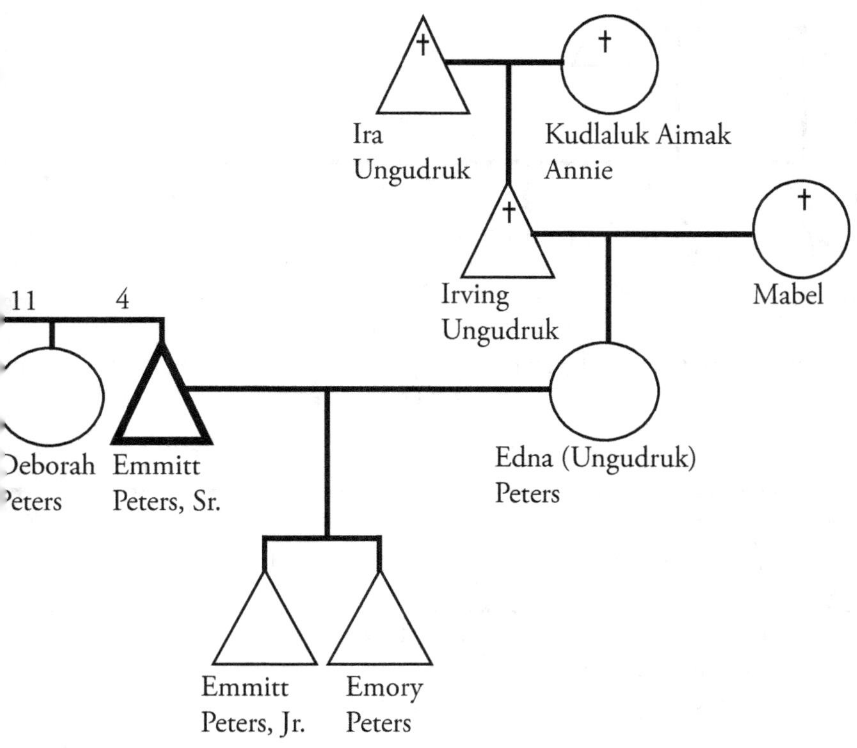

Ira
Ungudruk
Kudlaluk Aimak
Annie
Irving
Ungudruk
Mabel
11
4
Deborah
Peters
Emmitt
Peters, Sr.
Edna (Ungudruk)
Peters
Emmitt
Peters, Jr.
Emory
Peters

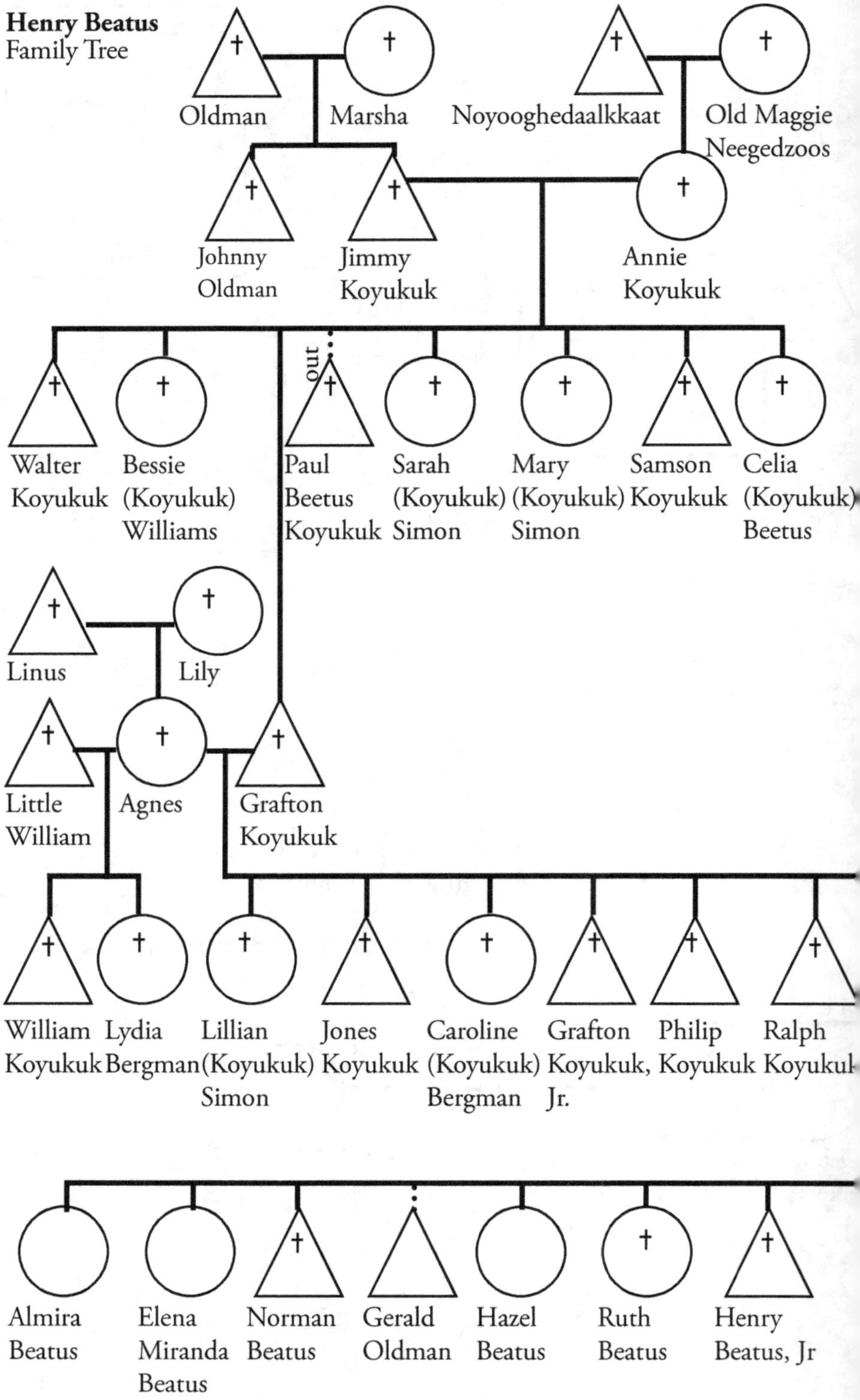

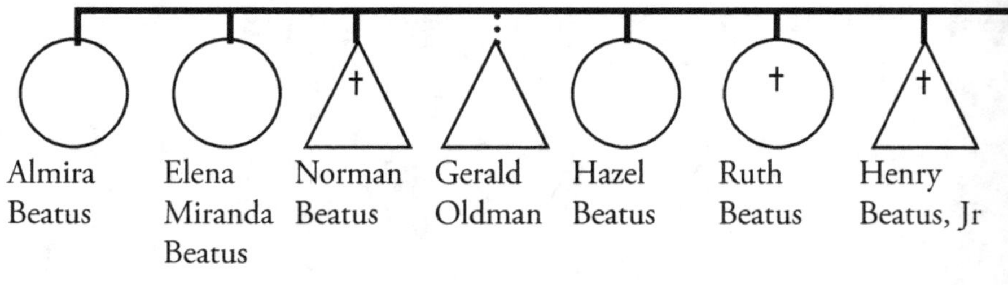

Henry Beatus
Family Tree

Oldman
Marsha
Noyooghedaalkkaat
Old Maggie
Neegedzoos

Johnny
Oldman
Jimmy
Koyukuk
Annie
Koyukuk

Walter
Koyukuk
Bessie
(Koyukuk)
Williams
Paul
Beetus
Koyukuk
Sarah
(Koyukuk)
Simon
Mary
(Koyukuk)
Simon
Samson
Koyukuk
Celia
(Koyukuk)
Beetus

Linus
Lily

Little
William
Agnes
Grafton
Koyukuk

William
Koyukuk
Lydia
Bergman
Lillian
(Koyukuk)
Simon
Jones
Koyukuk
Caroline
(Koyukuk)
Bergman
Grafton
Koyukuk,
Jr.
Philip
Koyukuk
Ralph
Koyukuk

Almira
Beatus
Elena
Miranda
Beatus
Norman
Beatus
Gerald
Oldman
Hazel
Beatus
Ruth
Beatus
Henry
Beatus, Jr

out

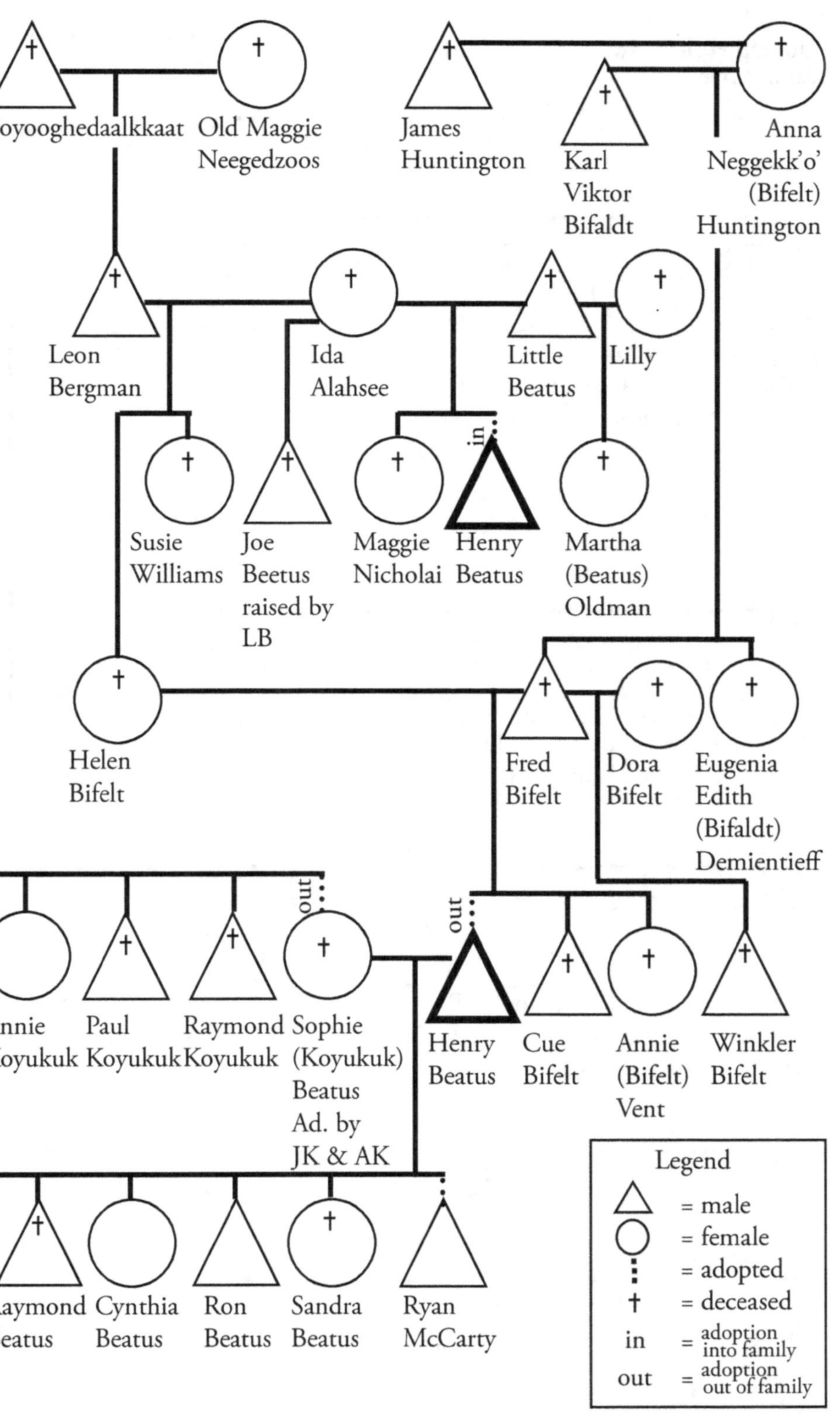

Noyooghedaalkkaat
Old Maggie Neegedzoos
James Huntington
Karl Viktor Bifaldt
Anna Neggekk'o' (Bifelt) Huntington
Leon Bergman
Ida Alahsee
Little Beatus
Lilly
in
Susie Williams
Joe Beetus raised by LB
Maggie Nicholai
Henry Beatus
Martha (Beatus) Oldman
Helen Bifelt
Fred Bifelt
Dora Bifelt
Eugenia Edith (Bifaldt) Demientieff
out
out
Annie Koyukuk
Paul Koyukuk
Raymond Koyukuk
Sophie (Koyukuk) Beatus Ad. by JK & AK
Henry Beatus
Cue Bifelt
Annie (Bifelt) Vent
Winkler Bifelt
Raymond Beatus
Cynthia Beatus
Ron Beatus
Sandra Beatus
Ryan McCarty
Legend
= male
= female
= adopted
= deceased
in = adoption into family
out = adoption out of family

Donald Honea, Sr.
Family Tree

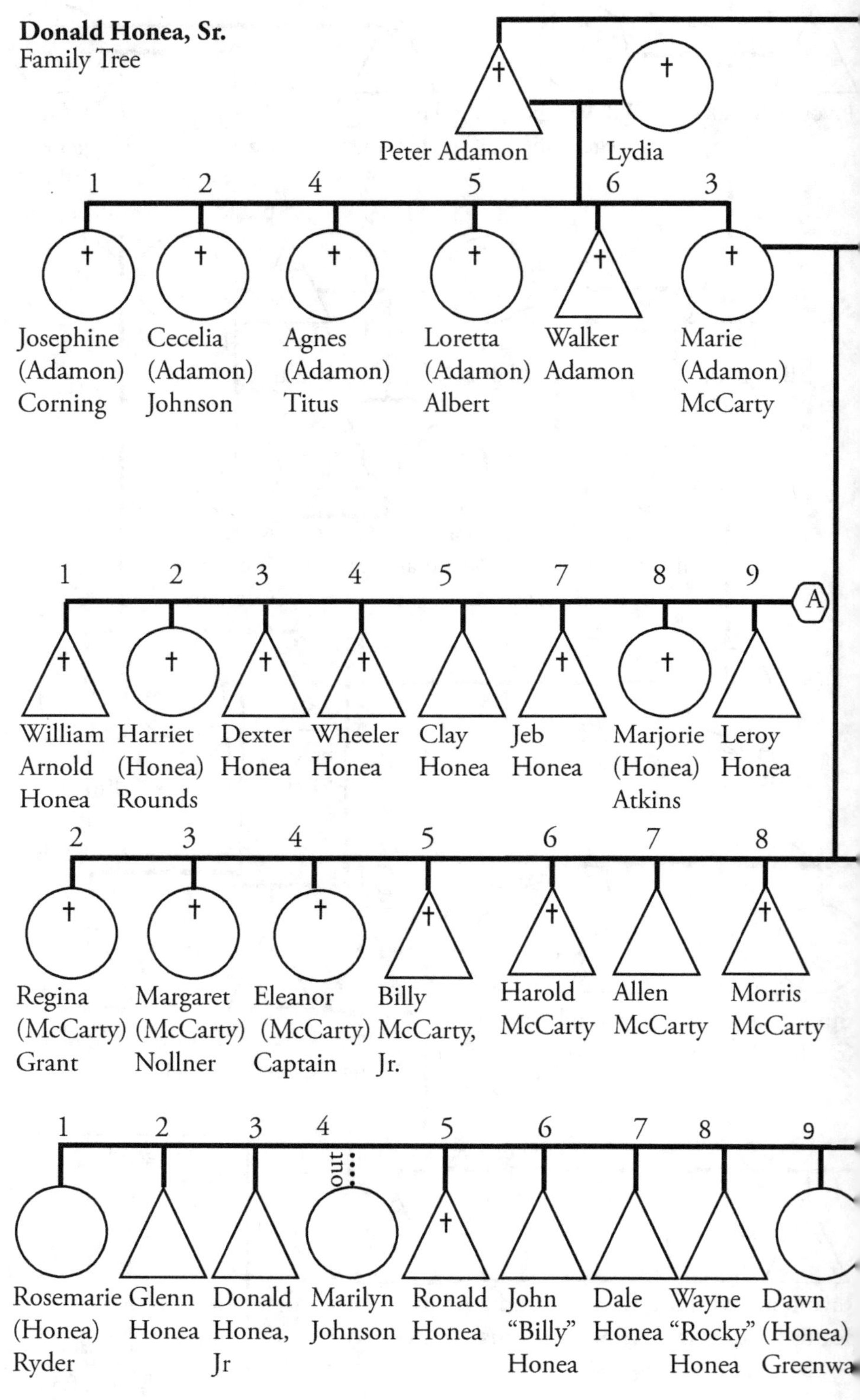

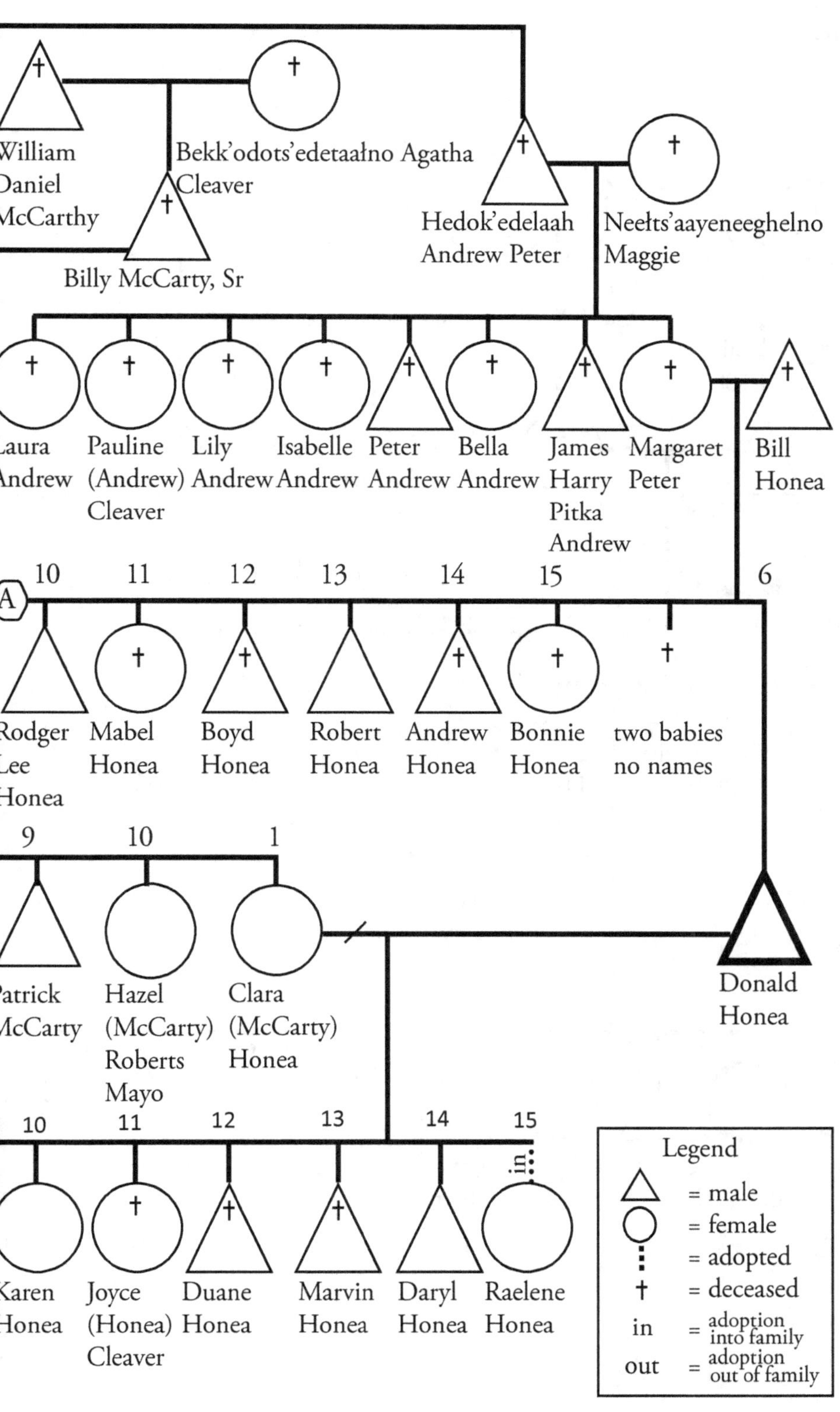

William Daniel McCarthy
Bekk'odots'edetaałno Agatha Cleaver
Billy McCarty, Sr
Hedok'edelaah Andrew Peter
Neełts'aayeneeghelno Maggie
Laura Andrew
Pauline (Andrew) Cleaver
Lily Andrew
Isabelle Andrew
Peter Andrew
Bella Andrew
James Harry Pitka Andrew
Margaret Peter
Bill Honea
A
10 11 12 13 14 15 6
Rodger Lee Honea
Mabel Honea
Boyd Honea
Robert Honea
Andrew Honea
Bonnie Honea
two babies no names
9 10 1
Patrick McCarty
Hazel (McCarty) Roberts Mayo
Clara (McCarty) Honea
Donald Honea
10 11 12 13 14 15
in
Karen Honea
Joyce (Honea) Cleaver
Duane Honea
Marvin Honea
Daryl Honea
Raelene Honea
Legend
= male
= female
= adopted
† = deceased
in = adoption into family
out = adoption out of family

Rose Albert
Family Tree

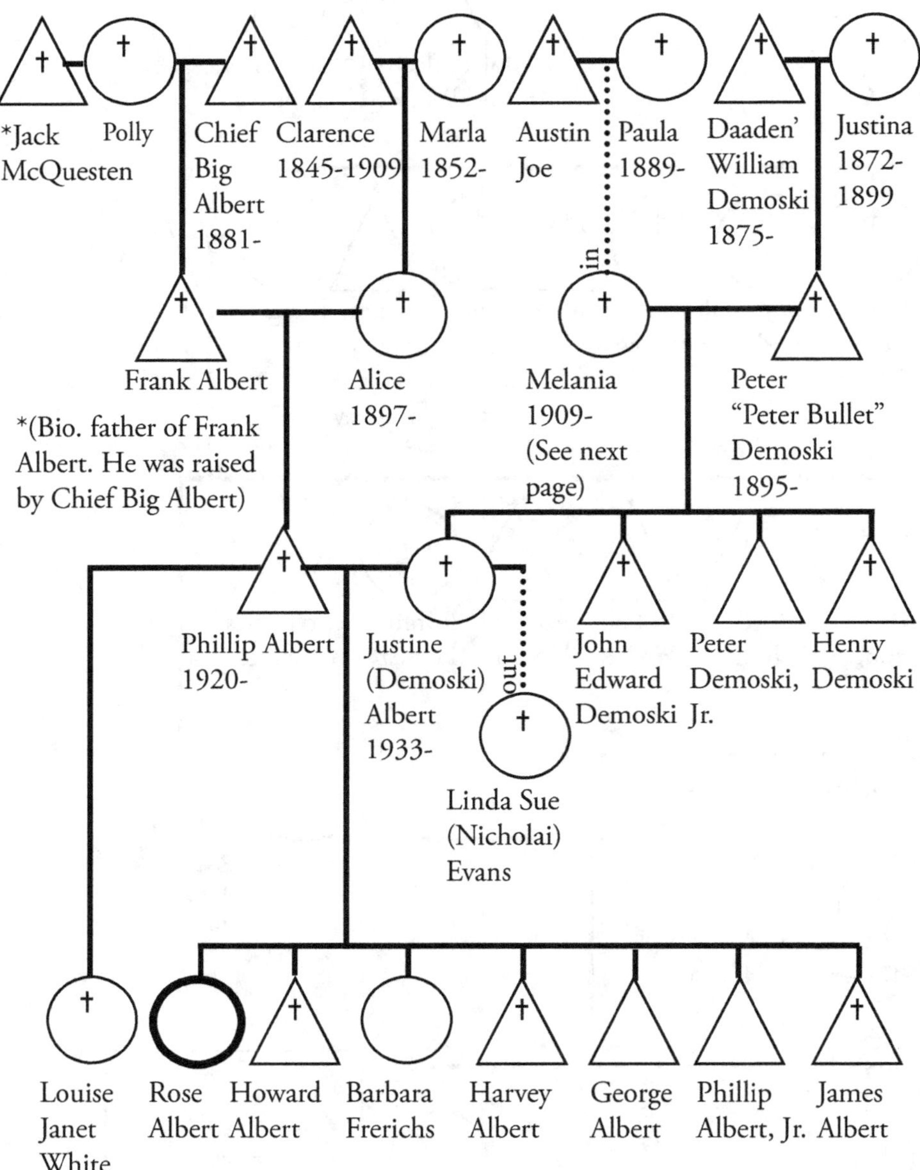

Rose Albert
Family Tree of Rose Albert's late grandmother Melania (Joe) Demoski's
biological family.

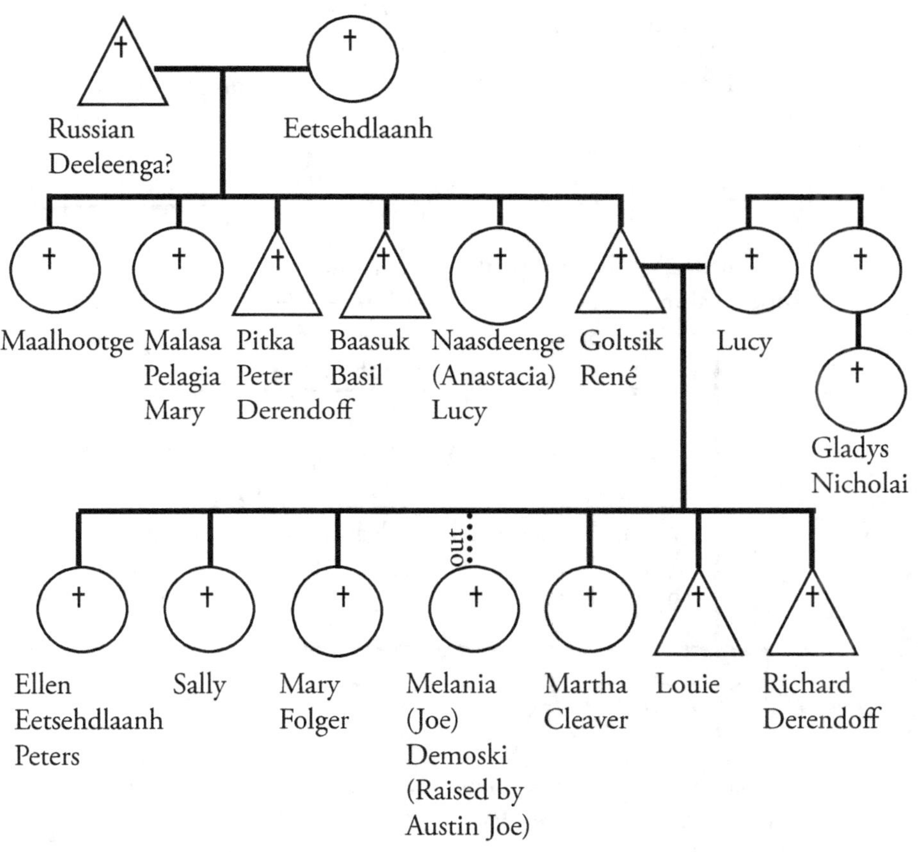

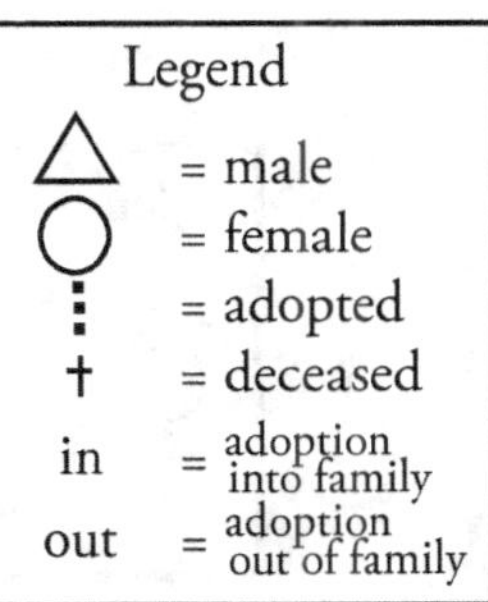

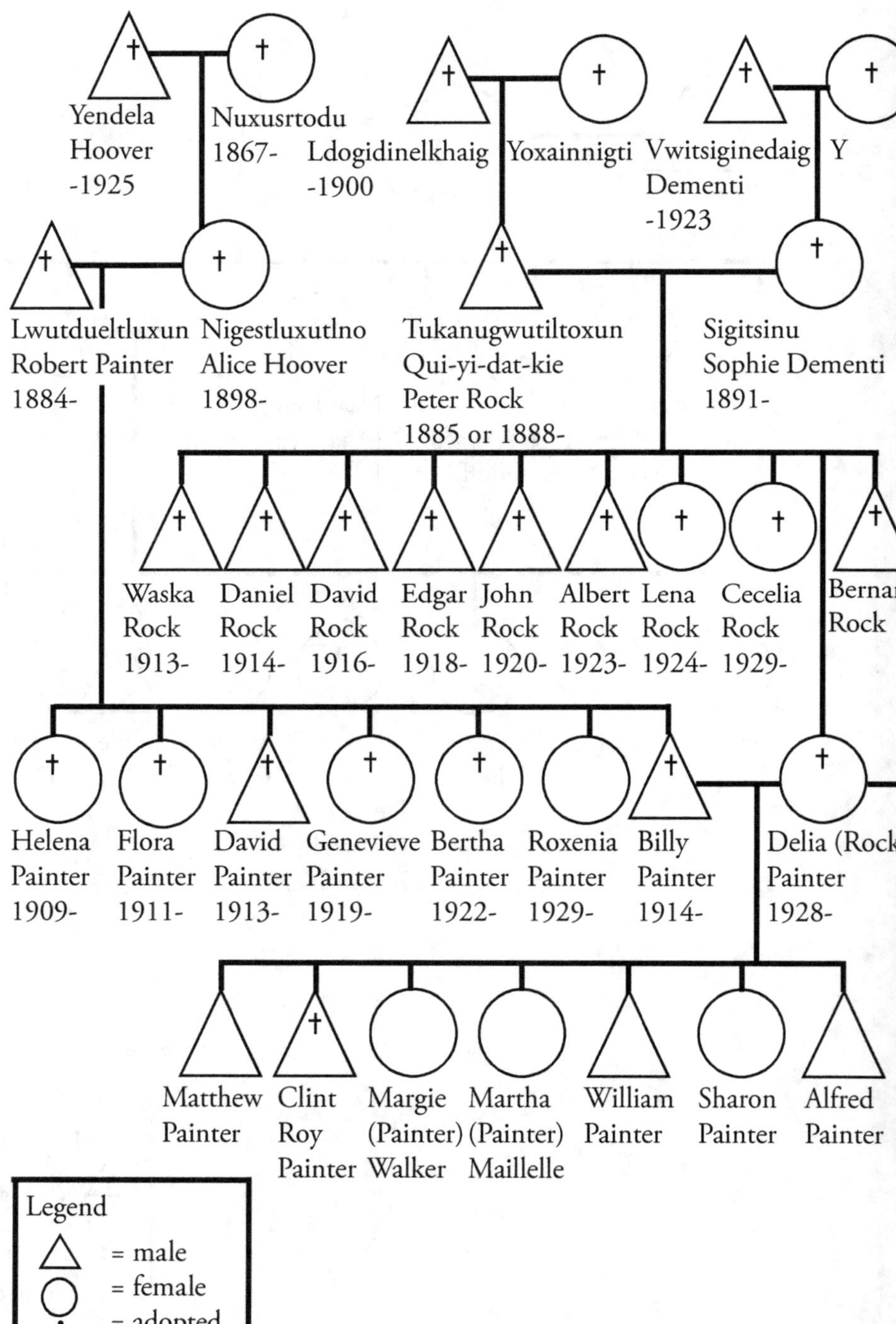

Dean Painter
Family Tree

Yendela Hoover -1925
Nuxusrtodu 1867- -1900
Ldogidinelkhaig
Yoxainnigti
Vwitsiginedaig Dementi -1923
Y

Lwutdueltluxun Robert Painter 1884-
Nigestluxutlno Alice Hoover 1898-
Tukanugwutiltoxun Qui-yi-dat-kie Peter Rock 1885 or 1888-
Sigitsinu Sophie Dementi 1891-

Waska Rock 1913-
Daniel Rock 1914-
David Rock 1916-
Edgar Rock 1918-
John Rock 1920-
Albert Rock 1923-
Lena Rock 1924-
Cecelia Rock 1929-
Bernar Rock

Helena Painter 1909-
Flora Painter 1911-
David Painter 1913-
Genevieve Painter 1919-
Bertha Painter 1922-
Roxenia Painter 1929-
Billy Painter 1914-
Delia (Rock Painter 1928-

Matthew Painter
Clint Roy Painter
Margie (Painter) Walker
Martha (Painter) Maillelle
William Painter
Sharon Painter
Alfred Painter

Legend
= male
= female
= adopted
= deceased

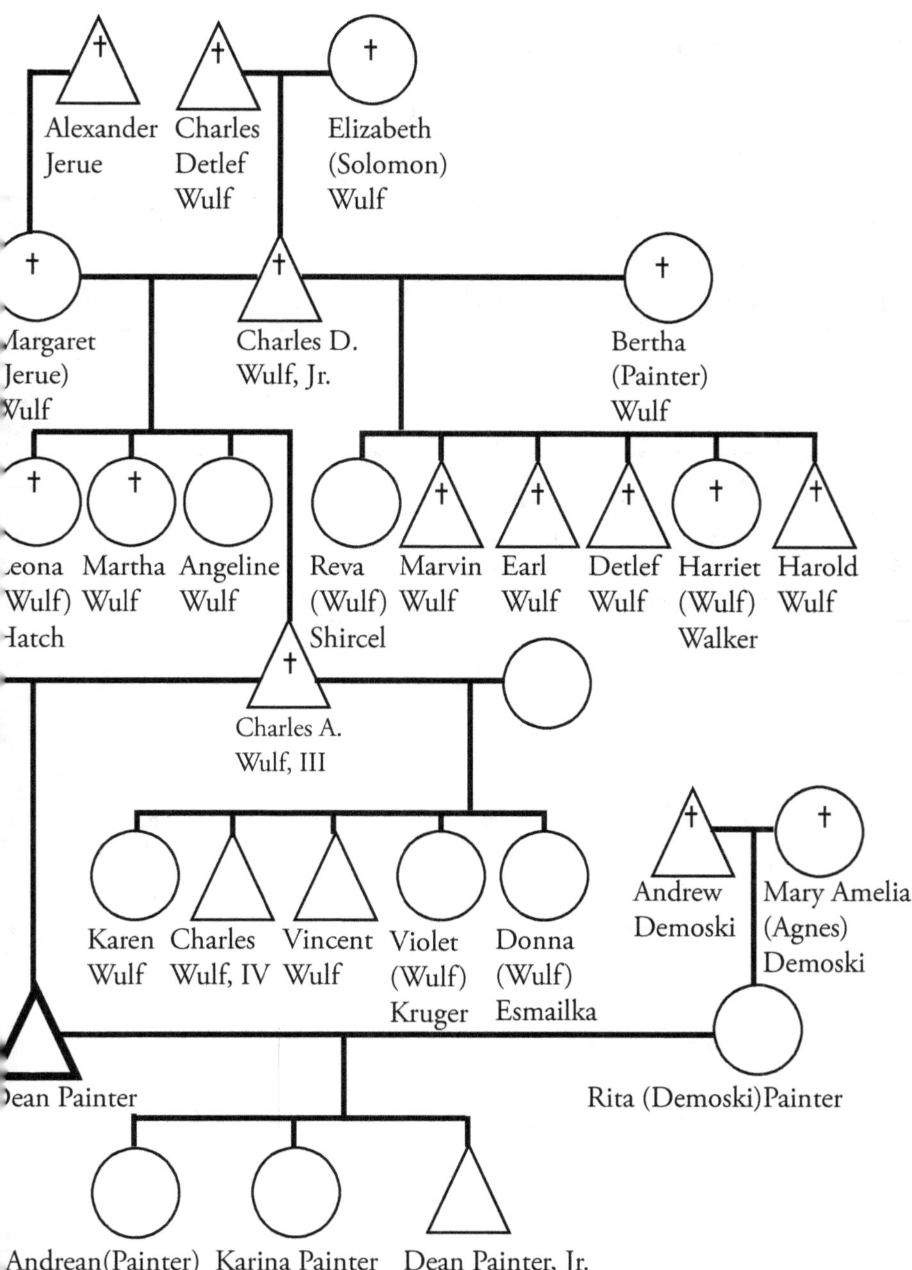

Alexander Jerue
Charles Detlef Wulf
Elizabeth (Solomon) Wulf
Margaret (Jerue) Wulf
Charles D. Wulf, Jr.
Bertha (Painter) Wulf
Leona (Wulf) Hatch
Martha Wulf
Angeline Wulf
Reva (Wulf) Shircel
Marvin Wulf
Earl Wulf
Detlef Wulf
Harriet (Wulf) Walker
Harold Wulf
Charles A. Wulf, III
Karen Wulf
Charles Wulf, IV
Vincent Wulf
Violet (Wulf) Kruger
Donna (Wulf) Esmailka
Andrew Demoski
Mary Amelia (Agnes) Demoski
Dean Painter
Rita (Demoski) Painter
Andrean (Painter) Madros
Karina Painter
Dean Painter, Jr.

Ramy Brooks and Roxy Wright
Family Tree

Henry Wright
K'ets'enokko Old Annie
Fred Eugene Rose
Louise Jacabena Damme

Joseph Wright
Bessie David
Arthur Rowe Wright
Myrtle Rose

1 Grace (Carter) Marks
2 Marion (Carter) Goldberg
4 Billie (Carter Opland

1 Arthur Eugene Wright
2 Alfred Wright
4 Donald Wright
5 Lawrence Wright
6 Jules Wright
7 Forest Wright
Miranda (Hildebrand) Wright
3 Gareth Wright

Shannon (Wright) Erhart

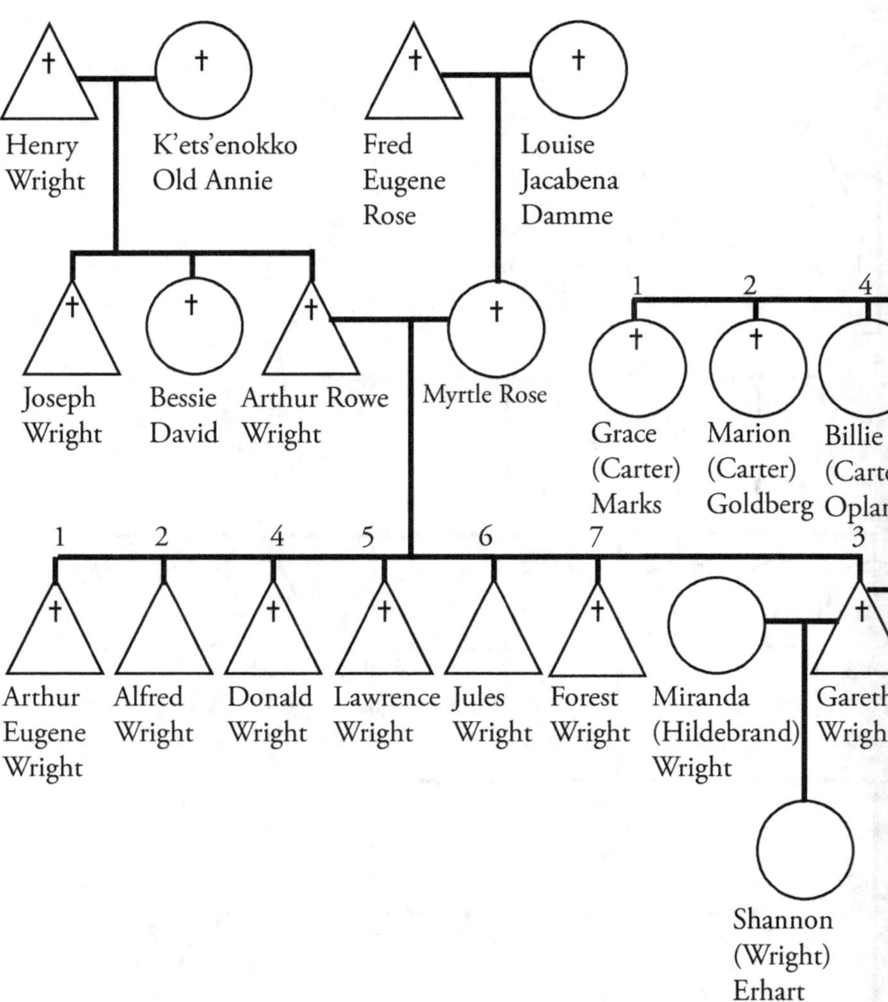

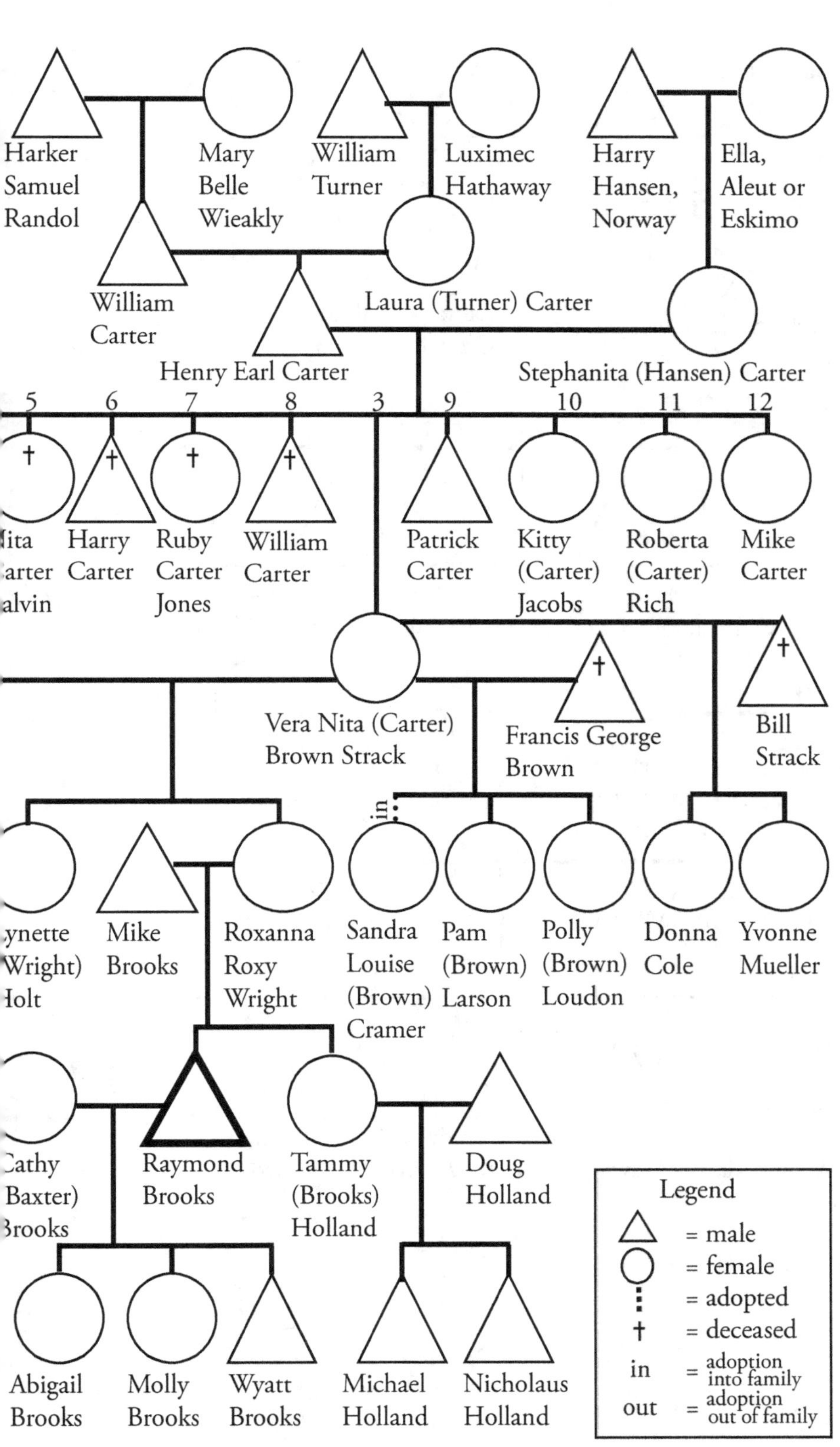

Harker Samuel Randol
Mary Belle Wieakly
William Turner
Luximec Hathaway
Harry Hansen, Norway
Ella, Aleut or Eskimo
William Carter
Laura (Turner) Carter
Henry Earl Carter
Stephanita (Hansen) Carter
5 6 7 8 3 9 10 11 12
†ita arter alvin
† Harry Carter
† Ruby Carter Jones
† William Carter
Patrick Carter
Kitty (Carter) Jacobs
Roberta (Carter) Rich
Mike Carter
Vera Nita (Carter) Brown Strack
† Francis George Brown
† Bill Strack
ynette Wright) Holt
Mike Brooks
Roxanna Roxy Wright
in:
Sandra Louise (Brown) Cramer
Pam (Brown) Larson
Polly (Brown) Loudon
Donna Cole
Yvonne Mueller
Cathy Baxter) Brooks
Raymond Brooks
Tammy (Brooks) Holland
Doug Holland
Abigail Brooks
Molly Brooks
Wyatt Brooks
Michael Holland
Nicholaus Holland
Legend
△ = male
○ = female
⋮ = adopted
† = deceased
in = adoption into family
out = adoption out of family

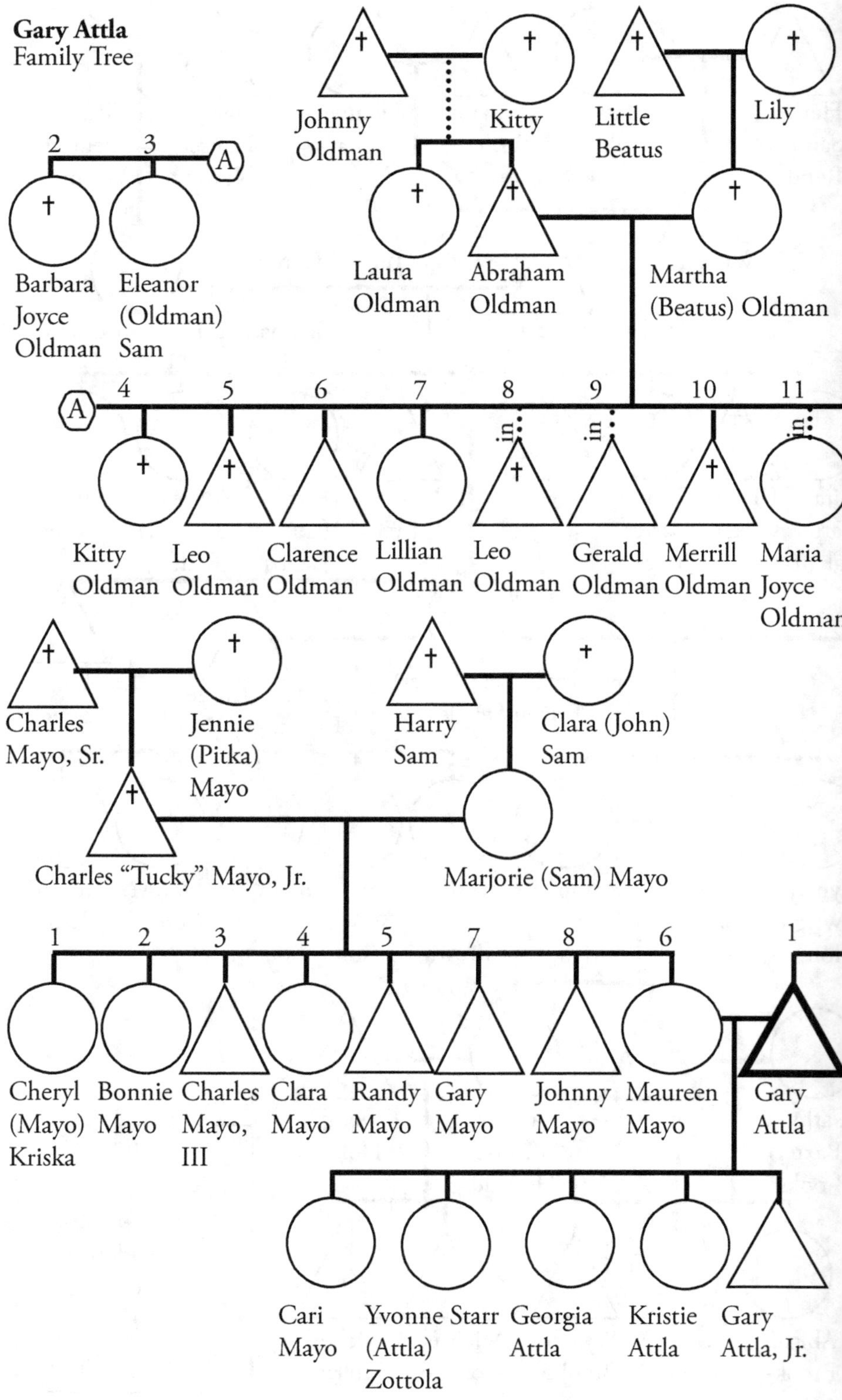

Gary Attla
Family Tree

Barbara Joyce Oldman
Eleanor (Oldman) Sam
Johnny Oldman
Kitty
Little Beatus
Lily
Laura Oldman
Abraham Oldman
Martha (Beatus) Oldman
Kitty Oldman
Leo Oldman
Clarence Oldman
Lillian Oldman
Leo Oldman
Gerald Oldman
Merrill Oldman
Maria Joyce Oldman
Charles Mayo, Sr.
Jennie (Pitka) Mayo
Harry Sam
Clara (John) Sam
Charles "Tucky" Mayo, Jr.
Marjorie (Sam) Mayo
Cheryl (Mayo) Kriska
Bonnie Mayo
Charles Mayo, III
Clara Mayo
Randy Mayo
Gary Mayo
Johnny Mayo
Maureen Mayo
Gary Attla
Cari Mayo
Yvonne (Attla) Zottola
Starr
Georgia Attla
Kristie Attla
Gary Attla, Jr.

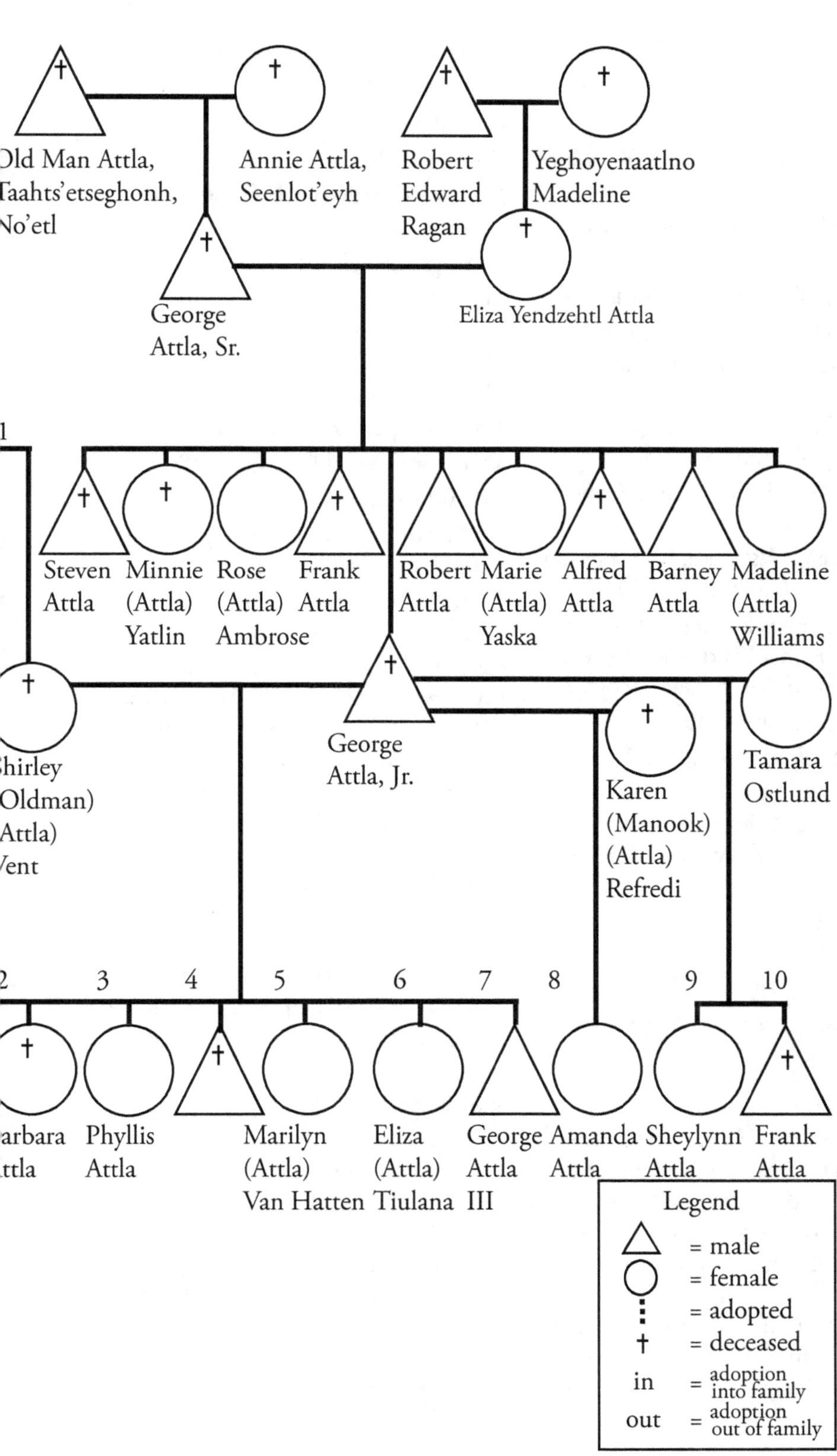

Old Man Attla, Taahts'etseghonh, No'etl
Annie Attla, Seenlot'eyh
Robert Edward Ragan
Yeghoyenaatlno Madeline
George Attla, Sr.
Eliza Yendzehtl Attla
1
Steven Attla
Minnie (Attla) Yatlin
Rose (Attla) Ambrose
Frank Attla
Robert Attla
Marie (Attla) Yaska
Alfred Attla
Barney Attla
Madeline (Attla) Williams
Shirley (Oldman) (Attla) Vent
George Attla, Jr.
Karen (Manook) (Attla) Refredi
Tamara Ostlund
2
3
4
5
6
7
8
9
10
Barbara Attla
Phyllis Attla
Marilyn (Attla) Van Hatten
Eliza (Attla) Tiulana
George Attla III
Amanda Attla
Sheylynn Attla
Frank Attla
Legend
△ = male
○ = female
⋮ = adopted
† = deceased
in = adoption into family
out = adoption out of family

We thank you for your support.
To order: contact the Yukon-Koyukuk School District
4762 Old Airport Way, Fairbanks, AK 99709; Phone: 907-374-9400;
https://www.yksd.com

∞

Look for Judy Ferguson's upcoming book:
*All the Right Stuff, When Smokey Can't…Alaska's Wildland
Firefighters Can!*

∞

Books and Materials by Judy Ferguson
Judy's eight other books are available in print as well as eBooks.

*Windows to the Land, An Alaska Native Story, Volume One:
Alaska Native Land Claims Trailblazers*

∞

*Windows to the Land, An Alaska Native Story,
Volume Two: The Iditarod and Alaska River Trails*

∞

Bridges to Statehood: The Alaska-Yugoslav Connection

∞

Blue Hills: Alaska's Promised Land

∞

Parallel Destinies: An Alaskan Odyssey

∞

Children's Books
Alaska's Secret Door
Alaska's Little Chief
Alaska's First People
Lesson plans available for each title on CD

Judy's Website: http://judysoutpost.com
1-907-895 4101; outpost99737@gmail.com; Box 130, Delta Junction, Alaska,
99737, U.S.A.

∞

Books and Materials by Yukon-Koyukuk School District

YKSD Website: https://www.yksd.com/Page/535

YKSD Biography Series (twenty-one) books,
featuring twenty-one elders